VOLTAIRE SIX

VOLTAIRE SIX

THE TOP TIGERS

Historical Fiction

JOHN R. COOKE

Writers Advantage
San Jose New York Lincoln Shanghai

Voltaire Six
The Top Tigers

Writers Advantage
an imprint of iUniverse, Inc.

For information address:
iUniverse, Inc.
5220 S. 16th St., Suite 200
Lincoln, NE 68512
www.iuniverse.com

ISBN: 0-595-23275-2

Printed in the United States of America

To the helicopter pilots and crewmembers that lost their lives while in the service of their country in Vietnam.

And to the Top Tigers.

"Greater love hath no man than this, that he would lay down his life for his friends."

—John 15:13.

Acknowledgements

I wish to express my heartfelt thanks and appreciation to my family for their strong and consistent support of this work. Without the strong support and encouragement from my wife, Astrid, our son, Kenneth, and our daughter, Patricia, I might well have never written this book. I am truly grateful to my brothers, Tom, Sam, and Rick; my sister, Kay; and my sister-in-law, Carolyn, for their steadfast support. And I am especially grateful to my brother Rick for the outstanding artwork he provided—the cover and the map. Also, I offer my sincere thanks to my former students for their encouragement. I am certainly grateful to Thao To and her family for helping me with my Vietnamese vocabulary and spelling. Moreover, I wish to thank my Army flight school classmates (ORWAC Class 66-2) for all of their encouragement, and especially their help in jogging my feeble memory regarding much of the technical matter. Like the Top Tigers, they remain always, truly stouthearted fellows.

Preface

This is in part a work of fiction. Although inspired by actual events, the names, persons, places, and characters are inventions of the author. Any resemblance to people living or deceased is purely coincidental. The few brief quotes from public or historical figures used in this work should be covered under the "fair use" provision of copyright law. The operational incidents described in this work are roughly based on the author's personal experiences while serving as a helicopter pilot in Vietnam during the conflict there. As many of the words and terms used in this work are rather unique to that particular place and time—South Vietnam in the 1960s—a glossary has been added at the end of this book.

Chronology

A Brief Chronology of U.S. Involvement in Vietnam

1950 President Harry Truman signs legislation granting $15 million in military aid to the French for the war in Indochina.

1954 President Dwight Eisenhower decides against U.S. intervention on side of French when the British reject his proposal for joint action.

May The French garrison at Dien Bien Phu falls to the Vietnamese.

July Geneva Agreements call for cessation of hostilities and divide Vietnam at the 17th parallel.

1955 U.S. begins to send aid directly to Saigon government and agrees to train South Vietnamese Army.

1960 John F. Kennedy is elected president. Some historians say that Kennedy was eager not to appear "soft on Communism" after being embarrassed by the Bay of Pigs fiasco in Cuba.

1961	President Kennedy speaks of a "long twilight war" and says that Vietnam will be the "proving ground of democracy." He sends U.S. military advisers to Vietnam.
	Hanoi forms the National Liberation Front for South Vietnam, later dubbed the Viet Cong (Vietnamese Communists).
1962	U.S. Military Assistance Command (MACV) formed in South Vietnam.
1963	Battle of Ap Bac, first significant set-piece battle between the Viet Cong and ARVN with American advisers and air support. Ap Bac was a clear VC victory. Five U.S. helicopters were shot down that day.
	South Vietnamese generals stage a coup and assassinate South Vietnamese President Ngo Dinh Diem (November 2). Three weeks after the assassination of Diem, President Kennedy is assassinated (November 22).
1964	Tonkin Gulf Resolution passed. U.S. aircraft directly bomb North Vietnamese targets for the first time.
	General William Westmoreland assumes command of MACV (June 20).
1965	Arrival of U.S. 173d Airborne Brigade in Vietnam.
	Air Vice Marshal Nguyen Cao Ky becomes prime minister of a military regime in Saigon.
	Arrival of 1st Cavalry Division (Airmobile); established base camp at An Khe in Central Highlands (September).
	Arrival of 1st U.S. Infantry Division in Vietnam; establishes base camp at Di An (October).

Battle of Ia Drang Valley in the Central Highlands; first major battle involving U.S. troops, the 1st Cavalry Division. U.S. suffers major losses—234 men killed in four days (November).

Operation Rolling Thunder begins; sustained U.S. bombing of North Vietnam.

President Johnson offers Ho Chi Minh participation in a Southeast Asian development plan in exchange for peace. The offer is rejected.

1966 25th U.S. Infantry Division arrives in Vietnam; establishes base camp at Cu Chi.

President Charles de Gaulle of France visits Cambodia and calls for U.S. withdrawal from Vietnam.

U.S. troop strength in Vietnam reaches nearly 400,000 by year's end.

1967 Operation Cedar Falls in the Iron Triangle and Cu Chi District (January).

Operation Junction City, a major U.S./Vietnamese operation near Cambodian border (February).

Secretary of Defense Robert McNamara testifies before a Senate subcommittee that U.S. bombing of North Vietnam has been ineffective.

Muhammad Ali refuses to be drafted into the U.S. Army.

Rev. Martin Luther King Jr. speaks out against the war.

1968 Tet (Chinese New Year) Offensive starts (January 31).

U.S. and South Vietnamese troops recapture Hue (February 25) after 26 days of bloody fighting.

Journalist Walter Cronkite speaks out against the war.

President Johnson rejects General Westmoreland's request for an additional 200,000 troops. President Johnson declares that he will not seek reelection.

My Lai massacre reported (March 16). U.S. troops kill approximately 100 Vietnamese detainees—men, women, and children.

Number of U.S. troops in Vietnam peaks at just over 500,000 men in April 1968.

Martin Luther King Jr. is assassinated (April 4).

"National Turn in Your Draft Card Day," is marked by much public draft card burnings (November 15).

General Creighton Abrams replaces General Westmoreland at MACV Headquarters.

Richard Nixon is elected president after campaigning on the platform of having a "secret plan" to end the war in Vietnam.

1969 Viet Cong raid on Cu Chi Base camp destroys 14 Chinook cargo helicopters.

U.S. troops capture Hamburger Hill (Hill 937), and Ap Bia Mountain, in Ashau Valley, only one mile from the Laotian border.

U.S. troop reduction begins.

1970 U.S. troops mount a major operation into Cambodia to clean out Viet Cong/NVA strongholds near the border.

Four Kent State University students are killed by National Guardsmen while demonstrating against the war (May 4).

	1st Infantry Division leaves Vietnam.
	25th Infantry Division leaves Vietnam.
1971	Publication of the Pentagon Papers.
1972	Richard Nixon is reelected president.
	Last U.S. ground troops leave Vietnam.
1973	Cease-fire agreement signed in Paris.
1974	President Nixon resigns (August 9).
1975	Communist troops capture Xuan Loc (April 21), the last South Vietnamese defense line before Saigon.
	Saigon falls to North Vietnamese troops (April 30).

— — —

1976	The unified Socialist Republic of Vietnam proclaims that Saigon has been renamed Ho Chi Minh City.
1977	Vietnam becomes a member of the UN.
	President Jimmy Carter pardons most of the 10,000 Vietnam War draft evaders.
1984	A federal judge announces a $180 million settlement against seven chemical companies—manufacturers of Agent Orange—after Vietnam veterans charge them with gross negligence.
1985	Famine spreads in Vietnam following the failure of the Communists' farm collectivization program.
1995	The United States open full diplomatic ties with Vietnam (July 11).

Contents

III Corps
Tactical Zone
Ho Chi Minh Trail
Cambodia
War
Zone C
War
Zone D
Les Trungs
Plantation
Nui Ba Den
Mountain
Pho Da
Tay Ninh
Ben Suc
Ben Cat
Xuan Loc
Bien Hoa
Cu Chi
Saigon
Long Binh
My Tho
Vung
Tau
South
Vietnam
South China Sea
Mekong Delta
III Corps Tactical Zone
VC Zone
Roads
Miles
0 10 20 30 40 50
0 10 20 30 40 50 60 70 80
Kilometers
N
THAILAND
CAMBODIA
SOUTH VIETNAM
GULF OF THAILAND
INDOCHINA
SOUTH CHINA SEA
14°
11°
102°
105°
108°

Chapter 1

Taking Fire

Halos, he thought. They looked like mystical halos. Magic halos. Halos of ice. Perfectly formed halos.

There before him, in the heavy, moist air over the jungles of South Vietnam, he could see five helicopters flying ahead of and slightly below him. They were flying out of Xuan Loc with a load of South Vietnamese soldiers, headed for an opening in the middle of nowhere called "LZ Battleaxe" (LZ—landing zone). Supposedly, there was a Viet Cong headquarters in that area that was to be cleaned out—neutralized, destroyed.

The big, broad rotor blades were churning through the heavy morning sky, and as they did so they appeared to actually be pulling the moisture right out of the air. Each helicopter seemed to be wearing a perfect halo of moisture just above the rotor plain—a big, broad, icy halo.

Lieutenant Clark later wondered to himself, Did anyone else notice it—the halo effect, the perfect frozen halos of water following, hugging the space just above the rotor plains of the graceful ships—airships which looked like schools of giant tadpoles—flying just above the broad green jungle canopy?

Maybe it was a special sign—a good omen. Frozen halos—yes. They are like halos of ice. Did anyone else ever notice it? He never asked and he never knew.

Lieutenant Clark had not been with this unit—this helicopter company—for long. It had been only a little more than two weeks since he had arrived at the Saigon airport, Tan Son Nhut, been processed in and assigned to fly with the 68th Assault Helicopter Company (the "Top Tigers") of the 145th Aviation Battalion. The battalion headquarters was in Bien Hoa, just north of Saigon, but the Top Tigers were temporarily assigned to Vung Tau, about forty miles southeast of Bien Hoa, on the coastline.

That morning, before daylight, they had started their mission from their home airfield at Vung Tau. They flew into Xuan Loc in radio silence and using only their running lights. Trying to fly at night in a tight formation using the running lights only was also something new to Clark. They had not done that in flight school. And now, here in Nam, there seemed to be tremendous emphasis on flying tight—*really* tight—formations.

Lieutenant Clark was flying with Captain Nowotney, his new platoon leader, and the captain strongly emphasized tight formations.

"Get control of the aircraft," Nowotney kept saying, "and tighten up the formation. Stay closed up. Tighten up. Come on. Tighten it up. This is supposed to be a military formation. It's supposed to look sharp. Don't straggle. Remember, if you straggle, you'll get run over."

Later the captain explained further: "A good tight formation demonstrates discipline and skill. When we fly into an area, people look up and they know it's us, the Top Tigers, when the formation is sharp and tight. That's our signature. It impresses people—not only other Americans but the enemy also," he said.

Captain Nowotney was a good man. He was a skilled pilot and an honest and conscientious officer. Lieutenant Clark liked him. The captain was doing his best to show Lieutenant Clark, the "newbie," the ropes. But this bold new idea had never occurred to Lieutenant Clark. He had done some formation flying in flight school, but not much—and it was rather loose to say the least. But now this: flying formations to impress the enemy—an air show for the enemy. What a concept, he mused. I thought that was what all these guns and rockets were about, or for—to impress—or *de*press—the enemy.

Lieutenant Clark developed something like a grudging admiration for the Top Tigers because of their tight formation flying. But he always harbored a suspicious feeling that loose and scraggly would have served just as well or better than tight and spiffy. Before his one-year tour of duty was finished he would know more than one man who had lost his life in the process of relentlessly trying to tighten the formation. One could not help but wonder about how the enemy was impressed when he looked up and saw the American aircraft crashing together, with bits and pieces flying in every direction.

"Tighten it up!" Captain Nowotney said. "Come on! Move in there! Move in! Close in. Close it up. Get tight! Tighten it up!"

Lieutenant Clark held the controls firmly. "Okay, okay," he said to himself. "If you say that it can be done, then we'll do it." He could see the running lights of the aircraft to his right. He eased in closer—and then still closer. Now he could see the red panel lights before the faces of pilots in the ship to his right and just a bit below his level. They were flying at an altitude of about 1,000 feet at 90 knots. It seemed as though his nose always started to itch when he started to fly in a tight formation. For a while he kept struggling with the controls, thinking that he absolutely had to scratch his nose. It was an absolute must that his nose be scratched, pacified, requited. He quickly brushed his nose a time or two with his gloved left hand. Then Captain Nowotney spoke up again.

"What's wrong with you?" he asked. "Leave your nose alone. Fly the aircraft. Come on! *Fly* the aircraft!"

So, that was the end of that. Clark's nose never seemed to itch again. It was as if it had vanished from his face. That sort of thing, the fierce itching, suddenly seemed physiologically impossible—totally prohibited and absolutely out of the question. Vanquished. Conquered. Subjugated. That problem was solved. It was a thing of the past. The nose problem was gone. And that was how things worked with the Top Tigers. The man says "do it," and we pick up and do it. That's how it works. Just like that.

After a while he started to feel that he was getting the hang of it. Sometimes it was almost as though the helicopters had no rotor plains, no blades to worry about becoming fatally entangled. Now they were like big fireflies on a morning breeze. They had discovered a miniature Gulf Stream or jet stream in Southeast Asia. With very little weaving and bobbing, onward they cruised like a school of fish in a narrow channel of clear, clean stream water.

They landed at the airstrip at Xuan Loc, which was a small outpost about forty miles northeast of Saigon. The sky was starting to lighten a bit in the east as the Vietnamese soldiers started to climb aboard the aircraft. (Vietnamese soldiers were usually referred to as "ARVNs," for Army of the Republic of Vietnam, pronounced "Arvins" by Americans.) Soon they were all aboard, with their rifles and equipment clattering and banging about, and the pilots were pulling power and climbing back into the sky, flying toward the northwest on a compass heading of 280 degrees.

They were still flying with running lights only but now the outlines of the aircraft could be clearly seen against the early morning sky. Lieutenant Clark adjusted the power settings. Because of the load of troops they had just taken aboard, he now had to pull in more power to hold his airspeed and altitude. Now they were flying at about 500 feet.

Lieutenant Clark pulled in close to the aircraft to his right. He picked a spot, a running light, and focused on it. He concentrated on that light, that spot, and he did his best to keep the formation tight. Captain Nowotney was silent. Everyone was silent, but the wide rotor blades whizzed, whistled, and popped through the heavy morning air. The cargo doors were wide open and some of the soldiers sat with their feet dangling out of the aircraft in the open air. Clark could smell the JP-4 (JP—jet petroleum), the turbine-jet engine fuel, but, fortunately, mostly he could smell the good clean fresh air rushing through his open window above the lush jungles below—a deep rain forest which had never known the sound and smell of the internal combustion engine.

They did not fly long before the CO, the commanding officer, Major Compton, came on the air and started to talk on the company's assigned radio frequency.

"Okay, guys," he said, "we're about five minutes out. The LZ appears to be cool. The pathfinders have their lights and panels out. Everything seems to be okay so far."

Major Marker, the operations officer, came on the line.

"Okay, I've got the lights. I can see the lights on the LZ. The pathfinders say we're all set. There's enough room for us to land all together in there. We'll be landing on this course, a northwest heading, roughly a heading of 280 degrees."

Two minutes later Major Compton came back on the line.

"Okay," he said, "I've got the LZ in sight. I've got the landing lights. Let's go on in. Let'em down easy." Major Compton, the CO, "Top Tiger Six," (the commander always had the radio call-sign suffix of "six") was a handsome man and an able commander. Everyone respected and trusted him. He had fought in the Korean War as an infantry platoon leader.

Lieutenant Clark started to reduce the power. He could feel the aircraft easing down, losing altitude, as were all of the aircraft before him in the formation. Now he could clearly see the watery halos over the aircraft ahead of him. Was this a good omen? Well, let's hope so, he thought. He glanced ahead and briefly picked up the green and blue lights on the landing zone. If no one had fired on the pathfinders then this should be a safe operation—a "cool" as opposed to a "hot" LZ.

The aircraft started to bounce and bob about a bit now in the rough airstream of the leading helicopters. As the five aircraft in front of him reduced their airspeed and altitude they created more rough air turbulence toward the rear of the formation. That was something one had to always expect and be prepared for. At the front of the formation one had clean air to work with—toward the rear of the formation, dirty air. It was something like following in a convoy of boats—riding the wake, the waves.

They flew low over the pathfinder's lights on the ground, continued to let down and soon were slowly sliding through and settling into the wet grass in the narrow opening in the jungle.

"Okay, get'em off," Captain Nowotney shouted to the crew chief and the door gunner. "Get'em off! Come on! Get'em off! Get'em off! Move it!"

The short little Vietnamese troops (they were rarely ever more than five and a half feet tall) quickly disembarked from their places on the helicopters, some pausing to look back to make sure they had not left anything behind. And then they started to move out slowly and cautiously toward the tree line, about fifty yards away.

The flight of Hueys sat briefly on the LZ. (The UH-1, Iroquois C-model helicopter had been originally been designated as the HU-1, and the nickname "Huey" came from that nomenclature.) Somehow it was like a flight of birds catching their breath before another long full-throated dash off against the wind.

Again, they heard the CO's voice on the radio.

"Okay, guys, are we all set? Everybody off-loaded? Are we ready to go?"

Several voices quickly agreed that they were all absolutely ready to "pull pitch," pull power and go—get back into the air.

"Okay," said Top Tiger Six, "Let's go. Let's get out of here."

The CO and the operations officer, with their crews, led the way. But as they got over and just past the tree line at the forward end of the LZ, someone came on line and said they were taking fire.

"Taking fire, Mustangs, taking fire!" Major Compton said. He was talking to the gunship platoon, the "Mustangs."

"Mustangs, get in here right now and suppress that tree line. Give us suppressing fire. We're taking fire. Get after that tree line. Get on 'em. Come on. Get on 'em *now*."

The "Mustangs" were B-models Hueys. They were small, boxy-looking aircraft modified to be loaded down with rockets and machine guns. The gunships had electrically rotated 7.62-mm machine guns mounted beneath the fuselage on each side and pods of 2.75-inch rockets above the machine guns. The rocket pods on each side of the aircraft contained seven rockets each. Some of the gunships, the ones called "Hogs," also had a 40-mm grenade launcher built into their nose boxes (the avionics box). The copilot aimed the weapons system with a cross-hair device that hung down before his face from the ceiling and fired them with buttons on that device. The B-model Hueys were not the slick-looking AH-1G "Cobra" gunships. The Cobras, or the "snakes," had not started to arrive in Vietnam at that time in late 1966. (This aircraft was called the "Cobra" because that was the radio call sign of the first gunship platoon in Vietnam.) The Huey "slicks" were C-models, somewhat larger, more elongated, and more powerful than the B-models, and were used for hauling troops and cargo. The C-model Huey would usually carry about six or seven American troops in combat gear, or about ten fully-equipped Vietnamese troops. Also, the C-models had one 7.62-mm machine gun mounted in each doorway that could be fired by the door gunner and the crew chief, when necessary.

The Viet Cong were just getting used to seeing the American banana-shaped H-21 Shawnee helicopters in the air when the Huey B-models were suddenly introduced in early 1963. The Viet Cong called the H-21s "Angle Worms," and the B-model Hueys were referred to as "Little Dippers." The UH-1 Huey became referred to as the "ubiquitous Huey"—the "workhorse of the Vietnam War," by some journalists.

"Focus…" Major Marker said, "I think you need to concentrate on the northwest corner there. I think that's where the fire's coming from—the northwest corner."

Lieutenant Clark was impressed with how calm and cool pilots always seemed to sound when they reported that they were "taking fire." He later came to realize that those words, "taking fire," would many times be the final words of some of these men, these pilots and crewmen.

The Mustangs usually flew just a bit behind the company formation and out to the flanks. They provided protection for the "slicks." The Mustangs were fast, efficient, and, above all, aggressive. They tended to always be bristling for a fight. No one ever seemed to have a complaint about the Mustangs. They were instantly firing on the tree line. They concentrated on the tree line at the northwest corner of the landing zone, but soon it seemed as though they were firing machine gun bullets and rockets into the complete circle of trees around the LZ.

"We got a man hit," someone said.

"Is it bad?" Major Compton asked.

"It's the foot. He's hit in the foot. It's Tuck. Mr. Tucker's been hit in the foot."

"Okay. Break off from the formation," Top Tiger Six said, "Go ahead and break off and head back to Xuan Loc. They've got a clinic there and they should be able to take care of him. We'll alert them and make sure they are expecting you."

"Roger that," said Mr. Swain, Mr. Tucker's co-pilot. "We're out of here and on our way."

One could almost tell by the attitude, the position of the aircraft against the skyline that Mr. Swain was quickly pulling a great deal of power as he broke away from the formation, nosed his aircraft over and downwards, and headed back toward Xuan Loc. The aircraft seemed somehow to react like a great steed responding to his master's demand for an urgent effort, a special endeavor, a special mission.

As Lieutenant Clark flew over the tree line at the far end of the landing zone the crew chief and door gunner in his aircraft opened fire with their machine guns at the tree line—just inside the tree line—firing almost straight down through the trees at times. The acrid smell of burning cordite was in Clark's system and it seemed to remain there for quite some time. The noise of the simultaneously firing M-60 machine guns was deafening—even with earplugs. But, at the same time, it was an exhilarating sound, a comforting sound that somehow seemed to bring with it a strange sense of security. Hot expended cartridge casings flew all over the metal floor of the helicopter and rolled about, many of them spilling out of the aircraft and falling into the roof of the jungle below.

After the Mustangs blasted away at the tree line for a few minutes, no more enemy fire was reported. The Top Tigers made three more trips between the airstrip at Xuan Loc and LZ Battleaxe that morning, bringing in more troops and then additional supplies. No more enemy fire was reported and there were no more casualties. Three days later they would extract this same Vietnamese unit from another landing zone about ten miles to the north of where they had been put into the jungle. (In operations, they never said they would collect or "pick up" the troops. It was always referred to as an "extraction." Likewise, during the operations briefings they never spoke of putting the troops into landing zones. They always spoke of "insertions.") The report was that they, the ARVNs, had encountered no resistance—no contact with the enemy—with the notoriously elusive "Charlie."

As it got later in the day, Lieutenant Clark noticed how formation flying seemed to get easier. It had to do with being tired, he later decided. The more worn out one is, the more one tends to relax. Being exhausted also helps one deal with fear, he discovered. If one is truly exhausted, then one tends to not get worked up over anything—except getting some rest, some rack time. At times he would be so exhausted that he felt as though, regardless of what happened, his body could not even muster the energy necessary to activate a rush of adrenaline—the stuff that put a man in that "fight or flight" mode—that natural high that caused some men to actually enjoy combat.

When the helicopter crews were all back on the ground again, on the PSP (perforated steel planking) airstrip at Xuan Loc, drinking coffee and

Kool Aid ("jolly-olly orange"), lounging in the morning sun, and eating C-ration cookies, they heard that Mr. Tucker would be alright. He had lost two or three toes, but he should be all right. He would not be a cripple or anything like that. Then someone who sounded authoritative said that Mr. Tucker had not lost two toes. He had only lost one toe or "one and a half toes."

Soon the men were making jokes about Mr. Tucker's situation. They started to speak of "the Legend of Mr. Tucker's Toes" or the quest for "whatever happened to Mr. Tucker's toe?" Someone came up with a little ditty that went something like this:

Somewhere in Marvin the ARVN's
Rice paddies,
Somewhere away over there,
Far beyond Buffalo, the Bills,
And all that fresh fallen snow,
Yes, there in the mud and grime,
A little part of America
Shall forever be,
I'll swear I truly know.
And that thing that lies there,
Forever and ever to our woe,
That thing that's out there and buried
Far, deep down below,
We all feel for certain that we know
That it's really so,
That thing, oh, yes,
That thing buried down there so deep
Is Mr. Tucker's toe!
Oh, yes, it's poor old Mr. Tucker's toe!
Poor old Mr. Tucker's…
Well, you guessed it, you know,
Oh, yes, it's poor old Mr. Tucker's tooohoooe!

So, all and all, everyone considered the mission at LZ Battleaxe a successful operation. They had experienced no fatalities or serious wounds. The ARVNs did not seem to find anything. Later Lieutenant Clark noticed that somehow they rarely ever met serious resistance when they were flying Vietnamese troops into operations. But when flying American troops, then things were often quite different. That was a different story.

Just at sundown, as the sky appeared to be aflame over the broad rooftop of the jungle to the west, the small formation of helicopters lifted off from the little airfield at Xuan Loc and headed back southeastward toward Vung Tau.

A little less than ten years later, on April 21, 1975, after a fierce two-week battle, the Communists would capture Xuan Loc, which would be the last South Vietnamese defense line before Saigon.

Chapter 2

The Diggers

It could have been a scene straight out of the pages of Kipling.

The wide doorways and high windows of the Pacific Hotel were open to the veranda, where a band dressed in white tunics filled the tropical evening with brassy music. The Australian officers were all dressed in white dinner jackets, black ties, and black trousers with broad red stripes down the sides. Everyone was shaved and clean and all the brass and leather was highly polished.

The place was the bright white stately Pacific Hotel in the southern seacoast city of Vung Tau. All of the free-flowing rum, music, spit, and polish represented the Australian army's "dining in" night. The Americans there discovered that it is traditional for the Australian Army to take their dress uniforms, or "full mess kit" as they called it, with them wherever they went, be it Tasmania, Tay Ninh, or Timbuktu. Conversely, the Americans would have considered it absurd to bring a dress uniform to Vietnam—to a combat zone.

The Top Tigers, the 68th Assault Helicopter Company, was assigned the job of training the newly arrived 5th Battalion of the Royal Australian Infantry Regiment in helicopter (or "heliborne") operations. And the Americans, to a man, found the assignment a most pleasant one. The Australians were an outstanding bunch of "blokes." One of the Australian officers said to Lieutenant Clark that everyone was more than pleased to be working with the Top Tigers.

"You guys are special," the garrulous Aussie said. "You guys are not *just* tigers. No, you are the *Top* Tigers. I tell you man, that says it all. *Top* Tigers—not just tigers, but *Top* Tigers. And we all know that you can't get no higher than that—the top. And that's were you guys belong—right there on the top—top of the whole smear—top of this whole business—this whole whirly-birdie business."

Many of the American helicopters wore the "badge of the Rising Sun"—the motif of the Australian Military Forces—on their Plexiglas windows. And likewise, many of the Aussie jeeps bore the prowling tiger sticker of the 68th Assault Helicopter Company, the Top Tigers.

After a fine steak dinner and all the proper toasts, the Aussies convened their "Baggy's Court." This was an original form of the Kangaroo Court, in which the lower-ranking company grade officers tried to punish the higher-ranking field grade officers for such farcical transgressions as wearing their hat at the bar, loitering, breathing in someone else's air, or some other such appalling misdeed. The American field-grade officers (in their dull green fatigue uniforms) did not have a chance. They were found guilty of all charges imaginable in a whirlwind of laughter, cheers, jeers, and bush-league jurisprudence.

One of the Aussies told Clark that kangaroos have little fear of man and out in the far reaches of the outback they commonly stand or sit staring at groups of people. During the early days of settling Australia, there were occasions when trials would be rather impromptu and rather informally conducted out in the open. Some started to notice the kangaroos sitting watchfully at a respectable distance and thought they might actually be some sort of a strangely attentive jury. Hence the term, "kangaroo court" emerged from the rugged regions of the old outback.

During a recess in Baggy's Court, the Australian commanding officer, Colonel John Wickham, of Melbourne, presented the American commander, Major Robert Compton, of Champaign, Illinois, with an Australian slouch hat, and in turn, Major Compton presented Colonel Wickham with a Montagnard crossbow. (The Montagnards are the aborigines of the Vietnamese highlands.)

This training arrangement soon developed into a real mutual admiration society between the "Diggers," (as the Aussies often called themselves) and the "Yanks." Each unit seemed to take great pride in its professionalism. The two units worked well together in training and in combat. Whether it was conduct at the bar or life-or-death combat operations, there was never a case of one side or the other not living up to full expectations.

Lieutenant Clark could hardly believe his luck when he arrived at Vung Tau and was quartered in the Pacific Hotel. This was certainly a long way from the tent or the Quonset hut that he had expected to live in when he arrived in Vietnam. The hotel quartered the Royal Australian 5th Infantry Battalion, the 68th Assault Helicopter Company, and the 106th (U.S.) Medical Support Battalion—and that was it. There were no civilian guests in the hotel. And the Pacific Hotel was a wonderful place to live. The food was good, the laundry was attended to, Vietnamese servants (mostly old women) cleaned and polished the officers' boots daily, there was a nice bar, and they usually had films or some other sort of entertainment to enjoy each night.

Upon his arrival, Clark was assigned to Room 217, which he shared with Warrant Officer Melvin Meeks, who was also newly arrived from the States. Clark lifted his heavy duffel bag and tossed it lightly onto his bed. The bag was stenciled **1/Lt Winston W. Clark** (the W was for Watson) with his serial number stenciled underneath his name. Clark introduced himself to his new roommate. Meeks was an amiable young man right out of flight school, as was Clark. Mr. Meeks was almost always agreeable, but there was something strangely melancholy about him. He always seemed just on the border of being depressed. He rarely smiled. Clark came to learn that Meeks deeply loved his wife and missed her a great deal. They had been married for only a short while when Meeks departed for Vietnam.

Clark and Meeks often dined and watched films together and, as "newbies," they were both being trained on local operations and procedures by the company check pilots, Lang and Hatch.

Company check pilots were almost always the senior warrant officers, usually with the most flying time. Also, they usually had a great deal of experience serving as instructor pilots. To Lieutenant Clark and most of the Top Tigers, Lang and Hatch became legendary figures. If ever there were men who could become one with their machine and work wonders with a helicopter, then these were those men. In another age, or time and place, these men might easily have been duelists, gun fighters, or Mississippi riverboat gamblers. There was a quite reserve about them that seemed to indicate that they were somehow in close contact with the powers of life and death. In a low-key way, both of them emanated a vibrant and potent presence. It was as if they were forever prepared to pull the plug or flip the switch that would change things in a fatal way.

Collins, the door gunner, would describe them as "cool." But that would be a gross understatement. These two were icemen. They were the kind of men that one could bet one's life on and not be disappointed. Clark always remembered them as two of the best men he had ever known. In their veins, he concluded, flowed a unique balance of warm blood and ice water.

John Lang was from Virginia and Bill Hatch was from Mississippi. Later, when Lieutenant Clark thought back about the Top Tigers, it came to him that the Top Tigers were predominantly Southerners—as he was. The CO, Major Compton, was from Illinois. Captain Nowotney was from Pennsylvania, as was Mr. Linville. Their door-gunner, PFC Collins, was from Ohio. Lieutenant Yamashi was from California, and Mr. Meeks was from Maryland. Aside from these few individuals, everyone Clark could remember in the company was from the South. He had heard the question asked a number of times: What was it about Southerners and the military? Clark later decided that it was a combination of economics and the Southern culture of guns and the pursuit of outdoor sports and adventure. Clark later thought it ironic that the Aussies referred to these men as "Yanks" when so few of them would consider themselves Yankees.

Lieutenant Clark enjoyed flying with both Lang and Hatch. He had enormous respect for both of them. But Lang—tall, rangy, blond, blue-eyed, handsome, and humorous—seemed to be the more commanding figure. Lang had a deep, clear, and distinctive voice. His voice was husky and distinctly masculine. It easily conveyed authority. Women of all ages and races were attracted to him. Lang was what some would call "a real stud of a man." Some men could find beer in a desert. Lang could find a willing woman there also.

"Now, backing up," Mr. Lang said as he demonstrated a hovering maneuver to Lieutenant Clark. "When it comes to backing up, always remember to do just as little of it as possible. A lot of accidents happen when people are trying to back up a helicopter—or even a car, for that matter. Just remember that the good Lord put your eyes in the front of your head—not the back. Therefore, you can see a lot better looking forwards rather than backwards. It's that simple. So, don't ever back up unless you absolutely have to. And when you do have to back up, back up just as little as possible. Don't push it."

When John Lang spoke of how to properly operate a helicopter, he spoke with such vivid and vital authority that for a moment, in his mind's eye, Winston Clark could visualize himself as the wide-eyed little farm boy, Joey, listening to Shane, the gunfighter, discuss the proper handling and operation of a revolver.

"It's that simple," Lang said.

Everything seemed simple to Mr. Lang. Perhaps that was one of the fundamental reasons that almost everyone liked him and enjoyed his company. He seemed altogether uncomplicated. When Lang was off duty he had a hearty laugh that would sparkle and crack right through the darkest storm clouds and bring instant sunshine and warmth raining down all around. No matter what the situation was, John Lang was always welcome.

Hatch's voice was softer. He was generally a quieter, more restrained person, and perhaps a little less sociable than Lang. Hatch once confided to Lieutenant Clark that he planned to run for sheriff when he returned to his home in Mississippi in a couple of years, after completing his twenty years in the army.

Clark had been with Lang several times when the pressure was on, and Lang worked what seemed like minor miracles with those flying machines they called Hueys. On one occasion, Clark was flying with Lang when they were tasked to pull an Aussie heavy mortar platoon out of the jungle. The Diggers had been under fire and they were exhausted. One of them was wounded, and they could not locate a suitably large opening in the jungle from which to be extracted. They were in a very small opening in the jungle, and they needed to be extracted without delay.

Chapter 3

Dead Man's Beach

Clark and Lang located the Aussies. There were only six of them, but they were carrying some heavy equipment. Lang flew into the wind and over the small opening and slowly eased down among the tall trees into the dark, dank open space. Down, down the aircraft went—straight down to land softly in the middle of the opening on the floor of the rainforest.

The weary, sweaty Aussies quickly climbed aboard, managed to get all of their heavy gear—base plates, tubes, ammunition, and pack-boards laced with fin-tailed little rocket bombs—in place and secured. The Aussies briskly settled in and signaled thumbs-up. They were ready to lift off. The wounded man appeared to be shot in his left armpit. He was shirtless, bandaged across his chest, and seemed to be in fair condition—as well as could be expected. He was smiling a tired smile. He winked and did a thumbs-up sign.

But now the aircraft was too heavy to be pulled straight up out of the little hole in the jungle.

"Now, where do we go from here?" Clark silently asked himself. "What about translational lift?"

"Translational lift" was the term pilots used for the critical point where the helicopter aerodynamically transitions from hovering flight into rapid forward and upward flight. After going through translation lift, the chopper blades cease to merely beat the air, but they gain the lift of a circular plain, or wing.

At its broadest point the space in the jungle before them looked not more than twenty yards wide. The space was not wide enough to make a dash for it, to get through translational lift and gradually up and into the sky. (The distance normally required to get a Huey through translational lift was about twenty yards.) But in this spot they had about twenty yards at most—and then there were tall trees to deal with. Additionally, they were working with a heavily loaded aircraft and in a no wind situation. Since there was no wind down in this little hole in the jungle, the wind factor did not need to be considered on take-off.

Mr. Lang was on the controls, and he was carefully monitoring the fuel level. They were down now to only about one quarter of a tank. Lang pulled up on the collective pitch lever, the power, and held the aircraft at a steady hover. He remained like that, more or less motionless, for what seemed like five minutes. He was gauging his power reserve—every minute more fuel was being consumed and the aircraft became a little lighter as a result. They took on weight with the mortar platoon but at the same time, as they hovered about, they were consuming fuel losing weight. Lang spoke to the crew chief.

"Okay, Jackson, watch my tail rotor. I'm gonna back into those trees and try to gain a little space here—a little running room."

Jackson came on line immediately. "Gotcha, sir. You're okay. Come on back. Come on. You're okay."

Lang carefully backed the chopper into what appeared to be a small opening in the trees and underbrush. Occasionally they could hear the blades—first the tail rotor then the main overhead blades—clipping and chopping at the foliage. Lang had the aircraft well in hand. He moved steadily, ever so slowly and carefully, hovering backwards inch by inch. He backed the chopper into the trees almost as though he was creating a parking place where he might sit it down and hide it for the night.

Finally, he got the machine to a position where a little more than half of it was backed into the trees. The undergrowth was such that apparently he could back no farther into the jungle.

"That's about it," Jackson, the crew chief, said. "I think you'd better hold it right there."

Lang then held it steady for a moment. He checked the power gauge. Lang stared forward at the open space before them—the available take off space. It certainly was not much. He gave the space an eagle's gaze. The available space was carefully being weighed and measured. This little piece of real estate was being most critically evaluated. Lang glanced upward toward the little circle of sky above them, and then straight ahead again at the open space before them.

"Now, what Mr. Lang is doing here," Lieutenant Clark was thinking, "is like a form of Zen—dynamic Zen."

"Okay, are you guys ready?" Mr. Lang asked. "Is everything secure?"

"Yes, sir," Jackson answered. "We're all set."

"Okay," Lang said. "Everybody hang on. Here we go, guys. Hang on."

With those words Lang eased the cyclic control stick forward bringing the nose of the aircraft down just a bit while simultaneously pulling in the power with the collective pitch lever. The helicopter raced forward toward the tall trees on the far side of the clearing. Lang continued to pull in the power as the aircraft quickly gained forward speed. When Mr. Lang consciously committed himself to this maneuver there seemed to be a silent conversation going on between him and the helicopter. His hands were firm and sure on the controls. The machine seemed to enjoy the way Mr. Lang handled her and she responded in a favorable manner. Later Clark was impressed with the powerful breathtaking roar of the engine as the machine dipped and moved forward. He imagined that he could almost hear the fire-breathing machine speaking to Lang and saying: *Alright, if you say we can do this, Mr. Lang, then we can—we shall do it. Yes, it shall be done.*

Just at the very moment when it appeared that they were all going to crash straight forward into the trees at the edge of the opening, Lang pulled back slightly on the stick and the aircraft popped upward. It seemed to move straight up the tall tree line—up, up, up—almost as if the aircraft was being pulled up on cables. Inside the cockpit it was a lot like being in an elevator. Lang gave the collective pitch lever a slight pumping motion and the airship continued to climb and finally it was above the trees. As the chopper peeped out over the roof of the jungle, Mr. Lang pushed the stick slightly forward and the nose dipped a bit as he simultaneously "milked," or gently pumped the collective pitch lever for more power. The machine moved forward over the green boundless top of the jungle. Lang instinctively looked for low places on the roof of the jungle. He would aim the aircraft into these pockets of space at the same time he continued to gently pump the power lever. The aircraft responded like an old friend. Slowly, it gained forward air speed and lifting power. Lang slowly turned the machine into the wind, and it slowly gained altitude. The engine now had a solid, completely certain, and almost triumphant sound about it. Everyone inside the chopper started to breathe again. The aircraft gradually climbed up into the air. Altitude—it meant security. Lang leveled the aircraft off at one thousand feet, and they flew quietly back to their home base at Vung Tau airfield. Clark noticed that the fuel level was quite low now, but they easily had enough to reach their home base. They could usually fly for about two hours before they needed to start looking for a refueling point.

"All things considered," Clark thought to himself, "with that wild run at the trees and all—well, you only get one chance at something like that. You cannot hesitate to reconsider Plan B or whatever. Once you are committed, you either make it or you don't. It's all or nothing—nope, no second chances in a place like that. Yep, Mississippi riverboat gamblers on station over the Mekong. Rolling those bones."

From the seat of his pants, the "pucker factor" of his buttocks, to the tips of his fingers and toes, if ever there was a man in tune with—*at one* with—his machine, that man was John Lang. When he turned his eagle's gaze on the console, he was seeing straight through to the heart and soul of the machine. No man could do more. This cocoon of rivets and metal suddenly became a flying metaphysical object and performed wonders.

"You know," Lieutenant Clark said to Lang, "not just anyone could do something like that—that which you just did back there."

But Mr. Lang acted like it was the most natural thing in the world. John Lang had cheated death on numerous occasions. It came with the territory.

"Just like drinking ice water on a hot summer day," said Lang with a broad smile.

Once Lang committed himself to that maneuver, there was no turning back. Just before he reached the point where they might crash into the trees, he had pulled back on the cyclic control stick just a bit, just slightly. But how much was slightly? If he did not pull back enough, they would have crashed into the trees before them. If he pulled back too much, the tail of the aircraft, the tailboom would have been too low and the tail-rotor blades would have sawed into the earth, the helicopter would have fallen backward onto the tailboom and they would have crashed back-wards. At the same time the pilot had to know just how much power to pull in with the collective pitch lever. If he did not pull in enough, the aircraft would never get above the treetop level and would lamely flutter back down to the ground for a hard landing—and perhaps explode. If he pulled in too much power, the engine would stall out and they would keel over to the side and crash. The pilot in charge had to know exactly when to pull the stick backward, and he had to know just how much power to pull—and he was not allowed to think about these movements. They had to be instinctive, "seat of the pants" movements. And they were. Mr. Lang taught Lieutenant Clark a great deal about developing a touch, a feel for flying helicopters.

"It's like Zen," Clark thought. "Aerodynamic, turbine-jet-powered Zen."

"Remember all that stuff they taught you in flight school," Lang said. "That was all basically good stuff and it works. Some people seem to believe that when they get over here in Nam that different rules apply—or that no rules apply. And that's not so. Fly the aircraft like they taught you in flight school and you'll be okay. You shouldn't get into trouble. The main thing you need to be mindful of over here is that the air is less dense and the payloads are heavier. And sometimes people are shooting at you, of course. So, you are going to need to stay alert and pay more attention to your available power and fuel load. You do those things and you should be alright."

Lieutenant Clark spoke up one day just after Mr. Lang had demonstrated a smooth maneuver. "I think I've got it," he said. "I've found the key."

"What do you mean?" Lang asked.

"The way to get the job done in this business, I believe, is simply to make no sudden movements in the cockpit. Take it slow and easy—no sudden movements. Everything slow and easy."

"Well, yes and no," Lang said.

"What do you mean?"

"Well, some people," Lang said, "like Mr. Meeks, your roomy, for instance, sometime appear entirely prepared to fly the machine slowly and easily right straight into the trees or the wires ahead. Slow and easy won't always get the job done. But it is a good general rule, I suppose."

Clark laughed and said something like, "Aw, come on." But he was surprised by what Lang had said. This was the first indication Clark heard that intimated that his roommate, Mr. Meeks, might be considered a loser by some in the company. Clark liked Meeks, but no one likes to be associated with a loser.

Lang and Clark were approaching the airfield at Vung Tau when Lang spoke.

"You see up there toward the end of the runway on the left—those bunkers there?"

"Yes, roger that," Clark answered.

"That's our ammo dump," Lang said. "And Rats almost blew the works a couple of weeks ago."

"Rats" was Captain Richard Ratcliffe. The Mustangs, the gunship platoon, were commanded by Major Wilson, a red-faced little man who always seemed somehow preoccupied with some sort of crisis management situation, often something of an administrative nature—the proper manner of completing this or that official form or report. Even though Major Wilson officially commanded the gunship platoon, everyone really considered Captain Ratcliffe, "Rats," to be the real platoon leader. Ratcliffe had a thick neck. He was a short stout man with very short reddish hair who seemed easy-going and filled with a natural and graceful sense of self-confidence. He had a ready smile and people seemed to like him in all instances, and he almost always liked the people he met. And when he spoke, people listened. Captain Ratcliffe instilled complete confidence in those around him, and he seemed to do it in a totally effortless manner. Even though he appeared to be completely casual, it did not take long to see that he also appeared to be a natural born warrior and leader. Ratcliffe was the supreme *samurai* of the Top Tigers. Some of the advisers called him "Buddha."

"What happened?" Clark asked.

"He was approaching the airfield just as we are now," Lang said. "He reached over to disarm his rockets and one of them fired. One of them fired and it exploded harmlessly over there on the left side of the airstrip. But it was dangerously close to our ammo bunker site there. Another fifty yards or so and he would have hit a bunker and we could have had a major fireworks."

"What caused the rocket to go off?"

"No one seems to know," Lang answered. "Rats said he thought it must have been some kind of weird electrical power surge or something like that. But no matter what he said, the enlisted men, those that were working in the area, seemed to think that Rats did it on purpose—just for kicks—just to see them scramble. Can you imagine that? They seemed to think that Rats simply wanted to liven things up a bit and get some attention."

"That sounds highly unlikely, I think."

"As far as Rats goes," Lang went on, "the men seem to think nothing accidental could ever happen with him. It's all got to be intentional and it's got to be just for kicks. I don't think the men could ever imagine Rats not being completely in control of everything—in charge and in control. That's their take on Rats. Some of them have started to refer to him now as the 'rocket man'—Rats the Rocket Man."

"Point is," Lang concluded, "Be careful around those gunships—those rockets. They do seem to act rather erratic at times."

The Sunday morning after the Australian "dining in," both Clark and Meeks were able to sleep late and then go to the nearby beach for a swim. "Dead Man's Beach" they called it. The beach was beautiful, with huge boulders as a backdrop and with no development around it. There were only a few more Americans and Australians enjoying the sunshine and beach. They had heard the place referred to as "Dead Man's Beach" and wondered aloud why the beautiful place had such a forbidding designation. Just before they prepared to roll up their towels and things and return to the hotel, a friendly GI briefly spoke with them and explained the beach's morbid nomenclature. Even though this beach was picturesque and inviting, the GI explained, it had a very tricky undertow. He had been told that every year at least one or two people were pulled out to sea by the deadly current and drowned. Also, there was a worrisome swarm of sharks that consistently lurked just off shore in the deeper water. The men could often see the sharks as the pilots flew low over the beaches coming in and out of the Vung Tau airfield.

Clark thought the beach was one of the most beautiful that he had ever seen. He had seen an old map somewhere that told him that the French called this place *Cap St. Jacques*. He loved it, but he also respected it and enjoyed it with caution. There was always a special place in his heart for this place—Vung Tau. He enjoyed the sound of the name—*Vung Tau*. Later he thought of it as a fitting metaphor for the American experience in Vietnam. The beach at Vung Tau was beautiful and inviting, but it could also be cruel and deadly.

Chapter 4

The Crew

It seemed to Lieutenant Clark that, as soon as he got settled in to the stately Pacific Hotel in Vung Tau, he started to hear rumors that the company would soon be relocating.

He soon discovered that this was more than a rumor. The 68th Assault Helicopter Company would be relocating to Bien Hoa Airbase within the next thirty days.

Clark had felt all along that Vung Tau, with the hotel and the beach, was too good to be true. And sure enough, it was. What he was presently hearing was that, now that the company had finished training the Royal Aussie's 5th Battalion, it would only be practical for them to relocate to Bien Hoa Airbase. There they would be nearer to their headquarters and their sister companies. Also they would be located more-or-less in the center of III Corps Tactical Zone, which was their assigned area of operations. That area roughly included the region from Vung Tau on the coast, westward to the Saigon/Bien Hoa/Long Bien area, on westward to Di An,

Cu Chi, and then finally to Tay Ninh district, near the Cambodian border. Di An was the base camp for the 1st Infantry Division and Cu Chi was the base camp for the 25th Infantry Division, both of which the Top Tigers would be supporting with their helicopters.

The III Corps area extended north of Saigon about seventy-five miles to Loc Ninh. The corps area also extended to the south almost to My Tho, which was about forty miles south of Saigon in the Mekong Delta.

Asian folklore held that the Mekong River, located about forty-five miles south of Saigon, represented a sacred serpent that wound its way down from Tibet to the South China Sea. Cambodian peasants supposedly considered their royal family—Prince Sihanouk's family—to be descended from the sacred serpent of the Mekong River. Early on the thought had occurred to Clark that the shape of Vietnam on the map rather resembled a dragon—slowly, furtively advancing down along the edge of the South China Sea.

Lieutenant Clark had finished his orientation training with Mr. Lang and now was flying with a regular crew—and a fine crew it was. Captain Nowotney informed Lieutenant Clark that he would be flying with Mr. Linville. So, now he had met Mike Linville and was looking forward to flying with him. Their crew chief was Sergeant James Dotson, a young black man from Memphis, Tennessee. Their door gunner was PFC Robby Collins, from Ohio ("near Cincinnati," Collins had said).

Clark felt especially fortunate to be flying with Mike Linville. Mr. Linville was from Pennsylvania, and he was a pilot of considerable experience and skill. He could not possibly have a temperamental bone in his body. Mike Linville was truly a man in possession of a sparkling personality. He was always laughing and joking. He seemed to carry a radiant torch of good cheer, light, and optimism with him. Everyone seemed to take great pleasure in his company. As Mr. Lang was to say one evening: "Linville, you know, I must say, I believe your Momma raised you right."

Mr. Linville had recently been awarded the Distinguished Flying Cross. Clark had never known anyone with such a high decoration. Actually,

Linville was the only man in the unit with such a distinction. Linville's reaction after being presented the award was to take a careful look at the medal and say, "Hey, that's a really pretty medal. Really."

"Yeah, I guess so," Clark said. "Charles Lindbergh was awarded the first one back in 1927. You remember Lindy, I'm sure."

"Oh, sure. Yeah," said Linville. "Lucky Lindy—good man."

"When you write your Momma," Mr. Lang joked, "you can tell her that you've now been decorated by Betty Crocker, and recommended by Duncan Hines."

One evening Linville came to tell Clark about the occasion that resulted in him being awarded that decoration.

"Not long after we had dropped these grunts into the LZ," Linville said, "we got word that they were in serious trouble. The landing zone, somewhere just north of Phuoc Vinh, turned out to be hot—super hot. The CO came on the line and asked us to go back to the LZ and pick up some serious casualties. We were closest to the site, I believe. Well, we went in okay—no problems. Nobody shot at us. Or, at least, we took no hits. But then as the grunts started to move out of the tree line to bring the wounded out to us, all hell broke loose. We were sitting there waiting for the litters, the wounded, and just before the grunts reached the aircraft, we started to take fire—really hot, intense fire from the tree line. And what happens? The grunts all hit the ground—and they would not get up. We're sitting there with our blades turning, waiting, taking fire, and these guys are hugging the dirt. Terra firma. They won't get up—and we're taking fire like crazy. We can hear the bullets tearing through the aircraft. We were being shot to pieces.

"I shouted to the crew chief and the door gunner," Linville continued. "I told them '*Come on*. Jump out there and get those grunts moving! Tell them to come on. We gotta go! We can't just sit here and get shot all to hell!'

"But those grunts just would not move," Linville went on. "Our guys were out there in the grass pleading with them to get up. Then it got so hot that our guys would have to hit the deck and hug the ground. But they kept on pleading with those grunts to get up and move and go, but no luck. They seemed to be frozen—frozen in place. In the meantime, we're taking hits like crazy. It was like we were just sitting there getting shot to pieces. We could hear the bullets whacking into the fuselage and others buzzing through the open doors. Zing! Zap! Zing! Ping! Some really hot stuff, man. It was like everything was coming apart. Now I'll tell you what—and I realize this is difficult to believe—but we had bullet holes through every window—the Plexiglas was riddled. There was not one window on the aircraft that did not have bullet holes in it—and no one was hit. No one."

"No one was hit?" Lieutenant Clark marveled.

"No one. Not a soul. Not a scratch. Not a body."

"How could that ever happen?" Clark asked. "It seems impossible."

"It was Ultimate Six," Mr. Linville said, after a pause with a wide grin. When he said "Ultimate Six" he was holding his right thumb pointing upwards. And he was smiling and glancing up in a heavenly direction as he made an upward gesture with his thumb.

"What else can I say? It was Ultimate Six that did it. Ultimate Six was looking out after us that day."

"Finally," Linville went on, "somehow there seemed to be a slight pause in the intensity of the fire, and our guys *finally* managed to get those grunts up off the ground and into the aircraft. It seemed like we were sitting there forever waiting for them with their wounded. It seemed like an hour and a half. But actually it was probably only about three minutes. So finally they were aboard the aircraft. We pulled pitch, and off we went—full of bullet holes but okay—everybody was okay. I was flying with Tucker that day—you know, good old toeless Tuck."

Now, Mr. Linville not only was a recipient of the Distinguished Flying Cross, the men referred to him as the "coolest of the cool." He simply sat there taking fire and waiting for the soldiers to bring their wounded. Napoleon had his Marshal Ney, whom he referred to as the "bravest of the brave," and the Top Tigers had their Mr. Linville—the "coolest of the cool." The sheet-metal workers (the sheet-metal platoon) counted something like forty-five bullet holes in that aircraft—and *no one was hit.* The sheet-metal workers declared Mr. Linville to be the "coolest of the cool" and none would disagree. Mr. Linville was truly cool—and, as was Marshal Ney, he was truly brave.

Both of the main rotor blades from Mr. Linville's aircraft had so many bullet holes in them that they were deemed unsafe and irreparable. Still, the blades were wide, heavy, and relatively strong. The maintenance team carefully laid them side-by-side across a drainage ditch they had been forced to hop over to take a shortcut back to the barracks. Beside this sturdy improvised bridge the sheet metal workers erected a neat little metal sign which read as follows: "Your tax dollars at work—This bridge cost $13,871.52"

Sergeant James Dotson worked hard and conscientiously. He was normally rather quiet. Oftentimes he might even go unnoticed. He seemed like the kind of man who enjoyed a challenge. As soon as a challenge came along, Dotson would undergo a quiet metamorphosis and suddenly become a firm and steady leader.

"Come on you guys," Sergeant Dotson would say in a loud nagging manner, "let's get this business done. Let's don't doodle around. Let's get it done, man, *done*! I mean, like, *done*, man! Done, done, finished, over and outta here!"

Dotson seemed to thoroughly enjoy being a crew chief, and moreover, he appeared to enjoy firing the machine guns. He also had a brother who was a crew chief in a different unit—a CH-47 Chinook cargo helicopter unit. The Chinook helicopter looked a great deal like a flying boxcar underneath a set of twin main rotor blades. Actually, "Boxcars" was the radio call sign of one of the Chinook outfits, the 178th Assault Support Helicopter Company. Sergeant Dotson's brother had been badly burned in a helicopter crash, a Chinook crash, but he had recovered and was back on flight duty. Despite terrible burn scars, he still seemed to love his job.

Robby Collins, the young kid from Ohio, had been a clerk. He said the paper work just about drove him crazy. He decided that he was adventurous, so he volunteered to become a door gunner. And he enjoyed being with "cool" guys—the pilots. He was more than happy; he was excited to be working with Mr. Linville, "Mr. Cool," the "coolest of the cool." Also, he immediately hit it off with Lieutenant Clark and soon concluded that Lieutenant Clark also was cool—at least cool enough to join the team. Clark became convinced that there was nothing that Collins would not do if asked to do it by his pilots, Clark, or Linville. And, in all likelihood, the same applied to Sergeant Dotson.

As Lieutenant Clark and Mr. Linville finished inspecting (or "pre-flighting," as they said) the aircraft for the mission of the day, they looked up to see Major Scully, the executive officer (XO) and First Sergeant Rodriguez walking toward them. It was a clear, hot, sunny morning and they were going to Saigon. Linville and Clark had been assigned to fly Scully and Rodriguez to Bien Hoa and Saigon to coordinate the company's impending move. They were all prepared to spend at least one night in Saigon, and they were all looking forward to a chance to look around at things in the capital city.

Major Scully was a nervous man. He perspired profusely, was always wrapped up in paper work, and usually spoke of only two topics: his dislike for being in Vietnam, and his desire to be back home in Georgia. He became really fervent when he spoke of how he disliked being in Vietnam, and he appeared to almost melt with nostalgia and sentimentality when he spoke of Georgia. He seemed to never exhaust these topics—especially the topic of Georgia.

Lieutenant Clark soon decided that the company could not have a better first sergeant than First Sergeant Ernesto Rodriguez. This man was clearly surrounded with an aura of unimpeachable authority. He was from Texas, and was cheerful, outgoing, and humorous. But when he got serious, everyone got serious. First Sergeant Rodriguez was a first-rate teacher. When a class of some sort was required for the enlisted men,

Rodriguez did not delegate the task down to another NCO, as he well might have done. Quite often, he stepped forward and taught the class himself. He could conduct quick, well-organized classes like no one else in the unit could ever dream of doing. Normally, Sergeant Rodriguez spoke in a pleasant, gracefully-measured, authoritative manner. However, if, for a moment, he got the impression that someone was not paying attention or being disrespectful, he would suddenly—without the slightest warning—go into a fiery tirade. He expressed instant and profound rage in no uncertain terms. Yes, he had a searing rage mode. But still, somehow, he never lost control. And he never lost his composure. Sergeant Rodriguez had that rare talent of effective ranting, but at the same time, he kept his dignity and continued to make sense. And his harangues were effective and achieved the desired effect. After one of his rants, no one dared to misbehave in his presence again. No, not for a long time, if ever, would that guilty soldier fail to pay attention while First Sergeant Rodriguez was speaking. If they had been assigned to an infantry unit, the troops would have all followed Sergeant Rodriguez into battle anytime and anyplace, because their fear and respect for him would certainly have superseded any fear or respect they might have had for the enemy. Major Compton's job as commanding officer was made infinitely easier simply because of the fact that he enjoyed the good fortune of having Master Sergeant Ernesto Rodriguez serving as the company first sergeant, the "first shirt," as the men would say.

That awful term, "fragging"—the murder of one's own NCOs or officers by fragmentation grenade—was, and would remain, alien to this company of men. This unit had excellent cohesion, primarily because they were not a patched-together company of replacements. Most of these men had trained together at Ft. Benning, Georgia for over a year and were then shipped to Vietnam together—as a unit—and that seemed to make a great deal of difference. American units in Vietnam seemed to have less and less cohesion after the rapid-build up of forces started in 1965.

Certainly there was no one else in the world like First Sergeant Rodriguez, and Lieutenant Clark never forgot that man. Clark considered Rodriguez to be one of the finest teachers that he had ever observed. Both Clark's mother and father had been teachers, so he felt qualified to make judgments on these matters. His mother taught English, and his father had taught History and then worked for almost fifteen years as a school principal back in Watauga, Clark's hometown. One year before Clark had shipped out for service in Vietnam, his father had died of a heart attack. With his parents' blessings and encouragement, Clark had attended the state university, studied History, and was also thinking of becoming a teacher. Clark's sister, Clara, who was three years older than he, was also a teacher. Her field was Biology.

The flight to Bien Hoa was a short and pleasant one. Bien Hoa airfield was located about fifteen miles north of Saigon, and it took them about forty minutes to fly there from Vung Tau. There they visited their battalion headquarter in Bien Hoa City, and then they visited Bien Hoa Airbase. On the way out they noticed how Bien Hoa was expanding, with a great population of refugees living in surrounding shantytowns. Many of the new shacks were constructed in a rather novel manner. The refugees scavenged empty beer and soda cans discarded at trash dumps, cut the cans open, pounded them flat, and nailed them to strips of scrap wood to make metal sheets for walls and roof. Later, the Americans were to learn that the Viet Cong could also make excellent bombs and booby traps from soft drink cans. One of the most common Viet Cong booby traps was simply to remove the safety pin from a grenade and place the grenade inside a tin can. When someone tripped over the tripwire, the pull on the tripwire would extract the grenade from the open can, which then automatically primed itself and exploded after about seven seconds.

They drove onto the airbase and to the area, where they were later to be quartered. There was not much there at the airfield at that time, except for the U.S. Air Force facilities. Vietnam had only three jet airfields at that time: Tan Son Nhut, at Saigon; Bien Hoa, just north of Saigon; and Da Nang, about four-hundred miles north of Saigon.

Chicken-coop-type structures were being constructed for the Top Tigers to live in at Bien Hoa Airbase, and a large swampy area had to be filled in and paved over. That would become the huge heliport out of which they would operate. Also, structures would be erected for maintaining the aircraft, ammunition, and equipment. Already, U.S. combat engineers were busy filling in the swamp (or was it a rice paddy?) and transforming it into some pretty solid real estate. Lieutenant Clark was impressed with the fast and efficient work of the engineers. Later, he would recall that he could hardly believe how quickly they transformed that area into an extraordinary heliport and base camp. When Clark learned of the plans and first viewed the area, he was really not sure that it could be done.

The first major attack against Americans by Viet Cong agents had been at Bien Hoa Airbase. Just before dawn on November 1, 1964, a shower of mortar shells fell on the base, and a chain of explosions shattered the still darkness. U.S. advisers tumbled out of their beds and appeared to running in all directions at once as gasoline tanks erupted in flames and debris flew through the air. Search parties immediately fanned out through the neighborhood to search for the assailants, but they had vanished without a trace. After daylight, when the losses were tabulated, six B-57 jet bombers had been destroyed and more than twenty other aircraft damaged.

Five Americans and two South Vietnamese were killed, and nearly a hundred were injured. And this certainly would not be the last major attack against the Americans at Bien Hoa Airbase.

Chapter 5

A Chivalric Code

They spent two hours at Bien Hoa Airbase and then they were off to Saigon. It was only a short flight.

As they drew closer to Tan Son Nhut, the Saigon airport, Clark noticed there was a great deal of air traffic. Everyone had to be on their toes.

After landing, they tied down the rotor blades and locked the aircraft. Then they succeeded in borrowing two jeeps from the local aviation unit, the "Deans," as they called themselves because their unit had been in Vietnam longer than any other helicopter company. They considered themselves the old pros, or the *professors*, who were there to demonstrate to all others who came after them just how helicopter support should be properly done. Their gunship platoon was called the "Razorbacks." (It was said that their leader was from Arkansas.) Now their primary job seemed to be flying VIPs around the Saigon-Long Binh area. Long Binh was a supply depot area just northeast of Saigon that expanded until it covered twenty-five square miles. It was inhabited by about 43,000 Americans at its height, in 1968. Additionally, there were more than 20,000 Vietnamese employed there by the Americans.

The Deans and the Razorbacks had been involved in the Battle of Ap Bac, in January 1963, which turned out to be one of the first serious battles of the war. Bac was a small village in the Mekong Delta, about forty miles southwest of Saigon. (In the news dispatches it became "Ap Bac" because *ap* was the word for "hamlet.") The Viet Cong knew what was coming there and they prepared to make a stand, even though they were outnumbered by roughly ten to one. The Viet Cong commander seemed to expect defeat that day. Someone later found his diary in which he had written: "Better to fight and die than run and be slaughtered." Approximately 350 guerrillas stood their ground that day and humbled an ARVN division that was supported with armor, artillery, helicopters, and fighter-bombers. This looked like the set-piece battle for which so many American advisers had been wishing. Within five minutes the Viet Cong had shot down four helicopters. Here the Viet Cong learned that if they could shoot down one helicopter—and they were prepared to take risk and stick it out—they could, in all likelihood, shoot down more. The chopper pilots seemed to adhere to a strict code of camaraderie. If one crew went down, they had to be rescued—without question and right away. Some older, more experienced officers tried to tell the pilots that this war was no place for such chivalric codes of conduct. But the pilots did not listen. They had their own deep-seated feelings about what was right. Before that long day was over, the Americans had lost five helicopters, with three crewmembers being killed. The ARVN division had seen approximately 80 killed, and the VC only 18. Roughly a decade earlier, the Viet Cong had fought and defeated the French on almost exactly this same battlefield. The Viet Cong had stood their ground, fought bravely, and overcome great odds to win an impressive victory at Ap Bac. This victory seemed to be an important morale-building turning point for them.

After the Battle of Ap Bac, a pilot or crewman—later no one could recall the author's name—composed a ballad about the fight. It was sung many times over beer and popcorn at the clubs at Tan Son Nhut. The ballad of *Ap Bac* was sung to the tune of *On Top of Old Smokey*, and it went something like this:

We were supporting the ARVNs,
A gang without guts,
Attacking a village
Of straw-covered huts.
A ten-copter mission,
A hundred-troop load,
Three lifts were now over
And a fourth on the road.
The VCs start shooting
They fire a big blast,
We off-load the ARVNs
And they sit on their ass.
One chopper is crippled,
And another sits down,
Attempting a rescue,
Now there are two on the ground.
A Huey returns now
To give them some aid,
The VCs are so accurate
They shoot off a blade.
Four pilots are wounded,
Two crewmen are dead,
When it's all over
A good day for the Red.
They all lay in the paddy
All covered with slime,

A hell of a sunbath
Eight hours at a time.
Now all you young pilots please take warning,
When that tree line is near,
Let's land those damn choppers
Ten miles to the rear.

Chapter 6

Pearl of the Orient

Lieutenant Clark and his friends climbed aboard the jeeps with their bags, and then they were off for downtown Saigon with Sergeant Rodriguez at the wheel of one jeep and Sergeant Dotson at the wheel of the other.

Immediately as one drives through the main gate of the Tan Son Nhut airport, which is located to the northwest of the city, one is almost overwhelmed by the traffic and the bustle of the expanding city of Saigon. The air was blue with a heavy offensive haze created by the dense traffic. The first area encountered is a series of squalid wooden and tin shacks, some of them built over murky canals where the children swim and women wash clothes in the sewage-contaminated brown water. The main road leading into the city is choked with thousands of bicycles, motorbikes, motor scooters, cars and trucks of all types and sizes, buses, rickshaws, and even an occasional oxcart—vehicles of every sort imaginable. The windows of U.S. military buses were screened with wire mesh as a precaution against grenade assaults.

One drives by an endless line of street vendors selling a variety of items—from charcoal, soap, beer, and soda, to rice cakes, hard-boiled duck eggs, and soup. The favorite local soup was called *pho.* It was a thick mixture of chicken with cabbage, parsley, soybean sprouts, and rice noodles, laced with garlic and the national condiment, *nuoc nam,* a strong smelling sauce made from fermented fish. It appeared to Clark as though the Vietnamese might be eating *pho* any time of the day or night. He never took this drive without observing dozens of old women, either barefoot or in "Ho Chi Minh sandals" (sandals made from pieces of old tires), sitting on their haunches just inches off the dusty road busily eating *pho.*

As Clark's jeep carefully negotiated the traffic with Sergeant Rodriguez at the wheel, the streets seemed ever more congested. Sergeant Rodriguez, the company's "first shirt," was talking to the traffic under his breath.

"Yes, yes, you should do that and do it *now.* Yes, that's right. Yes, that's your place. Now, you just stay right there. Yes, stay there. No, don't get restless. Don't get nervous. No, no, no, you should *not* do *that.* No, brother, no way, no way—back off! Back off and cool it!"

Sergeant Rodriguez seemed involved in a calm but half-desperate effort to find or create order in the chaos. Saigon was bursting at the seams, and it was hot and stifling.. Saigon—along with its sister city to the southwest, Cholon, their Chinatown—was filled with refugees. Since 1960 the population had more than tripled from just over one million to over three million. By the time the Communists took control of Saigon in the spring of 1975, the population would be estimated at approximately five million people.

Women and girls were seen everywhere in their traditional *ao dais,* the graceful, gossamery, butterfly-like Vietnamese dress, and their wide conical hats. They often covered the lower part of their faces with a handkerchief in a vain effort to avoid the dirt and the pervasive clouds of stinking blue fumes that overwhelmed everyone in or near all of the busier streets. Many of the young women appeared extraordinarily pretty and delicate in their gossamer silk or cotton *ao dais,* with its high-necked tunic and loose pantaloons. Some of the older women were terribly ugly, with black enamel-covered teeth and betel nut juice running down the corners of the mouths.

A powerful Vietnamese emperor of the fifteenth century, Le Thanh Tong, initiated some extraordinarily progressive reform measures that concerned the women of his empire. He strongly promoted education, and encouraged poetry and art contests. He encouraged his scholars to record the history of their country, and he issued the first complete map of Vietnam. His major achievement was a comprehensive and unusually liberal legal code. He was the Vietnamese Justinian, one might say. Its provisions protected citizens against abuse by mandarins, and entitled women to possess property, share inheritances, and repudiate their husbands under certain conditions. The legal code of Le Thanh Tong was said to be unique in Asia, and indeed, it was quite progressive compared to what was going on in Europe at that time.

With its spacious boulevards, botanical gardens, tree-lined squares, marketplaces, and fine public buildings, Saigon clearly bore the stamp of its French heritage. The French had taken control of the city in 1859. They had actually been in contact with the Vietnamese since 1627, the year that a number of Jesuits were expelled from Japan and allowed to enter Vietnam for asylum.

One of them was Alexandre de Rhodes, an accomplished linguist. Rhodes devised a system, still in use today, to transcribe the Vietnamese language in Roman letters instead of Chinese ideographs. Rhodes was a successful missionary in Vietnam for several years, baptizing almost 7,000 people—including 18 nobles. But then the emperor reacted out of fear that the Christians were eroding his authority. Rhodes was banished to the Jesuit headquarters in Macao. He sneaked back into Vietnam at the risk of his life in 1645. He was arrested and imprisoned for three weeks before being expelled again. Of the nine priests who accompanied him two were beheaded, and each of the other seven had a finger cut off. Rhodes returned to his native France to die in 1660. To the end of his life he continued to lobby among French religious and commercial leaders to support renewed missionary efforts in Vietnam. However, the French did not really start to apply themselves to their *grande mission civilisatrice* (the conquest of Vietnam) until the mid-nineteenth century. Many of the more educated Vietnamese happily embraced the French culture, while resisting French colonialism.

The first American to set foot in Vietnam was Captain John White of Salem, Massachusetts. His clipper ship visited Saigon in 1820. However, the royal court officials of the Emperor Minh Mang quickly rebuffed Captain White. The emperor considered himself to be the "Son of Heaven," and he was at the top of a hierarchy that—in the Chinese tradition—mirrored a static concept of order and harmony. The royal court was there to protect the kingdom from innovative and potentially disruptive ideas and practices. He severely punished Buddhists and Taoists, whose beliefs and teachings violated the doctrine of the emperor's divinity. The same certainly applied to those who preached Christianity. Minh Mang's establishment contained no department of foreign affairs. "The barbarians," he said, "were not worthy of any attention."

For some unknown reason, to Lieutenant Clark the name Saigon had always—since he first heard the name—represented the exotic in its most complete and absolute form. *Saigon.* He would say the name, "Saigon," and he could almost hear a gong sounding somewhere behind a curtain of bamboo and see a dragon descending the Mekong River. Saigon would, for Clark, provoke all of the feelings and smells and sounds of all of the mysteries of the Orient. Saigon was one with the mysterious, enigmatic, and inscrutable. Saigon, if we search carefully, thoroughly, and patiently, will you reveal your fabled secrets, your cultural wonders, your exotic prizes, your hidden treasures?

Clark and his companions were amazed by the traffic, but still he found Saigon dazzling. Clark had read everything he could find about Vietnam, starting with the French scholar Bernard Fall's *Street Without Joy.* Fall was killed in Vietnam in 1967 while accompanying a U.S. Marine patrol working out of Da Nang.

Not all of the streets in Saigon were narrow, dirty, and crowded. They drove down the wide tree-lined Boulevard Norodom, a handsome avenue that opened onto the Presidential Palace, an imposing structure that dated back to French colonial days.

The palace was now called the Gia Long Palace, in honor of a powerful eighteenth-century Vietnamese emperor, and it was also the former French governor's residence. White-uniformed police ("white mice," the GIs called them) were standing behind the high-wrought iron fence at close intervals, guarding that disputed place. A large flag of the Republic of Vietnam waved over the palace. The Vietnamese flag depicted three red stripes on a yellow background, a combination which gave rise to the unkind GI quip that, "When they're not red, they're yellow."

Lieutenant Clark could make out a few bomb craters on the palace grounds, and the palace itself appeared to still be pockmarked from large-caliber shells fired into it in February 1962, during an airborne assassination attempt by two renegade South Vietnamese pilots. The two pilots, flying AD-6s—World War II attack airplanes, models given to the South Vietnamese by the U.S.—circled the palace for almost an hour during the early morning hours, strafing and dropping bombs and napalm, and all mostly to no avail. Three guards were killed and thirty were injured. But the ruling family survived, uninjured except for Madame Nhu, who had fractured her arm while tumbling down the stairs to the bomb shelter.

But the attack caused the president, Ngo Dinh Diem, to become even more of a recluse and to relegate more power and authority to his younger brother, Ngo Dinh Nhu, who was considered by most to be rather unstable. Then, in November of 1963, the generals launched a coup d'état and seized control of the government. (Also, the renegade pilots survived the failed bombing raid-assassination plot and went unpunished.) The Vietnamese president and his brother (the "mandarins," as they were known) were assassinated after they attempted to surrender during the generals' coup. The president, Diem, was a Catholic presiding over a nation of mostly Buddhists. He was a short, plump figure always dressed in a white linen suit and a black tie. And it was generally agreed that he was not the most effective of national leaders (even though one journalist on an early visit to Vietnam referred to him as the "Churchill of Asia").

Most agreed that the president's younger brother, Ngo Dinh Nhu, was the real power—along with his pretty wife, Madame Nhu, the "Dragon Lady." (Her maiden name was Le Xuan, which means "Beautiful Spring.")

Madame Nhu, in her stiletto heels and her diamond-encrusted crucifix, appointed herself the arbiter of Vietnamese moral laws. One of the things the Dragon Lady wished to do was to make it illegal for Vietnamese women to wear "falsies." However, this idea was abandoned, because it created an unduly complicated problem of enforcement for the police. It was no secret that Diem believed that all Vietnamese should be Catholics. Religious freedom was not a crucial item on his agenda. After a Buddhist monk had burned himself to death in the center of a busy Saigon intersection in protest of Diem's treatment of Buddhists, the Dragon Lady's response was: "If the Buddhists wish to have another barbecue, I will be glad to supply the gasoline and matches." Some described the Dragon Lady as insensitive.

Madame Nhu said that the monks were all Communists or dupes of the Communists. Most Westerners who had met her husband, the powerful younger brother, Nhu, were quite skeptical of him as a reliable ally. It was commonly said of him that he was a heavy user of opium and an enthusiastic admirer of Adolf Hitler. He was already busy organizing his own corps of storm trooper Brown Shirts, but he dressed his men in blue shirts. As the United States continued to commit more and more resources to the war in Vietnam, there were persistent rumors that the CIA might have played a role in that bloody coup d'état in the heart of Saigon. After that coup, the war was quickly Americanized. Politically speaking, the South Vietnamese government had bottomed out—gone bust.

It was the Diem regime that came up with the term *Viet Cong.* The *Viet Minh*, a nationalist movement founded during the early 1940s by Ho Chi Minh to fight the Japanese and later the French, was sometimes referred to as the National Liberation Front. The Viet Minh were almost always closely associated with nationalism—not Communism. But the Diem regime coined the disparaging name "Viet Cong"—Vietnamese Communists—to describe all those groups that opposed President Diem, and to give them an image of ruthless and fanatical cruelty. The terms Viet Cong, VC, Victor Charlie, and Charlie survived the war and are currently used almost always without any pejorative overtones. (On Wall Street, a VC is said to be a "venture capitalist.")

When the crowds in Saigon learned that the ARVN soldiers had killed both Diem and his brother, Nhu, that was supposedly the first and only time in the history of the war that they cheered their troops. Girls gave the soldiers bouquets of flowers, and men offered them beer, soda, and tea.

Madame Nhu escaped the coup because she happened to be in the United States at the time. She and her children later flew to Rome. On November 22, 1963, just three weeks after the President of the Republic of Vietnam was assassinated, President John F. Kennedy was assassinated. When Madame Nhu heard the news of Kennedy's assassination, she said that it was as it should be, because, she said, Kennedy was behind the murder of her husband. Diem's older brother, Ngo Dinh Thuc, the Archbishop of Hue, also escaped. The Vatican called him to Rome in an effort to disassociate the church from the regime's behavior.

Both official and unofficial commissions and committees would exhaustively investigate the assassination of President Kennedy. But neither the American or South Vietnamese government ever conducted a public inquiry into the assassination of Diem and his brother, Nhu.

The assassination of President Kennedy created a unique moment in the history of the twentieth century in that it caused so much speculation about how significantly this tragic incident might have affected history. Not only serious historians but also the common people all across America seemed to ceaselessly ask themselves, "What would our relationship with Cuba, with Vietnam, with the *world* have been like if President Kennedy had not been assassinated?"

Many cynics have said that it would have all been about the same. Some have said things might have been even worse. But many of those would-be-optimists, those touched by the spirit of the "New Frontier" and *Camelot*, seem to believe that somehow it all might have turned out a great deal better than it did.

After the Bay of Pigs fiasco in Cuba and an unsuccessful summit meeting with the Russian Soviet leader Nikita Khruschchev in Vienna, President Kennedy said, "Now we have to make our power credible, and Vietnam is the place. Vietnam will be the testing ground of democracy."

Some have said that President Kennedy was preparing to pull the Americans out of Vietnam. However, others have said that he was consciously edging his country into what French President Charles de Gaulle had warned him would be a "bottomless military and political swamp." The early death of President Kennedy certainly represented one of the great might-have-been questions of the Vietnam War, and the history of the twentieth century.

After the assassination of Diem, the Saigon government was controlled by a succession of Vietnamese general officers, or juntas. There were several fairly quiet and bloodless coups over the next few years, as one clique of officers would replace another at the head of the government. The people of Saigon and South Vietnam seemed to hardly notice. Because of the great infusion of American money, Saigon was a gold rush city. In time, the Americans, those who considered themselves old hands around Saigon, would boast of being "coup qualified." Some called these coups a boneheaded game of musical chairs. The new American President from Texas—a big powerful man who clearly did not want to become the first U.S. president in history to lose a war—glowered at his military advisers and said, "I'm gittin' tired of this *coup* bull*khakha*," or words to that effect. But Saigon leadership remained erratic and paper-thin.

Next, Clark and his colleagues drove by the main cathedral. It was located in the middle of a wide tree-lined avenue, and seemed like an island with streams of traffic flowing around it on each side. It was a shady, cool, and attractive location. The Romanesque old cathedral was large and built of massive stones. It looked a very much like a cathedral one might expect to find in a small city in southern France. It was as if someone had plucked it up from its place there in central Europe and plopped it down in the faraway sweltering tropics of the esoteric East.

They stopped for a few minutes at the MACV Headquarters (U.S. Military Assistance Command, Vietnam) that was located on the Rue Louis Pasteur. This military headquarters was located in an attractive neighborhood of fine old well-maintained French-style villas—pastel-colored stucco villas with red tiled roofs, surrounded by protective walls and handsome palm trees. This was clearly the area in which the elite of the city resided.

After the short visit at MACV Headquarters, Major Scully led them down toward the center of the city. They drove through an area of nice shops and sidewalk cafes. Eventually, they arrived at the riverfront area. They parked near a moored large U.S. Navy cargo ship and waited while Major Scully went aboard to inquire about certain shipments of equipment and materiel that would be required to help get the Top Tigers reestablished at Bien Hoa Airbase.

Even though Saigon is located approximately 60 miles inland from the South China Sea, it is the chief port of South Vietnam. It lies on the Saigon River (*Song Sai Gon*, in Vietnamese—*song* is Vietnamese for river) and has three miles of quays along the river which are accessible to vessels of up to a 30-foot draft capacity. At that time, in late 1966, the port was handling a massive flow of war materiel, and by the end of the year there would be over 200,000 American soldiers in South Vietnam. Also, junks and many other shallow-draft vessels were busy bringing rice and other crops in from the Mekong Delta area to the markets of Saigon. South Vietnam was said to be the rice bowl of Southeast Asia.

After Major Scully had attended to his logistical business it was almost six in the evening, and they were ready to look for a hotel and settle in for the night.

They decided to stay at the Continental Palace Hotel. It was a fine old hotel right in the heart of the bustling, thriving city. The National Assembly Hall (the old Opera House) was located nearby at the head of Le Loi Boulevard. Immediately before the Hall, on opposite sides of the wide boulevard, were the Continental and the Caravelle hotels. The Caravelle was quite modern, air-conditioned, and considered first class in every way. The VIPs and top journalists usually stayed there. The Continental was altogether different from the Caravelle. To Lieutenant Clark, the Continental Palace Hotel was like a trip back in time—and it was, for him, a highly desirable experience. Yes, authentic time-warp type experiences are rare indeed, he thought.

The Continental Palace was an elegant relic that dated back to French colonial days, back to 1880, actually, and had counted among its guests Andre Malraux, Somerset Maugham, and Graham Greene. With its open front terrace and high arched doorways, Clark considered it just about the utmost in nineteenth century grace and elegance. There was no air-conditioning at the Continental, but the ceilings were high, and ceiling fans were slowly turning everywhere. It seemed cool, relaxing, and inviting in every way. There was a rather large courtyard in the center of the hotel that was filled with lush tropical greenery and tinkling, rippling fountains. It was the perfect place to sit and enjoy a cup of coffee or a cool drink on a hot day in the tropics. The Continental definitely seemed to be something straight out of the old world—back from a time when all things seemed slower, more gentle, and more forgiving—a time when time itself seemed to flow like a gentle river—refreshing, calm, and smooth—life sustaining and not life threatening. Looking back for a moment, Clark thought, was there not once a time that did not seem quite so burdened by Dow and Jones, or depleted by the thinning layers of ozone, or nagged by global warming or the hyper-anxieties of being lost in space—a time when time itself was not carefully measured and allocated in frugal allotments? Could that time not be recalled just for a brief moment here seated at the heart of the Continental Palace with just the right potation and companion?

In the rooms the beds were large and luxurious and covered with a fine mosquito netting. At night, when the fans were turning and the windows were open to the courtyard below, the gossamer net over the bed would flutter softly in the gentle breeze. And the person lying in bed, enclosed in the soft netting, the gossamer wings, enjoyed a feeling of gentle movement—like flying on a magic carpet. One might feel as though he were smoothly flying off into the cool, dark, star-studded heavens to sleep with the angels.

Lieutenant Clark and Mr. Linville shared a room at the Continental. Major Scully had a room immediately across the hallway from them. The three enlisted men found rooms four blocks away at a hotel that was leased by the U.S. government for the use of enlisted servicemen.

On Christmas Eve in 1964 Viet Cong terrorists planted a bomb in the Brinks Hotel, which had been leased to house U.S. officers. The VC agent, disguised as an ARVN officer, had rigged a car bomb and parked the car in a lot beneath the building. It was set to explode at six in the evening—at "happy hour." The explosion killed two Americans and injured fifty-eight others. The agent who planted the bomb watched the explosion from a nearby sidewalk cafe. The Viet Cong commanders later said they executed this daring venture in order to demonstrate to the people of Saigon that the Americans, with all their pretense of power, were vulnerable and could not be counted on for protection.

As they were washing up, getting changed into civilian clothes ("civvies"). While getting ready to go out and enjoy a nice meal, Clark said to Linville, "Hey, this place is really something—Saigon, I mean. What do you think?"

After a moment Linville replied, "Saigon? Oh, yeah. You know, back in the old days, Saigon was not just the capital of Vietnam. It was the capital of all of French Indochina, which included Laos and Cambodia. Someone told me that when the Frenchies were still in charge around here they called Saigon the 'Pearl of the Orient.'"

Chapter 7

The *Rue Catinat*

When Clark and Linville were washed and dressed and ready to leave the hotel, they met Major Scully in the hallway, and then walked out onto the busy street.

Saigon's wide Le Loi Boulevard before them was full and thriving. Le Loi became the greatest emperor in the history of Vietnam back in 1426 by defeating and expelling the Chinese. After decisively crushing the Chinese Army, Le Loi was generous in victory in that he provided the Chinese with sampans and horses to carry them home. Then, apart from a last abortive attempt in 1788, China never again lunched a full-scale assault against Vietnam. Le Loi established a dynasty, the longest in Vietnamese history, which became a model of enlightenment and lasted nearly 400 years. The myth of Le Loi was much like the Arthurian legend of old England. This legend depicts Le Loi as a simple fisherman who one day cast his net into a lake, only to bring up a magic sword that made him a super-warrior.

"Every man should accomplish some great enterprise," Le Loi supposedly said, "so he can leave the sweet scent of his name there for later generations to admire."

Across the way was the Caravelle Hotel, cool and modern, cold actually, like a huge block of polished marble, appearing to be bereft of a heart and soul. The Caravelle, crowned with a large but gracefully modernistic icon of an old Caravelle—an elegant sailing ship with its sails puffed full and yet still neat and trim—brought to mind a giant Christmas ornament. In contrast, the rambling old Continental Palace brought to mind a steamy rendezvous featuring Charles Boyer and Marlene Dietrich.

Tu Do Street was not far from the Caravelle. They had all heard of Tu Do Street, the street known for its bars, clubs, cafes, and restaurants, and they were eager to look it over, to "check it out," as Linville said. They walked across the wide boulevard just before the National Assembly Hall—the old Opera House—and immediately onto the narrow tree-lined Tu Do Street, which led down toward the riverfront. (Most Americans pronounced Tu Do as "Two Doe.")

During French colonial times Tu Do Street was called the Rue Catinat, in honor of one of Louis XIV's marshals. During the early 1960s, the Diem regime renamed it Tu Do, or "Freedom Street." Later, after the Communists took over the city in 1975, they changed the name again. They called it Dong Khoi, or "Uprising Street." But to the residents of Saigon, it seemed to always remain the *Catinat*.

Tu Do Street did not disappoint. It was pleasantly busy and clearly thriving on all the foreign money which seemed to be pouring into to the city at that time. They walked past one cafe or restaurant after another. Most of the restaurants displayed prominent signs that read, "French Cuisine," or "Haute Cuisine." They walked past bars with names like "The San Francisco Bar," "The Gay Paris Bar," "The Florida," or "The Chicago Bar." Bar girls in tight blouses and miniskirts would usually sit near the doorways, winking and waving at passersby, inviting them in for a drink.

"You buy me drink, GI." It was not a question and it was not a demand. It usually sounded more like an urgent suggestion.

If a customer entered and stood at the bar with a girl, he was expected to buy her a drink. The girls received a percentage from the drinks of colored water, called "Saigon tea," which the customer (usually a soldier or sailor, almost always a foreigner) had to purchase in order to enjoy their company. There seemed to be many sailors in town on that day. Just around the corner here and there they could see Turkish baths combined with massage parlors and "Cheap Charlie" tailor shops.

Before the arrival of the French in strength, only the Chinese residents of Vietnam had smoked opium, and in such small quantities that it was not worth refining locally. But in 1898 the French built a refinery in Saigon, where a blend was concocted that burned quickly, and thus encouraged consumption. Vietnamese addiction soon rose so sharply that opium eventually accounted for almost one-third of the colonial administration's income. With a more robust economy in mind, the French had set in motion a traffic that would attain monstrous proportions. Decades later, with usage still rising, the quest for the drug prompted French agents to manipulate the Hmong tribes of Laos, which traditionally cultivated opium poppies.. For awhile, French counterinsurgency groups used clandestine opium profits to underwrite operations against the Communists. Also, the French backed the *Binh Xuyen*—the Vietnamese equivalent of the Mafia—who tried to oust South Vietnamese President Ngo Dinh Diem soon after he took office in 1954. Later, some high level Saigon officials were to be involved in the importation of the narcotics that would, to a great degree, poison the American army.

At the head of the street they came out on the Saigon riverfront. This area was also bustling and teeming with activity. Just to their right was the Majestic Hotel, another rather nice hotel with a river view. Nearby was a popular floating restaurant moored at the dockside. Business was booming. This restaurant had recently been bombed by terrorists. Four people had been killed and about twenty-five injured. But now business appeared to be back in full force.

From time to time small groups of boys in dirty short pants with sores on their legs would pursue them calling "Hey, you! Hey, you, GI! Give me cigarettes! Give me money! Give me candy, gum—chew gum!" And when the boys were disappointed they shouted, "Hey, you number ten, GI! Yea, yea, you number ten, man!" This was local street talk for "You're no good. You are the absolute worst, the pits." Number ten was as low as one could go on the human chain in Saigon. And if they said that one was "*beaucoup* number ten," then that was even worse still.

The three of them walked back down Tu Do Street and selected an attractive restaurant for their evening meal. They enjoyed watching the passersby and the food was good. They all ordered fillet mignon or Chateaubriand, which seemed perfectly cut and prepared in every way. Something Clark noticed was that every time he dined "French style," everything, literally from soup to nuts, was offered. The nuts, the cashews, were freshly grown there in Vietnam. They enjoyed the food immensely, and with the food they drank Vietnamese beer. The brand name was "33," and that in Vietnamese was *Ba Muoi Ba*, but generally pronounced something like, "Bom'de'bom'." Of course, all the Americans thought that was the perfect name for the Vietnamese beer because if one had more than two bottles of it to drink, one certainly felt "bombed" by "Bom'de'bom' and suffered from a horrendous hangover the next day.

While they were eating, someone wondered aloud about what the enlisted men, their crew, might be doing at that time. Actually, it was good that they could not witness what their crew was doing at that time. Because at almost that very moment Sergeant Dotson and Collins were selling cigarettes on the black market just a couple of blocks away from where the officers were enjoying their steaks. And Dotson and Collins were just barely managing to escape an aggressive gang of Vietnamese black marketeers with their skins intact. First Sergeant Rodriguez had remained in their hotel and eaten there at the NCO Club, where he encountered some old friends.

After the meal was finished and the second bottle of *Ba Muoi Ba,* "33" beer was almost finished, Lieutenant Clark spoke to the others in a rather hesitant manner.

"You know, there's a guy, a civilian, from my hometown that lives here in Saigon," he said. "My uncle gave me his telephone number and asked me to promise to look him up if I got a chance." After a pause, Clark continued. "What do you think? Shall I give him a call?"

Linville spoke. "Well, sure, why not? Might be interesting."

In a rather indifferent manner, Major Scully agreed. "Yeah, I suppose so," he said. "Yeah, why not?"

"Let's walk over to the Brinks Hotel," Clark said. "It's not far from here and surely there's a phone there that we could use."

Clark telephoned at the Brinks, and after a couple of rings, Alan Clayton, from Old Catawba, came on the line.

"Hello, Mr. Clayton. This is Winston Clark from back home. How are you? Good. Say, I realize that you don't know me, but I'm sure you recall my father, Wendel Clark. Yes sir, my Uncle Fred asked me to phone you here in Saigon, if I got a chance. Yes, sir. I just arrived here in town today."

Clark chatted with Clayton only for a few minutes before hanging up the receiver. He looked at his companions and said: "Well, guys, he wants us to come over for a little visit. Are you up to it?"

Linville and Scully quickly agreed.

Alan Clayton had a nice, rather roomy, second-floor apartment down Le Loi Boulevard, just off of the main market place on Le Tanh Ton Street. Clayton, a large and distinguished-looking man in his mid-fifties, greeted them in a friendly and enthusiastic manner. He seemed honestly pleased to meet the three aviators and appeared truly delighted to be their host. He was quick to ask about Clark's mother and his Uncle Fred, as well as several other friends and relatives back home in Old Catawba. Clayton also asked about Clark's sister, Clara (the family called her "Claire"). Clara had taught school for several years in U.S. Air Force family ("dependent") schools in both Italy and Germany. She thoroughly enjoyed her travels and now, still unmarried, she was back at the state university working on graduate degrees. She hoped to eventually be able to teach at the university level.

Clayton offered his condolences for Clark's father, Wendel, who had died the year before. "He was a fine man," Clayton said. "Everyone loved your father. He had a good heart—a really good heart."

Clark remembered his father as a great puzzle, one of the great unsolved mysteries of his life. His father, Wendel Clark, had served successfully as the principal of the school in Watauga for over fifteen years. He was highly respected and popular. Everyone seemed to love him. They always said that he had "such a good heart." Some even said that he should have gone into politics. But somehow, he was not content with his life and himself. He started to drink more and more. One night, when the beer and whiskey were flowing freely at a back-yard barbecue, Clark had heard his father tell a friend that, if he had his life to live again, he would be a poet and live in Italy. He mournfully regretted that he had "never been anywhere, never seen anything, never done anything." He had never been more than 300 miles from Watauga, the place where he was born, in his entire life. He had missed both World War II and the Korean War because of a peculiar heart murmur that caused him to fail the physical examinations. As his drinking continued to increase, the family started to hear rumors that he might be dismissed as principal of the school. Someone was saying that there might be a job for him over in Covington County. And then one night just before Christmas he disappeared. Two days later they were notified that he had been found dead in a small motel not more than fifty miles from Watauga. The report said that he had died of a heart attack. He had been drinking heavily. So, the man who had been so good at demonstrating love, and who had been so beloved, had died of a defective heart. The man who dreamed of living as a poet in Italy, who had dreamed of conversing with Voltaire, Pascal, Benjamin Franklin, and

Abraham Lincoln, had died in a cheap motel back in Old Catawba. Clark thought of Tolstoy dying alone in an almost deserted country railway station. Clark's father's name, Wendel, was an old Teutonic name that meant "the wanderer." The wanderer died on the road.

During his last days Wendel Clark had talked of "breaking the chains," and of becoming "the man he was intended to be." He talked a great deal about Patrick Henry, Leo Tolstoy, and freedom. He spoke of the "Watauga curse," and the World War I Doughboy statue that stood at the head of Cherry Street (which was their main street). He said that he was like the Doughboy. He always had a leg up, but never seemed to be moving—never going anywhere. He was frozen in time and space, he said. It was the "Watauga whammy"—the curse of the American Gypsy class. The "living dead," living on wheels but never really going anywhere, he said. Route 66 was tobacco road and grapes of wrath paved over. Route 66 was, he said, a wasteland within a wasteland. Where is the soft underbelly of America, he asked. That has such a good sound to it, he said. "The soft underbelly..."

Winston Clark's Uncle Fred said that in some ways Winston's father, Wendel, had "never really grown up." And those words hurt. They hurt so much that Winston Clark never forgot them. They were branded indelibly onto his heart. He instantly prayed and resolved that no one should ever say that about him when he was gone. "He had a good heart, but he never really grew up."

"He spoke a good deal about Patrick Henry, Tolstoy, and freedom," Uncle Fred had said.

And he died "free," Winston Clark thought. He was born free, but then he became entangled in the emotional kudzu of life in Old Catawba, and his gyros became impaired. He lost his way. Every man seems inclined to seek the freedom to make a fool of himself. But his father was born free, and he died "free." Clark would always remember that the first thing that struck him when he saw the motel where his father had died was a large and prominent red neon sign which proclaimed: "**FREE** color TV." The "free color TV" sign was just above the room in which his father had died.

So, there you have it, Clark thought. Th-tha-that-that's all, folks. There you have it, in just a few words, another epic tale concerning the pursuit of happiness in 20th century America. His father had died with a good but defective heart—and free color TV. Albert Camus had discussed this sort of thing in his play, *Caligula*: "The simple truth is," he said, "men die and are not happy." Is that what it means to be "grown up"—to accept Camus and his Caligula and their cosmic dead-end?

Alan Clayton smiled broadly and offered them drinks. He had a Vietnamese servant in a tight beige vest and black trousers that took their orders at a nice, well-stocked bar. As Clark introduced his friends to Clayton, he filled them in on some of the older man's background.

"Mr. Clayton works for the U.S. Agricultural Department. Right, Mr. Clayton, or is it the State Department?"

"Well, both you might say," he answered. "I work as a U.S. agricultural advisor to the Vietnamese. We concentrate on the food crop—more food, more rice. And, I must say, we have been rather successful. The Vietnamese are now able to produce two rice crops per year. In 1945, at the end of World War II, Vietnam suffered a terrible famine. In northern Vietnam something like two million out of a population of ten million people starved to death. But now, since 1964, South Vietnam has actually been able to export rice. Why, who knows? I might work myself out of a job, if I'm not careful."

Chapter 8

Enter Monsieur Voltaige

Just as Clayton's servant, Nguyen, a pleasant, slightly stooped and graying older man, was handing out the drinks, there was a faint ringing sound that indicated to Clayton and Nguyen that someone was at the door.

"Will you get that, Nguyen?" Clayton asked.

Nguyen was quick to answer the door and usher in Mr. Clayton's newly arrived guest.

"Voltaige!" Clayton exclaimed. "Oh my, what an honor! Voltaige! Monsieur Voltaige, *mon ami*, come in, come in, please, by all means. Welcome, welcome to my humble abode. I'm so glad you could drop by—so pleased, really. We didn't realize that you were in town."

"Monsieur Voltaige, please allow me to introduce a *landsmann* of mine," Clayton continued. "Monsieur Voltaige, this is Lieutenant Clark. He is—as I am—from Old Catawba. Our families have been friends for many, many years. He just arrived in Saigon tonight for a surprise visit.

This is my evening for pleasant surprises, I suppose you could say. Lieutenant Clark, this is my dear friend, Monsieur Marcel Voltaige."

Monsieur Voltaige looked Clark carefully in the eye, offered his hand, and said, "*Bonsoir, Monsieur* Clark. It is my pleasure to meet you. *Oui, monsieur*, the pleasure is entirely mine, I assure you."

Clark shook the small but firm, cool, dry hand and gazed for a moment at the gentle and pleasing countenance of the little Frenchman.

Monsieur Voltaige had soft blue eyes that sparkled. His gentle, hypnotic eyes were his most dominant feature. Overall, his features—face and body—were well proportioned, and his small, pale face almost always wore a soft warm smile. His white hair was combed straight back and it always appeared to be fresh, clean, and shiny. It was difficult to estimate his age. He was one of those people who could be anywhere from 55 to 65 years of age—or perhaps even older. The general impression he presented to the world was of a kind gentleperson—a generous, urbane, humane, wise, and sensitive gentleman. But still, this man was something else, something more than that. What was it? This little man was someone special. Clark searched for the proper word. This little man was...*majestic*. That was the word. He was like a prince. That was it. He was a prince. His regal presence, charm, and grace seemed to fill the room. And from the first, Clark felt certain that he had seen that face somewhere before.

The gentle Frenchman met and shook the hands of Linville and Scully.

"Monsieur Voltaige owns and operates a rubber plantation just northwest of here," Clayton said. "Lieutenant Clark and his friends are pilots, helicopter pilots."

"Ah, pilots, *oui, aviateurs*," said Monsieur Voltaige. "*Tres bien*. Very good. Interesting. Yes, of course. Pilots."

"A rubber plantation," Linville remarked. "Now, with this war going on and all, how does anyone manage to operate a rubber plantation around here?"

"Ah, *oui*," answered Monsieur Voltaige, "One manages. As they say, it can be done. Sometimes it seems as though everything is difficult—as you say, tricky. But if one is careful and resourceful, one can prevail. As you say, 'We shall overcome!' Yes, one can manage. After all, life is a challenge, *n'est-ce pas*?"

After they chatted for awhile and had a few drinks, they decided to go out and take a stroll about the city and take a look at late night Saigon. By then it was close to midnight, and the city was quieter now; the air was cooler, and a somewhat fresher.

"This guy is really *some*one," Alan Clayton whispered to Clark as they prepared to leave the apartment. "Monsieur Voltaige—he is well connected—*quite* well connected."

They walked by several market places and some brightly lighted cinemas. Clark was amazed at the stacks and stacks of American cigarettes he saw available for purchase on the streets of Saigon, along with a great deal of whiskey, rum, gin, and vodka. Clark was surprised to learn that one of the hottest items—perhaps *the* hottest—article on the black-market was hairspray from the American base exchanges—aerosol cans of hairspray. The Vietnamese women just did not seem to be able to get enough of it. The streets were littered and dirty as at that time the sanitation services were in the process of collapsing as most of their people rushed away to labor at the U.S. military bases for much higher salaries than the municipality could pay. It was especially loud near the cinema entrances with popular Vietnamese music twanging away in a blaring singsong manner. Most of the heavy traffic was gone by that time and the air was cooler and fresher. They walked past a number of nice stores, shops, and cafes as they approached the area around what Monsieur Voltaige referred to as the *Catinat*.

Eventually, they returned to Tu Do Street, where Monsieur Voltaige pointed out a few especially good cafes and restaurants. (Monsieur Voltaige always referred to Tu Do Street as the *Rue Catinat*.) They walked a short distance down several side streets leading off of Tu Do and they were startled by what they saw. Almost every shop or apartment house entranceway was filled with street people, homeless people lying on the pavement seeking rest and shelter. Entire families, but mostly women with small children, and old people, were covered under filthy threadbare blankets, oil clothes, straw matting, tarpaulins, or whatever they could find for cover. Large rats seemed to be everywhere. They were fearlessly running about and over and among the bodies lying on the bare cement. The people did not panic as the worrisome rats ran about them often actually scampering over the reclining bodies. If they reacted at all, it was merely to shoo the rats as one might do with bothersome insects. The rats were huge, the largest Clark had ever seen—and bold, apparently fearless. Most of the young children were covered with sores, and one small child looked as though a major portion of her nose was gone. Clark could not help but to ask himself, "Was that a rat?" It was painful to ask, but he had to ask, "The child's nose…did a rat do that?"

As they came to a corner and turned around to walk back down toward Tu Do Street, Clark hesitantly spoke to Monsieur Voltaige.

"This is awful," he said. "Aren't these rats dangerous for these people? Especially these women with babies, I mean?"

"Ah, *oui, monsieur,*" said Monsieur Voltaige. "This is not so nice. Actually, it is a catastrophe, a calamity of war, I suppose one could say. *Catastrophique—oui*, it is *catastrophique.* The refugees, they are everywhere these days. They are trying to escape the war."

"Those sores on the kids there…do you suppose the rats are inflicting those injuries? Do you suppose…are those rat bites?" Clark asked.

Monsieur Voltaige seemed reluctant to answer. Finally, he said, "*Oui, monsieur*, I am afraid so. *Oui*, I fear that it is so. Here I believe that rats eat the people and the people eat the rats. It is not so pleasant. No."

Later Clark could remember several times walking through Vietnamese marketplaces and seeing dozens of rats hanging by their tails, butchered and cleaned and prepared for cooking and eating. One evening, back in Vung Tau, near Dead Man's Beach, Clark had been drinking beer at an open-air kiosk with a Vietnamese soldier and the soldier showed him a large insect that appeared to be something like a cross between a grasshopper and a locust.

"You can eat," the smiling Vietnamese said. The man took the large insect and popped him apart in the middle, squeezed out some greenish looking matter, and spoke with a broad smile that showed many gold-rimmed teeth.

"You eat," he said. "This is the best part. This—this is good. Yes, yes, you can eat," he said and then demonstrated by eating the insect and seeming to thoroughly enjoy it. The smiling soldier did not simply eat the insect. In what appeared to be a special favor for Lieutenant Clark, he emphatically savored it. When the soldier squeezed the insect and showed the internal green matter to Clark, it was very much like the soldier was saying, "Look, now, this is like a little cream puff, and *this*, this is the *crème de la crème*."

Clark was suddenly startled by a slim pale figure that stepped out of the shadows and seized him firmly by the wrist. It was a grim looking young woman in a tight fitting red silk dress, an *ao dai,* and conical hat. She was more than pale: she was white—as white as a ghost. "Powder? Was she completely covered with powder?" Clark asked himself. She was not so much like the average young Vietnamese woman, as she was like the ghost of a young Vietnamese woman. She had large, hard, sad black eyes, and long, yellow, sharp looking teeth. Her grip on Clark's wrist was cool and firm. She was standing quite close to Clark. "You come with me. You come. Come now with me. Come with me now," she said in an urgent sad sort of way.

"No, no," Clark said with clear anxiety on his face and in his voice. "No, no. Thank you, no, no, I should not. No, no, I could not. I cannot. No, no, thank you. No, I cannot. Really. Please, no."

The ghostly figure vanished as quickly as she had appeared. Clark could smell joss sticks burning and hear a cymbal tingling behind a thin wall somewhere not far away in the darkness.

Monsieur Voltaige was looking at Clark with both amusement and sympathy.

"Oh, *mon Dieu*!" he said. "One really never knows quite what to expect here. Saigon can be a dangerous place, Monsieur. Here there is said to be a great deal of the…what do you say? What did they call it in the old days? The sailor's pox? *Oui*, it was called the sailor's pox. Oh, yes, the pox. But of the most dangerous and insidious type. *Oui, insidieux*, indeed. *Catastrophique, oui*. Oh, terrible. Abominable. *Oui*, nasty. Truly a very nasty business indeed."

"That's true. Oh, yes, quite true. This place can be dangerous," Clayton said. "And especially at night."

"Hey, are you okay, Winnie?" Linville laughed. "Hey, man, you okay?"

"You okay, kid?" Major Scully appeared nervous.

"You acted properly, Monsieur Clark," Monsieur Voltaige continued. "Absolutely. Precisely. One must be discreet. One must be careful—very careful, indeed, in Saigon. *Oui*, this can be a dangerous place. One must learn, yes, one must learn one's way about. I hope that one day I will have a chance to show you about—to show you the nicer places to visit. Monsieur Clayton perhaps can show you about. Monsieur Clayton could show you the *Cercle Sportif*, for example, I am sure. Wonderful place. That is a wonderful place and you would meet many truly nice people there. Yes, I am sure of that."

"Why, yes," Clayton replied. "I would be happy to show them the Circle Sportif. It's a very nice place indeed. Many of our most distinguished journalists congregate there."

The Circle Sportif was an old French club where one could play tennis or swim and enjoy drinks at a poolside bar. It was Saigon's equivalent of the country club.

Finally, they returned to the Continental Hotel where they went to the bar and had one or two more rum and Coca Colas. Clark enjoyed getting to talk with Clayton about their hometown, Watauga, back in Old Catawba, and all the people they knew there. Clayton asked about the deserted old family mansion that stood on the northern edge of town, dilapidated and decrepit.

"I don't know what's going on with that place," Clayton said. "I thought it was torn down years ago. Lord knows what's going on in our scattered family. We're all over the place, and nobody writes; nobody communicates anymore. The family's kind'a busted up, I suppose. Everyone is busy with their own lives—their own problems. You know how it goes."

Clark had visited the old Clayton mansion on several occasions when he was a small boy. He was with his father who was visiting Alan Clayton's father, Brooks Clayton. Someone in the family, probably more than one, had been a serious sportsman, and they had provided some taxidermist with a great deal of business. Old man Clayton had three sons and they were all strong and ambitious men. Alan Clayton's elder brother, Lyle, was a successful banker in Memphis, and his younger brother, Curtis, had been a highly decorated hero in the Korean War. There were many mounted heads of deer decorating the walls. There was a bobcat, many birds—hawks, wild turkeys, ducks, wild geese, and even a snow owl—and some rather large fish. But now the old mansion was deserted and stood silent and empty on the hill in the trees on the edge of Watauga. Inside, the furniture was covered with dusty sheets and the bird, animal, and fish eyes were fixed, staring coldly straight out into the dusky emptiness. The once vibrant home stood now abandon and lifeless.

Monsieur Voltaige seemed especially friendly to Lieutenant Clark and just before they were preparing to depart and turn in for the night, the Frenchman invited Clark to visit him at his plantation, Les Trungs. He called his place Les Trungs.

"*Oui, s'il vous plait*. Come out to my place and allow me to show you around. Bring your friends. *S'il vous plait*," he added. "You must. You simply must."

"Where is your plantation?" Clark asked.

Monsieur Voltaige mentioned the name of a well-known French tire-producing corporation, and then he said: "The Merlette Plantation, perhaps you have heard of it. Of course, you have—it is quite well known—and my plantation is not far from there—only about twenty kilometers. I call my plantation 'Les Trungs'—Les Trungs Plantation. I am sure you can find it with your helicopter. We have our own landing strip and helipad there. And we have a swimming pool there. Yes, a refreshing pool! I will plan on your visit. I will be so honored. And you will find it safe and comfortable there. You and your friends must come to visit us—and at any time. Come unannounced, if you must. But come. I insist. Messieurs, Messieurs, I *insist*."

"Oh, wow! Sounds exciting," Linville said.

"Yes, yes, sure," Clayton spoke up. "You must visit Monsieur Voltaige. He has a marvelous place out there. And you must meet his daughters. Oh, *oui, mon cheri, oui*. You must meet his daughters. They are two darlings—absolute darlings, I must say. Beautiful girls, charming girls, they are indeed. Yes, Genevieve and Monique—two authentic beauties."

"Nice. You have daughters with you here, Monsieur Voltaige—here in Nam?" Clark asked.

"*Oui, oui*. My two darlings. Yes! Genevieve and Monique—they are with me there at Les Trungs Plantation."

"Well, I don't know. Visiting a rubber plantation out in the middle of no where here in Nam...well, sounds kind of chancy, kind of risky to me," Clark said.

"Oh, no, no, no!" Monsieur Voltaige said. "You can do it. It is safe. You will find it safe. You will risk nothing. Please, ask my dear friend, Mr. Clayton, here. He will tell you. He has visited with me at Les Trungs Plantation on more than one occasion. No, no, you will risk nothing. I promise you—absolutely nothing. Now, I must ask you, would I invite you if it were not safe? Now, would I? I have lived here for many, many years. And I ask you, Messieurs, would I have my daughters here—there at the plantation with me, if it were not safe? No, no, of course not. No, I would not! You know that I would not, I am sure."

"Well, we are sincerely grateful for your kind invitation, Monsieur Voltaige," Clark said, "and we will see what we can do."

Major Scully said for the third time that he was tired, exhausted actually, and had to turn in soon.

"Oh, yes! You must! And now I know we must all retire for the evening. I know we all have much to do on the morning," Monsieur Voltaige said. "So, Messieurs, *au revoir. Bonne chance.* Good luck, and Godspeed."

Just as Monsieur Voltaige was about to walk away with Clayton at the entrance of the rambling old Continental Palace Hotel into the dark cool streets of Saigon, Clark suddenly spoke again. The young lieutenant from Old Catawba was suddenly inspired. He had made a startling discovery. It came to him in a flash.

"Ah, that's *it*! *Voltaire*! Monsieur Voltaige, you are Voltaire! Yes, you remind me of Voltaire—of a picture I once saw of him in a book somewhere. I am sure of it. I can see it in my mind's eye right now. Voltaire, 'the happy philosopher,' they called him. That's it! Yes, that's it! You are *Voltaire* all over again."

Monsieur Voltaige smiled his charming smile and said: "There, there, Monsieur Clark. *Oui, mon ami,* I believe that I have heard that before. *Oui,* Voltaire. The *philosophe,* and a wise man of letters, that he was indeed. *Oui.* Monsieur Voltaire was a teacher of modesty and moderation, of tolerance and toleration—and of common sense."

"*Oui,* Monsieur Voltaige, that's it," said Lieutenant Clark. "You are the complete Voltaire except for your short hair. Voltaire, in this picture at least, I recall that he had shoulder-length hair. But still, yes, you are 'the happy philosopher.' You are Voltaire—Monsieur Voltaire."

"So, please, do not forget that you should come and visit us at my plantation. Please, come soon. *Au revoir,*" said Monsieur Voltaige.

The little Frenchman smiled broadly, waved a friendly goodbye, and walked off into the streets of nighttime Saigon. He was smiling. He seemed pleased. And the man seemed majestic. He was the Little Prince at 60.

"You are doing a great deal for this country," called Monsieur Voltaige. "Godspeed to you, Messieurs. Remember to be careful, Messieurs. Be careful. Remember, prudence and caution above all else—prudence and caution. Saigon can be a dangerous place. *Bon chance, Messieurs, bon chance.*"

"*Au revoir,*" he said from a circle of light on the corner. "*Au revoir.*"

Clark slept deeply that night in his large Continental Palace Hotel bed, with the gossamer mosquito netting billowing over him. As he felt the breeze he lifted off and flew through the star-studded night. He flew higher and higher over the dark mud of the Mekong kingdom, with Le Loi Land far below. But not far away was the apparition with the white face, the hard black eyes and the sharp yellow teeth saying, "You come with me now." There was an awful sadness there. Somewhere a terrible wrong had been committed. Could that wrong be undone? How could he refuse? How could he say no to those big sad black eyes? After all, had not the handsome young President said that we are prepared to "bear any burden, climb every mountain," and all that stuff. The huge rats scampered over his feet, tripping him, causing him to stumble and almost fall onto the damp cement. Now the wild turkeys from the old Clayton place were stalking him. And there over his shoulder was the beautiful but dead snow owl. The small child had no nose now, and the smiling Vietnamese soldier, with large half-gold teeth, offered the oozing insect and again said, "You can eat, yes, you can eat." Clark smelled burning joss sticks and heard cymbals tingling behind thin walls. And then—close to his face—the owl screeched—and screeched again! But we are here to help. How could he say no to all that—the rats, the insects, the yellow teeth? We were supposed to be lending a hand, right? Reaching out, yes, reaching out. They—those exotic creatures—they meant well, did they not? Or were they out to kill him? The ragged smiling little boy shouted, "Hey, you *beaucoup* number ten, GI." Beyond the Rue Catinat, beyond the Cercle Sportif, there was a gruesome circle of life, someone had explained. The people had to eat the rats before the rats ate them. There, there was

Monsieur Voltaige standing nearby. He stood alone in a circle of light under the lamp at the corner. "Life is a challenge, *n'est-ce pas*?" The little prince smiled and said, "Oh, yes, Monsieur Clark, Saigon can be a dangerous place. *Bon chance,* my friend, *bon chance.*" And the mud and the blood and the slime of the Delta-land was swimming by, far below in the dark distance, and the sharks were waiting just off Dead Man's Beach—and they demanded much more than Mr. Tucker's toe. And there was Le Loi on the paddy dike flashing his great sword about, this way and that. Now Clark could see his father, Wendel the Wanderer, standing soberly, serenely before the Doughboy statue. His father's face had a slightly mocking expression about it. And just above and behind the Doughboy statue one could make out a prominent red neon sign that said: "**FREE** color TV." And there 500 channels of ash and trash awaited them. Clark felt that his father had something to say to him, but he never said it. He just smiled that mocking smile and never said anything. Clark could see the wild geese live and liberated from the old Clayton mansion flying below in a wide inverted V formation. They were turning away from the Mekong Delta and starting to fly off in search of the Mississippi Delta. Then he could hear the powerful hum of a Huey helicopter—rotor blades popping. And with VHF in one ear and UHF in the other, his feet on the pedals applying just the right amount of pressure, with torque-plus in one boot and counter-torque in the other, with the cyclic control stick in his right hand and the collective pitch lever in his left hand, he flew on and on into the golden mist to bear any burden. And the little prince stood in the circle of light at the corner and smiled back at him.

"*Au revoir,*" he said. "*Au revoir.*"

Chapter 9

The Airbase

Lieutenant Clark thought the officers and men of the 68th Assault Helicopter Company were taking it all a lot like a group of school boys going off to summer camp for a couple of weeks.

During the early part of December 1966, the Top Tigers moved from Vung Tau to Bien Hoa Airbase. The days of packing and hauling were long and exhausting, and no one liked the idea of leaving Vung Tau. But finally they were finished. The last bag, rocket, bullet, and blanket had been packed into their helicopters and flown to Bien Hoa Airbase. They were now in their new quarters—and it was a far cry from their previous quarters in Vung Tau at the Pacific Hotel. But their spirits were high, and there was persistent laughing and joking as they moved into their dirty, dusty, chicken-coop-type barracks on the airbase.

The barracks were long low wooden buildings built on concrete slabs, with louvered sides to let the air (and dust) in and fine-mesh screen tacked on to hold out the mosquitoes. There was a small game or briefing room at each end of the building and the rest of the space was divided into two man cubicles. The roommate situation remained as it had been at the Pacific Hotel, and Lieutenant Clark found himself sharing a tight cubicle with Mr. Meeks.

For awhile the showers and latrines were in the open, later they had a separate building to fill those needs. After a few days, and a few brief but intense early morning rain showers, they discovered that they would have to protect the toilet paper underneath large tin cans.

One day about that time, after Lieutenant Clark became sarcastic with Major Scully in a good-humored sort of way, the weary major pensively said: "You know, Lieutenant, I've recently discovered there's only two things in life that I really can't stand. One is wet toilet paper—and the other is smart lieutenants."

Lieutenant Clark later remembered thinking that Christmas that year—1966—seemed less like Christmas than any other that he had ever experienced. There were few of the traditional signs of Christmas to be observed around the base at Bien Hoa. Several of the pilots received fruit-cakes, brownies, or homemade cookies in the mail (upon arrival the brownies and cookies were mostly just crumbs—bits and pieces). Also, there was a fine turkey dinner with all the trimmings at the Air Force Officers' Club on Christmas day. But that was the extent of it—hardly any tinsel, artificial snowflakes, or Christmas music was discernable anywhere in USARV-land (USARV—U.S. Army Vietnam). And perhaps that was all for the better, because Christmas is traditionally the season of serious homesickness for people away from home and serving with the military. The people in Operations tried to let everyone they could possibly spare off from flying on Christmas day. But still, as calls continued to come in from the field for helicopter support, roughly half of the crews ended up flying missions. Later, Clark thought that it was probably better that everyone was kept busy at Christmas time. Actually, there was very little time for the Top Tigers to get bogged down in homesickness.

Even as they were in the process of moving they continued to fly missions. They were becoming more familiar with what the Vietnamese Army called the III Corps Tactical Zone, which was roughly the area around Saigon, approximately 50 to 75 miles out in every direction. The terrain was generally jungle north and west of Saigon, and rice paddies south and east of the capital city. And the terrain was almost all flat. At the northern limits of the theater of operations, where III Corps met II Corps, one started to enter the mountains, or what is usually referred to as the Central Highlands. Nui Ba Den was the one exception to the flat terrain in III Corps. Nui Ba Den—the "Black Virgin Mountain"—was located about ten miles west of Tay Ninh. It rose abruptly, volcano-like, out of the surrounding plains up to an altitude of about 3,000 feet. Helicopters frequently landed on the helipad that served the small base camp and radio station located atop the mountain. However, so long as the Americans flew on and off of the mountain, it was never really secured. At any time on any given day, crews remained subject to take fire from almost anywhere around the heavily wooded sides of Nui Ba Den. One of the American advisers in Tay Ninh once commented to Lieutenant Clark: "We own the top of it (the mountain), and the bottom—and Charlie owns the middle. He's got countless caves and holes in there."

The crews of the 68th flew two types of missions: combat assaults ("CAs"), and administrative or miscellaneous missions—"ash and trash," they called them. They normally flew from dawn to dusk—or later—almost everyday. They usually flew seven days a week and then would get a day off to rest—and that day off was never a promise, never sacrosanct. Sometimes they would have an hour or two off between missions, but generally they maintained an exhausting flying schedule. Lieutenant Clark often thought that he felt like a dead man hanging over the controls of a flying machine—a machine that was kind enough, benevolent enough to almost fly itself. He learned to love the Huey, the workhorse of the Vietnam War. This machine, the old pilots said, was "forgiving"—meaning that occasionally a pilot could make a serious mistake and live to tell about it.

For awhile, Clark and Linville found themselves flying a number of missions out of Tay Ninh City, supporting the American advisers there. Tay Ninh City was about 65 miles west of Saigon and about twenty miles from the Cambodian boarder. It was located near a densely wooded area referred to as "War Zone C," and was considered an important crossing point for enemy troops and materiel coming down the so-called Ho Chi Minh Trail. Some said that Tay Ninh Province was the termination point of the Ho Chi Minh Trail.

Chapter 10

Uncle Ho and His Trail

The importance of the Ho Chi Minh Trail to the Communist victory in Vietnam in 1975 could hardly be exaggerated. This trail was an elaborate communications network just across the Vietnamese boarder that cut down through Laos and Cambodia. Its entry point in the north was just west of Hanoi and its termination point was about 700 miles to the south, just west of Tay Ninh, in South Vietnam.

The trail was nothing new. The Ho Chi Minh Trail, which threaded through southern Laos and northeastern Cambodia into the highlands of South Vietnam, was not a single track, but a complex web of jungle paths and trails. During the early 1960s one could usually fly over the region in helicopters and nothing was discernable, even at low altitudes, beneath the green canopy that seemed to stretch out endlessly in every direction. The Montagnards, the aboriginal tribes who had inhabited this area for centuries, hunting its tigers, elephants, and other wild beasts, and cutting and selling the prized teakwood, had carved out paths in their migrations. For millennia they had also served traders as guides, and as caravans of coolies transporting gold and opium from China to the cities of Southeast Asia.

The Viet Minh had used this trail as a link in the war against the French. In the initial stages of the southern insurgency, it became the route through which North Vietnam infiltrated cadres, or advisers, as well as modest shipments of arms, ammunition, and other materiel to the Viet Cong. But later it became like a superhighway to the south.

The Communist leadership in the north made the decision in the spring of 1964 to turn the primitive trail into a functioning modern logistical system. The decision was made that men could no longer simply carry supplies to the south on their backs and shoulders, like an army of ants, endlessly fighting the leeches, mosquitoes, and malaria of the vast jungles. If they were going to win on the battlefield, they had to have the ability to move things, to supply troops in the field at thousands of remote base camps in central and southern Vietnam.

The immense project of expanding the trail, which began in the middle of 1964, continued until hostilities ceased a decade later. Its architect was Colonel Dong Si Nguyen, who became Minister of Construction in North Vietnam after the war. Nguyen spared no expenses. He brought in engineer battalions equipped with up-to-date Soviet and Chinese machinery to build roads and bridges that could handle heavy trucks, tanks, and other vehicles. Anticipating the likelihood of relentless American bombings, he erected sophisticated antiaircraft defenses. He dug underground workshops, storage facilities, fuel depots, barracks, and hospitals. He had platoons of drivers, mechanics, radio operators, traffic managers, ordnance experts, doctors, and nurses on call. During 1964, an estimated 10,000 North Vietnamese troops went south. But this was only a trickle compared to the numbers three years later, when they were pouring into South Vietnam at the rate of 20,000 or more per month. With the enlargement and expansion of the trail the Communists had added a new dimension to the war. Now they would be able to stay one step ahead of their enemies as the war escalated.

One might think that bombing would hamper or block this trail. If it were visible it would appear to be like a series of blood veins and vessels running down the long limb of a great beast. No matter where it would be bombed or defoliated, the busy convoys from the north would simply branch off to the left or right and find another conduit that was open. And on the vast train of men, women and supplies would go, until it found its destination somewhere in the south. Even after major excursions in this borderland twilight zone, the Americans and the South Vietnamese were never able to destroy the Ho Chi Minh Trail.

But what of the man, this Ho Chi Minh, the man for whom the trail was named, and the man that Saigon was later renamed to honor?

That was not his real name. Ho Chi Minh was a *nom de guerre.* He was born Nguyen Sinh Cung in 1890 in Vinh, a small village in central Vietnam. Early in 1911, in Saigon, he signed on as a stoker and galley boy aboard a French freighter bound for Europe. Thirty years would pass before he saw Vietnam again.

Using a number of pseudonyms, he traveled the world in search of an education and a cause. During his travels he became fluent in English, French, Russian, and at least three Chinese dialects. In 1913, he crossed the Atlantic from France and visited Boston and San Francisco, before settling in Brooklyn as an itinerant laborer. The skyscrapers of Manhattan dazzled him as emblems of Western industrial progress and power. He was impressed with the success and status of Chinese immigrants in America. When he proclaimed Vietnam's independence from France in 1945, his speech would feature an excerpt from the American Declaration of Independence: "We hold it to be self-evident that all men are created equal."

After a year in the United States, he sailed for London, where he worked as a pastry cook, and enjoyed mixing with Chinese and Indian workers and getting acquainted with the Fabian socialists.

Ho was in France in 1919 during the Treaty of Versailles. He had hoped to meet with President Woodrow Wilson and speak with him about

Vietnam's status and future. However, that meeting never happened. Ho spent six years in Paris. And while he was there he was, to some degree, converted to France's *grande mission civilisatrice*, but at the same time, he mixed with various leftist groups and was converted to the Revolution. Ho said that France was the nation of Voltaire and Victor Hugo, who "personified the spirit of brotherhood and noble love of peace," the spirit that pervaded the French. But these people had betrayed their Revolution, and their devotion to "liberty, equality, and fraternity." Now they were determined to be great imperialists.

In early 1941, disguised as a Chinese journalist, traveling by foot and sampan, he slipped across the border back into Vietnam. He was back, after a thirty year odyssey. He told his compatriots that the time had come to liberate Vietnam. They must fight both the Japanese and the French. In the Confucian spirit, they respected him—he was their elder—and they called him uncle—"Uncle Ho"—in an attitude of reverent familiarity.

When he returned to Vietnam he had chosen his final pseudonym, Ho Chi Minh—which means "Bringer of Light," or some say, "He Who Enlightens." (This name choice actually seems to lift Ho up towards the pantheon of Buddha in that the word *buddha* is not a proper name but a title meaning "Awakened One," or "Enlightened One.") Ho had found his cause—nationalism and national independence.

"It was patriotism and not Communism that originally inspired me," he said. In 1945, as World War II was ending and all was chaos, he was desperately fighting to rid Vietnam of the Japanese. At that time he said that he would "welcome a million American soldiers, but no French." He told his closest friends that they could regard the United States as a good friend because, "It is a democracy without territorial ambitions."

The man considered the first American killed in Vietnam was Lieutenant Colonel Peter Dewey of the OSS. (The OSS, Office of Strategic Services, is said to be the predecessor of the CIA.) Dewey was gunned down just outside Saigon in September 1945. He was a remarkably accomplished young man who had already worked as a foreign correspondent in

Paris, fought in the Polish army, and engaged in espionage behind the German lines in France. As World War II in Vietnam was ending and the Japanese were in the process of surrendering, Dewey supposedly alienated French and British officers in Vietnam by contacting the Viet Minh and trying to work with them. He was accidentally killed in a Viet Minh ambush on the way to the airport. He had been told not to display the U.S. flag on his jeep. If he had been allowed to do so, in all likelihood, he probably would not have been ambushed and killed. He noticed several Vietnamese trying to block the road. Dewey swore at them in French and swerved around the roadblock. The Vietnamese replied with a blast of machine-gun fire that blew off the back of his head. His body was never recovered. He was only twenty-eight years old.

Peter Dewey was the first of almost 60,000 Americans to be killed in Vietnam. The French and Viet Minh blamed each other for his death. Ho Chi Minh sent a letter of condolences to President Truman. Americans who worked with Ho remembered him fondly after the war.

Ho's heart began to fail in early 1969, and by late August he could no longer work. On September 2, Ho died at the age of seventy-nine. He had never married. The North Vietnamese war effort did not weaken after the death of Ho Chi Minh. Quite to the contrary, his people appeared to be more inspired than ever. He personified his people's relentless pursuit of independence and unity. It was universally and ardently believed that the "Bringer of Light" should not have died in vain. The light was to be sustained.

After his death, Ho's body was embalmed and displayed in a granite mausoleum conceived by Soviet architects to imitate Lenin's tomb in Moscow. Every day, masses of Vietnamese shuffle through the mausoleum, weeping as they gaze at the waxen corpse of the man they consider their savoir. But this was not at all what Ho had in mind. His last wishes were to be cremated, have his ashes placed in three ceramic urns and buried on three unmarked mountaintops around the country.

"Cremation," he said, "is not only good from the point of view of hygiene, but it saves farmland." His successors said they were forced to go against his wishes because, "In death, as in life," they said, "he belongs to the people." He was the founder of the state, Vietnam's Lenin or George Washington, one might say.

Chapter 11

Ash and Trash

Lieutenant Clark found Tay Ninh to be an interesting little city. As one would fly over the city to approach the small PSP airfield (usually from the east), one could easily make out the main temple of the Cao Dai religious sect. The focal point of the temple was what appeared to be a central bell tower over the main entrance that exhibited a huge icon of an all-seeing human eye—the primary motif of this sect.

The Cao Dai sect was founded in 1919, by Ngo Van Chieu, a mystic who claimed to commune with a master spirit he called Cao Dai. The Cao Dai cult supposedly appealed to the Vietnamese taste for the supernatural, and eclectically held that the ideal creed ought to combine the best of all the other religious and secular beliefs. Its saints included Jesus, the Buddha, Joan of Arc, Victor Hugo, and Sun Yat-sen. The effigies of these "saints" supposedly graced the main temple in a kind of rococo wax museum at one time. By 1938, the Cao Dai counted 300,000 disciples, a number that quintupled in the years immediately after World War II.

However, like almost all movements in Vietnam, it became political and was crushed by the Diem regime.

The Hoa Hao was another southern sect that could not seem to find a secure place in Vietnamese society. The Hoa Hao, named for a village in the Mekong Delta, emerged in 1939 as a brand of reformed Buddhism invented by a faith healer named Huynh Phu So. The simplicity of the sect attracted thousands of poor peasants. But it also became essentially a private army that eluded control by the powers that be—the French, the Viet Minh, and, for awhile, the Diem regime.

The Americans were just starting to support the Diem regime in a big way in 1955, just about the time that Diem perceived these sects as being a bit too troublesome and defiant. The Americans bribed several of the sect leaders to rally to Diem, paying them as much as $3 million each out of CIA funds. The Hoa Hao were finally subdued in early 1956 when their guerrilla commander, Ba Cut, was captured and publicly guillotined in the French colonial tradition in Can Tho. The South Vietnamese government was to pay a price for this cruel and ruthless incident. After the execution of Ba Cut, several thousand of the defeated Hoa Hao and Cao Dai fighters moved into the recesses of the Mekong Delta and joined the Communist underground. They would emerge afterward to count among the Viet Cong guerrilla fighters.

One of those early "ash and trash" missions struck Lieutenant Clark as being rather unusual. They were assigned to fly ARVN payroll officers about 25 miles northeast of Phu Loi to a leprosarium, a leper colony. The Vietnamese officers were going out to pay the people who managed the leper colony. Of course, they did not land the chopper directly in the colony compound itself. They landed some 300 yards away from the colony entrance. The pay officers walked to the entrance of the colony to transact their business.

This was remarkable to Clark, because he simply did not realize that leprosy existed as a problem in the modern world. He associated it with biblical times. Later he spoke about this with several other officers and came to discover that Americans tended to call leprosy "Hansen's disease" and that there were leper colonies in Louisiana up until the early part of the 20th century. Clark learned that leprosy remains one of the three most dreaded diseases of the tropical parts of the world today, along with malaria and yellow fever.

Captain Thedeibeau was known for religiously saying, "Good morning, Vietnam!" every morning first thing when he arose from his bunk. With half-feigned joy, he seemed to be proclaiming and reminding himself that with the passing of each day he was getting one day closer to that day when he could say, "Goodbye, Vietnam!" Thedeibeau was from Louisiana and seemed to know all about leprosy—and "*Lou-zan-nah.*"

Captain Thedeibeau was afflicted with a bad case of hemorrhoids, and he sometimes carried with him to his chopper what appeared to be a small inner tube. Sitting on this "rubber doughnut" (as he called it) seemed to ease his misery somewhat. He was such a good-humored man that no one would ever make fun of him with his special seating arrangement. And if they did, he would laugh, and with a broad smile, and say something like, "You just wait, you ding-a-ling jackass. Your turn is a'comin', buddy. Everyone gets theirs in the end. Just you wait, old buddy."

Clark and Linville spent several days flying in and around Tay Ninh City. They flew a number of coordination missions with the ranking American advisers in Tay Ninh as they went out to visit and inspect satellite base camps and firebases in the district. One day they spent almost the entire day flying support missions up to the top of the mountain, Nui Ba Den. Acting much like a cable car, they repeatedly lifted loads of South Vietnamese soldiers, their families, and their belongings to the summit of Nui Ba Den. And there were always people up there who wanted to come down. So, they were lifted back down.

The Vietnamese would often bring live chickens and ducks—with the legs tied—on board the helicopter with them. But the final logistical haul of the day was, to Clark, a most memorable one. It was a load of live pigs. The swine were large and squealing, and in a most disagreeable and distressed state. As their skinny Vietnamese soldier-keepers lifted them aboard the aircraft, Lieutenant Clark noticed that the pig's legs were tied. But—at the same time—he thought, If one of those unhappy fellows breaks loose and crashes into the cockpit just about the time we go into our final approach to that little helipad on top on that mountain...well, it could be a really nasty scene. Really nasty. Was there not a better way to transport pork? Clark wondered.

Just before takeoff, Mr. Linville came on the intercom to speak with Dotson and Collins. "Listen, guys," he said. "Keep a close eye on these porkers, okay? If you think for one second that one of them is going to break lose, get'em outta here—out the open door right away. Don't hesitate. Do I make myself clear? Out of here right away, because if we get a wild 300-pound pig up here leaning on the stick, then that's all she wrote. And we can't have that. So, stay alert. Be on your toes. And watch those porkers."

Both Dotson and Collins quickly came back with, "Roger that, sir."

Lieutenant Clark was tired and ill at ease on that last crowded flight to the top of Nui Ba Den, but none of the porkers broke loose, and he was able to make a normal landing—intact—on that elevated helipad. Clark and his crew were quite relived to see the swine safely off-loaded by their four skinny soldier-swineherds and packed away to their new pens. Happily for all involved, Clark thought, there were no flying pigs spotted in the skies over Tay Ninh Province on that day.

Landing a helicopter atop Nui Ba Den was rather tricky, even under normal circumstances. Pilots in the III Corps area were used to landing on fields and strips that were only a little above sea level. Tay Ninh was about sixty feet above sea level. The air was hot and less dense than it would be back at Ft. Benning, Georgia, and the loads in Vietnam were usually much heavier than back in Stateside training exercises. But the pilots learned to slow down a bit and pull in a little more power, and the landings were fine—usually quite smooth. However, atop Nui Ba Den, up at just over three thousand feet, the air was even less dense. The air was thin. So, it seemed to Lieutenant Clark that he needed to pull in twice as much power as when he was landing at or near sea level. In addition to the thin air up there on the summit, the helicopter would be buffeted by unpredictable winds, updrafts which might hit the aircraft at any time from any quarter—especially just at the moment when the pilot was getting ready to put the ship down on the helipad.

Mr. Linville taught Lieutenant Clark a trick or two about landing a helicopter that increased the lieutenant's confidence considerably.

"Remember to lean into it this way," Linville said. "Your body language counts here. Landing up here is a motion, see, a follow-through motion just like this," and he demonstrated by moving his right fist slowly forward and simultaneously gently lifting his left hand, pulling it easily upward as he leaned forward.

"Don't worry about overshooting the pad," he said. "You're okay. You are tending to undershoot it. And that's okay—better to slightly undershoot than to overshoot. But stay ahead of the aircraft—always be out there about 200 yards ahead of the nose box. Just sort of lean forward and push the cyclic stick a little forward as you go, and then pull in some power with your collective pitch till you feel the blades catching hold. And that should put you right over the pad. Then you should be able to put her down nicely—on the money—on a dime."

There was a certain smooth rhythm to this whole business of flying choppers. Clark leaned into it, pushing the stick forward, pulled in the power, and the helicopter reacted just as it should—just as he knew it would. They were over the center of the helipad—at just over three thousand feet—and easing down smoothly with a full load of pork—in that bright, white, light, thin air up there on top of Nui Ba Den. The men and their machine were in complete harmony.

"*Possunt quia posse videntur,*" the Romans had said. "They can do it because they think they can do it."

Clark and his crew refueled at the PSP airfield just west of Tay Ninh City. And then, as the sun began sink behind the lush jungles of

Cambodia to the west, they lifted off and started back to the airbase at Bien Hoa, another day of "hauling ash and trash—and fresh pork and poultry—for Uncle Sam" behind them.

Chapter 12

Search and Destroy

While flying in Tay Ninh Province Lieutenant Clark and Mr. Linville had become quite familiar with the area. Within a short period of time they could instinctively, at a moment's notice, turn the helicopter and fly in the direction of any local airstrip or fire-base—with hardly a glance at a map—and arrive at the desired destination in a brief period of time.

Flying westward from their base at Bien Hoa, they became familiar with Di An, where the U.S. 1st Infantry Division had their base camp. Then a bit farther to the southwest was Cu Chi and the U.S. 25th Infantry Division base camp. The Cu Chi base camp was huge, and the Top Tigers often refueled there. It covered 1,500 acres and its perimeter was six miles around. It was home to about 5,000 Americans plus about 1,000 Vietnamese civilians who worked there. (It was later learned that these were almost all Viet Cong sympathizers and informers.) Supplying this base was a colossal job. It became a major ongoing military operation in itself. The base devoured so many resources that at least one combat commander there said that it became "the tail that wagged the dog."

Actually, Cu Chi base was in the heart of the most tunnel-riddled countryside in South Vietnam, and was the scene of some of the most destructive operations of the war. The tunnel network was to plague the Americans from the moment of their arrival to the time they left. It took the Americans over a year to locate and block all the tunnels that ran underneath the huge Cu Chi base camp. And after they did succeed in doing that, the Viet Cong created a complex structure of tunnels, trenches, and firing positions all around it. They called the ring of tunnels "The Belt." This was the same system they had used to defeat the French at Dien Bien Phu in 1954—by drawing the belt ever tighter.

Just north of there was the area that became known as the Iron Triangle. This forty-square-mile section of jungle represented the largest Viet Cong base nearest to Saigon. It seemed like a natural citadel of jungle and briar, beneath which was a honeycomb of VC bunkers and tunnels. In 1967 it had been a refuge for insurgents for over twenty years and had defied every attempt to conquer it. The southward pointing apex of the triangle was the junction of the Saigon and Thi Tinh Rivers, which formed two of its sides. The third side, or top base line, of this triangle was an imaginary line running from the village of Ben Suc eastward to the district capital of Ben Cat. Australian journalist Peter Arnett was credited with giving the place its menacing name in 1963. He was the first to notice that, with respect to enemy concentration and determination, it resembled the Iron Triangle of the Korean War.

Peter Arnett had a good reputation among almost all of the lower ranking officers and soldiers in the field in Vietnam—as did Neil Sheehan, the UPI and later, *New York Times* journalist. As good journalists should, these men seemed to have a special knack for always managing to be present when and where the action was unfolding. Sheehan was present at both the Battle of Ap Bac in the Mekong Delta in January of 1963, and—with Arnett—at the Battle of Ia Drang Valley in the Central Highlands in October of 1965—

two of the critical battles of the war. They would be there even if it meant renting a taxi in Saigon and driving there. They were good at quickly getting to know the key men involved in the operations, and they were willing to take risks. The ancient maxim that "a good soldier always moves toward the sound of the guns" seemed to apply to these men. Peter Arnett spent over twelve years in Vietnam.

Continuing northwest of the Iron Triangle, flying above Route 14 and the Saigon River, Clark and his crew entered Tay Ninh Province. Almost directly east of Tay Ninh City was the Merlette Rubber Plantation. And then just north of the Merlette Plantation, there along the Saigon River was Les Trungs Plantation, the home of the little Frenchman, Monsieur Marcel Voltaige, their friend from the night out on the town in Saigon. They managed to over-fly Les Trungs one day around noon and they could easily make out that, sure enough, the little prince did have his own airstrip (unpaved red clay), helipad, plus an impressive appearing villa. It looked a bit like a medieval fortress. And there beside the villa—just as he said it would be—was a swimming pool filled with clean sparkling water. The soil in rubber plantation country always seemed to be red clay. After spending a day working on or near one of the rubber plantation airstrips, the soldiers would be completely covered in red dust from head to toe from the dirt kicked up by the helicopters.

This caused Lieutenant Clark to recall an old Clark Gable film, with Gable and Jean Harlow. Winston Clark had seen that film one night on the late, late show while he was away at the university. The film was called *Red Dust.* Made in 1932, it was an unusual old Victor Fleming film about life on a rubber plantation in Vietnam—in Indochina. What an unusually exotic setting for a Hollywood production, Clark thought at the time. There was really something special about that film—and now about this place, Les Trungs. Clark and Linville were eager to land there for a look around, but the proper opportunity seemed to evade them. They were usually on a pretty tight schedule. One day soon, they promised one another. Yes, one day soon they would be landing there. That must happen. That was to be. Certainly it was meant to be. Les Trungs. It was written in the stars.

But before that could happen, it seems as though someone higher up wanted to focus on the war—and the Iron Triangle.

For the most part it seemed like the Americans and the ARVN were getting into the habit of simply avoiding the Triangle. There had been several modest attempts to pacify the area and to drive out the insurgents, but nothing seemed to really affect the enemy's firm situation there. Apparently the Viet Cong were deeply entrenched there and intended to remain that way. But finally, in early 1967, the top generals in Saigon decided that the time had come to seriously deal with the famous Iron Triangle.

The Iron Triangle dominated the strategic land and river routes into Saigon from the west—from Cambodia. A great deal of intelligence information had been carefully studied at the highest levels in Saigon and the conclusion was that urgent action was needed in the Iron Triangle. Pressure must be applied. Every kind of intelligence material imaginable—sampan traffic on the Saigon River, nighttime patrol activity, prisoner interrogation, electronic observation data—had all been carefully compiled and computerized and thoroughly analyzed. The pattern was clear. The Iron Triangle was a major thorn in the side of the ARVN and the Americans, and a major threat to Saigon. The top brass in the Saigon intelligence ranks said that saboteurs and terrorists working out of the Triangle seemed able to strike almost at will in the capital. There were more terrorist incidents in Saigon in 1966 than ever before, and apparently, most of that activity was planned and prepared in the Iron Triangle. The top leaders in North Vietnam had been promoting the idea of "popular uprisings" more than ever before, and it appeared as though they had designs on the capital, Saigon itself. The Communist leaders referred to Ben Suc, a village within the Triangle, as "the gateway to Saigon." The Iron Triangle could no longer be ignored.

Operation Cedar Falls was designed to destroy the Iron Triangle. Plain and simply put, that was the mission. This operation was designed to be a textbook example of the controversial strategy of "search and destroy," and it was planned to be thorough and ruthless.

Operation Cedar Falls was set to start on January 8, 1967. The chief aim was to locate the tunnel headquarters of the Viet Cong regional headquarters, explore it, and then destroy it, along with any other tunnels found there. The tunnels would be dynamited. Incredibly, later the Americans would learn the full extent and significance of the tunnels. They would discover that in Cu Chi district, in and around the Iron Triangle, the insurgents had excavated an estimated 48 kilometers of tunnels during the war against the French and they had been extended to approximately 200 kilometers by the time the American army arrived in force, in 1965.

First of all, the village of Ben Suc was to be emptied of people and razed. All other villages in the Triangle would be treated likewise. Once the civilian population had been cleared out of the Triangle, it was to be stripped of vegetation and declared a free-strike zone. Most of the area had been saturated from the air with the chemical defoliant known as Agent Orange, which killed the vegetation. Tragically, it was later determined that Agent Orange contained minute amounts of dioxin, a highly poisonous substance that also causes cancer, congenital deformations, and other afflictions in humans and animals. This dioxin accumulated from repeated spraying, lingering in the silt of the streambeds and entering the ecosystem of South Vietnam. After the war, scientific tests indicated that the South Vietnamese had dioxin levels in their bodies three times higher than inhabitants of the United States.

The operation was preceded by a weeklong softening-up, (or "LZ prep," as it was called) of bombing missions and artillery strikes. It was safe to assume that the approaches to Ben Suc would be mined and booby-trapped, and that perhaps a battalion of VC would be prepared to defend the village. There would be a total of about 16,000 ARVN troops and over 30,000 U.S. troops involved in Operation Cedar Falls. The American and ARVN troops would be flown in by helicopter, and driven in by armored personnel carriers (APCs) and tanks. It was the largest military operation in South Vietnam to date.

Lieutenant Clark and his crew would be a part of this mighty armada of helicopters. An entire battalion of 1st Infantry Division soldiers, 500 men, commanded by Lieutenant Colonel Alexander Haig (a future Secretary of State) was airlifted into the middle of the village by sixty helicopters. This was the largest number of choppers ever used for such an attack. Fortunately, the Top Tigers found all of their LZs to be cool during the operation, and they suffered no casualties.

The Viet Cong leaders later said that the Americans were nothing if not predictable. The Americans almost always started their operations shortly after eight in the morning and were usually ready to call it a day by six in the evening.

They lifted off from Dau Tieng base at 7:30 a.m., flying in two parallel lines of thirty helicopters (Huey "slicks") clattering across the hazy morning countryside and into what the GIs aboard imagined would be a hot landing zone. The formation suddenly swooped down to treetop level and zoomed in to land in the center of the village of Ben Suc.

Chapter 13

The Iron Land

They took no fire on the way in. As the GIs swiftly unloaded and ran to take up defensive positions, another helicopter appeared, flying about in low circles above the village. It had loudspeakers attached and announced in Vietnamese that no one should run away. If they did they would be shot.

"Stay in your homes and await further instructions," the loud voice said. As the soldiers landed in the village, preplanned artillery and air strikes exploded in the Thanh Dien forest to the north, to cut off escape routes.

Late in 1966 the Viet Cong had received advanced intelligence regarding Operation Cedar Falls. The main-force units in the area had already been withdrawn to a sanctuary near the Cambodian border. Only a small force was left behind. There was no significant resistance in Ben Suc. The only American casualties were caused by booby-traps. The village was sealed and the inhabitants, mostly women, children and old men, along with the inhabitants of surrounding hamlets, were interrogated by the South Vietnamese soldiers.

Simultaneously, as the 1st Infantry Division soldiers landed in Ben Suc, the 11th Armored Cavalry started to crash across the Iron Triangle with their tanks from Ben Cat to Ben Suc on the Saigon River. They experienced no contact with the enemy as they forced their way through the tangles and thickets to join up with the air-landed infantrymen in the ghost town of Ben Suc. The tankers then turned back southward and battered their way to the far point of the Triangle at the junction of the two rivers. So, theoretically, the Triangle had been overrun and conquered.

The next day all the villagers were shipped out—over 10,000 of them—with whatever belongings they could carry and animals they could round up. They were transported in trucks and big Chinook transport helicopters. Some of the people had never seen huge helicopters like the Chinooks and seemed thoroughly convinced that—as they were forced aboard—they were entering the belly of a giant beast that would surely devour them.

Some of those involved said that on January 8, 1967, the village of Ben Suc—former population of about 4,000—was wiped off the face of the earth. When the last truck, helicopter, and boatload of people and animals had left the village, the demolition teams moved in. The grass-roofed huts were soaked with gasoline and razed, leaving spindly black frames, charred furniture, and the entrances to the ubiquitous bomb shelters. Then the bulldozers went to work, flattening all the more solid buildings, fences, and graveyards.

In retrospect, what happened there at Ben Suc seemed—in every way—dreadful, monstrous, terribly cruel, and wrong. In a land of ancestor worshipers the Americans destroyed the graveyards and attempted to remove the people from them.

Vietnam is primarily an agrarian society. Essentially, it is not a land of important cities, nor does it have an urban-based technology. Vietnam is a land of peasants, whose deeply traditional lives are characterized by constant repetition, by the sowing and reaping of rice and the maintenance of customary law. The Vietnamese worship their ancestors as the source of their lives, their fortunes, and their civilization. In the rites of ancestor-worship the death of a man marks no final end. Buried in the life-giving rice fields that have without break sustained his family, the father lives on in the bodies of his children and grandchildren. And there was something special about rice farming that helped to prepare the Vietnamese for war. Planting rice is hard work and it requires much patience, physical labor, and persistence. And it requires teamwork. These are all excellent prerequisites for first rate guerrilla armies. "Vietnamese soil is sacred," Ho Chi Minh once said to a French friend. "Vietnamese soil is flesh of our flesh, and blood of our blood."

The land is the continuum of the Vietnamese peasant family. The father is not so much the owner of the land as the trustee of the land, which will certainly be passed on to the children. To the Vietnamese, the land itself is the sacred constant element. Western concepts of land profiteering and mobile societies are beyond the comprehension of the Vietnamese peasant. The traditional peasant spends his time in one place, and is bound by long tradition to the rice land of his ancestors. His world is a small place, and the earth takes precedence. As the source of life it is the basis for the social contract between the members of the family and the village. Without land, the farmer would have no social identity. He would be a tramp, a landless vagrant. The Vietnamese believe that if a man moves off his land and beyond the village limits, his soul stays behind, buried deep in the earth with the bones of his ancestors.

Ben Suc was strategically situated at a major crossing point on the Saigon River in Cu Chi district. It was the western point of the Iron Triangle. It had been a prosperous village. Most of the villagers were peasant farmers, raising crops like melons, grapefruit, and cashew nuts. Because a market was held there each day, the place could boast many shops, a pharmacy, and a few rather primitive restaurants.

After the bulldozers had done their work, the 1st Division engineers stacked 10,000 pounds of explosives and a thousand gallons of napalm in a crater in the center of the ruined village. Then they covered all that with earth, and tamped it all down with bulldozers. A chemical fuse triggered the five-ton explosion. It was thought that it would certainly destroy any undiscovered tunnels in the vicinity. The gigantic explosion caused the earth to tremble for miles around the village. One officer involved in the operation said:

"The village of Ben Suc no longer exists."

However, this gargantuan effort to depopulate and destroy Ben Suc failed. By the end of the year, over a thousand villagers had drifted back to Ben Suc. Many of the returning villagers lived in their old bomb shelters or dug new chambers and tunnels. After the monsoon rains the grass started to grow again on top of these refuges, concealing them from view. The guerrillas who had managed to hold on and survive got busy reconstructing the tunnels so necessary for bringing main-force Viet Cong back in from the Cambodian border—back into the Iron Triangle.

"The enemy might—from time to time—occupy the face of our earth," said the legendary North Vietnamese General Vo Nguyen Giap, "but our people would always occupy its bowels."

The Viet Cong usually fought on their own land, to which they felt closely tied. Some of the guerrillas there started to refer to the Iron Triangle as "the Iron Land," or "the Land of Fire." They wrote poems and songs about that land, how it shielded and sustained them and about the "sacred salvation of the nation."

"Mother Earth herself is our protector," wrote the poet Duong Huong Ly.

The partridge in the night cries out
Our love of our native land.
Your entrails, Mother, are unfathomable.
The noise of picks

Shakes the bosom of the earth.
Columns, divisions, will arise
From you, and the enemy
Will quake and flee.

The massive raid on the Iron Triangle did turn up some significant discoveries. A number of tunnels, bunkers, and rice caches were uncovered. A rather large medical complex containing what appeared to be an operating room, and a plentiful supply of medicines were discovered. Maps of the Saigon area and Tan Son Nhut Airport were found. And there were some Viet Cong flags and thousands of documents. Some of these were lists of Viet Cong sympathizers—including a list of all the barbers working at Cu Chi base, the U.S. 25th Infantry Division Headquarters.

The U.S. command in Saigon hailed the operation as a triumph. Approximately 750 Viet Cong were reported killed, and the Americans suffered 72 killed and 337 wounded. But by the end of the year, the Communists had returned to the devastated area and reconstructed the sanctuary. And later they used it as a springboard for their assault against Saigon in the Tet Offensive of early 1968.

The pattern seemed to be repeated time and again. The Americans would repeatedly conquer territory that could not be held. The war was a test of endurance in which the side able to last longer would prevail. As for the war of attrition, the "body count war," Ho Chi Minh said to the Americans the same thing he had said to the French over twenty years before.

"You can kill ten of my men for every one I kill of yours, but even at those odds, you will lose and I will win."

Sir Robert Thompson, the British counterinsurgency adviser to the Saigon government, saw clearly that time would work against the United States and its South Vietnamese allies unless they could isolate the Viet Cong from their peasant support. Thompson proposed a more modest anti-guerrilla approach, rather than the massive operations that tended to squander resources and devastate and alienate the peasants and the countryside. Thompson warned the highest levels of the American command that the Communists could deadlock the conflict and exhaust the U.S. forces.

"In a revolutionary war," he said, "you lose if you do not win."

Lieutenant Clark and his crew refueled one more time at Cu Chi base before lifting off just at sundown for the short flight back to Bien Hoa Airbase. It had been a long, hot, and frantic day. And Ben Suc was no more. Helicopters of all sorts and sizes were buzzing about everywhere—and so were artillery shells. The helicopter crews had to take extra careful precautions to avoid flying through areas of concentrated artillery fire which might be shooting out of any base camp at any time of the night or day. More than once, helicopters in Vietnam were brought down by "friendly" artillery fire. By the end of 1967 the Americans would have over 3,000 helicopters in Vietnam.

Clark's head was filled with a kaleidoscope of images of helicopters, APCs, enormous bulldozers, GI and ARVN soldiers, shouting NCOs, wailing civilians, reluctant water buffalo being herded off, and earth-shattering explosions. Clark was not at all sure of what to make of all this—this man-made tempest. What was happening here? Was this tempest really necessary? This tempest—did it represent the burning out of the cancer? Or did it represent the sowing of the seed, the implanting of the cancer? The American commanders seemed to always be speaking of equipment, technology, logistics, and statistics. They rarely ever spoke about the Vietnamese people—their condition, their mind-set, their immediate needs, their environment, and their future. Or actually, was there to be a future in Vietnam? The village had to be destroyed in order to be saved someone had said. Exactly where in the scheme of things were the rice farmer, his family and their water buffalo, and their piece of land when the centurions spoke only of fire and sword. But what should the centurions do? Was not that their craft—the application of fire and sword? Who—if anyone—*should* be here at the vortex of things in the heart of

Ben Suc, in the marketplace? Who should it be—Buddha, Confucius, Sun Yat-sen, Victor Hugo, Henri Dunant, Gandhi, Albert Schweitzer, Mother Teresa, Adam Smith, Karl Marx, Harpo Marx, or Johnny Appleseed? Who should it be? Who is it that knows what is to be done here?

When Lieutenant Clark spoke with the Vietnamese they were always talking about their likes and dislikes, their problems, and their immediate needs. They almost never spoke of technology. Once a young boy asked Clark how many engines were attached to a B-52 bomber. But that was about the extent of it for technology with little Nguyen. Yes, the B-52 was a mighty flying fortress, an impressive machine, and an overwhelming terminator of life. But was it there where it should be in Vietnam, in a guerrilla war, an insurgent war? Was it not this environment that the handsome young president had in mind when he created the Green Berets, with all of their hands-on, face-to-face tools and techniques? Do we win hearts and minds with technology—or with people?

What was happening here? Was someone out of touch? But who are you to ask? Clark asked himself. You are just a lieutenant, a fly-boy, and your place is in the helicopter, in the cockpit hauling ash and trash. Don't get out of line here. Get back into the cockpit. Yes, our place is in the helicopter—the cockpit. You are not a policy person. Mind your ash and trash. Get on with it.

"Some days," Linville said, "when I climb into this machine I feel as though I'm mounting a marvelous flying carpet. On others days I feel like I'm climbing into a metal coffin. You never know, actually, what it's gonna be on a given day. But we shan't dwell on it. Let's turn the crank—turn them blades, guys. Let's go."

Tell us, Marvin, what was this all about? Were we—the Americans—really helping these people? Or were we simply keeping busy, moving about from point A to point B, dispensing chemicals and ordnance, and filling out forms and after-action reports, and compiling statistics that might be fed into a computer somewhere? Were the computers really so important? As they move inexorably down the Ho Chi Minh Trail the

Americans say the Vietnamese are like ants. And what are we like? Body snatchers from Planet X? We must be like crop dusters set on automatic pilot. But instead of dusting boll weevils and other insects with DTD, we are dusting people and their environment with Agent Orange and napalm—and CS (tear gas/riot-control gas) and hair spray. And while we were preoccupied with Our R&R, our DEROS dates, and getting our tickets punched, Ben Suc is no more. What about the rice farmer who actually had to hide and shelter his water buffalo underground? What about displaced ancestor worshipers who were now in search of ancestors?

Are we simply whistling past the graveyard? To Lieutenant Clark, the whistling was starting to sound like the crack of doom.

Chapter 14

Les Trungs

The Top Tigers flew a number of follow-up combat assaults in and around Cu Chi district and then Operation Cedar Falls started to be regarded as history, concluded, over with, done, finished—*fini*. The LZs had all been cool, surprisingly enough, and that was most agreeable to the pilots and crews of the 68th Assault Helicopter Company.

Lieutenant Clark and Mr. Linville and crew were back again, flying mostly administrative missions in Tay Ninh Province. They had just finished flying one of the U.S. adviser officers, a Captain Torres, back from one of the outlying firebases to the airstrip at Tay Ninh City and were refueling when they learned that they were being released early that day. Clark was impressed with how Torres seemed to be such a "lone eagle type." Usually U.S. advisers travel in pairs out to the local ARVN firebases, but not Torres. He traveled alone, and one might see him anywhere. He seemed to get around more than any other adviser that Clark had come to know. Somehow Clark got the impression that Torres had some sort of special authority or relationship with the Vietnamese. They seemed to really hang on his every word and every nuance. Torres appeared to be fluent in the Vietnamese language.

Captain Torres climbed off the chopper at the airfield and, with a friendly smile, told Lieutenant Clark they were released for the day. It was only 1600 hours—4:00 p.m.

Lieutenant Clark was on the controls. He had just made the takeoff from the Tay Ninh airstrip and was turning northeastward toward Bien Hoa when Mr. Linville spoke.

"Hey, what do you think?" he asked. "Shall we swing by the little Frenchman's place and see what we can see?"

"Sure," Clark answered. "Fine idea. Let's do that."

As Linville took the controls of the aircraft and took up a more northward heading, Clark turned slightly in his seat and asked the crewmen, Dotson and Collins, "Hey, guys, you got any problem with that? Or do we need to get back to home base right away?"

"Hey, drive on," Sgt. Dotson said. "I got no problem with that. Let's go see what we can see."

"No problem here," Collins said. "Groovy, man. Let's go. Let's do it."

It was only a short flight to Les Trungs, Monsieur Voltaige's rubber plantation from Tay Ninh. The Frenchman's place was only about 16 miles ("as the crow flies") from Tay Ninh City, just across the Saigon River.

As they approached the plantation they could hardly believe their eyes. Just as they over-flew the place they saw a small dark helicopter swooping down over the airstrip and rapidly hovering over to a helipad that was fairly close to the villa, or *chateau*, as Monsieur Voltaige would refer to it.

"Hey, get a load of this, guys," Linville said. "The little frog has his own cute little chopper—his own private helicopter! Wow! This guy must really be somebody."

"You think so?" Clark asked. "You think that's him?"

"Well, shucks, I'll tell you what," said Linville. "Let's drop down there for a couple of minutes and check it out. What do you say?"

"Well, yeah, I suppose we could," Clark answered.

"Listen guys," Linville continued, "if anyone that's anyone just happens to spot our ship down there and have questions, we can always say we got a warning light that we had to check out, right?"

"You got it, Mr. Linville," Sgt. Dotson answered. "We gotta check out this warning light. It might be a hydraulics problem. Who knows?"

"I'm with you, man," Collins said. "Better not take chances. Better safe than sorry."

Linville did a sharp right turn and then swooped down with the Huey over the red clay airstrip. He made his approach to the midway point on the strip and then continued on down the strip at a high fast hover. He put the chopper down at the top of the strip not far from the helipad just as the two men—Monsieur Voltaige and his pilot—were climbing out of the small, sleek-looking helicopter.

Linville quickly shut down the Huey and he and Clark climbed out of the aircraft while their crewmen prepared to tie down the rotor blades. The two pilots walked toward Monsieur Voltaige. He turned in their direction, and they could clearly see that he apparently recognized them and was pleased to see them.

"*Bonjour, bonjour, Mes amis! Mon Dieu, c'est possible? Salut, salut!*" Monsieur Voltaige said as he extended his open arms and extended a hearty greeting to them. He was dressed in a loose, well-cut safari-type khaki outfit.

"Hey, what's this?" Mr. Linville asked nodding toward the small helicopter on the helipad. "Is this yours—your very own little flying machine?" he asked.

"*Oui,* Monsieur Linville," Monsieur Voltaige answered. "*Oui, oui,* it is my own. Oh, yes, a bit of luxury here I must admit. But it is necessary. We must be able to travel, to get about, *n'est-ce pas*? We must be able to attend to business, *n'est-ce pas*? And please allow me to introduce to you my pilot. Gentlemen, this is my personal pilot and good friend, Paul Picair."

Clark and Linville greeted Picair and shook his hand. A fit looking man who appeared to be in his early forties, Picair wore the wary look of a soldier-of-fortune type who might also be serving his *patron* as a body-guard and chauffeur. He wore a well-tailored, neat-looking, dark-blue flight suit. Gold colored pilot's wings were embroidered on the suit over the left breast pocket.

"What make is it? Who's the manufacturer?" Linville asked again, nodding toward the small chopper.

"An Alouette. It's an Alouette," Picair answered with a slight hint of pride.

Linville and Clark gave the machine a quick walk-around inspection with Picair.

"Hey," Linville said with great feeling, "a really nice machine. I mean, this is like really nice. A super little toy to play around with. Excellent!" he heartily approved.

The Alouette was painted dark green, which caused Clark to think for a moment about the perpetual "black chopper" stories and mythologies. On a fairly frequent basis Americans stationed at places near the Cambodian border, places like Tay Ninh, would report seeing—usually late at night—a mysterious black chopper. And, in all likelihood, a dark green chopper would appear to be black at night. The Americans could never establish contact with it or really describe it very well. But they were persistent in insisting that they had seen a black unmarked helicopter near the Cambodia border. And the clear inference was that there was some kind of high ranking North Vietnamese or Viet Cong commander in the area there that had his own chopper and seemed to use it mostly quite late, on quiet, moonless nights. Clark maintained his serious doubts about the story. But for a moment the idea did come to him:

"Were people perhaps seeing Paul Picair and his flying Frog friend swooping harmlessly about the area?"

At that moment Lieutenant Clark noticed the registration number painted on the side of the little chopper. In large yellow letters and numbers it read: VT 6007.

"That's it!" he said. "That's it! Now I've got you," Clark said looking over at Monsieur Voltaige with a smile and a gleam in his eyes.

"Yes, I know you. I've got you. Yes, that's you," he continued pointing at the registration number on the helicopter.

"You are VT 6007. You are *Voltaire Six* with salutes, salutations, and compliments from 007, your counterpart in murder and mayhem. That's you: Voltaire Six, the Count of *Catinat*, the Marquise of Tay Ninh Province, and Prince of Les Trungs."

"Oh, yes," Monsieur Voltaige replied with a gleeful smile. "*Oui, oui,* Monsieur Clark. I believe you are on to me. You have me. I have been discovered, and you, my cavalier, have discovered me. It is blind intuition, I am sure. Of course, what can I say? You have the measure of the man—and you are a chivalrous young gentleman and a scholar of distinction."

They all laughed together, and then the little Frenchman continued.

"Ah, but I know you, also," he said. "*Oui*, I have you, also, monsieur. From the beginning I have suspected that you are...yes, you are...No, not Tom Sawyer! You are *d'Artagnan.* That is you, *mon ami.* You are d'Artagnan, from the Gascony. The third...no, no, the fourth musketeer. What do you think, Monsieur Linville? Am I not correct—Lieutenant Clark is Monsieur d'Artagnan? He is the one, *n'est-ce pas*? Yes, yes, I believe Monsieur Clark is a perfect d'Artagnan, the quixotic Gascon, one of the giants from the pen of Dumas—*Oui*, Monsieur Alexandre Dumas."

"Yes, by all means. That he is," Linville said. "He is d'Artagnan. And I would venture so far as to say that when he grows up he just might become Don Quixote, the man from La Mancha. Yes, sir, this young man has a bright future—Whirly Birdie Express, Windmills Incorporated. He's on a quest, you see. He would like for everyone to be a good guy. It's just that simple. He wants to see the Evil One vaporized—evaporated. Gone. Outta here. Long gone. Plain and simple."

"Now, come on, Winnie," Linville continued. "What was it that Benjamin Franklin said? What was it, come on, now?"

Linville beamed at Clark.

"Well, now—Oh, yes," Clark replied with a rather diffident smile. "Franklin said that he thought that the world would be a much nicer place if only men would not be such beasts to one another. Is that what you mean?"

"Yeah, that's it. That's it," answered Linville. "You see, my man here is on a quest. He's in search of the Lost World of Norman Rockwell."

As he laughed Monsieur Voltaige looked up toward the chateau, smiled broadly with his eyes shining and said, "Ah, *oui, messieurs*, look who we have here. Yes, now, let us look here directly before us. Who do we have here? *Oui*, *oui*, my daughters! My darlings! Yes, here they are. *Voila!* Genevieve and Monique!"

Both of the young women waved and shouted.

"Papa, Papa! Hello, Papa! Hello! Hello!"

Monsieur Voltaige greeted his daughters, warmly embraced them, and then introduced them to all present. Sergeant Dotson and Collins had finished securing the Huey and had just joined the others.

Genevieve was 22 and Monique was 24. And they were both very attractive women. Here they were standing on the edge of War Zone C in South Vietnam, and they looked as though they could have just stepped off of the Champs Élysées on a warm summer's afternoon in Paris. They were each dressed in pastel-colored plain-cut sleeveless cotton summer dresses, and they wore white patent leather shoes.

The natural beauty of Genevieve struck Lieutenant Clark with a unique force. She was a marvelous creature, and her sweet smell and powerful presence physically jolted him. When she stood close to him, he was dazzled. He feared he was gaping. He feared embarrassment. He feared appearing to be a complete idiot. But Clark remained under her spell, and to a great degree, he was helpless.

Just to touch her..., he thought. Yes, just that—just to touch her. To touch her hand. There he felt sure he would find the stuff of magic.

When their eyes met a page turned in the book of life for Winston Clark. Almost instantly he entered a new level of the universe, and he found it to be a tranquil and harmonious place, but—at the same time—exhilarating. For better or worse, he would never go back to being the same person, and he found that quite suitable. He suddenly felt liberated. He was a more complete person now. He had arrived. No more wild turkeys, no more wild geese in the pursuit of desiccated scarecrows. He was entering a new dimension. He stepped up onto this new plain suddenly and yet it felt eternal—timeless—as if he should have been there all along. He had been a sleepwalker before. This new dimension—it had always been there just below the surface, just beyond the veil, awaiting him. Clark felt immeasurably better just knowing that Genevieve existed. She was a part of the universe, their universe. Regardless of what happened they were together. Yes, she was there, and he was there, and he was whole, incorruptible, and ageless. Genevieve stood there next to him in the red dust of War Zone C—and at the center of the universe—and he was a nobler man.

Linville nudged Clark gently and muttered, "Hey, man, this is definitely *not* the stuff of Norman Rockwell. What do you think?"

Monsieur Voltaige was speaking to them. He said, "This is wonderful. This is all very special, I assure you. Now, here, yes, we have you here with us at last. And it is such a pleasure to have you all here," he opened his arms to them all as he spoke. "*Oui*, to have you all here as my guests...this is very, very special I must say. And so, please now, *s'il vous plait*, join us for our evening meal. Have some wine and dinner with us, please, *s'il vous plait*. Please."

Lieutenant Clark quickly glanced at Mr. Linville, who hesitated for a second and then gave a kind of uncertain shrug and looked down at the ground.

"I don't think so," Clark said looking at Linville. "I'm not so sure we can do that—lovely as it sounds."

"Right," Linville spoke up. "We don't want to push our luck too much with the powers that be. We are a bit off our flight plan here right now. But, hey, maybe another time. It would be great!"

"Oh, this is unfortunate," Monsieur Voltaige said. "So unfortunate. I do wish you could find a way to dine with us and share a bottle of wine with us. It would be quite enjoyable I am sure. But, I understand. By all means, I understand. You are pilots. You have things to do—missions to fly. A schedule to keep. Duty calls. Of course, I understand the military. I know how it is. All of us know the military. But now, wait just a moment. Would you like to take a refreshing swim in our swimming pool? This is something I am sure we would all enjoy. It would be quite refreshing, and I am convinced that it would not take up so very much of your time. Come now, what do you think? A little swim in our pool? It would refresh you, I am sure. What do you think?"

At that moment Monsieur Voltaige seemed to be especially eyeing Sergeant Dotson and Robby Collins. "A little swim in our pool? Yes, what do you think?" he asked.

Both Dotson and Collins appeared to be quite flattered at this kind consideration and invitation. Their excited expressions told Lieutenant Clark exactly what their feelings were regarding this matter.

"Well," Clark said, "I'm afraid we don't have our swimming stuff, trunks and all, with us, so—"

"Ah, that is of no consequence," Monsieur Voltaige immediately inserted. "That is certainly no problem here. We have everything here at Les Trungs. Everything, I tell you, Monsieur Cavalier. *Absolument tout.* We have it all. If you need swim wear, we will provide it ten-fold. How does that sound, *Messieurs*, ten-fold?"

Dotson, Collins, and Linville all faced Lieutenant Clark with broad smiling faces. The girls, Genevieve and Monique smiled prettily, their eyes sparkling. The crew was more than eager for a little adventure, some variety in their ash and trash lives. Clark made a conscious effort not to look Genevieve in the eye, and then he spoke.

"Well, alright," he said, "I suppose we could find another thirty minutes or so for a little dip. Sure. Why not? It is awfully kind of you to invite us, Monsieur Voltaige. But, remember, guys, just a little dip. We can't get water-logged and hang around here forever."

"Ah, *oui,* Monsieur Clark, *mon cavalier, oui.* Follow me and I will provide you with everything, yes, everything you could possibly need," said Monsieur Voltaige. "I wish we had more time so I could show you around. But we must do only that which we must do—what time allows, *n'est-ce pas?*"

The crew was led to a bathhouse that stood at the head of the swimming pool. There, momentarily, Monsieur Voltaige and a Vietnamese waiter brought two large baskets—one filled with bathing suits and the other with towels. Also, some sun tan lotion was offered to the soldiers.

"*Voila*!" said Monsieur Voltaige. "I think you will find everything that you need here. Please, *s'il vous plait*, let me know—personally—if you have any unfulfilled wishes, yes, if you wish for *anything*. Just say the word, *messieurs*, just say the word, and we will do our utmost to make you happy. You are my guest, and we wish to please. We wish that your visit with us be a most pleasant one."

At that moment Monsieur Voltaige appeared to suddenly remember something, and he spoke rapidly to the Vietnamese waiter in French. The Vietnamese man quickly departed to accomplish his assignment. And then the Frenchman turned again to Lieutenant Clark and Mr. Linville.

"Ah, the beekeepers!" he said. "We must invite them to join you. *Oui*, the beekeepers—*notre apicultrice*—you must meet them."

"Beekeepers…?" Clark said with a questioning expression.

"*Oui*, *monsieur*, beekeepers. Yes, you will see. Now, let us get changed and into the water—the refreshing water. There is nothing like it," said Monsieur Voltaige as he walked away.

As Monsieur Voltaige departed the bathhouse, Clark looked at Linville and rolled his eyes. Linville replied to Clark's gesture in a heavily exaggerated French accent:

"Now, *messieurs*, if you have any unfilled wishes, please, *s'il vous plait*, just ring my bell. After all, you *are* my cotton-pickin' guests, you see, *n'est-ce pas*?"

Within minutes the airmen had found swimming trunks that suited them, were changed, and then they were quickly in the pool. The water was just right—not cold and not warm. They were all impressed with how clean the water was despite all the red dust that was commonly in the air around the rubber plantations.

They were adjusting to the sparkling waters when they all looked up to see the girls approaching the pool to join them. Genevieve and Monique were dressed in thoroughly revealing bikinis. Clark thought for a moment that he might lose his breath, his ability to speak, or even move. He thought that without any doubt whatsoever, he had never seen such breath-taking beauty. He was focused on Genevieve as she entered the water, and her perfect form, her overwhelming beauty must certainly be unique. For a moment it was as though she was the first woman he had ever seen. He had never seen the likes of her. As far as Clark was concerned, she was unique in every way. Again, as he struggled to regain his composure, he suddenly felt embarrassed for the entire crew for they all seemed suddenly quiet—and quite close to speechless. Clark later thought of the great irony in the nature of young men. One could fire machine guns at them, and they would have something to say—perhaps a great deal to say—but put the stunning sensuality of rare feminine beauty before them—and they were dumbstruck—speechless.

The two daughters of Monsieur Voltaige made a little small talk, apparently about the water, and then they were in the pool. At that time Monsieur Voltaige and Paul Picair approached the pool with two Vietnamese girls. These young damsels were also well formed and dressed in the slightest of bikinis.

"And so, *messieurs*," spoke Monsieur Voltaige, "How do you find the water? Come now, is this not refreshing?"

Linville spoke: "We find the water—and the company—to be first class—top notch, four stars—no, *monsieur*, five stars."

"And now," said Monsieur Voltaige with a broad smile, "please allow me to introduce *notre apicultrice*—our beekeepers—the charming and lovely Le Lanh and Mai Bec." Monsieur Voltaige then proceeded to introduce the Vietnamese girls to each of the Americans separately.

"Beekeepers...?" said Clark with a curious glance at Monsieur Voltaige.

"*Oui, monsieur*, beekeepers." Monsieur Voltaige replied. "We keep bees. These girls attend our bees, and they provide us with the freshest and sweetest honey one could ever wish for. Here at Les Trungs, we try whenever and wherever possible to be self-contained and self-sustained. Actually, Monsieur Clark, I think you would find that we have just about everything here." With a glance at the Vietnamese girls who were standing near him in the water now, he continued: "This is Le Lanh, and we often call her 'Lee Ann.' And this is Mai Bec. We often call her 'Becky.'"

Dotson and Collins seemed quick to befriend the Vietnamese girls, the beekeepers, and drift off to one corner of the pool. Dotson seemed quick to befriend Mai Bec, and Collins seemed quite pleased to be in the company of Le Lanh. Out of the corner of his eye, Clark could see that Linville had started a conversation with Monique. So, he thought, things seemed to be working out in a most amazing and wonderful way.

Clark swam closer to Genevieve and started to make small talk with her. And it was not half so difficult as he had imagined it would be. Both Genevieve and Monique spoke passing English, and the Vietnamese girls also seemed to know some English. Genevieve seemed outgoing and friendly. Well, I suppose that's part of being a glamorous person, Clark thought. And he did find himself coming back to that word—glamorous—time and again.

I really believe, Clark said to himself, that she is the only truly glamorous person I have ever known. The honey-colored hair, the pink lips, the greenish-blue eyes—such an abundance of perfection—gracious, harmonious perfection. Her voice was enchanting to his ears. She made the world a better place just by walking on it, Clark thought. '*The grass stoops not, she treads on it so light.*'

She asked him what his life was like as a helicopter pilot in Vietnam.

"Oh, it's not bad," he said. "Most of us love to fly."

"Oh, but *le risque*, the danger," she said. "I think it must be very dangerous, that what you are doing. Is it not? Is it not very dangerous?"

"Well, yes, sometimes," Lieutenant Clark answered. "But not entirely. Sometimes we simply fly Vietnamese officers and their families—and their chickens and ducks—, from here to there, and so forth. Some say we are like truck drivers in the sky. But we like our work—most of us like it."

Clark asked Genevieve about her life. She had spent most of her life in France, and gone to school in Paris, where her mother was presently living. She normally did not spend a great deal of time in Vietnam with her father—usually six months at the most. She said that she and her sister had only recently arrived and were not at all sure of how long they would remain in Vietnam, at "Les Trungs."

"Why 'Les Trungs?'" Clark asked. "Why does your father call his place Les Trungs?"

At the very moment that Clark had asked his question about the plantation's name, Monsieur Voltaige spoke up. He was now there beside them in the water.

"This name, Monsieur Clark," he said, "is a salute to the Vietnamese people and their undying courage and fortitude." Monsieur Voltaige proceeded to tell the story of the Trung sisters.

"In their ancient history, the Vietnamese have had repeated clashes with the Chinese. Many times the Chinese were apparently obsessed with the idea that they should assimilate the Vietnamese. But the Vietnamese would have no part of it. Never. A Vietnamese princess named Trung Trac was determined to avenge the murder of her dissident husband by a Chinese commander. She led the first major Vietnamese insurrection against China. This was in the year 40 AD. She and her sister, Trung Nhi, mustered other defiant nobles and their vassals, including another woman named Phung Thi Chinh, who supposedly gave birth to a baby in the middle of the battle yet continued to fight with the infant strapped to her back. They were victorious over the Chinese. And with the Trung sisters as their queens, they set up an independent state that stretched from Hue into southern China. But the Chinese crushed them only two years later, and the Trung sisters committed suicide by throwing themselves into a river. The Vietnamese still venerate them, and they honor them with a national holiday each year. Even the Viet Cong acclaim the Trung sisters as pioneer nationalists. And Madame Ngo Dinh Nhu, the sister-in-law of South Vietnam's former President Ngo Dinh Diem, erected a statue in Saigon in 1962 to commemorate their patriotism—and also to promote herself as their reincarnation. Vietnamese women have played prominent roles in the history of this country. A young woman named Trieu Au led the nation in the third century. She became the Vietnamese equivalent of Joan of Arc. She also fought for Vietnam's independence against China. But tragically, she was defeated, and—at the age of 23—she also committed suicide. And she is still worshiped as a sacred figure for this nation."

"That's interesting," Clark said. "Very interesting. I had no idea."

"Nor I," Mr. Linville said. "Well, really, it sounds like this country has got quite a history."

"Oh, yes, indeed it does," said Monsieur Voltaige. "And, yes, I commonly find that the Americans—the majority of the Americans—appear to be totally ignorant of the history of this nation. And yet, at the same time, your nation is investing so much blood and treasure here."

The diminutive Frenchman paused briefly and then continued to speak.

"Ah, *oui*, *messieurs*, the Vietnamese have struggled long and hard to become a nation—an independent nation. Some say for a thousand years—for a thousand years they have struggled to become a nation. And yes, it is true, some are now saying that they are prepared to struggle for another thousand years to gain that independence—that nationhood. I often think that the Americans are mistaken to speak so disparagingly of this so-called 'Charlie,' and 'Marvin the ARVN.' I believe that you will find that these people, the Vietnamese people are very strong—yes, very strong indeed."

Just prior to departing the rubber plantation Clark stood alone for a moment with Genevieve to say goodbye. Her smell was uniquely fresh and sweet. It made Clark think of springtime in the high meadowlands of the mountains. It was a lovely smell—vital and life renewing and sustaining.

Clark was walking slightly ahead of Genevieve as they left the patio and slowly walked toward the airstrip. Genevieve softly grasped his arm and said:

"'Don't walk in front of me. I may not follow. Don't walk behind me. I may not lead. Walk beside me and be my friend.' Those words are from Camus," she said. "Albert Camus. Do you know Camus?"

"Camus? Yes," Clark said. "Camus was an interesting man. I have read some of his works."

"I hope you can return soon to visit us," she said.

"I would like that very much," he said. "I promise you that I will do my best. It must be possible—somehow."

"Your thoughts? What are your thoughts now—at this moment?" she asked.

He looked down at his awaiting helicopter, sitting alone on the red dirt strip with the jungle behind it, and then back at Genevieve. He looked at her hands. Lady fingers, he thought. Perfect lady fingers. Such absolute perfection.

"I was thinking of power," he said, "how power is sometimes so hard, and then again, sometimes so soft. I was thinking of the awesome power of rare beauty—such rare beauty…such rare beauty as I have come to know today. This will be a day to remember," he said.

"And what are your thoughts at this moment?" Lieutenant Clark asked.

"I was thinking of how much I have enjoyed your visit," she answered. "And I was thinking of how much I would like to see you return soon and visit us again—perhaps often. I feel that this must be possible—somehow possible. I feel that you must return to us. I was thinking that I would like—very much—to get to know you better. I would like to be your friend."

"Yes," Clark said, "Yes, I too would like that very much."

She looked down at the awaiting helicopter and then back to him.

"We have enjoyed your company very much," Genevieve said. "Please come back to us soon. I would be very pleased. *Oui*, very pleased. You have…How do you say?…a standing invitation. Yes, you have a standing invitation to visit us at any time."

"I assure you that I will do my utmost," said Clark.

"Can you communicate with us?" Can you inform us of your plans?" she asked.

"Well, I really don't know. I will investigate that, believe me," Clark replied.

"It would be very nice if you could pay us a proper visit," said Genevieve. "We should have dinner. We would have a party. You should come and spend a few days with us. Yes, you must! Surely your friends can release you for a few days. And I know my father can arrange it. You know my father. He can arrange anything. Oh, our Papa, he knows everyone and everyone knows him."

"Well, yes, somehow I find that quite believable," Clark answered.

At that moment Monsieur Voltaige approached them. They were standing near the helipad.

"What is this now? Did I hear someone say that Papa should arrange something?" Monsieur Voltaige asked with a twinkle in his eyes.

Genevieve spoke with her father in French. She seemed rather excited. He readily reassured her and she seemed requited, pleased.

"Tell me," Monsieur Voltaige said to Clark. "What is your commanding officer's name and unit designation? I believe that I heard one of you say that you are the tigers, correct—the Top Tigers? I have met your executive officer, I believe. That would be Major Scully, *n'est-ce pas*? Major Scully? *Oui, oui.* I would like very much to speak with your commander—and get to know him—your commanding officer. Yes, please, what is his name?"

Lieutenant Clark hesitated for a moment, but then furnished the Frenchman with the requested information. Then Clark added:

"Now please. Let us not be rash. Let us not be too presumptuous, too overwhelming. I really would not like for our commander to get the idea that we have been spending all of our time hanging around your pool and bar—and your beekeepers. That would not be so good—no, not at all. I am sure you understand, Monsieur Voltaige."

"Monsieur Clark, *cher ami*," Monsieur Voltaige said as he put his arm around Clark's shoulder. "You know that you can trust me. You can have full confidence in me. I am nothing if I am not discreet. I am sure that our mutual friend, Monsieur Clayton, would be happy to reassure you that I am a most discreet person—most discreet—and reliable. A good friend. Trust me, *mon ami*, trust me. You can believe that I have only your best interest in mind."

Monsieur Voltaige looked directly at Genevieve and said to her in reference to Clark: "*C'est mon ami.* Yes, he and all of the Top Tigers. They are our friends."

Lieutenant Clark started to speak again, but Monsieur Voltaige made an impatient gesture and said: "I will hear no more, Monsieur d'Artagnan, *mon cavalier, mon* musketeer. Be on your way, and *bon chance.* Fly away in your bird. Be careful and take good care of yourself and your fine crew—your beloved colleagues. Remember: 'All for one, and one for all.' That is a wonderful philosophy. I am sure that we will meet again—and soon. I am sure of it. And now...*Au revoir*, my friends, *Au revoir*."

Lieutenant Clark waved goodbye to the group as he walked out onto the airstrip toward his helicopter, walking in powdery red dust.

"*Au revoir, mon ami*" Monsieur Voltaige said.

His daughters, Genevieve and Monique, waved goodbye.

"*Au revoir,*" they said.
There was music in their voices.
"*Au revoir.*"

Chapter 15

Nocturnal Lumberjacks

They were on a night flight—a night mission.

Lieutenant Clark was watching what appeared to be a small black and white television screen attached to the middle of the helicopter console. He found it difficult at best to detect any nighttime enemy activity—or anything else—on the snowy little screen.

"What do you see?" Captain Ratcliffe asked.

"Not much of anything," Clark answered. "It looks like snow, mostly."

"Don't stare at it too long," Ratcliffe said, "or it will mess up your night vision."

Clark was flying with Captain Ratcliffe and his crew for a few days and nights. Some extensive maintenance was being performed on Clark's regularly assigned aircraft, and therefore he and Mr. Linville had been split up to work with other crews for a few days. Sergeant Dotson and PFC Collins were staying with their aircraft and assisting the men in the maintenance platoon, helping to get their ship prepared for further operations.

This break in the routine allowed Lieutenant Clark an opportunity to fulfill a harbored wish to fly gunships for awhile—and especially to be able to fly with "Rats," Captain Ratcliffe, the 68th Buddha, the informal leader of the Mustangs, the gunship platoon. Some of the American advisers had started to refer to "Rats" as "Buddha," mainly because of his short stout build and serene composure and stoic attitude. Clark and his roommate, Mr. Meeks, had entertained the idea of trying to join the gunship platoon for some time, but thus far the opportunity had not presented itself. The gunship platoon was actually a great deal like a tight-knit private club, and sometimes it took a transfer or a death to get admitted to the club. The first step in getting into the gunship platoon seemed to be to get chummy with the platoon members themselves—getting on their right side. Now Clark had his chance, for a few days at least, to experience flying with the Mustangs.

It was 2200 hours—10 p.m.—and they were flying over Tay Ninh Province, over War Zone C. The mission was to electronically detect nighttime enemy activity. They were flying at about one thousand feet over an area that was considered a likely enemy infiltration route between the Cambodian border and the Iron Triangle—the main route toward Saigon. This area was actually not too far from Les Trungs, Monsieur Voltaige's rubber plantation.

The newly-installed electronic device was designed to be a heat-seeking instrument of sorts. It detected body heat. If there was a column of enemy troops below them they should appear on the screen as a string of light dots, something like a small army of white ants. But the device would also pick up the body heat of other creatures down there, for example a water buffalo, a tiger, or an elephant. So far, Lieutenant Clark could only make out sporadic snowy dots here and there all over the screen, but no consistent pattern. At this point both Clark and Ratcliffe were convinced that there was no immediate enemy activity to be reported in their assigned area of responsibility. They systematically flew a back-and-forth pattern over the area for another forty minutes, and then they flew back to the airstrip on the western side of Tay Ninh City.

After refueling the aircraft they pulled it off to a quiet place beside the PSP runway to relax for a while before going back out for another reconnaissance patrol. They drank Kool Aid and coffee, chatted, and ate C-ration cookies. It had been a longer day than their usual long day of flying, and after a while they decided they all felt like catching a little nap before performing their next late-night air patrol.

Captain Ratcliffe, the Mustang Buddha, made a little mound of sandbags, laid his flack vest over the burlap, and then lay down on the PSP just in front of the rocket pod, on the left side of the helicopter. He stretched out to make himself comfortable. And then he stretched a bit more until he was actually resting his head on the warhead of one of the rockets. He folded his hands over his belly, pulled his cap down over his eyes, and seemed prepared to doze off and enjoy a little slumber under the sparkling stars. After a moment, however, Sergeant Mahone, the crew chief, laid his hand gently on Captain Ratcliffe's shoulder and said, "Captain Ratcliffe, sir, you know you have your head resting on a warhead—on a rocket—on the tip of the thing. And you remember, I'm sure, that they're kind of tricky. Sometimes they do strange things—like cook off. Right? You know what I mean? Don't you want to rest somewhere else? What do you think?"

"Oh, yes," Captain Ratcliffe immediately responded. "Oh my…what…what on earth am I thinking about? Heavens to Betsy! I must be zonked out of my mind. This is crazy—yes, crazy to say the least. There must be a better place around here someplace—anyplace."

He stood up and after a moment decided to lie inside on the cargo floor of the helicopter.

Captain Ratcliffe had been stationed in Korea for two years before being assigned to serve in Vietnam. While in Korea he had met and married a Korean woman. Lieutenant Clark had overheard Ratcliffe say on several occasions that he was married to a "gook."

After about an hour on the ground, they were back in the air again. They were in War Zone C, about twenty miles directly west of Tay Ninh City. They were flying very close to the Cambodian border. It was after midnight. After flying for about thirty minutes they detected an indication on their screen that there was some sort of activity taking place pretty much directly below them on an east-west line. The pattern on the radar screen did look something like a rather active train of fat white ants. Captain Ratcliffe flipped his radio switch and reported back to the U.S. advisers' command and control station at Tay Ninh City.

"Hey, I think we've got something here," he said.

He relayed to them that some positive signals had been detected and he was going down to check them out—get down on the deck. Captain Ratcliffe gave the adviser map coordinates and after a couple of minutes the adviser came on line and said there should be a road there, roughly at that point on an east-west heading.

"Okay," Ratcliffe said. "We're going down to have a closer look."

Captain Ratcliffe made a tight right turn and started down in a steep dive toward the eastern end of the white dot column that had been sighted. His altimeter registered just below 500 feet when he flipped on the landing light. The landing light was attached underneath the aircraft on the forward end of the belly of the machine. It was, in effect, a spotlight that could be freely turned and manipulated in almost any direction. As the aircraft zoomed down over the target area the helicopter crew could make out what appeared to be a slight break in the tall trees of the War Zone C rainforest. That was the unpaved road mentioned by the adviser. And then suddenly they could all make out a great jumble of frantic activity just under the canopy of the tall dense forest. Lieutenant Clark's first thoughts were that it appeared to be some sort of stampede. And that was exactly what it was. At first glance it appeared to be something like a wagon train that was suddenly driving madly ahead, seeking shelter from a storm.

Captain Ratcliffe pulled the aircraft up and to the left. They always tended to try to consciously keep the aircraft pointed toward the south to be double sure they did not collide with the mountain, Nui Ba Den, just northeast of them. Ratcliffe got back on the radio to command and control in Tay Ninh City and reported the sighting. After a moment the adviser came back on and said that the area was a free-fire zone and no one should be in that area.

With Captain Ratcliffe on the controls, the helicopter swooped back down for a closer look at things. Ratcliffe switched on the landing light and then made another pass over the contested area. This time he slowed the aircraft somewhat and the Americans tried to take a more careful look at what was going on below them on that remote jungle trail. Again, they observed the chaotic scene, the panicky wagoners driving their reluctant oxen, trying to force them to suddenly move faster than they had ever moved before. The oxen appeared to be pulling carts that were heavily loaded with timber. There appeared to be a single column of about eight or ten carts. Each cart appeared to be pulled by two oxen and accompanied by two drivers.

Again Captain Ratcliffe got on line and reported what the crew had sighted. After a few minutes Lieutenant Clark got the impression that the U.S. adviser was speaking with someone else there at his station and he had additional information regarding the puzzling midnight jungle convoy.

"I've been told," the adviser said, "that those guys are probably lumberjacks. They go into that area late at night and steal timber every now and then. There's some teak out there, and some mahogany too, I believe, and that's pretty valuable stuff, they tell me."

Ratcliffe seemed puzzled. He keyed the radio switch.

"Well, what do we do?" he asked. "Is there any action required on our part?"

After a moment the U.S. adviser came back on line.

"Well," he said. "They know they're not supposed to be out there. And it's a free-fire zone. Everybody knows that, you know. Everyone. So, you can shoot 'em up if you wish."

These words hit Lieutenant Clark like a slap in the face. Salty sweat ran into his eyes. He could hardly believe his ears, and yet these words somehow did not come as a total surprise. He had a deep feeling of dread that had been telling him for some time now that this might be the result of their reconnaissance and late-night report.

"You can shoot 'em up if you wish," the man had said—just like that. It was so casual. "Shoot them if you wish. Fire 'em up."

Every word, every syllable spelled death—violent death. Were those lumberjacks men, or were they ants—or just snowy blips on a radar screen?

"Everybody knows this is a free-fire zone," he had said. "Everyone." Well, how can we be so damned sure? Were these aircrews men or were they crop dusters from hell? Were people involved here with their domestic animals, or were they discussing boll weevils? What did the crop involve tonight—cotton, corn, tobacco, timber, or people—a body count? The words were *so casual.* The silence of the crew and the cold *whop, whop, whop* sound of the rotor blades in the cool black night air all cried out against it—against casual death, against the casual destruction of life, against murder.

No, it was not supposed to be like this. These are *people* we are talking about.—And the animals supported a livelihood for these men, who were fathers and brothers and uncles. These animals sometimes lived under the same roof with these men and their families. But they are stealing timber in a free-fire zone. And where is Charlie in this business? Is Charlie also in the timber business? Was Charlie really into virtually everything—the timber business, the drug business, and the body count business? Was this supposed to be search and destroy, or was it cold-blooded murder? What to do? The aircraft—and all those inside her—were approaching decision altitude. What to do?

Lieutenant Clark could feel Captain Ratcliffe's presence more than see him. Clark did not dare to look directly at Ratcliffe. He was afraid to look him in the eyes. What would be the reaction of the Mustang Buddha? Would he very casually roll the aircraft to the right, reduce power, arm the weapons systems, take of the safeties, and start the dive down toward the frantic convoy and casually condemn them to a violent death with the words: "Okay, guys, let's give it to 'em"?

Did this Mustang, this aircraft commander, feel the urge to be generous, humane, sane, and reasonable—or did he feel the need to do something, expend some ordinance, to create some action, to generate a body count? What was it they had learned from Teddy Roosevelt, the Roughrider? "I would not be a spectator," he said. "No. Always I would prefer to be the man in the arena—always. Don't just sit there!" T. R. said, "Get action! Fortune favors the bold!"

Americans are the pragmatic people of action, are they not?

Lieutenant Clark really did not know Buddha—Captain Ratcliffe, the 68th Buddha—that well. The matter could easily go either way. Clark did not like the idea of disobeying an order. No, especially not when Captain Ratcliffe was standing behind the order. This man had special authority. He had clout—special authority. People listened when he spoke. Everyone was aware of that special authority that he carried. No one defied the Buddha. No one would challenge Captain Rats. But what would he do? Lieutenant Clark simply did not know. Was it possible? Could he really shoot these creatures as they fled in a panic down a nighttime jungle-logging trail? The perspiration burned in the corners of Clark's eyes. Ratcliffe, the corn-fed American Deaths-head, the Death Valley Buddha—what was he thinking? What would he say? What would he do? What was his wish, his desire, his command? The 68th Buddha was presiding over life and death and he seemed to be in his element.

Without a word, Captain Ratcliffe made another pass over the panicky convoy of carts, bellowing oxen, and running, shouting men. They appeared to be more frantic than ever and apparently there was no real shelter available to them. As the great boxer, Joe Lewis had once said: "You can run, but you can't hide." They were revealed. They were exposed on a jungle firing line trail in a free-fire zone. They were in the electronic valley of death. They were prisoners of darkness and despair. And they were close to the very heart of War Zone C.

Finally, Captain Ratcliffe spoke.

"Well," he said slowly, thoughtfully. "These guys are crazy. They're stupid. But I think they are harmless. Evidently this timber means an awful lot to them. They're in a mighty dangerous business, I'd say. But, as I said, I think they're harmless. So, let's look the other way and pretend that we didn't see them. Let 'em go."

Buddha had spoken.

These words were so sweet to Lieutenant Clark. "Let 'em go." These words chimed sweetly through his head. He would never forget the moment. He could breathe again. He was thoroughly pleased with Captain Ratcliffe and his decision-making process. After all, Buddha meant "the enlightened one." And he said, "Let 'em go." There would be no firing on men and oxen tonight. No firing on fathers, sons, brothers, and uncles tonight. The potential nightmare vanished in the cool black air over Tay Ninh Province, over War Zone C. The 68th Buddha had spoken. And there—flying in the shadow of Nui Ba Den—he had said, "Let 'em go."

Go home, nocturnal lumberjacks. Go home, larcenous loggers. Sleep well tonight. *Bon chance.* Beware of free-fire zones. Go over to Les Trungs and work for Monsieur Voltaige. He must have something for you to do—something safer for you to do—surely. Attend his rubber trees. Clean his swimming pool. Work in his kitchen. Learn to be gardeners, beekeepers, anything. But stay away from Death Valley. *Bon chance.*

"Yes, that timber must mean an awful lot to them," said Lieutenant Clark. He could somehow sense that everyone in the aircraft was more relaxed now—breathing easy again. Buddha had voted for life and not death.

Captain Ratcliffe reported his decision back to the U.S. adviser in Tay Ninh City. And the adviser accepted the verdict in the same casual manner that he apparently would have received an estimated body count report or anything else. Lieutenant Clark felt as though he could actually see through the radio—down the line, over the airwaves. What was on the other end? "It's a free-fire zone, and everybody knows it," the voice had said. And now to the coffee. And now to that egg sandwich. And that paperback book. Where was he? Yes, there he was—Louis L'Amour—a man to ride with. But no body count tonight. No special log entries tonight. Not much happening tonight.

Above the facade of the Cao Dai temple the all-seeing eye peered down at the empty dusty nighttime streets of Tay Ninh City. A few miles to the west the dark mountain, Nui Ba Den, stared southward through the darkness toward the slow flowing Mekong River. The logging trail deep in the rainforest where oxen had recently tread was now still and quiet in the moonless night. And overhead the helicopter's heavy rotor blades went *whop, whop, whop* in the cool black sky over Tay Ninh Province.

Buddha, the Enlightened One, had overruled the child of darkness and blocked the way of the crop dusters from hell.

The 68th Buddha climbed and, turning the helicopter slowly and gracefully toward the east, he flew off back toward Bien Hoa Airbase, and toward the light.

Chapter 16

Fire at Hotel Bravo

Top Tiger Six, Major Compton, was at the head of the long line of helicopters that was approaching to land on a wide-open dusty field a few miles west of Tay Ninh City.

Lieutenant Clark, now flying with Mr. Linville and his regular crew again, landed just two aircraft behind the CO, Major Compton, and the operations officer, Major Marker. The operations officer came on line and told all pilots to come up forward to the CO's aircraft for a last minute briefing.

It was late in February 1967, and they were preparing to launch Operation Junction City, which was to be one of the largest air-mobile assaults ever, involving a 240 helicopter sweep over Tay Ninh Province—or War Zone C, the dense rainforest backed up against the Cambodian border. This operation involved over 22 battalions, some 30,000 U.S. troops, and an additional 5,000 ARVN troops. The operation would last for over 60 days.

When Lieutenant Clark stood at the front of the formation and looked back over the field, he was awestruck. "I don't believe I have ever seen so many helicopters at once," he said.

"No, this is quite a gaggle, to say the least," Linville said. It appeared as though Hueys were lined up as far as the eye could see in almost every direction.

The pilots, tactical maps in hand, all gathered around Major Compton's aircraft for the last minute briefing. Everyone seemed rather impressed with the size and scope of the operation. It looked and sounded like they would be quite busy for the next few days, lifting troops in to a number of landing zones and then bringing up reinforcements where needed, as well as additional ammunition, water, and supplies. They were told that a large number of VC and NVA (North Vietnamese Army) troops were expected to be in the area—*if* they had not skedaddled over into Cambodia. The goal of Operation Junction City was to destroy VC-NVA bases in War Zone C, and especially along the Cambodian border. As far as resistance goes, no one had any idea of what to expect. But, to a large degree, the Americans had already given away the element of surprise by using bulldozers to clear off the huge field west of Tay Ninh upon which the helicopter armada was now marshaled. This massive rendezvous point was called "Hotel Alfa." Also, a number of likely landing zones had been pre-burned. This was becoming something of a standard procedure in this area. The tall elephant grass most often caught fire during the "LZ prep"—tactical preparation fires from the artillery, the gunships, and the Air Force Tactical Aircraft fire. Now a large number of possible landing zones had been pre-burned to avoid the fire hazard. The helicopters would have to deal with some smoke, dust, and ashes, but hopefully not blazing fires.

Again, the pilots were warned to keep their eyes open and be prepared for anything. The enemy in this area was said to have .50 caliber machine guns, and these were known to be some of the best antiaircraft weapons in existence—and the enemy knew the Americans were coming. On the first day or two of the operation the Top Tigers would be working with ARVN troops and then they would be transporting mostly U.S. 1st Infantry Division troops and also troops from the U.S. 173rd Airborne Brigade. Required radio frequencies were issued and the pilots were told where to fly the casualties.

"Remember," said Major Marker, "remember to keep your heads on swivel sticks. Keep your eyes open. There's going to be an awful lot of traffic around us today. The sky is gonna be full of helicopters. You can count on it."

The pilots all trudged back to their aircraft just as the Vietnamese troops were marching out among the machines and starting to climb aboard. The first load looked like good, tough, experienced troops. They were Vietnamese Rangers, among the very best of the ARVNs.

Top Tiger Six came on line and asked if everyone was ready to "pull pitch." Everyone was ready. No one seemed to have a problem.

"Okay," Major Marker said, "Let's pull outta here and head for our first objective, LZ Hotel Bravo."

The two parallel lines of eight heavily loaded Hueys each pulled up off the dusty marshaling field—"Hotel Alfa"—made a gentle turn northward and pulled up to only about 300 feet in the bright tropical sky. No matter which way the pilots turned, the sun seemed always to be in their faces. They all had their sun visors pulled down and appeared a great deal like robots with light green heads and metallic dark green faces. They wore green and gray gloves to give them some protection from a fire in the aircraft. The pilots wore flak vest with heavy metal breast protectors zipped inside. (The crews usually referred to the breast protectors as "chicken plates.") The pilots were pretty much completely covered, and the chairs they sat in also provided some armored protection. Hardly any skin was showing. Mr. Linville often even pulled his .45 caliber pistol and holster over between his legs to cover what he called his "vital parts."

Landing Zone Hotel Bravo was not far from a place called Bu Dop. This village was very close to the Cambodian border and was said to be a known way-station along the infiltration route leading into War Zone C from the bottom of the Ho Chi Minh Trail. The pilots could make out thick pillars of dark smoke here and there on the horizon marking the pre-burned landing zones that dotted the area.

They had not been in the air long, maybe ten minutes, when Top Tiger Six came on line and said: "Okay, LZ Hotel Bravo is dead ahead about two minutes. Let's be ready. Keep your eyes open."

Lieutenant Clark could see the smoke ahead that marked the landing zone. Out of nowhere he suddenly thought of Genevieve, the most glamorous person he had ever known. In his mind's eye he could see her on the Champs Élysées. There behind her, just over her shoulder, was the Arc de Triomphe. Also, he could see her standing in the red dust near the landing strip at Les Trungs. She was always elegant, beautiful, graceful—regardless of the setting. What would she be doing right now, at this moment? Could it be possible that he would never see her again? Again, with vivid instant recall he could see both Genevieve and Monique standing there near the red dirt airstrip, waving goodbye.

"*Au revoir*," they said. "*Au revoir*." Les Trungs Plantation was not more than thirty miles behind him, to the northeast of where they were now flying combat operations.

Hotel Bravo was just ahead. What would Hotel Bravo have in store for them, the Top Tigers? The LZ was in sight. There it was—they were now over it. It was burned black and smoking. "Hotel Bravo" was an oblong opening in the rainforest and appeared to be just large enough for their flight of sixteen helicopters. The Mustangs had just finished "prepping" the tree lines around the LZ. At that time—8:40 a.m.—there were flights of approximately sixteen helicopters now landing at ten other different remote positions all over War Zone C—an area of approximately 2,500 square miles

Mr. Linville gently landed the helicopter on the black smoldering turf. Ashes from the burned elephant grass were flying everywhere, and everyone was making a conscious effort to protect their eyes and to keep the stuff out of their noses and mouths.

Linville came on line to the crew, Dotson and Collins.

"Okay, guys, come on, come on. Let's get 'em off. Get 'em off. Come on, come on. Get 'em moving. Let's go, let's go, let's go!"

The Vietnamese Rangers were quickly off the helicopters and slowly, cautiously moving off toward the northern tree line.

Top Tiger Six came on line. "Okay, guys, is everybody ready to clear outta here?"

Everyone was ready.

"Okay, let's pull pitch. Let's get going. Let's move it," said Major Compton.

Mr. Linville had flown the aircraft into the landing zone, and now Lieutenant Clark would fly it out. Linville was the "AC," the aircraft commander. Because he had more flying experience than Clark, Linville would usually sit in the left seat, the chief pilot's seat, and he would be responsible for all decisions regarding aircraft utilization. Lieutenant Clark, because he outranked Linville, would be the responsible officer with regard to any administrative matters. Of course, Clark was expected to move up to aircraft commander status within a matter of weeks—depending on how much flying they were scheduled to perform.

Clark took the controls. He put his feet firmly on the pedals and started to gently pull in additional power with the collective pitch lever. The helicopters lifted up about four feet off the ground, moved slowly forward, gained some forward air speed, went through translational lift, and were soon moving up above the treetops and into the sky. Just beyond the forward end of the landing zone there was a narrow space that appeared to have been untouched by the pre-burning and the LZ "prepping." Just as Lieutenant Clark glanced down and noticed this small clear area, it seemed to suddenly come alive. It opened up. It flipped open. What appeared to be two large hidden cellar doors covered with grass suddenly opened wide, revealing two .50 caliber machine guns, each with two-man crews. The two machine gun pits were separated by about twenty feet of open space covered with tall, yellow elephant grass.

Lieutenant Clark and his crew appeared to be directly above these two pits when the Viet Cong suddenly opened their doors as if to say, "Surprise! Surprise!" The .50 caliber machine guns immediately opened fire. But they did not fire on Clark and his crew. They fired instead on the next two helicopters just behind Clark and Linville.

"Pop smoke!" Linville shouted over the intercom. "Pop smoke! Mark those fifties!"

Both Sergeant Dotson and Specialist Collins (who had recently been promoted from PFC) instantly threw canisters of bright red smoke down toward the .50 caliber gun pits.

"Marking with red smoke," said Sergeant Dotson.

"Dropping red smoke," Collins said.

And then the pits—the pits of death—were behind them.

Those large bullets from .50 caliber machine guns did terrible things to helicopters—and to men. In a very fast sequence of events things started to happen. Someone came on the line and said, "We're taking fire. Fifty caliber. We got a man hit. *Got a man hit*!" And then after a few seconds there was a tremendous, earth-jarring explosion. One of the helicopters had crashed and exploded almost directly beneath Lieutenant Clark's aircraft.

"Oh, God!" Mr. Linville said, "What was that?" They all dreaded to say it, but they all knew what it was. Next they heard someone say:

"We got a man hit! We got a man…." someone said on line.

And then after a slight pause, they heard another terrible explosion.

Major Compton was on the line.

"Two fifty caliber positions there at the head of the LZ—in that little open area there. They're marked with red smoke. Mustangs, get on 'em! Mustangs, go after those fifty cal pits *now*! They're marked with red smoke. Shut 'em down! And shut 'em down now! Hit 'em and hit 'em *now*! Let's go! Come on, let's go! Hit those fifties! Shut 'em down!"

Without hesitation the Mustangs came in from rear and flanking angles and fired everything they had at the VC gun pits. Then it was quiet for a moment. The Mustang door gunners managed to get red smoke grenades closer to the gun pits. It was not clear to anyone whether or not the gun pits had been neutralized. The camouflaged pit doors appeared to be closed for the moment. Still, no one really felt sure that the gun pits were neutralized. Suddenly a U.S. Air Force tactical air support pilot came on line and was speaking with Major Marker.

"Hello, Top Tigers, this is Air Force Phantom 3446. I'm on station over Hotel Bravo and I've got cluster bombs and napalm. I'm hearing something about some fifty calibers. Shall I take a shot at 'em?" the Air Force pilot coolly asked from the cockpit of his F-4 Phantom at an altitude of eight thousand feet.

"Yes, by all means," said Major Marker. "I would recommend a good shot of napalm as soon as possible. They're at the top of the LZ, the west end, and they're marked with red smoke."

"Roger that," the Air Force pilot said. "We've got the red smoke in sight."

As the helicopters cleared out of the area the Air Force Phantom jet zoomed down and dropped a napalm bomb that seemed to clearly cover the two enemy gun pits. It appeared to be a perfect hit. No one could tell if the machine gunners had been burned or if they had escaped through a connecting tunnel. But nevertheless, for now the gun position seemed to be shut down, out of business. To the Top Tigers napalm appeared to be an awfully effective weapon. The Top Tigers landed three times more that day at Landing Zone Hotel Bravo and experienced no more hostile fire there.

Almost as soon as the first helicopter crashed, Captain Ratcliffe had fired his remaining seven rockets at the gun pits and then landed his chopper near the tree line. He unstrapped himself, climbed out of the machine, and instructed his copilot, Mr. Gibson, to circle around for a few minutes and then come back in and extract him.

"Give me about ten minutes," Ratcliffe said.

Captain Ratcliffe, his red wet face darkened by ashes from the recently burned landing zone, single-handedly managed to locate and extract two bodies from the wreckage. Later it was said that he thought these two men—Mr. Ingram and Sergeant Wade—were still alive. No one ever knew for sure. But they were declared dead shortly after they were brought into the field hospital at the U.S. 25th Infantry Division Headquarters near Cu Chi. The Top Tigers lost two complete crews on the first day of Operation Junction City.

Two other aircraft took hits that day, but no crewmembers were hit and the helicopters were not seriously damaged. But gone from the midst of the Top Tigers were Chief Warrant Officer Ingram; CWO Gray; Sergeant Wade, crew chief; Specialist Henley, door gunner; CWO Grimes; CWO Carter; Sergeant Sweet, crew chief; and Specialist Cottle, door gunner. Slowly the notion came to the men of the 68th Assault Helicopter Company that the voices of those men who had laughed and joked in their midst—who had been so close to them, had eaten C-rations with them, and drank beer with them—their voices were now stilled forever. Some men struggled to express the idea that it hardly seemed possible that those men could be so suddenly gone forever. But Lieutenant Clark was surprised to learn that some officers in the company merely said, in effect, "*C'est la guerre,*" "That's war. That's how it works."

Captain Ratcliffe was later awarded the Silver Star Medal for his single-handed attempt to go into the wreckage, under fire, and save lives at Landing Zone Hotel Bravo.

Operation Junction City ended after 72 days of frantic combat operations throughout War Zone C, mostly near the Cambodian border. American troops succeeded in capturing large quantities of enemy stores, equipment, and weapons, but there were no large decisive battles. The largest encounter was at Landing Zone George, which was also near Bu Dop and the Cambodian border. In the area around LZ George the Americans claimed to have killed an estimated 200 Viet Cong. At the conclusion of the operation the Americans reported 2,728 VC/NVA KIA—killed in action. Two hundred and eighty two Americans were reported killed in Operation Junction City.

Now Lieutenant Clark knew just what Hotel Bravo had in store for the Top Tigers. He though of the pits of death and he wondered how many more Hotel Bravos there would be awaiting them in the future.

Late that night Clark laid back exhausted on his bunk–bed. He closed his eyes, and he could clearly hear the voices and see the forms, the smoke, and the colors.

"Red smoke! Red smoke!"

"Pop smoke!

"Popping smoke!"

"Marking with red smoke!"

There in the middle of everything was the 68th Buddha—his eyes filled with an adrenaline glow and his red face shining and covered with sweat and ashes.

"Taking fire!

"We got a man hit!"

"*Au revoir*," she said through white teeth and perfect lips.

"*Au revoir*."

Chapter 17

An Island of Civilization

The pilots were drinking beer and throwing darts in the small game room-bar at the end of their barracks when Top Tiger Six walked in. He looked cool and fit, as usual.

"Say, Clark," he said, "do you know a Frenchman—a guy named Voltaige?"

Clark looked at Linville and grinned broadly as if to say, "Uh oh. Here it comes. Here we go."

"Oh, yes, Monsieur Voltaige. Yes, sir, I've met him," said Lieutenant Clark. He went on to explain how he had met the Frenchman through his hometown friend, Mr. Clayton—Alan Clayton. Clark did not mention the impromptu visit to Les Trungs that he and Linville had managed some weeks ago.

"Well, this guy evidently talks about you as though you were his long lost prodigal son," Major Compton said. "I've been told by someone higher up that he wants us to pay him a visit, and soon, at his plantation.

And I've been told, in effect, that this is something that we *will* do—and we will do it soon."

Clark appeared to be surprised, as he was to some degree. So, the little Frenchman really did have pull.

Top Tiger Six had definite plans to fly out to meet Monsieur Voltaige, the influential plantation owner. Major Compton instructed Lieutenant Clark and Mr. Linville that they should be prepared to fly their aircraft to Les Trungs plantation for a social visit on the very next day—which would be a Sunday. Major Scully, the executive officer, and First Sergeant Rodriguez would accompany the CO. Also, Captain Ratcliffe was invited to come along with his co-pilot, Mr. Gibson, and their crewmembers. A total of thirteen men from the company would be visiting Monsieur Voltaige and his family at their plantation in Tay Ninh province. The estimated arrival time would be 1400 hours—2 p.m.

The weather was hot, bright, and sunny as usual the next day, when they lifted off from the airbase at Ben Hoa. They climbed up to an altitude of about two thousand feet and took up a northwest heading for Les Trungs. The flight took them only about forty minutes and then they had the red clay airstrip at Les Trungs in sight. After a closer look, Lieutenant Clark could make out "Voltaire Six's" little helicopter—**VT 6007**—on the helipad near the villa. Mr. Linville had tuned in the Armed Forces Radio Network on the radio and as Clark turned the helicopter to line up with the airstrip he was listening to the popular Pete Seeger song, "Turn, Turn, Turn."

The broad thick rotor blades started to pop—*whop, whop, whop*—as the flight of three helicopters descended toward the dusty, unpaved airstrip.

As the pilots shut down their engines and climbed out of their cockpits, the crewmembers picked up their tie-down lines and prepared to catch the slowly turning rotor blades and tie them down to the aircraft tail booms.

Top Tiger Six and Major Scully stood awaiting Lieutenant Clark and Mr. Linville. It was clear that the Company Commander expected

Lieutenant Clark to do the honors and introduce everyone. When Captain Ratcliffe and Mr. Gibson had joined them they all started to walk up the red dirt strip toward the villa. They could see Monsieur Voltaige with his daughters, Genevieve and Monique, accompanied by both Alan Clayton, the agricultural adviser from Old Catawba, and Paul Picair, the private pilot, standing together in a group at the head of the airstrip awaiting them. Monsieur Voltaige gave them a friendly wave.

"Hello, my friends, *mes amis*," he said.

Lieutenant Clark stepped forward to greet the Frenchman with a hearty handshake. Monsieur Voltaige gave the lieutenant a warm embrace and welcomed him effusively. Clark gave Genevieve a nod and a knowing look, and then proceeded to introduce everyone.

Monsieur Voltaige displayed graceful deference toward the Commanding Officer, Major Compton, and First Sergeant Rodriguez. The Frenchman tended to treat Major Scully like an old friend even though they had met only briefly, weeks before in Saigon. And then Lieutenant Clark turned to introduce Captain Ratcliffe. And something strange happened at that time. Lieutenant Clark was not sure that anyone else noticed it but him. After Clark introduced the Frenchman to Ratcliffe there was a slight pause before the two men greeted one another and shook hands. Or was there really a pause, a hesitation? As he introduced them, an instant coolness materialized that Clark could almost physically feel—almost touch. It actually made the flesh crawl on the back of his neck. Did he imagine all this? For a moment Clark felt strangely awkward.

"Have you two met before?" he quietly asked.

"Oh, no, no, no," gushed Monsieur Voltaige, smiling broadly. "I assure you," he said, "that I have not had the privilege before today of meeting Captain Ratcliffe. I am sure of that—quite certain. And I wish to assure you, by all means, to say that the honor is all mine—entirely. I am indeed pleased to met you, Captain Ratcliffe, and I am happy to welcome you to my home here at Les Trungs Plantation."

"Sure. Sure. By all means," Ratcliffe said. He was cordial but cool. He did not smile.

When Monsieur Voltaige introduced his daughters to Captain Ratcliffe, they too seemed to communicate an odd sort of deference toward the 68th Buddha. The two young women seemed friendly but ill at ease with Ratcliffe. Throughout the visit they seemed to respect him but not relish his company. It was if they sensed that he represented something in which they were not at all interested.

As the crews trudged up from the airstrip to join the main party, Monsieur Voltaige introduced his daughters to everyone and then lastly, he introduced his pilot, Monsieur Picair. The trim swarthy pilot was again dressed in a dark blue jumpsuit and he seemed proper, but somewhat reserved and detached. Something about Picair struck Clark as being sinister, but again, the lieutenant suspected that he was perhaps being overly imaginative.

Monsieur Voltaige invited everyone to join them for poolside refreshments. A small army of servants holding small baskets of white, steaming hot face towels stood near the pool prepared to serve the crews. Using tongs, they distributed the neatly rolled steaming hot little towels, one to each of the guests. Each soldier readily applied the hot cloths to their faces, hands, and necks and appeared to find the effects thoroughly refreshing. The Americans were presented with a first class buffet and every sort of drink imaginable. Because they were flying, the CO managed to spread the word that they were all to be allowed not more than one drink containing alcohol, but then after that, it had to be juice or carbonated drinks.

The Frenchman sent for the beekeepers, Lee Ann and Becky, and their "friends," and soon the aviators were surrounded by a very attractive collection of young Vietnamese women. Several of the women were noticeably taller, and they were said to be Chinese. They were all dressed in colorful bikinis.

"Uh oh," Sergeant Dotson said, "here come 'dem honey bees. Here 'day are! Here 'day are! Whoa, now—whoa, whoa, whoa! Look out now! It's honeybee time! Yeah, yeah, sho'nuff, it be's honeybees time!"

After they had picked over the buffet for awhile, Monsieur Voltaige suggested that everyone take a swim and arranged for everyone—including Top Tiger Six—to be suitably attired. Within minutes, the aircrews were all in the cool sparkling waters. Lieutenant Clark noticed that the Frenchman seemed to be concentrating his hospitality on Top Tiger Six, their commander. All the crewmembers—and especially Dotson and Collins—seemed to be thoroughly enjoying themselves.

Alan Clayton had the shape of a giant potato. He did not swim and remained attired in his loose safari outfit. It was fresh and neatly starched. Monsieur Voltaige also remained in his freshly starched and pressed safari outfit. Clayton seemed eager to make small talk with Lieutenant Clark about their hometown. But after a few minutes it became clear that there really was not much news emanating from Old Catawba.

"Monsieur Voltaige really knows a lot of people," Clayton said to Clark in a lowered tone.

"He knows people at embassy level. He knows people at MACV—at the top levels of MACV. He carries a lot of weight around Saigon. And he likes you, Winston. I know he could do you a lot of good. So stay on your toes, boy, and watch how you play your cards."

"Yes," Clark responded, "that sounds like good advice, I would say. It's evident that he's got pull."

"And, Winston, I must say, I believe that he is the most charming man I have ever met. Absolutely."

Clark finally found the opportunity to visit with Genevieve, and he noticed that Linville had quickly paired off with Monique. Collins was entertaining Lee Ann, and Dotson was chatting with Becky. All the crewmembers gathered around Lee Ann to admire her hair. She was standing near the pool and she had combed it out in full over her shoulders. They called to Lieutenant Clark and the other officers to come over and have a look. Lee

Ann had beautiful shiny black hair that was so long it almost reached the ground behind her. It was the longest hair any of them had ever seen. She appeared to be rather proud of her tresses.

Captain Ratcliffe was in the pool, but he seemed quite subdued and distant behind his sunglasses. He stood in the shallow end of the pool chatting with his copilot, Mr. Gibson. A muscular, taciturn man, Gibson appeared to be entirely devoted to flying gunships and heeding Captain Ratcliffe's every wish and word. One almost never saw Captain Ratcliffe outside the presence of Mr. Gibson (everyone called him "Hoot"). Gibson also remained restrained and distant behind his army-issued aviator's sunglasses. There was something about Ratcliffe that day that seemed to convey the message that he had chosen not to be especially impressed with Les Trungs and its host.

They spent about an hour in the pool before Monsieur Voltaige suggested that they allow him to show them around his place. He suggested that everyone remain in swimsuits, as that would be much cooler than the usual aviator's attire. Monsieur Voltaige had Vietnamese servants provide the Americans with towels and sandals.

The servants at Les Trungs were women, mostly, with a few old men. The young men were almost all either in the military or away somewhere avoiding the military. Monsieur Voltaige referred to some of those working for him as his Cambodians—men who supposedly did not have to worry about being involved in the Vietnamese war on one side or the other.

The Frenchman showed them everything—his rubber trees, his rubber processing buildings, his powerhouse, his generators, a sawmill, the pineapple and peanut crops. He showed them his vegetable gardens, his mangoes, his coconuts, his banana trees, his cinnamon trees, his sugar cane, his beautiful flower gardens, his beehives, his honey, his domestic animals, and his stables. He even had horses. Also, Les Trungs was equipped with a skeet shooting range and tennis courts. Later, Clark thought, actually, this remarkable little man seemed to have just about everything.

"Honey," said Monsieur Voltaige, "is not only a food. No. Ah, *oui, messieurs*, honey is not only quite tasty on our breakfast rolls, it is also a medicine. Honey has been known by generations of Vietnamese to be an antiseptic. *Oui*, as it acidifies, it kills bacteria. This is what we call 'folk medicine,' *n'est-ce pas*? Folk medicine, yes, but it works.

"At one time," Monsieur Voltaige continued, as he stood near the fragile little evergreen trees, "cinnamon was the most profitable spice traded by the Dutch East India Company. Cinnamon was once actually more valuable than gold. In Egypt it was once used in both witchcraft and embalming. It is used in much more than our pastries, you know. It is also used in perfumes and drugs. It remains today a most profitable product."

"Oh, yes, that's quite true," Mr. Clayton agreed. "This is indeed a profitable crop. The Vietnamese Army, the high command, has actually had a few quiet little turf wars over who should control the cinnamon business. There was one general who was once referred to as 'the Cinnamon General.' War or no war, everybody is out to make a buck, right? The soil and the climate here are perfect for cinnamon—and making a buck, actually."

"*Ah, oui*," said Monsieur Voltaige. "I believe it was your Ayn Rand who once said, 'Wealth is a monument to man's ability to think.' Indeed, everyone here is thinking. And everyone is out to make a buck. That seems to be the natural order of things."

Lastly, Monsieur Voltaige showed them around his chateau. The place seemed to be something of a cross between a fortress and a palace. It had a grand dining room, a large, well-appointed kitchen with a great deal of polished and shiny brass everywhere, a really comfortable and inviting library, complete with an extraordinary collection of books, and some impressive works of art—mostly impressionist works. The woodwork throughout the chateau was marvelous. To Clark it appeared to be mostly mahogany—and, for a moment, it made him recall the nocturnal lumberjacks and their dangerous excursions into War Zone C.

Monsieur Voltaige displayed an impressive gun rack just off the library in which he had about fifteen fine, expensive-looking hunting rifles locked. Lieutenant Clark noticed that the last rifle on the far end of the rack was an AK-47, a Russian-designed Kalashnikov, the automatic rifle most commonly used by Communist troops—and often times preferred by U.S. advisers over the American-made M-16. An adviser once told Clark that the AK-47 provided more firepower and did not seem to jam as easily as the M-16.

"Don't forget," Clark had heard one GI quip to another, "your weapon was produced by the lowest bidder."

Near the library there was a small family chapel. Also, there was a small theater for viewing films or live entertainment, and there was even what appeared to be a small ballroom. Lastly, they quickly viewed the small but well-stocked wine cellar.

It was all there. And it was all rather dazzling. Clark would never have imagined that someone could get so much under one roof—especially here on the outskirts of War Zone C. It was like a mixture of the Palace of Versailles, with its hall of mirrors, and the yellow brick road and the Palace of Oz. For a moment the old 1933 James Hilton novel, *Lost Horizon*, and Shangri-La came to Clark's mind. But there were no great mountains and valleys here—and no lamasery. Only red clay and rubber trees mostly, and Nui Ba Den standing tall and foreboding like a lone sentinel at a distance to the south.

As Monsieur Voltaige showed them around, several times he emphasized self-sufficiency, and truly, he appeared to be just that—self-sufficient to an amazing degree. Major Compton asked Monsieur Voltaige about the name, "Les Trungs," and the Frenchman explained about the Trung sisters and how the name pertained to an important part of ancient Vietnamese history.

"Perhaps," said Monsieur Voltaige, "perhaps I should have called the place, '*Les Delices.*' *Oui, Les Delices* instead of Les Trungs."

"Why?" asked Lieutenant Clark. "What does that mean—*Les Delices*?"

"*Ah, oui, mon ami*," the Frenchman said. "You are the one who called me 'Voltaire,' *n'est-ce pas*? Voltaire, the prince of letters—the prince of eighteenth century wit and wisdom."

"Oh, yes, that's right," said Clark. "Voltaire Six, that's you. Voltaire Six, the Prince of Les Trungs, Marquis of Tay Ninh Province—and confidant of 007."

"*Oui, Monsieur d'Artagnan, oui*," said Monsieur Voltaige. "You have the gift—the gift—a vision of human nature. You know men. You possess a special insight. You are quite discerning. And yes, you know people. It is a gift. That I believe, my *cavalier*. You go at once to the core, the heart of the matter. And you said to me: 'You are Voltaire.' *Oui*, Voltaire, and we all know him: Voltaire, the great man of letters, and great friend of humanity and humanism—the central figure of the Enlightenment. Voltaire was, you know, one of the few great men of letters who wrote in every literary form. He wrote poetry, plays, novels, history, science, biography, and essays—he did it all—and he did it exceedingly well. Anatole France—what did he say? *Oui*, he said, 'In Voltaire's fingers the pen runs and laughs.' That is what he said. With Voltaire 'the pen runs and laughs.' With all of his incomparable wit, energy, and literary skill, Voltaire fought for those timeless truths and principles: that men should be reasonable, rational, sane, and tolerant. They should not be beasts to one another. He made his stand beneath the flag of the human spirit and ceaselessly opposed tyranny, oppression, and blind, heartless bureaucracy. A prince of all those who would be magnanimous and civilized. And as you know, I am sure, he lived a long life as a courageous crusader against tyranny, bigotry, and cruelty. 'Tend your own garden,' he said. And those were the wisest words uttered in a thousand years. Take care of our own—our own business, your own affairs, before we go around trying to take care of the business of others."

"Because of his controversial—some say revolutionary—stances on a wide range of issues," the Frenchman continued. "He was sometimes forced to seek asylum away from his homeland. Indeed, he was often banished and imprisoned. But he smiled back at the world and remained 'the happy philosopher.' At one time he sought asylum in Geneva, and there he purchased a lovely villa called *Les Delices,* 'The Delights.' There he spent some of the most enjoyable years of his life. And that is what this place is to me: Delights, delights, delights through and through. Some say that our estate is to be found on the backside of the moon. But, be that as it may, I love it. I love it without reservations. It is vital and whole—complete. It refreshes my soul. This location is very special, I assure you. Sometimes I look at this red soil and I see the blood of my family—my people. We have become a part of this place—a part of this land."

"And Les Trungs," he continued, "is filled with delights. Voltaire taught men to think and to think clearly. He valued common sense. He was not against religion, as so many seem to want to believe. He was simply against fanaticism—against blind hatred and senseless cruelty."

For just a brief moment, Clark thought that Monsieur Voltaige was looking at Captain Ratcliffe when the Frenchman voiced these words regarding hatred and cruelty. And was there a trace of cynicism and cruelty in Ratcliffe's eyes as he gazed back at the diminutive Frenchman? If Les Trungs was for sale, Captain Ratcliffe was not buying. And if Ratcliffe was for sale, it appeared as though the little prince had not yet arrived at the proper bid.

"Finally, in the end," Monsieur Voltaige continued, "Voltaire, believed this to be the best of all possible worlds, and that we should work together to cultivate it. *Oui*, our world, God's green earth, our fair planet—it is a garden, he said, and we should cultivate it. 'Let us cultivate our garden,' he said repeatedly. This man, Voltaire, he was all about that simple question: 'How should men live their lives?' Do men wish only to be amused and deceived? Do men want only bread and circuses—television, beer, and chips? Voltaire was not seeking perfection. He sought balance—only balance. Like Socrates and Diogenes before him, he carried a light. He carried a lantern, a torch. He was seeking that delicate balance that would support a decent society. What he said men needed in their daily lives was merely good common sense—what he called *le bon sens*. And some skittish souls would blame him for the Revolution—for the French Revolution! But it was he who informed us that common sense is not common. No, unfortunately, that is the case. Monsieur Voltaire was our crowned prince of letters and his letters represent the great monument of French literature. And he was refreshed and revitalized at *Les Delices*, the Delights. He stood there under the flag of the human spirit and *le bon sens* at *Les Delices*. And at this time and place, it is with great pride that I call my estate, this little island of civilization, Les Trungs, for the Trung sisters—for, yes, they too were fighting tyranny, injustice, and cruelty."

After a long moment, Major Compton spoke.

"How do you manage to maintain your plantation here with this war being fought all around you?" the major asked.

Monsieur Voltaige paused and then answered.

"It is sometimes a delicate situation—truly. But we have been here a long time, *monsieur*—a very long time indeed. Many of the people here—in this area—they are like family to us. And we hope to remain here. We are vigil. We make no assumptions. We take nothing for granted. We move forward a day at a time. We keep our eyes open, and we do our best."

"Yes, that's all one can do," Alan Clayton agreed, "our best. We can only do our best with what we have. 'You must live your life, that is your first duty to yourself—and to God.' That's what Thoreau said, I believe."

"*Oui, oui*, and, I must say," the little Frenchman added, "We work hard. We must cultivate our own garden. Yes, what was it that our friend Voltaire said about work, my friends? He said, 'Work, yes, it keeps us from the three great evils of life: boredom, vice, and need.' So very true, *n'est-ce pas*? Yes, we work hard."

"Mind you," Monsieur Voltaige continued, "I recently visited the office of an American friend in Saigon, and he had this remarkable little sign hanging on the wall of his office. To me, it was really quite striking—this little sign. I looked upon this sign and I will swear to you that I started to feel a bit like the prophet Daniel when he read the mysterious handwriting—in flames—on the wall for King Belshazzar. This little sign read simply, '*Keep trying.*' The letters on this little sign were all crooked and several of them appeared to be actually about to fall off the signboard. '*Keep trying,*' it said. And I thought to myself, 'That is brilliant! Absolutely brilliant! These words are so banal, so commonplace, and yet so supremely penetrating, so perceptive, so profoundly astute—breathtakingly wise.' For indeed this little twisting serpentine sign said it all, my friends. That is our duty to God, the universe, our forefathers, ourselves, and our posterity—to *keep trying.* Simply that. As Daniel would say to Belshazzar, 'Do not lose your way and become too pompous, too puffed up, too sophisticated. Ignore this simple wisdom at your peril. Ignore these words and you will be found wanting.'"

"Absolutely," Clayton said. "Well said—well selected words, indeed."

"*Oui,*" said Monsieur Voltaige. And then with a broad grin, he said, "Come now. Now we shall grill steaks. We do not wish to become 'puffed up,' however, we *are* preparing a fine meal for you. Come now! *Bon appetit, messieurs, bon appetit!*"

The smell of grilled steaks filled the air around the swimming pool. Everyone seemed to be having a wonderful time. The Americans seemed to have quite unexpectedly landed in paradise. Monsieur Voltaige, his daughters, and his servants seemed to be everywhere at once, soliciting and fulfilling every conceivable wish that the Americans might have had. The Top Tigers commented to one another, in effect, that they had never known such generous and overwhelming hospitality. Some of the Americans seemed to convey the impression that they could hardly believe that such a place, such an oasis of gracious and generous hospitality could possibly exists in war-torn Vietnam. Others, however, seemed to be at the other end of the spectrum. They seemed to convey the impression that this country struck them as being so strange and exotic ("weird" was a word they often used) that anything might be expected. It seemed apparent that some of the crewmembers had enjoyed more than the prescribed amount of alcoholic beverages—but not the aviators. They were all enjoying themselves, but were clearly sober. Captain Ratcliffe and his sidekick, Hoot Gibson, appeared relaxed and at ease but still lacked enthusiasm for the ambiance that suffused the party at Les Trungs.

A live combo played soft jazz just off the swimming pool area. They called themselves "The Voltaige Players," and seemed enormously talented. They demonstrated their ability to play almost any type of music—popular, folk, country, jazz, and even classical. It was said that—with Monsieur Voltaige's sponsorship—three out of the five players had studied music in Paris. Several of the crewmen started to dance with the girls at the poolside.

They enjoyed a delicious onion soup, and a salad. Next they had a choice of meats. They could enjoy a fine beef steak, pork, or ham. Lobster and shrimp were also offered. New potatoes dripping with hot melted butter, fried potatoes, and stir-fried vegetables were served. Wine and liqueurs were offered. After the meal they were served fruit and nuts. The bananas grown in Vietnam were not large and yellow like those the Americans had known at home. The bananas in Vietnam were small and green, but they had a nice sweet taste. When they were a bit over-ripe they had a honey-like flavor. Yes, it was all there—soup to nuts. And that was the way it always was at Les Trungs—nothing but the best of everything. Lieutenant Clark and most of the other Americans felt as if they were living—just for awhile—in a dream world.

"Hey, man," said Specialist Collins, "it just don't get no better than this, man. No way, man. No way."

Winston Clark finally managed to be alone with Genevieve for a few moments. They stood against the back wall of the stable, and just as soon as they were certain that they were out of sight of everyone, they embraced and kissed passionately. They were both totally intoxicated with love. The power of their feelings left nothing else to be desired. They desired only one another. Les Trungs did not exist. The Champs Élysées did not exist, nor did Old Catawba. The war did not exist. Only their love existed. And nothing else mattered. Their feelings were clearly mutual—he wanted her and she wanted him—and they needed no words to express their frantic feelings. They kissed time and again—hungrily. Their love was stimulating and exciting, almost to the point of being debilitating.

"You must come here and be with us—be with me," she said breathlessly.

"I don't know how, but yes," he said. "Somehow I must be with you. It must be possible. We must make it happen." Clark thought that he felt weak, but at the same time, he felt as though he could fly without wings.

"Can you...could you leave the military?" she asked.

"No," he answered. "Not at this time. But yes, yes, I know we must be together—and we will be. Nothing is more important. Somehow, I know we can work something out. Is that your wish—for us to be together?"

"*Oui, oui*!" said Genevieve with great intensity. "*Oui.* Yes, yes, of course! How could you ask? *Oui, oui,* we must be together—and soon, I believe. It must be possible. You can feel my heart beating—beating out of my breast, I am sure."

"Genevieve, Genevieve!" It was her sister, Monique, calling.

"*Oui*, what is it?" asked Genevieve.

"Come," Monique said. "You...you and Monsieur Clark should join us by the pool. Now. Come!"

"*Oui, oui*," said Genevieve. "We are coming. We will join you in a moment."

"Come," she said to Clark. "Now we must go."

Winston Clark felt as though he were glowing from head to toe—yes, glowing in the dark. Surely others would now stare at him in wonder, but so be it. He was possessed and he possessed something so supremely special and extraordinary that no one else could ever take it from him. It was his alone. It was part of him now. No one else could ever touch that part of him. It made him whole—complete. His encounter with Genevieve behind the stables lasted perhaps less than five minutes, but he felt as though he had just captured a golden moment that would last forever. It was timeless. Later he thought it was like a spiritual experience. He felt so totally uplifted. He no longer feared pain, poverty, sickness, or death. He had known something so sweet, so precious, so riveting, so exhilarating, so fulfilling that probably nothing else in life could ever come close to this celestial zenith, this unexpected brief encounter in the middle of nowhere. This delicate triumph of peace on the edge of War Zone C. This girl with the honey-colored hair and the Arc de Triomphe behind her, with just a kiss, she had given him a priceless gift. He held it close and it warmed his heart. He had no needs, no wishes. He was wrapped in a magical cocoon. Now he knew that his soul was clearly indestructible. He felt that no matter what happened now, his life was somehow complete and whole in a very important way.

They joined the others at poolside.

Everyone enjoyed the food, drinks, and company and no one seemed to want to think about or speak of flying back to Bien Hoa. But finally, at 10 p.m., Major Compton said they had to go. There were missions to be flown in the morning—at dawn, as usual. The Top Tigers needed to fly back to the base and they would need to be briefed on their Monday morning missions still that night or early the next morning at "O' dark-thirty," as Major Scully said.

So, Top Tiger Six started talking about going home at 10 p.m., but it took them another thirty minutes before the men were actually lacing up their boots and starting to say goodbye. The men clearly did not want to leave. Several of them said, in effect, that for once it would not hurt for them to stay out all-night and then go to work at dawn. They were young and strong and could handle it.

First Sergeant Rodriguez quickly ended the discussion by directing the soldiers—in his own special way—to get moving.

"Listen to your commander," he said, and the way he said the word "*listen*" was almost like a whiplash. One could almost see some of the soldiers cringe.

"Did you hear the commander? Did you hear the CO? Well, okay," he said, "So let's go. Let's move. When your commander says let's go, then you jump, okay? Yes, by God, you jump! You understand? Okay. So, get moving. Let's go. Let's clear outta here. Right now. Let's go."

End of discussion. The men instantly reacted to his words and were soon ambling back down toward the airstrip and the helicopters.

Monsieur Voltaige, accompanied by Alan Clayton, spoke with Lieutenant Clark just before he left the poolside area.

"Your commander," said Monsieur Voltaige, "*ah, oui*, he is a good man. He is—I am sure—a first class commander. I am completely convinced that he has a brilliant future before him. Mark my words: he will have a distinguished career. One day he will be a general officer. *Oui*, he is a truly first-class officer."

Lieutenant Clark smiled broadly in complete agreement.

"Yes," he said. "I can assure you that we all feel privileged to have him as our commander. I don't believe we could ever have a better commander. Yes, indeed, he has our full confidence, and we are proud of him. Top Tiger Six, you bet. He's our man."

"Yes, truly he is a fine officer and a gentleman," echoed Alan Clayton. "I have thoroughly enjoyed getting to know him."

"Your First Sergeant," Monsieur Voltaige said, "Sergeant Rodriguez, he too is a very solid soldier—a good man, a strong man, a remarkable man. He strikes me as being the very picture, the very essence of a first-class noncommissioned officer. You may rely on him totally in every circumstance, I am sure of it."

"Yes. Absolutely," Lieutenant Clark agreed.

Then something like a troubling cloud of doubt passed over the little Frenchman's facial expression.

"And your Mustang commander," Monsieur Voltaige said, "The gunship commander, Captain Ratcliffe…ah, yes, he is a very powerful personality—a strong man. In his case…well, yes, in his case I believe that he too has a brilliant career before him. This man, Monsieur Ratcliffe—he is a warrior, a fighter. But still there is a bit of the philosopher king in this man. Do you know what I mean? This man must grapple with life. He must take it in his hands. Yes, he must take the horns in his hands. He must seize life by the throat. He wants always to go to the heart of the matter. He cannot be still, this man, no, no. He is possessed by a special spirit and power that is seeking a mountain to climb, a dragon to slay, a battle to fight, a hard victory to grasp. He is a crusader. *Oui*, he is a strong man, and I could see him rallying the troops to his banner—under fire—and leading the charge. Yes, I am sure that he will have a heroic future."

"Ah, yes, most assuredly," Clayton agreed. "Captain Ratcliffe is an impressive officer. Yes, he certainly is—a strong personality. That's true—quite true. I believe that the ranks of the Top Tigers are filled with remarkable men, actually."

Monsieur Voltaige and Alan Clayton said goodbye to Lieutenant Clark and wished him well. They insisted that he plan to visit Les Trungs Plantation again in the near future.

"Monsieur d'Artagnan," Monsieur Voltaige said in a whimsical sort of way. "*Mon* d'Artagnan, our musketeer, *mon cavalier*, take care of yourself and your comrades."

"*Oui*," Lieutenant Clark said, "and Voltaire Six, our Marquis of the Cambodian marches, our Count of Tay Ninh, and gracious Prince of *Les Delices,* with full and glad hearts, we thank you for your gracious hospitality."

Monsieur Voltaige warmly took Lieutenant Clark's hand in his, looked the young man in the eyes and said: "Ah, *oui*, *mon* d'Artagnan, *mon cavalier*, you will look after yourself, will you not? We treasure your company. *Bon chance*, my friend, *bon chance.* And please remember, as I said to your fine commander and your friends: the men of your company, the Top Tigers, are all welcome to visit us here at Les Trungs at anytime. Anytime, I say. We will welcome the Top Tigers here at Les Trungs. You and your men should think of Les Trungs as a port in the storm. They are special, your people, the Tigers—truly special. The next time you visit we must drink together arm-in-arm. We must drink the friendship drink—the drink of brotherhood. And we must cultivate the art of good living, *n'est-ce pas*? *Oui, oui. Bon chance, mon ami, bon chance.*"

Before Clark departed Les Trungs he managed to speak with Genevieve for a few minutes more, and then her father joined them to say farewell.

"We must speak," Genevieve said. "We must communicate. I must know where you are, and how you are, and what you are doing—and when we can be together again." Breathlessly, she said: "Monsieur Clayton! Yes, that is it! That shall be our plan. We can communicate through Monsieur Alan Clayton. If you can send messages to him, he will get them to me. So, please, that is what you must do—communicate with me through Monsieur Clayton."

"Yes, okay," Clark said. "I'll do it. Yes, that should work. I feel certain that I can communicate with Mr. Clayton through the APO—the Army Post Office. We will communicate through Alan Clayton, and somehow we must see one another again soon. We *will* see each other again soon. I know it. I am sure of it."

She smiled excitedly and squeezed his hands together between her hands.

"Words cannot tell you," Genevieve said, "how terribly much I will miss you. But that must be. We must endure it. So be it. It will make us stronger—more determined. Somehow we will work something out. We will be together. I feel it. I feel it deeply. I will not return to Paris until I know that you will accompany me or follow me there. For now I will keep you here," she said as she touched her left breast. "You are here in my heart."

"And you are here in my heart," said Clark. They kissed and he walked away.

After everyone was strapped in and the machines were all run up to operating speed, the helicopters lifted off the dusty airstrip at Les Trungs. As they gained altitude, they turned slowly to the east, back toward their home base at Bien Hoa.

Lieutenant Clark was at the controls of the helicopter and he leveled the machine at three thousand feet and took up the easterly heading. Ahead of them he could easily make out the running lights of Top Tiger

Six's aircraft and also the lights of the gunship being flown by the 68th Buddha, Captain Ratcliffe. Mr. Linville was tuning the radios. Clark still felt as though he were glowing. He loved the feeling but he almost prayed aloud that it would not show. Mr. Linville seemed to be quite close to Monique. But something was not exactly right with them. Linville later confided to Clark that he found Monique "strange."

Mr. Linville tuned in AFN radio. And as they flew away from War Zone C with their exhaust pipes glowing fiery red in the inky black night, they could hear Jim Morrison singing the hit song, "Light My Fire."

Chapter 18

The Storm

Captain Jarvis Giles almost always came in hot. He clearly tended to land with too much power and airspeed. He zoomed in, nose up, with the rear end (the "heels") of his skids dragging and his tail rotor dangerously close to the ground. Captain Giles was what is commonly known in pilot circles as a "cowboy."

It did not seem to matter whether Captain Giles was attempting to lead a group of men or machines, either way he did not really lead them so much as attempt to herd them—to force them this way and that. He did not fly the helicopter so much as he attempted simply to jerk it around. That was his concept of aircraft control.

Captain Giles seemed void of feelings for the aircraft. The dynamic Zen that was brought to the art of flying by people like Mr. Lang was completely missing in the cowboy's flying technique. And if this whole concept of flying—dynamic Zen, the spiritual dimension of the art of flying—had been discussed with Captain Giles, his response certainly would have been something like "Hogwash!" or "Horsefeathers!"

Giles—who had only recently been promoted to captain—did not listen. And finally, the result would be that, to some degree, he would lay a curse on the entire company. Captain Giles would put an ugly curse on the Top Tigers. The time would come when no one in the unit would ever want to mention his name again.

Recently there had been some personnel changes in the company. There was an attempt to balance the experience factor between the aviation units that had been in South Vietnam for some time and the newly arriving units in the III Corps area. Major Wilson, who had been serving as the gunship platoon commander, was now being transferred to another company, where he would be serving as executive officer. Two other pilots out of the gunship platoon were transferred out. The Mustangs, the gunship platoon, would be taken over by the recently promoted Major Ratcliffe. This was a change that seemed to please everyone.

Another recent change was that a CWO Wesley Hobbes had transferred into the company and was assigned to the gunship platoon. He had served for awhile with the 11th Armored Cavalry Regiment in the Lai Khe area, and was said to have some gunship experience. Hobbes was small and fair skinned, with freckles—and he was aggressive. He was from West Virginia, and seemed like a harmless country boy. When Lieutenant Clark looked at Hobbes Clark could almost telepathically see a hay-straw dangling from Hobbes' mouth that was not really there, but should have been. Eventually, Clark came to think of Hobbes as a sort of deconstructed Billy the Kid, a dismal throwback to the cold-blooded old-range war days on the American frontier.

Some of the enlisted men heard Mr. Hobbes talking in a rather animated way one day about how the Americans would soon be "paving over" the Ho Bo Woods, one of Charlie's favorite hiding places just northwest of Cu Chi. Shortly after that they started to refer to him behind his back as "Hobo" Hobbes. Later, Clark overheard one GI, a crew chief, refer to Hobbes as a "stone cold killer."

Lieutenant Clark's roommate, Mr. Meeks, was now to be counted in the ranks of the Mustangs. He had been requesting a transfer to the gunship platoon for some time, and finally it happened: he was a Mustang. At first, he seemed really happy about the change. And then he had been paired off with Captain Giles, as the cowboy's regular copilot. After that Meeks seemed to become increasingly discontent and depressed.

Mr. Hobbes had flown with Captain Giles for a while and then Hobbes had been assigned as Mr. Mills' co-pilot. Mr. Mills was another little man. He was surly and aggressive, but not vicious.

At first Major Ratcliffe seemed concerned about Captain Giles' jerky flying techniques. But the cowboy was a big, strong man who seemed to be enthusiastic and aggressive about everything he did, so the Mustang Buddha remained cautiously patient and seemed to believe that time and experience would temper Giles and improve his techniques. Mustang pilots were expected to be instinctively aggressive. Nevertheless, Major Ratcliffe expected all of his men to grow professionally and personally as individuals and team players. He told them that in just those words.

However, Captain Giles did not seem to change—or grow. Lieutenant Clark could hear the whole story from his roommate, Mr. Meeks, who appeared increasingly disturbed.

Shortly after Mr. Meeks had been assigned to fly with the Mustangs they had been given a special assignment to support a group of rangers who were stationed at a small firebase in the middle of nowhere. Their base camp was deep in the heart of War Zone D, which was across Highway 13 and about thirty miles east of War Zone C. These men-–the rangers—were doing a great deal of long-range patrolling. And everyone knew that this was some of the most demanding, challenging, and dangerous duty any soldier could be assigned to perform in Vietnam. Often these men would serve as trail watchers—they would simply lay low in some remote piece of jungle somewhere trying to detect enemy activity.

They usually worked in groups of four and avoided contact with the enemy. They were meant to be observers and reporters—and that was all. Don't twist the cat's tail, they were told. If somehow they did make contact with the enemy, it could be disastrous because they were almost always outnumbered and away from their support base. They could attempt to find a clearing in the jungle, "pop smoke," and call for the helicopters, but the choppers had to get there quickly—or it was all over for the "Lurps"—or LRRPs—Long Range Reconnaissance Patrols.

The rangers needed fast support from the choppers, and that is why headquarters, for a while, started to assign a number of helicopters and crews to simply stay with the Lurp teams for as long as they were required. So, it seems that the Top Tigers and the Mustangs were closely supporting the "Oscar Team" (as these rangers were called for some reason—O for Observer and O for Oscar, perhaps) for quite some time.

The "slick," troop carrying helicopters supporting the Oscar Team with insertions and extractions would be rotated every four or five days. But the same two Mustang light-fire teams (there were two gunships in a light-fire team) supported the "Oscars" for several months. And those two light-fire teams included Major Ratcliffe and his copilot, Mr. Gibson, Mr. Mills with Mr. Hobbes as his copilot, and Captain Giles and Mr. Meeks. It soon became apparent that some of the gunship pilots had a great deal of admiration for the Lurps, the rangers, the jungle experts—the men who "walked with the phantoms of the night," as one Vietnamese interpreter put it.

Somehow Mr. Hobbes came into possession of a homemade carbine rifle. Some Viet Cong gunsmith had manufactured it and it was a marvelous piece of work. It was almost exactly like the U.S. Army-issued M-2 carbine, but it was apparent that it had been handmade from scratch. One of the rangers had picked it up on a recent raid. It was quite a souvenir, and evidently Mr. Hobbes had made a good trade with the adviser with something else he, Hobbes, had picked up somewhere. Mr. Hobbes started to cut notches into the stock of this crudely carved and forged rifle to indicate the number of enemy troops that he knew that he had personally killed. Lieutenant Clark never knew anyone else who did that sort of thing. William Bonney, Mr. Billy, solemn soldier of the Lincoln County War, meet Mr. Hobbes, the deadly dude from War Zone D.

One Sunday evening in the game room, after the evening meal, it had just started to rain outside when Lieutenant Clark spontaneously invited Mr. Linville to join him in a game of darts. Mr. Linville did not often mention Monique to Clark. But that evening, somehow the topics of Les Trungs, Voltaire Six, and his daughters did arise.

"I think you are getting mighty sweet on that Genevieve," Linville said. "Whooy wow! What do you think? She's a cool chick, huh?"

"Whooy wow! What can I say?" Clark answered. "Yes, mate. *Oui, oui, monsieur*. I think it is safe to say that I am a bit sweet on her. And how, may I ask, do you, my good man, feel about Monique?"

"Monique?" Linville started as though he had never heard of a beautiful young woman named Monique.

"Well, yeah, she's okay to make out with, I suppose," he said. "But I sense that she's bored. Yeah, she's sort of strange. She's something else."

"What do you mean?" Clark asked.

"Well," Linville, the Coolest of the Cool, said, "Sometimes, actually, I'm not sure. But I believe that Monique is from the deep end of the pool. I think she's bored with Americans in general, and with army guys in particular. You know me. I'm just a blue-collar flying stiff—a chopper driver. She's a jet setter. Yeah, man, a jet setter supreme. She knows the bright lights of the world—you know what I mean? The great watering holes. 'So, *monsieur*, shall we dine at Maxim's tonight—or what do you think—maybe the super-colossal-whopper-gargantuan-jumbo-mammoth-burger-house and shack? What shall it be, *monsieur*? And what wine would you prefer with your French fries, *Mademoiselle*? What is your wish, *monsieur*?' You know what I mean?" he said, in his exaggerated French accent.

"Needless to say," he continued, "that's not exactly my element—not exactly my beer. Monique goes first class and only first class. Just think—that broad's got her own pilot, for cry'n out loud. Her own chopper! And me, I go any way I can—sometimes by bus. Monique takes it only when it pleases her—only when it's just right. But me—I take it any way I can get it. You know what I mean?"

"Yes, yes, I see what you mean," Clark said in a subdued tone. Clark said no more on the topic. But he did not really agree with Linville. Winston Clark did not believe that anyone was too good or too far up the totem pole for his friend, Michael Linville, the Coolest of the Cool. As far as Clark was concerned Linville could run for President of the United States.

"I've got to give it to 'em though," Linville said. "I must say, there is something especially glamorous and amorous about those French women. Hmmm."

After a long pause Linville mentioned that Monique had said some things that would lead him to believe that her father was grooming her to take over his business one day.

"Yeah, she said a few things that would lead me to believe that her old Daddy is grooming her to take over the family business one day when he moves on—on to the great beyond."

"Now, listen," he continued. "Can you imagine how the guy will have it that marries up with her one day? Oh, wow! An empire at your feet! Overnight you would be running a great rubber empire. But, oh, man, here in Vietnam! Can you imagine spending the rest of your life here in Nam?"

"Well, but perhaps with a few visits to Paris sandwiched in now and again, yes, perhaps," Clark said.

"Well..." said Linville with a broad grin and a bright sparkle in his blue eyes.

On several occasions some of the Oscar Team members had spent the night in the Top Tigers barracks at Bien Hoa. They were treated as guests of honor. The aviators and the rangers seemed to enjoy one another's company. One evening they had stayed up rather late, drinking and playing cards and darts, when one of them went kind of crazy. For a while they had been tossing the darts, when this one Oscar—apparently rather intoxicated—started to throw a hatchet at the dartboard. He had trouble getting the hatchet to stick in the dartboard, so suddenly the man attacked the dartboard in a rage. He hacked and hacked and the dartboard was soon in pieces and the man continued to hack at the barracks' wall where the dartboard had been hanging. He hacked and hacked in a frantic rage. And no one seemed to react.

By the time one of his friends pulled him away from the wall and got him under control, the man had almost chopped a hole completely through the wall.

The next morning the Oscars sheepishly apologized and said they would replace the dartboard. And they were good to their word. The dartboard was soon replaced (and put over the hole in the wall). The Oscars gave the Top Tigers a case of beer in a further effort to patch up things.

Mr. Hobbes had been working with the Oscars for not much more than a month or so when ugly rumors started to be associated with his name. There was hushed talk of Hobbes being involved in some gruesome atrocities. A strong feeling of revulsion gripped Lieutenant Clark when he heard the talk, and he immediately decided that the less he saw of the benign-looking Mr. Hobbes, the better it would be.

Lieutenant Clark heard these stories from Mr. Meeks, and they seemed to have an awful ring of truth about them. These stories seemed even more revolting and loathsome somehow because of Mr. Hobbes' youth and innocent appearance. One story was that Hobbes was closely associated with rangers who had thrown enemy prisoners out of Hobbes' aircraft at high altitudes in order to frighten the other prisoners into being more cooperative and talkative. Clark heard this story more than once. Another story was that one day Hobbes was seen playing soccer with a couple of the Oscars, and they were using the severed head of a Viet Cong prisoner for a ball. They seemed to be enjoying themselves immensely while playing kick-ball with a bloody head of another human being. The word was that Major Ratcliffe had heard of this grotesque kick-ball game and was considering a request to have Hobbes transferred out of his platoon—perhaps out of the unit.

Somehow Clark got the impression that somewhere along the line in Hobbes' life's experience he had picked up the idea that cruelty and cold-blooded murder were parts of the rites of passage toward becoming an adult—a real man. It seemed like something he must do—practice cruelty. To Hobbes this seemed to be the very definition of power—the practice of cruelty, to have someone at your mercy. It was as though he felt he owed it to the race of people from whom he sprang. Hobbes did not seem to be at all influenced by what someone called the 1950s Saturday matinee Bijou "Code of the Buckaroo." This was the concept that one should wear a clean white hat and stand up for fairness and justice at all costs. Never kick a man when he is down, look out for the women, kids, and old folks, and never shoot anyone in the back—never ever. (But, with an evil flicker in his eyes, Hobbes would say, "Never say never.") And, through all the travail and consternation, in the cavernous Bijou it was clearly predestined that the good guy and justice would always prevail in the end.

One evening after washing up and eating, Mr. Meeks seemed unusually disturbed. He was drinking beer and his face was flushed—but he was absolutely sober—terribly sober. He had just finished reading a letter from his wife when suddenly he stood in the middle of the cubicle, faced Lieutenant Clark with red slightly teary eyes, and started to speak.

"Listen, roomy," he said, "if I die in this stupid war, be sure you tell everyone that I died for nothing. That's right—absolutely nothing—really."

After a pause he swallowed hard and then continued. "This is such a stupid war! What are we doing here? Can you answer me that? You're a smart guy, right? You've been to college. So, come on—tell me! Answer me that! What are we doing here in this stupid war? Yes, I mean it. If I die in this stupid war, tell 'em I died for nothing."

Lieutenant Clark tried to calm Meeks.

"Hey, hey," Clark said, "Come on, come on. Calm down. Take it easy for a minute. What is it? What's going on with you? What's the matter? Is somebody dumping on you?"

"I'll tell you what's the matter," Meeks said. "I've been assigned to fly with Giles—Captain Giles. That's what's the matter. You know how he operates, right? The guy is a complete idiot. Every take off and landing is like a life-changing experience. You seriously wonder if you will get to experience any more life as your hair is changing to totally white and your pucker factor is gnawing and tearing at the seat covers. The guy's crazy. It's that simple. He's crazy. He's an idiot. And he doesn't know how to fly a helicopter. He probably can't even ride a bicycle. So, all things considered, you could say that he has some serious short-comings. Now, come on. Don't you think you would agree?"

"Okay. Well, yes. What did he do?" Clark asked. "What's he been up to?"

"I'll tell you what he did," Meeks continued in an almost breathless manner.

"He almost landed us in a mine field today. That's right. He came in hot at the little airstrip up by Phu Duc. He came in so hot that he completely overshot the airstrip and ended up hovering over the minefield planted around the perimeter. So, there we were at a weak and shaky two or three-foot hover, looking stupid and trying to figure out what to do next. Well, Giles finally managed to ease it over to the end of the runway and put it down. Then we get into a shouting contest about how to fly a helicopter. He tells me that the aircraft is a dog—it's under-powered, he says. And it's a hog—it soaks up too much fuel. About that time Major Rats walks up and we both try to explain to him—explain to Giles—that if an aircraft is under-powered, then you simply modify your fuel and cargo or ammo load. You cut back on your weight. And Giles' reaction is like this is some sort of strange new concept he's never heard of. The last time he took off from the airfield at Tay Ninh, it was like he was aiming for that Cao Dai temple, the steeple over the temple. He only missed it by a couple of feet. I thought maybe he was hypnotized by that big eye—that big evil Cao Dai eye."

Meeks seemed to slow down for a moment.

"I wanted," he said, "to tell Major Rats that's it for me. I don't want to fly with him any more—period. No way. That's it. But Major Rats tells me to calm down and get on with the mission. 'Just do your job,' he said. 'I'll take care of cockpit assignments,' he says. So, that's it. What can you do?"

Mr. Meeks looked down and shook his head in a woeful, melancholy manner. He appeared to have tears welling up in his eyes.

"I don't know," Lieutenant Clark said after a long pause. "Just stay on your toes. Watch him, and if he gets too crazy, then you've got to demand a different assignment—a different job, or whatever. Watch him—try to work with him. But if he doesn't improve, you have got to demand some attention—and get some action. If everyone refuses to fly with Giles, then perhaps Major Rats will see there's a problem there. I think the guy's a threat to everyone who has to fly with him. I think he's an accident waiting to happen. We've just got to catch Major Rats at the right time and convince him that we've got a problem here with this guy."

Mr. Meeks sat on his bunk gazing at photographs of his wife. He said nothing.

The summer-time monsoon months had arrived in South Vietnam. The Americans stationed at Bien Hoa Airbase now usually awoke in the morning to pouring rain, and then again, at just about time for the evening meal, the rains poured down again. And sometimes it also rained at noontime. These monsoon rains were usually quite intense but brief. Within thirty or forty minutes, the skies would usually clear, it would be hot and steamy again, and then pilots could go on about their business of flying combat assaults or ash and trash missions.

One evening after Lieutenant Clark had returned from his daily ash and trash mission, he had his evening meal, read his paperback book, and—after deciding to turn in a little early—he lay down on his bunk and tucked in the mosquito netting. He had found the paperback book in a book box at the end of the hallway. He was enjoying the book. It was about the search for the source of the Nile. That is what life is to most of us, Clark thought. It's a quest. We are all searching for the source—the source of life, love, sustenance, vitality, mystery, awe, and adventure. Yes, life's a quest—a quest for that which it takes to make life complete.

What is it that makes life complete? Clark asked himself. And is it the same for everyone? Freud said that it was love and work, I believe. But what did Freud know? Then again, perhaps he was onto something there. Love and work.

Clark looked up in the dim lighting and could see the netting billowing in the breeze. It seemed unusually quiet that night. Then it started to rain—gently at first. Then he could see bright flashes of lightning and hear explosive crashes of thunder. Soon the rain was beating down on the barracks roof with great intensity and being blown between the louvered and screened walls into Clark's face. It was like a fine spray in his face as he lay there on his bunk. After several long ripples of powerful detonations of thunder, it soon became apparent to him that an unusually violent storm was breaking over the area—and Clark was instinctively thankful that he was not out on such a night trying to fly—trying to get safely back to the airbase. The thunder roared and raged over the air base and barracks. The storm seemed filled with interminable wrath and violence. It was like a dark and deadly barrage from above, a colossal cannonade from the infinite seething, surging sky.

Then Lieutenant Clark looked across his cubicle at the empty bunk where Mr. Meeks would normally be sleeping.

Oh, no, Clark thought to himself. Those guys are out supporting the Oscars. I know they are. And when you are supporting the Oscars, you could be out over the jungle at any time of the night or day. This is bad. This is not good. No. This is not good. No, not at all.

Clark had never heard such violent explosions of thunder. The fierce explosions seemed to be right there over his head. Clark had a strong feeling of foreboding, a deep-seated sense of dread. This storm was extraordinary—that was for sure. And it seemed to be growing even worse. This apprehension of the unknown was powerful. It was burdensome. And it was utterly dejecting, Clark thought. Somehow he felt sure that some of the Top Tigers were out there trying to fly through that awful storm.

Clark heard the violent crack of the storm and gazed at the empty bunk across from him. He felt a strange sense of feebleness and helplessness when he considered the terrible storm, the sense of dread, and thought of what might be happening out in the night sky over War Zone D.

As Clark lay there on his bunk trying to sleep, he could feel the misty rain blowing in through the louvered walls and through the mosquito netting on his face. Even though it seemed as if it never would, eventually the storm moved through the area and Clark dosed off into an uneasy slumber.

By the next evening everyone knew what had happened out in War Zone D during the night, during the storm. Lieutenant Clark was drinking a can of beer with Captain Nowotney, his platoon leader, and Nowotney provided some of the details. Captain Nowotney usually spent very little time at the bar drinking.

One slick and a light-fire team had been out just at sundown working with the Oscars. Captain Nowotney was flying the slick with his copilot, Lieutenant Albert Yamashi. The light fire team included Major Rats and Mr. Gibson in one ship and Captain Giles and Mr. Meeks at the controls of the other. Nowotney and Yamashi did an insertion, putting some rangers into a hole in the jungle. Then, within less than an hour, they got a call. Someone said that the Oscars were in trouble and were requesting an immediate extraction. It took about twenty to thirty minutes to locate the Lurps, but finally, they were able to get a McGuire rig—a Jungle

Penetrator—down through the thick jungle canopy and pull the rangers up. One of them had a serious arm wound. Captain Nowotney immediately turned his aircraft southward and started to fly back toward the Oscar Team base camp. They heard some bullets popping nearby—near misses. Someone reported taking fire and the Mustangs made several passes around the extraction area, firing their weapons and trying to neutralize the source of hostile fire. Because of the seriously wounded soldier, Captain Nowotney decided that he had better fly on to the clinic at the U.S. 1st Infantry Division Headquarters at Lai Khe.

While all this was going on, the aviators did not notice the violent storm that was rapidly building and then suddenly crashing down upon them. The storm seemed to have developed right over them—precisely there where they were working in the middle of War Zone D. This storm had not been forecasted by the weather experts. It was really like a malevolent monster storm that was suddenly there from out of nowhere. It seemed to have a mind and a purpose of its own. It suddenly raised its malignant head and it seemed prepared and eager to swat down anything in its way. Mostly the monsoon storms were rain, tons of rain, oceans of rain. But this storm was explosive, filled with vicious winds and venomous streaks of lightning. The up and down drafts were incredibly powerful and impossible to resist.

Captain Nowotney was a little ahead of the storm. He was riding on the forward edge of the monster, but still he said there were times when he could hardly tell if his aircraft was upright or inverted.

"I had vertigo," he said. "For a few minutes there I didn't know if I was up or down."

Captain Nowotney confided to Lieutenant Clark that he was almost ready to give up. He had just about decided that they were lost, done for, going in—probably inverted. But then he actually became inspired by the calm professionalism of his copilot, Lieutenant Yamashi. The young lieutenant, fresh out of flight school, seemed to vividly remember everything he had just recently learned about flying IFR—instruments flight rules.

Yamashi calmly tuned in the main navigational radio beacon to Saigon at Tan Son Nhut Airport, and calmly announced:

"Hey, look! We've got a good signal. Now all we've got to do is level off at about a thousand feet and follow this signal down to Saigon."

Lieutenant Yamashi took the aircraft controls, climbed up to one thousand feet, leveled off, and slowly and calmly turned southward in the direction of Saigon—and safety. At once, Captain Nowotney was greatly relieved. Everything was going to be all right. They were not going to die in that stormy night over the jungle. Nowotney was amazed—and thrilled. How cool Yamashi was! He was a perfect copilot.

The crew chief later told Lieutenant Yamashi that he was awfully happy to see him take the controls that night. Captain Nowotney confided to Lieutenant Clark that—even though he had completed ten years in the army—he would probably leave the service after returning to the United States, when his "tour of duty" was finished. He said the future looked to him like nothing but back-to-back Vietnam tours.

"And, believe me, I can do very well without that," he said.

"Just prior to election time," Captain Nowotney continued, "the top brass always says they can see the light at the end of the tunnel. That light they are talking about is a mirage, an illusion. It was a French general who first referred to that elusive light at the end of the tunnel twenty years ago. But the elections are real. And this open-ended war is real."

The Mustang light fire team was a little behind Captain Nowotney and they were somehow caught up in the full fury of the storm. They fought to control their aircraft. It was like being awash in a great black ocean of violent winds. While the pilots struggled, the helicopters would quickly ascend and descend—of their own volition it seemed. Working with the power settings and control levers hardly seemed to matter. The little boxy aircraft flew this way and that, like a toy in a wind tunnel. The pilots were soon lost. The violent movements of the aircraft were such that they could hardly read a compass or tune a radio navigational instrument.

As the pilots struggled to control their aircraft, they tried desperately to determine which direction to fly to reach the Oscar base camp, or Lai Khe, or Phu Loi, or Cu Chi, or Tay Ninh—or anyplace where they could safely land. They desperately needed to get away from that vast sea of jungle and rainforest known as War Zone D. They needed to be on the ground. They needed shelter and they needed it straightaway.

There was hardly any communication going on between the two gunships. The understanding seemed to be that each crew should seek their own refuge wherever it could be found. Look for lights, signals, or whatever, they said. Simply find that safe haven, that port, and slip into it as quickly and smoothly as possible. But the two helicopters continued to be battered by the storm, and that much-desired haven seemed nonexistent. Suddenly, fuel range became another imminently threatening factor. And Captain Giles said that he was flying a fuel hog.

Moments later, Captain Giles radioed to Major Ratcliffe that his fuel warning light was on. This meant that under normal circumstances they would have about twenty minutes more to fly. A violent and frantic ten minutes went by as though it were only two. And now Captain Giles was on the edge of panic—and by the time he went in, into the trees, into the jungle canopy, he had panicked.

Major Ratcliffe suddenly saw some faint lights ahead and managed to land safely at the 1st Infantry Division base camp at Lai Khe. He came in low and hot. They knocked down several radio antennas on their way in before skidding to a halt on the landing strip. Communications wires were hanging from their skids. They all felt lucky to be alive.

Captain Nowotney and Lieutenant Yamashi flew safely into Tan San Nhut near Saigon. An ambulance quickly took away the wounded Oscar. They later heard that his arm was amputated. But they had survived a terrible tempest, an evil wind. It was a dark and desperate night that none of them would ever forget.

But Captain Giles did not make it. Captain Giles panicked. This was the curse. Top Tigers never lost their composure. That was the ultimate sin—to panic—to lose your composure. These pilots had been taught to be professionals—and to conduct themselves as such—all the way, right down to the end.

"What is a professional?" Mr. Lang had asked. "A professional is someone who has everything under control. Or if he does not, he is systematically working to regain that control. And he never gives up. He continues to try everything he can possibly think of right down to the bitter end. Even if you go in, you go in flipping switches, turning knobs, pulling levers. You never give up. It's not in the cards."

Captain Giles did that which no one wished to speak of—and no one wished to recall—ever. He lost control. And he lost his composure—the ultimate sin among pilots. He frantically begged for help. And there was no help forthcoming. Help was beyond reach. He was on his own. He panicked and it even sounded as though he wept on the line.

"Somebody please! Someone please, please help us!" he cried. "We're running out of fuel! We're out of fuel! Oh, God help us! There's no place to put down—no place to land! What can we do? We're going in! What can we do? We're going in! Oh, God help us! We're going in!"

And that was the last they heard from him. He went into the dark thick jungle canopy of War Zone D. He took Mr. Meeks with him—and a crew chief named Price and a door gunner named Gilbert. Apparently they made no mark on that vast canopy when they went in. The rainforest swallowed them. It appeared undisturbed.

Captain Giles died as he had lived. He died trying to force things to happen.

Even though the Top Tigers and the Oscars searched extensively, the bodies were not found until over a year later—and then by accident. The people that found the remains—a Lurp team—said the body parts had been thrown around as though some wild beast had its way with them. The helicopter had crashed but not burned.

"Every man should accomplish some great enterprise," the Vietnamese Emperor Le Loi said, "so he can leave the sweet scent of his name there for later generations to admire."

Captain Giles did not benefit from Le Loi's wisdom. Captain Giles lost control—and no one wanted to remember his name. He did not "leave the sweet scent of his name there." What he left behind was a curse. Top Tigers did not talk about the storm, nor the people it claimed that black night over War Zone D.

Captain Giles said that he was flying a fuel hog. Could not, or should not someone have done something about that? He ran out of fuel. The others did not. Captain Giles had been told to adjust his fuel load. Had he done that—modified his fuel load and capacity? No one knew. The jungle swallowed those who knew about the fuel load that dark night. But he ran out of fuel. And the others did not. Some men would think about this for a long time. And this was a curse. No one wanted to remember what happened that night during the storm. And this was a curse. Captain Giles, in his panic, had demonstrated to them how not to die. This was something no one wished to know. And this was a curse.

Top Tigers never lost their composure. That was not meant to be. "It's not in the cards."

That night Lieutenant Clark heard the rain falling on the barracks roof as he sat on his bunk and gazed at the empty bunk across from him in the dim light of the small cubicle. And he felt the curse very close by.

"Be sure you tell 'em I died for nothing," he had said.

Chapter 19

The Burning Bush

Smoke rings, he thought—almost perfect smoke rings. They were flying the pathfinders' helicopter, the "smoke ship." Lieutenant Clark and his crew were blowing smoke from a helicopter. And now they were creating artificial clouds, smoke rings, around the top of a mountain.

Captain Phillips, the assistant operations officer, a tough, little, swarthy, no-nonsense type man, normally flew the smoke ship. But he was on leave, taking some R&R in Bangkok. And while Captain Phillips was out of country Lieutenant Clark and Mr. Linville had an opportunity to fly the smoke ship. They welcomed the change of pace. Clark later gained the impression, however, that actually there were not many pilots who wished to fly the smoke ship and be addressed on line as "Smokey." Clark did not realize this until later when he was in the process of training a new captain on how to work with the smoke ship. After one mission the captain, appeared a bit grim and bewildered, and quietly but firmly said,

"A man could get killed doing this." Somehow that officer managed to get a different assignment. He was never to be addressed as "Smokey."

"That's how it goes," said Mr. Linville. "That's it...as the worm turns."

The smoke ship was a UH-1C Huey "slick" modified with a smoke-generating apparatus attached just behind the exhaust pipe. This aircraft was normally used to transport the pathfinders, who were responsible for investigation and preparation of the landing zones. But it had recently been modified so as to have a smoke option, the ability to create smoke screens—artificial barriers intended to provide a few moments' protection for the troops as they jumped off the helicopters during insertions. In a no-wind situation the smoke screen would usually last at least five to ten minutes before it drifted away. In order to lay out that barrier the smoke ship pilots would usually fly down one side of the landing zone, flipping the smoke switch at just the right moment, and then the other side of the elongated opening in the jungle. They would usually be flying at an airspeed of 60 or 70 knots and at an altitude of only about six feet off the ground (the "deck").

Flying helicopters in Vietnam was generally considered "hazardous duty," but Clark soon determined that flying the smoke ship was generally considered *perilously* hazardous duty. While flying the smoke ship one had opportunities to "get right in Charlie's face," and fly at high speeds just a few feet above the turf. If things went wrong one just might become part *of* the sod. If one suddenly had a problem in that situation, like for instance, a well-placed bullet or two through the cockpit or the control systems, then one was quite likely to "buy the farm" within milliseconds. But for Lieutenant Clark and Mr. Linville, flying the smoke ship was a change of pace. They enjoyed it.

The Top Tigers were doing a series of combat assaults at the northern most sectors of the III Corps Tactical Zone. They were now in the area where the flat Mekong Delta plains gave way to some hills, the piedmont area just before getting into the II Corps Tactical Zone and the mountainous Central Highlands. They were now transporting and inserting troops of the U.S.

173rd Airborne Brigade into a landing zone located about five miles away from a small tree-covered mountain. The mountain rose up like a small volcanic peak, and had a commanding view of the surrounding area.

Major Marker, the operations officer, personally briefed Lieutenant Clark on the impending mission.

Niles Marker was a likeable man, made very much in the same mode as Major Compton, Top Tiger Six. Marker was tall, handsome, sharp, and commanding. The major difference between the operations officer and the CO, Major Compton, was that Major Marker was younger and physically larger than Major Compton. Major Marker seemed to be extraordinarily insightful. He was exceptionally good at cutting right to the heart of the matter. Major Marker impressed Lieutenant Clark as being the perfect operations officer.

"We feel almost certain that Charlie has observers on this hilltop," Major Marker said as he placed his finger on the appropriate place on the map. "We plan to insert troops over here—right in front of this little mountain, you might say. Now what we want you to do is put some smoke rings around this mountain top so the observers there—if there are any—will not be able to make out our LZs—will not be able to make out exactly what we are doing in their neighborhood."

"Okay," said Lieutenant Clark. "No problem."

"Fine," said Major Marker. There was something about the man that instilled confidence, and he and Clark got on quite well. Clark had a couple of chances to fly with Major Marker, and he found the operations officer to be a cool and talented pilot and a pleasant traveling companion.

One day while preparing for an operation (Operation Junction City), Lieutenant Clark had met Major Marker as he walked up the line of awaiting helicopters and crews. Clark commented to Marker about how most of the crewmembers and troops seemed to be seeking and usually finding shade in every conceivable space in and around the helicopters and napping.

"They always seem to be either sleeping or eating," Clark observed.

"Yes, you're right," Marker replied. After a pause Marker continued to speak. "Supposedly, just prior to the Battle of Waterloo, a young officer asked the Duke of Wellington for his best piece of permanent military wisdom, and the Duke's reply was, 'Piss when you can.'"

"I would agree with the Duke," Marker said. "But I would go a little further and add to that by also saying, 'Eat and sleep when you can.'"

Lieutenant Clark soon learned the wisdom of this fundamental and unadorned counsel.

Now, as Clark and Linville approached the small mountaintop, the obvious questions began to present themselves. Who, if anyone is up there, and, what will be their reaction to being walled in by smoke? Experience had proven that Clark and Linville thought a lot alike. That is why they were a good team and good friends. There were tense moments when very little discussion was required. Each of them seemed to instinctively know what the other was thinking and how he would react.

Major Marker came on line: "Okay, Smokey, go in now. Go on in."

Now they were on a short descending approach to the mountaintop. They were a little tense, but it did not show. There was no chatter, no chitchat. They were immensely curious about what awaited them as they neared the hilltop. Was this mission simply a peculiar precaution, or did someone have some intelligence that had not been shared with the pilots? Was there a known enemy position up there? No, surely not. Major Marker would have said so. But maybe he did not know. What did fate have in store for them? Was this a really dangerous mission? Or was it simply an opportunity to do some fun flying? But what if…? The bad guys could have a .50 caliber machine gun perched up there somewhere. They might have twin fifties. They might have a ring of steel all 'round this thing. They might be flying directly into the jaws of death. Yes, there may be a couple of big machine guns up there, and then again there might be a Burma Shave sign up there—or a "See Rock City" sign. Or who knows what is up there? What did fate have in store for them?

"Get on those guns, guys," Mr. Linville said. "Be ready. Here we go. Be steady and be ready, guys. Here we go."

Both Dotson and Collins quickly came on line with their "Roger that," "Roger that," acknowledgements.

Lieutenant Clark was on the aircraft controls, and Mr. Linville was poised, ready to flip on the smoke switch. Clark zoomed in close to the upper western side of the mountain. He then said "smoke," and Linville flipped the switch. Thick white smoke billowed from the outlets just behind the exhaust pipe. Clark took quick sidelong glimpses of the mountaintop. He could see no signs of life, activity, or enemy gun positions. It looked like virgin forest all around.

They completed one circle, one trip around the mountaintop. And then a second, and then a third. They took no fire. The tree-covered hilltop was quiet and peaceful. And now it was encased in white smoke. Some neat flying, Lieutenant Clark thought to himself. And some neat smoke rings. He and Linville offered one another congratulatory smiles.

"Atta boy," Linville said, "we did good. What da'ya think, guys?" he asked the crew.

"Looks good to me," Sergeant Dotson answered.

"Good show, man. Cool." Collins said.

Simultaneously, just as the smoke ship was completing its third trip around the mountaintop, and the smoke rings were looking rather well formed, the Top Tigers, led by Top Tiger Six and Major Marker, were turning to line up for their final approach to their selected landing zone—"LZ Bluebonnet." They were soon on the ground. The troops quickly dismounted from the helicopters, and then after a brief pause, the aircraft lifted off the ground, moved forward, and then flew off the LZ and into the air about 300 feet over the treetops. They brought in two "lifts"—troop loads—more that morning from Loc Ninh, and then the insertions at LZ Bluebonnet were finished. No one had fired a shot. And for "Smokey" it had been a fun mission. If there was a .50 caliber machine gun in the neighborhood, no one could tell. It was silent.

Next day the Top Tigers found themselves working with the U.S. 1st Infantry Division out of their base camp at An Loc. They would be making three combat assaults, three insertions somewhere on the western edge of War Zone D.

Lieutenant Clark and Mr. Linville were still flying the smoke ship. Major Marker gave them a late night briefing. First, he thanked them for their fine performance on the mountaintop smoke job. Then he got down to the business at hand.

"This is LZ Jackhammer," he said, pointing to the map before them. "Your mission will be simply to fly in first and drop off the pathfinders. And then, lift off, get in orbit, and when I give you word, get back down there and give us some smoke screens on both sides of the LZ—a pretty straightforward mission, guys. Do you have any questions?"

"No questions," Clark replied.

It was just after dawn the next morning and the Top Tigers were flying in the direction of LZ Jackhammer. They were about ten minutes out. Clark and Linville had lifted off earlier with the pathfinders. They were less than five minutes out from the LZ when they noticed black smoke on the horizon in the direction of the LZ. Just at that moment Major Marker came on line with a certain sense of urgency in his voice.

"Say, Smokey," he said. "We just got word that something is going on up there on the LZ. There's a LOCH, a scout, down in the LZ. It's some guy, a scout pilot, flying with the 1st Division, I believe. So, be on your toes. This LZ may be hot. But go on in and drop off the pathfinders, if you can. We plan to go ahead with the insertion."

"Roger that," said Lieutenant Clark.

"Well, well. The landing zone is marked by a burning LOCH," Linville said pensively. "Dandy—fine and dandy. Now this sounds like a dicey mission indeed. 'Land on the burning LOCH,' the man said. '*If* you can,' I might add. '*If* you can.' 'Aye, aye, sir, three bags full! And damn the torpedoes, and sit on your tubes, Mr. Gridley.' Okay, guys, be ready for anything. This could be a hot one."

Lieutenant Clark thought for a moment about the girl on the Champs Élysées with the Arc de Triomphe just over her shoulder. She was so fair, so beautiful, and she was smiling. This girl possessed magical powers. There was magic in her eyes and sorcery in her perfume. '*The grass stoops not, she treads on it so light.*' Without any effort at all she could make a man fly. And Winston Clark knew this girl, and he had always known her—would always know her. War Zone C could not contain the angel's wings.

Now they were on their short final approach to the landing zone. They could clearly see the small burning helicopter on the upper—western—end of the LZ. The aircraft was an OH-6 Cayuse ("OH" for "Observation Helicopter"). The Cayuse was usually referred to as a "scout" ship.

They saw no bodies—no signs of any activity of any type. The Huey's heavy rotor blades were popping—*whop, whop, whop*—as they descended and made their final approach into the landing zone. They came in hot and made a sliding full stop in the middle of the LZ. The pathfinders—four of them—were quickly off the helicopter and taking a cautious look around, rifles at the ready, before setting out to perform their tasks.

"Okay, guys, are we set? Are we ready for lift off?" Lieutenant Clark asked. He got a thumbs-up sign all around.

They lifted off, flew directly over the burning chopper, and out of the landing zone. Lieutenant Clark turned to fly a slow pattern to the left, the south. No one had fired on them. The LZ was "cool." They were all a bit puzzled. They were all thinking almost aloud: "What's the deal with the LOCH? What's the story with the burning LOCH? What happened? We didn't take any fire. Did he? Where's the scout pilot? Is he alive? What's going on here?"

They climbed up to 500 feet, and then heard Major Marker talking on the line. They answered his questions as quickly as possible. They explained that the landing zone—thus far—was cool. They had taken no fire. They could see no bodies and no activity. The pathfinders were down and out and were not reporting any enemy contact.

"Well, sounds good to me," said Major Marker. "Let's get on with it. Get back in there, Smokey, and give us some cover—give us some smoke. We're about three minutes out."

"Roger that," Lieutenant Clark said as he turned the aircraft to line up for a final approach on the northern edge of the landing zone. He rapidly approached the spot he was aiming for. And then they were just over the ground.

"Smoke," he said in a marvelously cool manner. It was almost as though he was asking for a drink of Kool Aid. Clark was flying from the left seat.

"Smoke," Linville said as he flipped the switch. "You got it, my friend. You got it." Mr. Linville would always remain the Coolest of the Cool. The title was all his.

Now they were hurling over the ground at 70 knots, helicopter nose down, tail up, and just six feet above the sod. The tree line was just to their right. It was there, not more than ten yards away from the cockpit. The tree line remained serenely silent.

Charlie, are you there? Linville was thinking. Charlie, where are you? Are you there?

This is it—flying like the devil, Lieutenant Clark thought to himself. Blazing saddles. Hell for leather. No. We're making angel's dust. That's what we're doing. This place cannot shut out the flutter, the beat of angel's wings—and life-sustaining angel's dust.

Lieutenant Clark pulled the aircraft up as he coolly commanded, "Smoke off."

Then they were up above the treetops again, gaining altitude and turning to make their next pass at the landing zone. Next they would put a smoke screen in front of the trees on the south side of the LZ.

Lieutenant Clark reported to Major Marker that they still had not taken any fire in LZ Jackhammer. "It's still cool, as far as we can determine," Clark said.

"Roger that," Major Marker acknowledged. "The LZ seems to be cool."

"Sir," Specialist Collins came on the line. He sounded excited. "Sir, I think I saw him—that pilot—the LOCH pilot, the scout."

"What?" Clark asked. "Are you sure?"

"Well, yes. I'm pretty sure," Collins said. "Almost certain. When we made that last pass, I think I saw him lying behind some bushes. He's up toward the top of the LZ, on the northern side. And he's smoking like he might be on fire. He might be burned."

"Uh oh," Linville said. "We better see what we can do—and quick." Clark agreed.

By that time they were on their final approach toward the south side of the landing zone. They put down their smoke screen just as they had done on the opposite side of the LZ.

"Smoke off," Lieutenant Clark said. He then popped the aircraft up above the tree tops at the end of the LZ, did a very tight turn in the air over the western end of the clearing, and then came back down to land just west of the burning LOCH.

"Where is he?" Linville asked Collins. "Where's that guy hiding—the scout pilot?"

"Pick it up, sir, and hover over there," Collins said. "Come on. Over there toward the other side—the northern side." Collins pointed toward the point he had in mind.

Lieutenant Clark hovered over in the given direction for a couple of minutes, and then Collins came on line and shouted, "Okay! Okay, sir, put it down! Put it down right here!"

Lieutenant Clark set the chopper gently down in the tall grass. And before anyone could say or do anything, Specialist Collins had unbuckled himself, was out of the aircraft, and running toward the northern tree line. As they watched him run, after a moment, they thought they could make out a thin pillar of blue smoke emanating from the undergrowth there just ahead of Collins. This thin pale bluish pall of smoke was distinctly not from the same source as the heavy white smoke from their newly created screen.

They soon observed Collins bending over to attend to something—or someone. Then for a few long moments he was entirely obscured by some of the white smoke that had drifted his way. And then Collins emerged from the smoke carrying someone cradled in his arms. He quickly trotted back toward the awaiting aircraft. Sergeant Dotson went out to meet him. Together they gently laid the badly burned scout pilot onto the floor of the helicopter. The crew could immediately smell the burned hair and flesh. The pilot's hair was almost all burned away and about half of his uniform was burned off his body.

Clark and Linville were instructed by Top Tiger Six that there was a "burn unit" at the American hospital in Long Binh, so they flew the pilot there just as fast as they possibly could.

The Top Tigers completed their mission at LZ Jackhammer without any other complications. The landing zone remained "cool"—uncontested.

Later they spoke with some officers from the 1st Division, and they learned a little more about the unfortunate LOCH pilot, a CWO Steven Lassiter. Steve Lassiter (his father called him "Buddy") had been a good-looking young man. His hair was shiny and blond like fresh woven gold, and his eyes were a sparkling sky-blue. They were told that he had been voted most handsome boy in his high school senior class. And he had married a beautiful girl—his high school sweetheart. Then he joined the army and went to flight school—into the army helicopter program.

Lassiter had been flying alone that day at LZ Jackhammer—"checking out the LZ," he said. He came in for a low slow pass over the LZ, and then there was this terrible explosion. He came down hard and was burning when he got out of the chopper. He frantically rolled in the grass in an attempt to put out the flames. That was not so easy, he said. In his efforts to extinguish himself, he set the grass on fire. But finally he managed to get the flames out. And then he tried to hide. He figured that Charlie would be on him at any minute. So he hid behind some bushes, but he was not at all sure that he would survive. He later said that his situation was almost funny. His main concern was that the VC would see his smoke, and soon transform him into a KIA (killed in action), or have him doing a long hike up the Ho Chi Minh Trail. He felt helpless. No matter where he tried to hide, no matter what he did, he continued to smoke. He was a living, breathing smoke bomb. He was a walking burning bush, he said. He thought that even if he took off his clothes and discarded them, he would probably continue to smoke. Now certainly he would never be the same. His face was badly scarred. And his hands were in bad shape. Right away in the burn unit, the doctors said that he would require "extensive restoration work." But he was alive. He lived. He was a survivor.

The burned scout pilot, Mr. Lassiter, was the only casualty experience by the Americans that day in War Zone D. The Top Tigers were quite proud of their door gunner, Specialist Collins, for his rescue efforts at LZ Jackhammer. With Major Scully's help, Lieutenant Clark wrote up a recommendation for Collins to be awarded the Soldiers' Medal for heroism.

This was the first the Top Tigers had heard of it, but the Viet Cong had invented a helicopter mine, or booby trap. And that was what had brought down Mr. Lassiter, the scout pilot. The Viet Cong had developed a little mine that was roughly the equivalent of the U.S. manufactured Claymore mine—which was actually a rather powerful little bomb. The VC called it a DH-10, for some reason. And the DH-10 mine was something the pathfinders would be looking for in the future. The VC, ever mindful that the rotor blades of a helicopter always created a downdraft, decided to place the mines at the tops of trees in an area where the helicopters could be expected to fly fairly low, or where they might be lured to fly low for surveillance. A rather sophisticated friction fuse was connected to the branches of the tree or a fairly tall bush, which bent under the helicopter's downdraft thereby detonating the mine that exploded under the machine. It was an ingenious little weapon and it succeeded in doing its nasty business on a number of occasions.

It worked at LZ Jackhammer. And no one there that day would ever forget it—certainly not the scout pilot, Steven Lassiter. He would recall it vividly for the rest of his life. When his father next saw him he would plaintively ask:

"Oh, Lord, what have they done with our Buddy?"

Chapter 20

Rock City

They were on final approach to Rock City. The rotor blades were loudly popping in the heavy moist morning air.

The Vietnamese called the village Pho Da. But the GI's called it "Rock City" because it was built on huge boulders. And this little village clearly struck Lieutenant Clark as being unique. It was certainly like nothing he had ever seen before.

An old woman living there told Lieutenant Clark that many, many years ago the gods became angry with a witch in Pho Da. The gods were upset with the witch for causing the early death of a beautiful young girl—a very special girl who represented only love and sweetness to the people in the village. The girl was called Len Lee and the people had only to look upon her smiling face and they would be glad. They would see her and they would be filled with joy and happiness. Everyone adored her and cherished her company, and she added much sweetness and strength to the lives of the people of the village. And so they—the gods—had thrown all of their stones at the old witch and buried her there for allowing the lovely little girl to die so young. The result was Pho Da, Rock City.

From an altitude of about a thousand feet, Pho Da had the appearance of a pile of petrified dung beetle balls. But these balls were boulders, huge boulders weighing tons. And strangely enough they mostly appeared to be of a more-or-less standard size. They were all piled up there at Pho Da—and nowhere else. Pho Da was about 25 miles northwest of Xuan Loc—in the middle of nowhere. It was surrounded by thick jungle. There were no other villages nearby, nor were there any boulders like these—all piled up out in the middle of nowhere—to be found anywhere else in the country.

How could people live in such a place? Clark thought to himself. How and why? But they did. About six hundred people lived there. And they seemed to live among the rocks like lizards. With canvass, bricks, boards, some mortar, and tin they had somehow managed to create numerous shelters—a complete shantytown—on, in, and among the huge rocks, in the middle of nowhere.

Lieutenant Clark and Mr. Linville were done with their stint as "Smokey" pilots and were now back in their regular helicopter and with their regular crew, Sergeant Dotson and Specialist Collins. Again they were flying mostly miscellaneous ash and trash missions around the northern half of the III Corps Tactical Zone. On that day, as they approached Pho Da, they felt that their mission was rather special. They were flying the battalion flight surgeon, Captain Charles Quackenhauer, M.D., out to Pho Da for a Civil Affairs medical support mission. This program involved U.S. Army doctors occasionally visiting remote villages—ones considered pacified and friendly—to provide some much needed medical services for the villagers.

Captain Quackenhauer was a competent and pleasant young physician who enjoyed exceptional popularity among the officers and men. He kept busy and he appeared to thoroughly enjoy his work. The enlisted men liked to say that it was nice that they had their own "quack." And recently, for Dr. Quackenhauer's birthday, the men had given him a pet duck they called "Quack-quack."

After landing at the local heliport, Lieutenant Clark climbed out of the cockpit and accompanied Dr. Quackenhauer as he walked toward what appeared to be a small marketplace just to the west of the huge pile of giant boulders. Mr. Linville said that he would remain with the chopper and catch a nap. Lieutenant Clark was carrying Doc Quackenhauer's medical case as they approached a large, roughly-constructed table on the edge of the square.

There were eight or ten battered old wooden folding chairs spread around the large table. Mostly women with infants were occupying the chairs. Some of the infants were crying and appeared to be suffering from various fevers and infections. Doc Quackenhauer's medical case actually seemed rather heavy to Lieutenant Clark.

He's prepared for anything, I suppose, Clark thought to himself.

Dr. Quackenhauer and Lieutenant Clark were met by "the elders"—a group of about six or seven old men and women, mostly wearing black pajama-type pants and white cotton shirts. Most of them appeared smiling and happy and gave the impression that they already knew Dr. Quackenhauer. They appeared to eagerly anticipate his visit. Clark stepped forward with the medical case and was about to place it on the large table when suddenly Dr. Quackenhauer stopped him.

"Wait, Winston," said Dr. Quackenhauer, "let them do that. Let one of them take the case and put it on the table."

Dr. Quackenhauer made a motion to one of the more able-bodied men, and the man stepped forward smiling, took the case, and placed it firmly in the middle of the table.

Lieutenant Clark gave Dr. Quackenhauer a puzzled glance, and the doctor explained.

"A couple of weeks ago," he said, "a doctor I knew walked into a place like this and when he placed his bag on the table, it exploded. It was booby-trapped. And he was killed."

Clark gave the doctor an incredulous look, shook his head, and then turned to look over the crowd of awaiting villagers. They appeared to be so pitiful, so helpless, so much in need of support of almost every kind. For Lieutenant Clark it was hard to believe that some of these downtrodden people would have *them*—the Americans—dead—and the sooner the better.

Dr. Quackenhauer was mostly occupied with taking care of the mothers with their infants. Their problems ran the gamut of ailments, sicknesses, and diseases, but there were quite a few who were suffering from malaria. Other common illnesses in these little villages were fungal skin infections, amoebic dysentery, and intestinal parasites such as hookworm, roundworm, and tapeworm. These blood-sucking parasites were a common cause of chronic anemia among the Vietnamese. Malaria and a protein-deficient diet also contributed to the chronic anemia.

Dr. Quackenhauer worked quietly and patiently among them for several hours before he started to give Lieutenant Clark little hints that perhaps they should start preparing to depart.

One of the elders who had greeted them looked decidedly discontent. He was clearly not happy. He appeared to be in pain. His face was swollen. After getting the impression that Dr. Quackenhauer was preparing to leave, he became a little frantic and started to make excited gestures and point to his swollen jaw. Finally, he opened his mouth and pointed inside, making a long moaning sound as if he wanted to make it perfectly clear that he was suffering from grievous pain.

"Okay," said Dr. Quackenhauer. "It's okay."

Everyone everywhere in Vietnam seemed to understand "okay."

Dr. Quackenhauer made it clear to the man that he would do whatever he could to help him, to ease his pain. He made a quick examination inside the man's mouth, and he seemed to spot the problem right away.

"Okay. An abscessed tooth," Dr. Quackenhauer said. "Yeah. It looks really rotten."

"What can you do?" Lieutenant Clark asked.

"Extract it," Dr. Quackenhauer calmly answered. Everyone—the Americans—realized, of course, that Captain Quackenhauer was not a dentist.

"Sergeant Dotson," said Dr. Quackenhauer, "go and get the tool kit out of the helicopter."

Sergeant Dotson looked at him in disbelief.

"Doc," he said, "you're not serious?"

"Oh, yes, I am," Dr. Quackenhauer answered. He was very matter of fact about the whole business. "I'll give him a shot of Novocain to numb it, and then take it out with your wire pliers. This should be no problem—no problem at all."

As they all watched, Dr. Quackenhauer did just that. And within less than an hour he had the rotten tooth out and the patient appeared somewhat dazed but relieved. Dr. Quackenhauer was good. His professionalism was extraordinary, and some of the Top Tigers actually started to call him their "legendary doc."

"Here," said Dr. Quackenhauer as he handed the wire pliers back to Sergeant Dotson. "You can put these back and your tool box, and we can get ready to go now."

As Lieutenant Clark was climbing back into the cockpit and getting strapped in, he noticed a beautiful little girl standing back out of the way just off the helipad. She was only about eight or ten years old. She smiled and waved at him happily. Her eyes were bright and shining. Clark thought of the old woman's story about the beautiful Len Lee.

"She made them glad," the old woman said. "They would see her and they would be filled with gladness. Her bright eyes were filled with good cheer and love. She was dearly loved."

Goodbye, Len Lee, Lieutenant Clark said softly to himself as he waved back at the girl. I hope and pray that the gods are good to you. Farewell, little princess. Farewell to you and Rock City.

After their departure from Rock City they flew westward to An Loc, which was in rubber plantation country. They dropped off a couple of

Vietnamese officers there. In addition to the two ARVN officers they transported, they also carried a tall lone Montagnard into An Loc. This man was a striking figure, over six feet tall—quite tall for a native in Vietnam—and he was dressed only in a white shirt. Later Clark noticed that the man was wearing tight black short-shorts underneath, but at first glance he appeared to be a tall dark native wearing only a shirt with long sleeves and long tails. The long sleeves were rolled down and buttoned in the tropical heat. And the shirt was so white and clean. Clark thought that it looked as if it had just been purchased right off the shelf in a men's shop in Watauga, back in Old Catawba. The man's hair was long, straight, black, and shiny. He smiled almost all the time and his teeth were white and healthy in appearance. The Montagnards (the GIs called them "Yards") were the local aborigines, an ancient people who had been on the land longer than the Vietnamese. This man made Clark think of Chingachgook, from James Fenimore Cooper's *The Last of the Mohicans.* Or was he more in the spirit of Queequeg, from Herman Melville's *Moby Dick*? But the Montagnard was not tattooed. The man looked as though he should be carrying a spear. But perhaps he had set it aside for the helicopter ride. The only baggage the man carried was a small shiny black bag with drawstrings. (A silk purse, perhaps?) The bag appeared to be filled with sand or rice (or perhaps gold dust). Clark had seen the man emerge alone from the trees near the helipad, speak shortly with the Vietnamese officers, and then, with a broad smile, climb aboard the helicopter. Clark would always remember this man. There was a snapshot of this most striking figure in some special chamber of Clark's brain. He traveled light, carried only a small bag, looked as though he should be carrying a spear, and appeared to be healthy and happy. This man appeared to be Rousseau's Noble Savage. Here he stood in the flesh. He really *did* exist. Here was Chingachgook, in the Vietnamese Highlands.

After refueling at the An Loc airstrip they headed south, flying over National Highway Number 13. Their next destination was Les Trungs.

Monsieur Voltaige had heard of Dr. Quackenhauer and spoken about him with someone important in the chain of command. And now their flight surgeon was scheduled to make a visit to the Frenchman's plantation to check on his people—his army of servants and workers. Lieutenant Clark and Mr. Linville, and no one else, it was said in the operations office, were to fly the doctor to Les Trungs.

The crew had experienced several rather severe thunderstorms that day and now a low overcast was developing. To avoid flying in the clouds, Mr. Linville descended down just off the deck over the highway. There was not much traffic on the highway, just a couple of small convoys of military vehicles, and occasionally some old, battered, and overcrowded Vietnamese buses. The buses even had some people riding on top, on the roofs.

Mr. Linville was on the controls. They were listening to music on AFN. As they cruised along over Highway 13 they could hear the Beatles singing "Ticket to Ride." Lieutenant Clark looked down at the roadside and he could make out strips on both sides the highway here and there where the foliage appeared about half brown and dead. This half-dead-looking area marked places that had been sprayed by the defoliate known as Agent Orange. Apparently, this area had been sprayed some time ago and was probably about due for another spray-job. These defoliants were supposed to make the roads and waterways safer by providing better visibility and some protection from enemy ambushes. Some soldiers said that the spraying really did not seem to make that much difference. It simply meant that instead of the Viet Cong hiding in green stuff, Charlie would simply hide in brown stuff.

However, as almost everyone later discovered, Agent Orange left quite a mark—quite a legacy, actually—a legacy of consternation, abomination, and horror. By 1967, 1.5 million acres a year of forest and crops were being destroyed in an effort to deny the Viet Cong food and places to hide. This program was first called "Project Hades," and then it became "Operation Ranch Hand." The Americans started to use Agent Orange in

Vietnam in 1961 and they stopped using it in 1971. During this time, nineteen million gallons of herbicides were sprayed over 20 percent of the forestland in South Vietnam.

The most common defoliant was Agent Orange. ("Agent Orange" was a code name taken from the orange colored identification band used to mark the fifty-five gallon drums it was stored in.) This chemical herbicide contained minute amounts of dioxin, a highly poisonous substance. The dioxin accumulated from the repeated spraying, lingering in the silt of the streambeds and entering the ecosystem of South Vietnam. Twenty-five years after American involvement in the Vietnam war ended in 1973, US public health researchers said that residents of Bien Hoa City showed dioxin levels as much as 135 times higher than in residents in Hanoi, the capital of North Vietnam. Bien Hoa Airbase was a major chemical depot during the war.

Thousands of Americans and perhaps more than a million Vietnamese were exposed to Agent Orange. And this herbicide has now been identified as a cause of cancer, congenital deformations, birth defects, miscarriages, and other afflictions among both humans and animals. The widespread use of this chemical brought on a reign of destruction that would haunt both the Americans and the Vietnamese for many years into the future. Agent Orange became one of the major curses of the war—one that would haunt both friend and foe alike.

Lieutenant Clark was just starting to sit back and relax when he looked straight ahead—and then looked again. Suddenly, there straight before them, at exactly the same level, same altitude, he could make out a huge U.S. Air Force cargo plane flying straight at them. And it was not far away. As the air traffic controllers would have said, "It was closing fast." This airplane was trailing a great sea of smog that billowed up and drifted out behind it. This was a specially equipped C-123 U.S. Air Force cargo plane being used to spray Agent Orange. It was down on the deck re-spraying National Highway 13—and it was headed straight for Lieutenant Clark's helicopter.

"Do you have the target there?" Lieutenant Clark asked Linville, "straight ahead—dead ahead—on our level?" There was a sense of urgency in his voice.

"Uh oh, yeah," said Mr. Linville, "yeah, I got it."

Simultaneous with those words, Mr. Linville pulled up the nose of the helicopter, pulled in additional power, firmed his feet on the pedals, and made a rapid climb to the right. The timing was perfect. The big Air Force C-123 cargo plane continued straight ahead up Highway 13 just as though the helicopter had never been there. The two aircraft folded smoothly over and under one another, almost as if this had been a practiced maneuver.

When the helicopter crew looked back below them they could easily make out the wide sea of blue smoke, the ocean of herbicides covering the road and all that was on it. The soldiers in the convoy suddenly found themselves in the middle of a great corrupt cloud of biting blue smoke. They immediately filled the blue smoke with blue language as they fought and struggled for clean air, while they cursed the perpetrators of this cruel chemical plague.

The Vietnamese crowded into their battered buses were astounded to suddenly find themselves surrounded by this poisonous cloud of thick blue smoke. The bus driver pulled over and stopped the old bus. How could this be happening? What was this all about? The Vietnamese, mostly women, children, and old people, screamed and cried out in vain. Why was this happening to them? Who was doing this—and to what purpose? Did someone wish to destroy their land and all that was on it? What had they done to deserve this cruel punishment? They wept and cried out in abject helplessness and despair as Operation Ranch Hand lumbered along its toxic way.

The cloud cover had now moved up to about a 1,000 feet. Mr. Linville continued to climb until he leveled off the aircraft at 800 feet.

"I think I can see the Frenchy's place from here," Linville said.

"Les Trungs, yeah," Clark agreed as he gazed through the Plexiglas at a dark spot on the distant horizon.

They decided to leave Highway 13 at that point and fly directly cross-country to Les Trungs. Actually, they all found themselves a little eager to arrive at the Frenchman's plantation, and to once again experience his grand hospitality. The charming Frenchman and his hospitality could fairly well be described as irresistible.

Lieutenant Clark glanced back over his shoulder, back toward the poisoned highway—the contaminated convoys and buses—and back toward Pho Da, Rock City.

Farewell, Lieutenant Clark thought, Farewell, Len Lee, little princess. Please avoid derelict buses. And beware: neglected bus stops in War Zone D can be fatal. Beware of those highways and byways of cruelty and death that abound in your land. And Pho Da, that somber Stonehenge of malady, destiny must call upon you, Len Lee, to make your exodus from beneath those toadstools of death. Perhaps your tender body is protein-deficient, but there is a glad heart inside that does not know it. No, it knows no deficiency. There is a life and shining light inside of you that will surpass all else in this awesome universe. That sweet radiance which enriches your soul—and brings gladness to those around you—that which is there inside of you, that spark, that translucence will glow and shine and live long after the dark shadows of malaria and beriberi have passed over the stones of Pho Da and on into the abyss of time and space.

The gods have thrown rocks at you, Len Lee. But now I pray that they will protect you from this ill wind, this sinister stranger known as Agent Orange. Farewell to Rock City, and farewell to thee, sweet princess. Fare thee well—and goodbye.

Chapter 21

Of Moses, Barbecue, and Beer

The visit to Les Trungs with Dr. Quackenhauer was pleasant and successful. Captain Quackenhauer was duly impressed with the Frenchman, Monsieur Voltaige, his personal charm, his family, his plantation, and above all, his hospitality.

Of all Monsieur Voltaige's army of servants and workers there was only a relatively small group that turned out to await the doctor's visit. Dr. Quackenhauer later commented to Lieutenant Clark that the people at Les Trungs appeared remarkably healthy when compared to the average group of Vietnamese villagers that Quackenhauer had come to know. The diet was remarkably better at Les Trungs—as was the sanitation. These, he said, were the essential elements, the keys to good health.

"Right, along with avoiding hostile gunfire," Linville injected.

The primary health problem at Les Trungs was malaria, the predominant health problem all over South Vietnam. After the war it was reported that the second greatest cause of death among the Viet Cong—after battlefield wounds—was malaria. The most common strain of the mosquito-borne fever in Vietnam was *falciparum*, which appeared to be resistant to the standard anti-malarial drugs. The Americans took their prescribed anti-malarial drugs on a regular basis, but they also suffered a large number of malarial casualties.

Monsieur Voltaige offered refreshments, and spoke of a refreshing swim, but the Americans said they were running late and could not stay long. The crew all looked longingly at the sparkling waters in the pool, and scorned the idea of having to rush right on back to the airbase. But they realized they had no choice. There were missions to be flown. The guys in operations seemed to be keeping everyone quite busy lately. However, they each found a few moments of companionship with the fair young women with whom they had become acquainted. Lieutenant Clark had the impression that Sergeant Dotson was pleased in Becky's company, and Specialist Collins seemed quite serious about his relationship with Lee Ann. Also, Clark was distinctly impressed that Monique was more interested in Mr. Linville than he had recently indicated.

To Winston Clark, every moment that he could spend with Genevieve was a treasure—a feast. But they had difficulty finding an opportunity to be alone. They met near the swimming pool and talked for about fifteen minutes. Genevieve was as sweet, alluring, and enchanting as ever, but she also seemed to be growing more demanding. She said that he must come *soon* and stay—yes, *stay*—with her. She seemed impatient and frustrated with his reasons for not being able to comply with her wishes. He repeatedly assured her that her wishes were his wishes also. He pleaded with her to remain patient a little longer. Surely, somehow they would find a way to be together. Winston Clark had no idea how he would satisfy her wishes, but he had decided to trust fate. He was convinced in his heart that when feelings this powerful were involved, something extraordinarily special and good had to come from it. As he had heard Monsieur Voltaige recently say in another context, "Let us reduce selfishness, and embrace simplicity and serenity. Let us all be optimistic—and *keep trying*. What else can we do?"

Lieutenant Clark had been able to exchange notes with Genevieve through Mr. Clayton, and he reassured her that he could continue to do that, and soon he would somehow work out an arrangement which would allow them to spend more time together. It had started to cloud up and suddenly there was a great crash of thunder just above them. The sky quickly darkened as tears started to trail down her face. He kissed her, and then she watched him walk away in the rain toward the awaiting helicopter.

As Clark climbed into the cockpit he was soaked and downcast. Rain was dripping off the end of his nose as he pulled the restraining straps over his shoulders. Linville spoke.

"Come on, Winnie. Get it on and let's jive, man! Yeah, let's jive on outta' here! Ya' know what I mean?"

"It's time to go to da' house!" Sergeant Dotson said from behind Lieutenant Clark.

"You got it, man," Specialist Collins said. "Let's get it on!"

Mr. Linville tuned the radio and as they pulled increased engine power and gained altitude, they could hear Ray Charles on AFN singing, *I Can't Stop Loving You.*

— — —

One evening, not long after their visit to Les Trungs, Clark and Linville were standing in the barracks game-room-bar talking about their visit to the Frenchman's plantation with Dr. Quackenhauer. They were talking about the relatively good health of those living and working at Les Trungs. Major Ratcliffe, the Mustang Buddha, happened to be passing through the room when, for some reason, he turned his head, came over to them, ordered a can of cold beer, and talked with them for a few minutes. The short stout major talked just long enough to drink one can of beer and get something off his chest.

"I think you are making a mistake," said Major Ratcliffe, "if you get too close to that guy and his girls and all that business out there."

"What da'ya mean, 'that guy'?" Linville asked, appearing a bit puzzled. "You mean the Frenchy, Voltaige?"

"That's right," answered Ratcliffe. "You know who I mean—Voltaige."

"Aw, come on, now," Lieutenant Clark said. "What do you have against the Frenchman? He's a charmer. He's been good to us. He's a prince. Have you got something against the French? After all, let us not forget that Lafayette was a Frenchmen—was he not? What's wrong with him—Voltaige, I mean?"

"You can't tell me…" Major Ratcliffe started to answer, "Well, no one can tell me that guy can run a plantation like that one he's got out there where it's located without an agreement with Charlie—no way."

"An agreement with Charlie…" Clark said. "What do you mean?"

"Well, come on. Think about it for a minute. I think you know what I mean," Ratcliffe said. "An agreement with Charlie…I mean that he is probably paying taxes to both sides. That's how he stays in business. I was talking with a guy I know in Saigon, and he said that it's common knowledge that some of these Frenchies are doing this sort of thing. They're are paying off both sides, so then no matter who wins the war in the end, the Frenchies—with their plantations—will also win."

"Well, I hadn't really thought of that," Clark said.

"No, not really. Nor had I," said Linville. "But, well, really, it seems sort of reasonable, actually. It's a family business, you know. It's been there for years—forever. And everybody needs the rubber, right? Where are any of us going without tires, right? What are we gonna do, put our pickup trucks on skids—or blocks? No, to me it looks like a matter of survival. He's gotta do what he's gotta do, wouldn't you say?"

"No. No, I would not say that," Major Ratcliffe said, "Anybody that's paying off Charlie is working against us. You can't have it both ways. Can't you see that? As old Honest Abe said once, 'You can't fool all of the people all of the time.' Mark my word, sooner or later, this guy is going to fall between the stools."

"Well, who knows?" Lieutenant Clark hardly knew what to say. He had enormous respect for the Mustang Buddha, but he also had a great place in his heart for Monsieur Voltaige, the little prince—and his daughter. Genevieve, the girl with the honey-colored hair, absolutely filled his heart.

"You guys should not get so close to those girls out there that you forget what you were sent over here for. Be careful that you don't end up behind the eight-ball," Major Ratcliffe said as a sort of parting shot as he walked away.

Monsieur Voltaige had cordially offered his home as a "port in the storm" to Lieutenant Clark and all of his Top Tiger friends. Now, from what Clark was hearing increasingly, air crews in his company were somehow finding opportunities to stop off at Les Trungs to enjoy themselves anywhere from an hour or so, to a couple of days.

Sergeant Moses Merlins, the maintenance platoon sergeant, a black man from Yazoo City, Mississippi, had stopped off there on several occasions and prepared barbecue for the men. Sergeant Merlins was famous for his homemade barbecue sauce. The men all fervently swore that there was no better sauce anywhere in the universe.

Monsieur Voltaige appeared to be absolutely inspired by Sergeant Merlins and his barbecue. Monsieur Voltaige said that they should team up and open a chain of restaurants together and get rich. Monsieur Voltaige said they should call it "Moses' Majestic Barbecue," and that the menus should have the form of stone tablets like those that Moses brought down from Mount Sinai. Merlins was charmed by the Frenchman, as everyone seemed to be, and appeared ready to accommodate the plantation owner in any manner possible. Monsieur Voltaige said that Sergeant Merlins had special powers, that he was a magician, and certainly sorcery was involved in the concoction of his special sauce. The Frenchman expressed a great determination to have the recipe.

"*Oui, oui*," the Frenchman said, "it is absolutely addictive—this sauce—irresistible! *Oui*, we must discover the secret ingredients."

"Sergeant Merlins," said Monsieur Voltaige, "instinctively knows those special ingredients for which the body and soul cry out. These are the elements from the very heart of the earth that we crave and must have."

Lieutenant Clark anticipated his return to Les Trungs with great fervor. However, he was beginning to be somewhat haunted by some disturbing thoughts and rumors. Major Ratcliffe's words weighed heavily on his mind.

"You can't have it both ways," the Mustang Buddha had said. "Anybody that's paying off Charlie is working against us. Wait and see: one day this guy Voltaige will fall between the stools. And his fall will be a great crash. He'll come down heavy."

Increasingly Clark was hearing the enlisted men talk about *everything* being available at "the Frenchy's place." And by "everything" they seemed to essentially mean music, food, entertainment, movies, erotic films, women, alcohol, and even drugs—hashish and opium. Winston Clark was experiencing a robust clash of mixed emotions. On one hand, he was happy to hear that the men had a safe place to enjoy themselves, but, on the other hand, he hardly wanted to hear that they were becoming addicted to drugs. But then he thought that perhaps he should take a closer look at himself. We all carry our weaknesses with us, he thought. What about being addicted to a woman? Can one be addicted to an angel? Can love become an addiction—a bad thing, a negative force?

Captain Nowotney, Lieutenant Clark's platoon leader, mentioned to him one day that Clark was due to be scheduled for R&R soon. Most of the officers and men that Clark knew went to Bangkok to enjoy their R&R, and some flew to Hong Kong. Most of the more senior officers tended to fly off to Hawaii to meet their wives there. Mr. Lang had just returned from Bangkok, and he was absolutely overflowing, gushing with enthusiasm for the place. He suddenly seemed to be a bottomless reservoir of adventurous, amorous, and exotic tales and anecdotes. Lang never told "war stories" about war. But he could tell endless stories about love. (Lang once mused that perhaps sex was not love but it was an exciting imitation.) John Lang seemed to have the ability to transform his Bangkok trip into the working man's Sheherazade of the *Thousand and One Nights.*

The thought had recently occurred to Lieutenant Clark that perhaps he might spend his R&R somewhere else besides Bangkok—someplace different. The thought had come to Clark that maybe he could spend his R&R at Les Trungs, Monsieur Voltaige's rubber plantation right there on the edge of War Zone C. What an idea! What a place to go for "rest and recreation!" War Zone C!

But perhaps it was possible. Nothing on earth could appeal more to Clark than an opportunity to be with Genevieve. And it hardly mattered where they met—just so they were together. To spend an entire week with her sounded like a sojourn in paradise to Clark. He longed for the touch of her skin, her scent, her smile, and her angelic profile. He longed to have her at his side—under his arm. His powerful feelings made him think that surely anything was possible—even a vacation in War Zone C.

Lieutenant Clark discussed his idea with Major Scully, the executive officer. Naturally, Major Scully appeared somewhat surprised that anyone would want to spend an R&R leave anywhere in Vietnam.

"Some place for a vacation," he mused. "There's also Laos and Cambodia, you know."

As usual, Major Scully was covered with sweat. His brown soggy t-shirt clung to his tired, scrawny body in a hopeless desperate sort of way. Linville once said that Major Scully made him think of one of the characters from the comic strip *Peanuts.*

"I think it's that kid called Pigpen," Linville said. "The one that carries dirt and disorder with him wherever he goes. Yeah, that's him."

Major Scully shook his head, took a long thoughtful pull on his cigarette, and said that he would "check it out" and let Clark know as soon as possible.

Clark discussed this idea with Genevieve through Alan Clayton. Genevieve was deliriously happy about the idea. Monsieur Voltaige heard of Clark's proposal to visit them for a week's vacation, and he heartily approved of the idea. The Frenchman discussed the idea with a friend in Saigon. The next day Major Scully called in Lieutenant Clark and said his request to spend his R&R at Les Trungs had been approved.

Somehow Lieutenant Clark was given the day off the next day. However, Major Scully told him to be in the operations office at 10 a.m.—and to be there on time and in a clean uniform. Clark enjoyed getting to sleep a little longer than usual that morning. But he was in the operations office as directed at 10 a.m. sharp—and in a fresh uniform with clean boots.

The CO was there, Major Compton, looking pleased, poised, and composed, as usual. Major Scully, the XO, was there—and in a freshly starched uniform for a change. First Sergeant Rodriguez was there to make sure that everything was just as it should be. Also, Lieutenant Clark was surprised to see the battalion commander, Colonel Perry, there along with the battalion Sergeant Major Merritt. And Lieutenant Clark's crew was there, Mr. Linville, Sergeant Dotson, and Specialist Collins—all smiling and happy. Clark was puzzled and quickly asked himself, What's going on here?

The tall colonel spoke: "Alright," he said, "Let's all stand at attention while the Sergeant Major reads the order."

The Sergeant Major started to read. The order was about First Lieutenant Winston W. Clark. He was being promoted to captain.

After the order had been read, Colonel Perry pinned Clark's new captain's bars (Dotson and Collins referred to them as "railroad tracks") onto his collar, and everyone heartily congratulated him. The colonel stood with Clark in the corner before the flag and someone snapped a photograph or two. "Be sure you get the flag in there," Major Scully said. Colonel Perry said that promoting Clark was a special pleasure because he had heard so many good things about him. Really? Clark thought to himself. From whom?

"But everyone knows the Top Tigers," the colonel said while looking over at Major Compton in an approving manner. "You fellows have been doing some fine work. Outstanding job—all the way 'round. First-rate performance, men. first-rate. Keep it up. We're proud of you."

Everyone was very cordial to the newly promoted officer—and especially his crewmembers. They were truly like brothers. They felt it then, and they would feel it even more in the future. Hot coffee and large fresh-baked sugar cookies were there from the mess hall, and everyone seemed to enjoy them with a special eagerness and pleasure.

"Good show, Captain Cool," Collins said. "Next thing you know you'll be a full-bird colonel—you just wait and see. You'll probably skip the other ranks. You know you've always been rank enough for us."

They had a good laugh. It was always easy to laugh with these men, Clark thought. It felt awfully good to Clark to receive praise from such men as these.

Officers in the U.S. military usually had a fairly good idea of when they would be promoted. However, this little ceremony caught Clark complete off guard. He was not expecting to be promoted for roughly another six months. He was thrilled at his good fortune, but also rather puzzled. He later briefly discussed this matter with Major Scully.

"Early you say?" Major Scully asked. "Well, I don't know about that. I don't think so. I think your promotion was right on time. Don't concern yourself, young man. Start thinking about being promoted to major. Be happy. You should have a bright future ahead of you. And congratulations again, captain."

Captain Clark was happy. He was more than happy. He was exhilarated. The daily grind of ash and trash and combat assaults seemed to weigh less heavily upon his shoulders now.

And now his thoughts turned to Les Trungs and R&R—and paradise—a sojourn in paradise—or in the golden dominion of *Les Delices*—The Delights.

Chapter 22

R&R

To Captain Clark, flying in to Les Trungs was like flying home. They were all there to meet him on that hot, sunny Saturday morning—Monsieur Voltaige, Genevieve, Monique, Paul Picair, and Alan Clayton.

Clark turned to wave goodbye to Linville and the crew. They had flown him out from Bien Hoa after a brief stopover at Tay Ninh. A new pilot, a young warrant officer named Plummer, would be sharing the cockpit with Linville during the week that Clark would be at Les Trungs. Linville lifted the chopper up to a five foot hover, did a pedal turn to his left, tipped the nose down a bit, pulled in some additional power, and off they went in a blinding cloud of red dust.

"*Au revoir. Bon voyage, mes amis,*" shouted Monsieur Voltaige.

Genevieve showed Clark to his room, which impressed him as being spacious, well-designed, airy, and comfortable. She instructed him to put away his things, change into his swimsuit, and come down for a swim and a buffet lunch. They kissed and glowed with warmth and anticipation of the time they knew would soon be theirs to spend alone together. Before Genevieve left him, she walked a short distance down the hallway hand-in-hand with him, pointed toward a closed door, and said: "This is my room."

When Clark joined the others down at poolside, he saw a beautiful buffet all laid out, complete with what looked like a fancily decorated birthday cake. It appeared as if Les Trungs was prepared for some sort of celebration. In large bold blue script letters the cake simply said: "*Felicitations*!" "Congratulations!"

There was a small United States flag on the right side and an equally small French tricolor on the left side of the cake.

Monsieur Voltaige popped open a bottle of champagne and announced that they were delighted to have the honor of celebrating the promotion of Captain Clark "with the man himself. So, here is to *mon ami*, Monsieur Winston Clark—and d'Artagnan, *cavalier*, patriot, captain of the guard, and stalwart protector of honor, purity, propriety, and justice."

They all drank to Clark's health and good fortune, and then Clark and Monsieur Voltaige drank the "friendship drink," arm-in-arm.

"And now, my friend," the Frenchman said. "We shall always be—as the red man would say—blood brothers. Always."

"*Oui, oui*," said Monsieur Voltaige after taking another sip of champagne, "Yes, by all means, we will wine and dine together and I shall teach you the art of good living. Yes, yes, I know this is a phrase that is almost totally alien to Americans. But I will teach you because you are our d'Artagnan, *bon vivant*, and delightful youth from Gascony. Americans, they consume and spend, but they know very little of the art of good living. Americans are the masters of the fast repast—of what they call 'fast food.' But perhaps it is now time to consider the art of 'slow food'—yes, slow food. When it comes to the consumer and consumption, the point is, you see, it is not how much you purchase, it is what you purchase and how you use it. One must learn how to prepare a fine cup of coffee, or tea, and how to drink it—where to sit, with whom you sit, and *when* to sit. These things matter with regard to the quality of our lives. Ah, *oui, oui*, these things matter! They are vital! Life can be enchanting if one appreciates it—savors it—only if one savors it. If life is to have any meaning at all, one must learn how to respect it, to revere it...how to relish it. For life is sacred. We must all realize that. Let us rejoice in our good fortune—the good fortune to be alive here and now."

All of those present clearly received the impression that these words came from deep within Monsieur Voltaige's innermost being—from his heart. He smiled in a melancholy way and sipped his Champaign.

Clark enjoyed the wonderful celebration. It was certainly like no other he could remember. The food, the wine, the companionship, the music—it was, as far as Clark was concerned, incomparable. For Winston Clark the afternoon became a dazzling kaleidoscope of eating, swimming, singing, drinking, and dancing. The girls were enjoying doing the dance called "the Twist," and later—when they were on the ballroom floor alone—Genevieve would teach Clark how to waltz and even to tango. Just before sundown two Top Tiger helicopters landed. Linville and the rest of Clark's crew had arrived, and they joined the party for a few hours. The kaleidoscope of joyful, bacchanal celebration and dizzying revelry continued to gain momentum until Linville bade them all an affectionate farewell. It was almost midnight.

"Oh, man," Linville had said to Clark just prior to departing, "Don't forget to wear your chicken plate tonight when you climb into that old cockpit. Your gonna need it. It's clear for all to see that you are in for some heavy-duty hand-to-hand combat. Beware of the Free French in the Free Fire Zone. Beware, I tell you. Beware! I feel a heat wave a'comin' on. Beware, my friend. Take no prisoners, but play fair. *Bon voyage* and *bon chance*!"

After that Clark did not remember much. Because of the hospitality of the Frenchman and his family, Clark definitely felt as though he were king for a day. He remembered having a final "friendship" drink with Monsieur Voltaige, and then Genevieve and Monique escorted him up the steep stairway to his room. He was quickly out of his wet clammy swimsuit—free of everything that binds and inhibits.

"Let's hear it for the Free French. *Oui, oui*, free is always better—*oui*, better than unfree. Free is the way to be. If we are not free, we are nothing. Nowhere, Nowheresville." He mumbled, "*Viva la* France!" and then he collapsed into the bed and fell immediately into a deep sleep.

He awoke the next morning with the sun in his eyes. After a moment he could feel the warmth of Genevieve's hands on his chest and shoulder, and he could see the beautiful glow of the morning sun shining through her honey-colored hair as she sat beside him and gazed down at him. He experienced no headache from the drinking the night before. He was delighted to awake at Les Trungs—and not at Bien Hoa Airbase with its ceaseless roar of helicopter and jet aircraft engines. The power of her beauty and the force of his love for her made him feel feeble and fragile, but light as air.

"Come," she said, "Let's have breakfast by the pool."

"Sure," he answered. "I'll be there. Just give me a few minutes."

Clark enjoyed his stay at Les Trungs immensely. It was the most joyful and exhilarating time he had ever known. He had wondered what Bangkok and Hong Kong would be like. But Les Trungs—on the edge of War Zone C, not twenty-five miles from Tay Ninh City, and not twenty-five miles from the Ho Chi Minh Trail—what could ever compare with this marvelous experience? He was enjoying the companionship of the most glamorous woman he had ever known. They swam together, went horseback riding together, they shot skeet together, played tennis, enjoyed films together, dined and danced together—and he could hardly believe that it was happening. Sometimes he really did think of pinching himself.

Pinching is not enough, he thought one day. Perhaps I should shoot off a toe—or something even more drastic.

Surely, while he was not paying attention some Valkyries had carried him off to Valhalla. This is R&R writ large, Clark thought. This was beyond the lost horizon. This was Shangri La. Nothing else in the world, he thought, could hold a light to this. He was rising up, arching, and gracefully sailing over the zenith, the high water mark, of love and joy and adventure in his life. And it was all so effortless. It was all so natural. He was thoroughly convinced that no memory in his life—not if he lived to be one hundred and ten—could ever be so sweet, so blissful, so fulfilling as this, his stay at Les Trungs. He was completely happy. He had it all. His life was as full and as complete as it could be.

Clark found that at Les Trungs they had a nice collection of films by Fellini, Bergman, and Truffaut. Also, one of the little things that he enjoyed discovering while spending time at Les Trungs, which for some odd reason he would recall for many years, was that the French seemed to have a great deal more appreciation for the American writer Edgar Allen Poe than the Americans did. While visiting at the Frenchman's plantation Clark had enjoyed several first-rate films based on the works of Poe. He recalled that in America the works of Poe seemed to always end up being represented by B-grade movies in which the story line usually did not much reflect the original work.

On the second night at Les Trungs, at the proper time, he had found his way down the hallway to Genevieve's room. The billowing gossamer wings that greeted him, the gauzy, delicate, dim, but fresh and shimmering character of the room was in harmony with the nature of the woman who lived in it. Her nest, her room was of another world—and it welcomed Clark with open arms.

"Come home, sailor—home from the sea," it said to him. "Come home, warrior—home from the boundless jungle." "Come home, Top Tiger—home to *Les Delices*, and the infinite delights of Les Trungs, the wondrous watering hole of War Zone C."

My Dulcinea, thought Clark, if you are in reality the spider woman, then I go gladly into the pit. I am happily entangled, entrapped in your web. I wear the webs that you spin like laurel wreaths about my head. Yes, my fair Dulcinea, I am gratified—I am elated to do combat with the giant windmills of this world—the honeycombed rotor blades and windmills of

War Zone C—for your smile and the warmth of your embrace is my refuge. Paradise exudes from your presence—your open arms.

When Clark considered the force, the seismic magnitude of the physical attraction between the two of them, he absolutely marveled. When they were re-united after being apart for awhile, they virtually collided like two planets in space. They merged in a fiery explosion of love and passion. They crashed together as if they were embarked on a desperate quest to vanquish a frenetic ravishing hunger, some strange and unique condition that certainly no other lovers in the history of the world had ever known or had to contend with. He had heard a great deal about drug addiction, but he remained completely convinced that no drug could ever be more stimulating, or have a more powerful effect than the nectar of her love.

In his dreams one night at Les Trungs, he found himself flying low over the nighttime jungle canopy. The moonlit canopy spread before him like an endless pale blue undulating desert. He could then make out some sort of dark barrier ahead, an obstacle. It was the Cao Dai Temple with the Giant Eye glaring directly at him. They flew ever closer. They were going to crash into the temple. They could not turn away. The controls did not respond. They were under the spell of the all-seeing eye. They flew straight into the retina of the Giant Eye. But there was no crash, no bone-jarring collision—no explosion.

He sensed that he was falling or descending on a great invisible slide. The smooth slick slide was not metallic—it was soft plastic or leather—or skin—human skin. Yes, it was the skin of a Titan.

Then, suddenly, he found himself in a quiet, dark place. He was alone in a large dark space. It was a dungeon. It was a slimy, dripping, hollow, echoing, rat-infested dungeon. It was the Bastille, he decided. Yes, it was the lower depths of the infamous Bastille, the mighty bastion with walls that were thirty feet thick. And he was chained to a wall—a prisoner of darkness, of desire, of passion—a slave of love.

"Don't forget what you were sent over here for," the 68th Buddha said.

Clark had become addicted to love. Someone said he had gotten carried away. Too much ambrosia, someone said. Was it all too much for him? Had he lost his balance? He was out of touch with Watauga, the land of the honeysuckle and turnip greens. He was cut off—excommunicated—from the honeysuckle and the kudzu.

Had he lost all interest in being an army officer—that which his father had never been? At first he had so loved the uniform and cherished the idea of being commissioned to serve "at the pleasure of the president." The words honor, duty, and country had seemed ever so potent to him. And early on becoming a pilot had great appeal to Clark. Yes, to be a pilot—to be licensed to operate an aircraft, to be a *pilot,* a helmsman, a guide, one who leads, seeks, finds the way, and directs the course. To be someone who points the way. Yes, this meant a great deal to him. And now had the pilot lost his rudder, his direction, his compass, his giros, his ballast, and his balance?

Someone was pushing a dim lantern into his face. Who was it? Who carried the lantern? It was Diogenes, the Cynic. Yes, it was dirty old Diogenes the original homeless mensch and street person. He lived in a barrel in the middle of Athens, and always carried a lantern, always on the lookout for an honest man. Diogenes was accompanied by two others, no, three others. They were Aristotle, Voltaire, and Virginia Woolf.

A distinguished cast of characters, indeed, I must say, Clark thought.

"There," observed old Diogenes, "There! He stirs."

"Look!" cried Aristotle. "He is becoming whole now. He has been a slow one, but now he is catching on. He has branched out and discovered his other part. Yes, some would even call this—his other part—his better half."

"You are recalled to life, my boy. Yes, it is time for you to be recalled to life," Diogenes said.

"Actually, one could say that it is time for his *call* to life, for he has never really been alive before. He has merely been going through the motions," Virginia Woolf declared.

Aristotle had just finished explaining his theory that when the gods created the great race of Titans these giants were found to be too powerful, too arrogant, too god-like. So the gods divided them into two parts. They called one part the male, and the other the female. This arrangement weakened the Titans considerably—especially after Pandora, the first woman, opened her box and released all the troubles of the world. But the gods no longer felt threatened. And these two different parts of the Titans were condemned to be seekers—be forever in search of one another in order to become more complete, more perfect, to become whole. Life was a quest. They were forever in search of that missing element. Just as Clark sought Genevieve and she sought him. Apart they were simply incomplete. They ached and burned to be reunited. Apart they were nothing. Together they were everything. The hidden power of love brought them together.

"*Oui, oui,* he stirs!" said Voltaire. "He has discovered the fair Genevieve, the glass-slippered maiden, the patron saint of the City of Light. She bridges his Hellespont. Now he can cross over."

"Oh, yes!" exclaimed Virginia Woolf with sad seaweed hanging in her hair. "Yes, and what God hath joined together, let no man put asunder. And now to the lighthouse with him! To the *lighthouse*! Darkness is destructive. Light begets life. And life begets life. Don't tarry, young man. You have an important mission to fulfill. Yes, much more than just blowing smoke rings and trying to deceive the denizens of the jungle. You, *you* are destined to be fruitful and multiply. So, now, out! Out of the darkness. Yes, out here where the air is light and you can breathe. Breathe and move on—on to the lighthouse! Follow the light. We shall meet you on the Dover Road. Move toward the light. Be gone, young man, go forth and be a man! Fulfill your destiny. Follow the light! Be a man, and be gone! Be gone!"

Winston Clark hurried down the winding path to the lighthouse and there he found the girl with the honey-colored hair awaiting him. He found Genevieve, the stalwart girl who had saved Paris from the Huns—and she found him. And together they happily found themselves much more complete, more whole—nothing was missing and nothing was amiss. It was all there. But still, they retained a great hunger for one another. But that mutual hunger was a gift. It was famishing, but stimulating and exhilarating. It was always there to relish. It brought them together as one. And it was eternal. It could be relied upon. It accomplished wonders. It made one feel as light as air.

— — —

From out of the rice paddy the GIs clambered aboard the helicopter. Wet and muddy. Exhausted. Desperate. These young men were drained. Depleted. And now they had webbed-feet. Water flowed across the metal floor of the aircraft underneath their afflicted feet. They had been in the water so long that now they had webbed-feet. When they looked up at him their eyes asked him, "What are we going to do with these feet? People back in the world don't have webbed-feet. No one would understand. We'll be different when we get back. We won't be the same. No. We'll never be the same." He pulled the lever and the helicopter ascended out of and moved away from the rice paddies. "Hang on, guys," he said. "Hang on. And we'll fly you out of here. We'll lift you up to the light. We'll hold you up to the light. Follow the light, fellows. Always follow the light. We'll hold you up to the light. We'll dry you out. There's the sun. We're moving now. Moving toward the light—into the healing sunlight. Hang on, guys. Hang on. Look! There's the sun!"

— — —

"Move toward the light," Virginia Woolf said with the sad seaweed in her hair. "Move toward the light. Move, move, move...."

Genevieve, the girl who had defied Attila and saved Paris, was his beacon. Her light quickly vanquished the darkness—the darkness that concealed death, decay, and destruction. With her hand in his, they stepped out of the shadows, out of the lighthouse, out of the darkness, and into the warm, purifying sunlight.

"There's the sun," someone said.

Clark awoke from the dream with bright sunlight in his eyes. And then the girl with the honey-colored hair leaned forward and was in his arms. A golden haze of passionate intensity settled over them. In the most delicate and exquisite of canoes (it was fashioned from porcelain) they drifted down a vaporous river of placid bliss. They dipped into a bottomless spring of love and desire. Silently, effortlessly they dipped their paddles into the placid river. They dipped them again and again. Together they glided quietly onward through the balmy vapors toward the inexhaustible and abounding mysteries of love and life and the natural world. The river was boundless—endless. They had achieved a kind of universal atonement. They were at one with the river.

Clark had arrived. For his R&R he had traveled to Nirvana. He soared and his experience was untouchable.

Clark had now come to notice that Top Tiger crews were finding the time and opportunity to stop off at Les Trungs with increasing regularity. He was pleased, but puzzled. Again, he was pleased to see the men of his unit enjoying themselves, but—considering the intensity of their regular schedule—he was rather amazed that they could find such an abundance of opportunities to grab so many of these little abbreviated R&Rs.

Now, now, watch yourself, Clark, he thought. Don't get the notion that you can have it all to yourself. Don't be selfish. Voltaire Six said that Les Trungs is open to *all* of the Top Tigers—not just d'Artagnan.

Recently Clark had even heard a rumor that Sergeant Moses Merlins was considering leaving the army and going to work for Monsieur Voltaige in his kitchen. What next? Would he next be hearing that John Lang would become Paul Picair's copilot?

But, as far as he knew, Clark remained the only U.S. military man to get to spend his entire R&R leave there—a full seven days. Actually, he was starting to feel quite at home there. Sometimes he fantasized about living and working there permanently. Linville started to tease Clark about becoming the *burgermeister* of Les Trungs.

Mr. Hobbes, the Hobo Kid of Bien Hoa, had stopped off at the plantation several times recently. He tended to drink too much, talk too much, and now Clark heard a rumor that he had abused a couple of the girls, pushing them around and treating them roughly. Captain Torres, an adviser from Tay Ninh City, was seen at Les Trungs from time to time, and it was said that he had sternly advised Hobbes to "Back off and lighten up."

"Cool it, young man," Captain Torres said, "or you might find yourself in a world of hurt."

Now it was said that Hobbes harbored a great resentment for Torres. Hobbes was heard referring to Torres as, "That Dago captain."

One day Linville turned up with the crew, and they managed to spend an entire day together with Clark and the girls. Clark noticed that Collins was getting quite attached to Lee Ann. And then he heard that they might even be planning to get married. An air of foreboding came over Clark when he heard that. He was not sure why, but he had an intuitive feeling that they might be in for a hard time. There was plenty to get in the way of love and marriage in Vietnam. There was the war, the drastically different cultures, the bureaucracy, and—most of all—the mission. When they were busy flying 12 to 15 hours a day, six—sometimes seven—days a week, where would one find the time to do the paperwork and make the arrangements to get married?

Finally, it was the day before Clark was schedule to end his little vacation and get back to duty, when Alan Clayton showed up at Les Trungs just before sundown—and he was not alone. Two other men accompanied him.

One of the men was Captain Torres, the adviser. Torres was the officer that Linville had described as the "lone eagle type," because he seemed to travel all over the province alone. He might be seen quietly talking with the Vietnamese officers anywhere and anytime in Tay Ninh Province. The Vietnamese always seemed to show him a special deference.

The other man with Clayton appeared to be about forty years of age, tall, strongly built, and distinguished. He was wearing the usual civilian khaki safari-type uniform, and definitely possessed a military bearing.

When Genevieve saw the three men walking up the hill toward the patio and pool, she seemed to suddenly grow tense. She mumbled something like, "Uh oh." A strange feeling of uneasiness came over Clark.

"What is it?" he asked her.

"Oh, nothing. It is nothing," she answered. "It is okay—okay. No, really. I will talk with you later."

After greeting Monsieur Voltaige and the girls, Alan Clayton looked toward Clark and shouted a friendly greeting.

"Winston," he said, "Come here, come on over here. Right now, my boy. I've got someone I want to introduce. Come here, son. Do you know who this is?"

Clark shook his head slowly, thinking that perhaps the stranger did look remotely familiar. He searched his mind but could not place the distinguished face.

"No," Clark said slowly. "No, I'm afraid not. Should I know him?"

"Why, yes, my boy," Clayton gushed. "This gentleman is from Old Catawba, just as you are—and I am. Winston, this is my brother Curtis. Curtis, this is Winston Clark. Now, Curt, I'm sure you remember Winston's father, Wendel Clark, the school principal. I'm sure you remember all of his family."

Curtis Clayton was Alan Clayton's younger brother, the one who had been a highly decorated hero in the Korean War. Curtis Clayton looked thoughtfully at Winston Clark and then spoke.

"Oh, yes," he said, "I remember them well. Good people." Curtis Clayton looked Clark over quickly but carefully and then seemed to be glancing past him and looking toward Genevieve. He appeared to be trying to catch her eye.

"I remember them well," he repeated. "And so, Winston, how are you, and what are you doing here in Vietnam—and here at Les Trungs?"

"I'm flying choppers," Clark answered.

"Flying choppers, you say? Oh, well, that sounds like an exciting business," said Clayton. "But as for right now, you really seem to be enjoying yourself. What kind of duty allows this sort of thing—poolside duty with all the beauty and charm and cultural amenities of the Continent right here at hand?"

Clark explained the arrangements for the unusual R&R.

Curtis Clayton stepped past Clark and took each of the girls—first Genevieve and then Monique—by the hand and gave them each a cordial greeting. Clark started to get the impression that Curtis Clayton had been there before, that he knew his way around. Apparently, Curtis Clayton had previously met Monsieur Voltaige and his daughters. Soon Clark discovered that was indeed the case. And now Clark thought that he detected a strange tenseness between Genevieve and Clayton.

Clark found an opportunity to speak with Alan Clayton about his brother.

"What's Curtis doing here in Nam?" Clark asked the elder Clayton.

"He's with the State Department. He is a Foreign Service Officer," Alan Clayton answered, "and it seems that he really gets around. He knows this area quite well."

Clark was never able to get any more specific information about exactly what Curtis Clayton did in his Foreign Service job. To Clark, this man seemed quite patronizing, and he never did feel at ease with him. Clark never had a proper conversation with Curtis Clayton. The tension grew palpable between the two of them.

They all had a nice evening around the pool and then an unusually fine dinner in the formal dining room. Monsieur Voltaige said that a special meal had been prepared in honor of Captain Clark and the final night of his splendid visit. But also, he was quick to add that they at Les Trungs were proud and pleased to be able to "welcome and honor Curtis Clayton, the dear brother of their cherished friend, Alan Clayton."

As usual at Les Trungs, they enjoyed live music in the evening after the meal. There was some dancing. Clark enjoyed a few slow cheek-to-cheek dances with Genevieve. But at one point, Curtis Clayton had danced with Genevieve and that feeling of anxiety and apprehension settled over them again. Curtis Clayton displayed an unusually serious demeanor while he danced with Genevieve—and she appeared reluctant to look directly at him—Clayton—when he conversed with her.

As the evening progressed Monsieur Voltaige opened some of his finest bottles of wine, and everyone seemed—on the surface, at least—quite cozy. Table talk flowed freely and the little Frenchman seemed more loquacious than ever. Somehow, the topic of American politics arose, and Monsieur Voltaige seemed to quickly warm to the subject.

"Ah, now, American politicians," he said. "They are a marvelous race of rodents. A great clumsy, storming, charging, yammering herd of little piranha—no, a herd of little fat men wearing cowboy boots—high heeled boots, mind you. These little men in snakeskin boots—the very embodiment of the grotesque! And in big hats, they run against the government, *against* their very own government, the system they built block by devious block—a system they love, they absolutely adore. Yes, they built it block by vile block. And it is a system they worship—a system they are delighted to be a part of. Oh, but they are brilliant! Ah, yes, that is for the whole world to see. They run against the government—a government they carry in their pockets—and they win time and again. There is no other place on the face of the earth they would rather be than right there, precisely in the middle of it, right there on Pennsylvania Avenue, right there in old 'Foggy Bottom,' 'where the action is,' as they say. Yes, it was for political purposes that this dirty little war was initially escalated. Yes, excessive greed and ambition fanned the flames. And now, still today, this war is played every day like a political piano. Every major move out here has a great deal to do with someone very high up back there in Vanity City getting re-elected. Yes, for someone back there—back there in Vanity City, the capital, the heartland of the homespun honeybears—it must be supported at all costs.

And since the assassinations, you have a tiger by the tail, *n'est-ce pas?* And now all of the slime, the dirt, and the blood—it is on your hands, and that is not very agreeable, not very pleasant is it? No, I fear—no, not at all.

"Yes, this is an old story," Monsieur Voltaige said in a lower tone, almost as though he were speaking to himself. "The misuse of power is so often responsible for oppression and war.

"It has been written," said Monsieur Voltaige after a brief pause, "that the Emperor Caligula, after planning to invade ancient Britain, stopped his army at the coastline of the North Sea. There he decided against his campaign, and suddenly abandoned his plans of conquest. Rather than ordering his cohorts to go and fight in Britain, there on the seashore he ordered his soldiers to pick up seashells instead. People started to think of him as mad. But now, in retrospect, perhaps that was not such a nonsensical decision—picking up seashells on the seashore.

"Yes, Vanity City is alluring, seductive, and captivating," Monsieur Voltaige continued. "And some of them—these congressmen—they remain there until they are a hundred years old and tottering about with nurses on each arm to give them balance. Balance! Ah, now there is a good word. That is just what they need—balance, more balance. The Greeks called it the 'golden mean.' Yes, but with excessive greed, balance is always lost. That is what we all need—balance. When we lose it, then we fall. And nothing can save us. We go over the edge not to rise again. They speak of a war on poverty, a war on drugs, but what about greed? Why not—for just once—make war on greed? And what would be the reaction to that bright idea? I fear there would be a great rush for a great many to suddenly start to do their banking in Switzerland.

"Ah, but these purveyors of snake oil in snakeskin boots, fat little rodents in high-heeled boots, there are no men like them on the face of the earth, and certainly no men half so clever—not exactly wise, mind you, but clever, oh, so clever. Their greed and ambition know no bounds. Even the seediest of them can readily visualize himself one day following in the footsteps of Lincoln or the Roosevelts. They are dwarves, and they would dare to speak of the legacy of Lincoln! Their arrogance is absolutely breathtaking! They are endowed with unlimited vision—yes, narcissistic visions of power, grandeur, and greed—without limits. They get terribly puffed up, but it is never enough. And that unbounded greed, you see, that makes it all possible. 'Think big,' they say.

"They are, I tell you," Monsieur Voltaige continued, "a marvelous race of rodents. They become swollen and puffy and corrupt. But their little teeth remain razor sharp—always razor sharp and ready for their prey, the soup *du jour*, a magnificent bill of fare, the soft underbelly of America—no, of the world! And with those sharp teeth they gnaw at the electrical lines of the universe, time, life, and matter—yes, the entire cosmos—and they create a great time warp of wealth and sweet opulence. These men live like kings! Yes, these homespun, down-home, so-called 'good ol' boys' are living like kings in velvet slippers. It is all too much, but they never lose their taste for it. They are the princes of…What do you call it? Payola? Oh, yes, that is a beautiful term—payola. It sounds like something sweet and healthy—something fun and life sustaining. Yes, that is it! They are the Pharaohs of the Potomac, the Princes of Payola, and the Dukes of Deceit, and the Harlots of Babylon, all rolled together in one—or rather two—chambers. They are unique, and they are brilliant, I tell you. There has never been anyone like them before in the history of the world. These men have assiduously brought political and corporate corruption to unprecedented levels. They are like cockroaches and spiders. They never die. An earthquake would not touch them. They can never be exterminated. They remain there, always prepared to absorb all the life they find within their grasp. They look and sound like harmless country fellows, like hayseeds. But in reality they are brilliant—brilliant seducers. I tell you there has never been anyone half so clever in the history of the world as these simple peddlers of snake oil. They are brilliant! Absolutely brilliant, *n'est-ce pas?*"

There was an awkward silence around the table. Curtis Clayton gazed at the little Frenchman, and his facial expression seemed to convey a clear hint of disdain and disapproval.

"Well, well," said Alan Clayton, "What can I say? Yes, politics can be vexatious."

Just after midnight Clark and Genevieve were able to be alone again together in her room. Outside the open window the rain fell softly and steadily.

"So what's going on with this guy, Clayton—Curtis Clayton?" Clark asked.

Genevieve took his hands softly in hers.

"Nothing," she said. "Nothing is going on. I have met this man before, and he seemed nice, and…well, for some reason, I think he likes me…and…"

"And what?"

"And nothing," she answered with a slight hint of frustration. "It was simply just like that, as I told you. We met and we enjoyed being together for awhile, and then…well, and then you came along. You came along in your helicopter and everything changed."

Clark gave her a long searching stare. An air of uncertainty and doubt hung heavily over the quiet, gauzy room. Outside the falling rain made a steadfast, almost hypnotic sound on the rooftop of the fortress-like chateau.

"Yes. And then you came along," she continued, "And blinded me to everything and everyone else. When I first saw you it was like looking directly at the sun. I could see nothing else. It is that way still. You are like the sun in my eyes. I see only you. You have changed my life. My life will never be the same."

They kissed and she continued to endeavor to reassure him. His doubtful gaze deeply disturbed her.

"Don't worry about that man," she said forcefully. "No. Do not worry about Curtis. He will go away soon, I am sure. I am certain of it. He will not trouble you. He will not trouble us."

Again and again they kissed. Regardless of what red warning lights might be flashing before his wary face, his love and desire for her was insatiable. When they touched they became light as air. Again, they embarked on that vapory river of placid bliss in that delicate canoe—a canoe carved from ivory. It was, he thought, a river of no return. And that idea was pleasing to him. It could be no other way with the girl of the Champs Élysées. If she touched a man, if she kissed a man, then for that man there was no return—no going back to things as they had been before.

Genevieve talked with Clark about leaving the army. She spoke of it in such a casual way and yet with increasing intensity.

"Can you not simply leave and come here and stay with us? Can you not simply inform them that you no longer wish to fly their helicopters for them?" she asked. "There are others, I am sure, who can fly the helicopters for them."

"No. It's not that simple," he explained. "I have a contract with the army. It's a serious, unbreakable contract. I love being with you, you know that—God knows you must know that. But I cannot break my contract—I could not desert the army. That would be a disgrace—a disgrace that I would never live down."

Genevieve honestly did not seem to understand. They were two people in love and should be together, she said. And that was all that mattered. Who could deny them their love and fulfillment—their happiness?

"Your commander, Major Compton, he seems like a nice man. Go to him," she said.

Clark repeated that he loved her dearly but he could not desert the army. He would do all in his power, he said, to re-unite them as soon as possible. But she had to understand that he could not—at this time—leave the army.

He thought of *A Farewell to Arms*, the story by Ernest Hemingway about a man who falls in love in Italy and casually leaves the army. But that was different. That was a long time ago, in a different army—and a different world. Yes, that was long ago and far away in time and space. And that was just a story—fiction. Hemingway was from the Land of Lincoln, and he would never do anything like that in real life. And this was real life, even though he did sometimes feel that he had entered the Valley of the Blue Moon and Shangri La. This was War Zone C in South Vietnam. And he was a Top Tiger. Nui Ba Den was right over there about fifteen miles away, and the VC were there now in their caves and tunnels sharpening their *punji* sticks (sharpened bamboo stakes, spikes, and spears) and making deadly booby traps. There was a real war going on and he had contracted to play a part in it. He had gone to flight school. Yes, even after what seemed like twenty EKGs (electrocardiograms) he was accepted. And he had gone to flight school knowing full well that he would fly in Vietnam. The doctor had said something about an unusual heart rhythm or murmur. But Clark looked healthy and strong, and the doctor also said something about the army needing helicopter pilots at that time. So Clark was admitted to the program. It was to be flight school and then lots of "OJT" (on-the-job-training) in South Vietnam.

How could anyone ever seriously consider deserting the army? Clark asked himself in the dark as the monsoon rains continued to fall just outside his bedroom window. How could he ever face his mother again, or his sister, or the memory of his father? How could he ever face anyone back in Old Catawba again after doing such a thing? After all, he had grown up in the shadow of the Doughboy statue at the head of Cherry Street. That doughboy stood like a rock, a stone icon at the very heart of his core. The exalted spirit of that statue was in the very essence of his being. It was a major part of who he was.

"I'll meet you down by the Doughboy," the kids all said when he was in high school.

What about the Rotarians, the Lions, the Elks, and most of all, the American Legionaries? Those men—all friends of his father's—were like uncles to him. They had helped raise him. They had counseled him, supported him, and cheered him on. They had helped to form him. They had helped in the formation of his values, to model his character, and structure his soul. His shame was their shame. How would they feel about Winston Clark as a deserter, a deserter in a combat zone, a deserter "in the face of the enemy," as the phrase went? His name would be erased from the collective memory of Watauga. No. This was real life. And one might just as well be dead rather than disgrace the family name and become a ghost, a leper, and a living symbol of shame, the very embodiment of dishonor.

Clark thought of Kipling's poem, *Boots.*

Boots, boots, boots,
Moving up and down again.
There's no discharge
In the war.

Early the next day Genevieve led him to the family chapel. Together they knelt at the altar, and she prayed for him and lit a candle for him.

"For your safety," she said as she firmly placed the small candle near the feet of a small image of Saint Mary.

"For your safety and for the angel that will hover over you and bring you safely back to me. I want to have a child with you. We shall have a boy, a son," she said.

After breakfast a pair of helicopters zoomed in to pick up Clark and fly him back to the Bien Hoa Airbase. Linville and Plummer were at the controls of one of the choppers and Major Ratcliffe and Mr. Gibson flew the other aircraft, the gunship. All four of the officers came up to the patio area to greet Monsieur Voltaige and his daughters. The Frenchman also introduced them to Curtis Clayton, who was standing nearby. For some reason Clark got the impression that Major Ratcliffe and Curtis Clayton established a quick rapport. The relaxed and obvious empathy there easily gave one the impression that these two men had met before.

"Kindred spirits, perhaps," thought Clark.

At one point, Clark walked past Curtis Clayton on the patio, almost brushing against him as he passed between the chairs. Clayton gazed up pensively at Clark and then, rather whimsically, he said:

"I really don't know about this helicopter business. A friend of mine recently said to me that all these helicopter pilots do around here is get shot down with monotonous regularity."

Clark smiled and walked on, saying nothing.

Winston Clark's R&R was over now. His sojourn in paradise was a memory now. He said goodbye to Genevieve on the patio near the pool.

He kissed her hands. Lady fingers, he mused as he looked at her hands. Finely formed, exquisite lady fingers. Perfection, he thought. These are the kind of fingers that bring succor and bliss to a man's life. These fingers were formed to reach out and offer golden apples and goblets of ambrosia and love to a valiant prince.

"D'Artagnan," she said, "you are my gallant cavalier, my prince. God bless and keep you. Come back to me soon."

"Soon," she said.

"Dulcinea," he said, "lovely Dulcinea, stay just as you are."

She waved as he walked off toward the awaiting helicopter with the golden tiger head painted on the nose box. And her warm magic followed him.

Chapaer 23

Secret Places

I lived like a king, Winston Clark thought to himself. It was only for a short period of time. But at least I have that, my R&R in Shangri La—no, in War Zone C. I have lived like a king—at least this once. And that cannot be taken from me. It's mine forever.

Clark was quickly absorbed back into the daily grind of the combat aviation support provided by the 68th Assault Helicopter Company. The American units—the 25th Infantry Division stationed near Cu Chi, and the 1st Infantry division stationed near Phu Loi—seemed to be unceasingly harassed by Viet Cong hidden away in the tunnels in that area, just northwest of Saigon. The Top Tigers were engaged in an endless cycle of combat assaults and ash and trash missions with those troops in the III Corps area.

"We do it every day," one of the Mustang gunship pilots said in a rather dejected manner one evening at the bar. "We shoot and get shot at every day—and in the same areas. It can get on your nerves, you know, after a while. They say we have pacified an area—and then Charlie resurfaces. Then we do it all over again a month or so later. It's an awful lot like going around in circles. Yeah, and you know what I mean? It really gets old."

The company stayed completely occupied with flying, maintaining aircraft and weapons systems, and more flying. Up at dawn, and coming in hungry and dirty at dusk—and sometimes much later. Clark wondered if he ever would be able to communicate with Genevieve—much less see her and touch her again.

Robby Collins, the door gunner, had a pet monkey now. Collins was often the last to finish his chores in the evenings. He had to clean the machine guns. He also expressed concern that he might never see Lee Ann again. One Saturday night Collins got terribly drunk, climbed into his bunk, tucked himself—and his pet monkey, "Dinky"—in with his mosquito netting, and fell into a deep sleep. He slept like a rock on his back, hardly moving, all night.

The next morning Collins awoke to find himself covered with monkey feces. It was an awful mess, and he appeared to be smeared from head to toe. Someone said the monkey had also been eating chips and smoking and drinking with Collins the night before and may have become rather sick.

Collins flew into a rage when he awoke that morning. He tore his way up and out and from under the mosquito netting at the same time reaching for poor confused Dinky as though he intended to throttle him. Next Collins was chasing Dinky between the barracks and then down the road toward the main gate to the compound. Collins looked awful. He was dressed only in dirty stained GI under shorts. His thin body was half plastered with muck and dung. His dog tags hung around his scrawny neck like a great chain weight. He also had one of those little P-38 C-ration can openers on a dirty string hanging around his neck. And he had murder in his blurry red eyes. Dinky scampered screaming and squealing through the compound gate and into the palm and breadfruit trees, never to be seen again by any of the Top Tigers. (The Vietnamese term for "crazy" is *dien tai dau*, roughly pronounced "dinky-dow.") For days after that episode with his monkey, Dinky, Collins seemed depressed.

About that time, Captain Clark was promoted to "aircraft commander." He had sufficient experience now, so from now on he would be mostly flying in the left seat—the "AC" (aircraft commander) seat. Mr. Linville would be moving on to another aircraft, another crew, and another new copilot—Mr. Plummer. Captain Clark's new copilot was Mr. Bauer.

Bill Bauer was from Tennessee, and Clark took an instant liking to him. Bauer was a quiet man. But when he spoke, he had something meaningful to say. He had been a sergeant in the Marines, in logistics, but got out of the Marines in order to enter the army helicopter program. Most people found him to be reticent, but absolutely "mission ready," focused and reliable. He was a good man to have around under any circumstances, and Clark welcomed Bauer as his new roommate. Captain Clark felt good flying with Mr. Bauer. Clark himself felt confident and mission ready. "Prepared for whatever comes down the pike," as he commented to Mr. Linville.

Just after Clark had completed his R&R and departed Les Trungs to return to duty, Curtis Clayton had a private—and rather tense—conversation with his older brother, Alan, there at the plantation. And the primary topic was the character and fate of their host, Monsieur Voltaige.

"The guy's anti-American," Curtis said to Alan. "He stinks. He smells like a Red to me. Did you hear what he had to say about our political system?"

"Yes, I heard what he said," Alan answered. "But listen, you know you don't have to take everything he says too seriously. He was just clowning around. The guy's philosophical. He likes to talk. And, you know one might even find a pearl of truth in some of what he said. I found it all pretty witty, myself."

"Well, maybe you have been out here hanging around with him and his bunch a little too long," Curtis said. "I think it's affecting you—the climate out here is getting under your skin. I think it's time for you to go home. Perhaps you need a change.

"He calls our people seducers," Curtis continued. "And look at him with all these half-naked Chinese women running around here. The next thing you know these GIs will be deserting to hang out at this plantation. Voltaige is the seducer. He's really one to be calling anyone else a seducer."

"Ah, come on. Don't get carried away," Alan said. "Now come on. Tell me about you and what you've been doing. What have you been up to lately? What have you doing with yourself?"

"Well, actually," said Curtis thoughtfully, "I was just about to get to that. Did you ever hear of Operation Phoenix?"

"Phoenix? Yes, I certainly have," Alan answered. "I think everyone has heard about Operation Phoenix. Say, are you working with the company, the agency?"

"This business is all Top Secret, you know?" Curtis said slowly, his voice just above a whisper. "But yes, I am with the agency now. And anything I tell you now—or at any other time—is strictly just between the two of us. You got that? That's important. It's vital. I hope you understand."

Alan Clayton gave his younger brother a long cold stare, and then he slowly spoke. He seemed to be choosing his words more carefully now.

"Yes, I understand. This Phoenix business, it's all about assassinations, isn't it—death squads and that sort of stuff, something like Murder Incorporated, isn't it?"

"Operation Phoenix is a special program intended to destroy the communist infrastructure in South Vietnam. That's what it is. No infrastructure, no Viet Cong," said Curtis Clayton.

"That could get mighty complicated—and nasty. Yes, this sounds like it might be a very dirty business to me."

"It can be," Curtis responded, "but it's a necessary business. And it is clearly becoming more effective everyday."

"Are you playing a role here—locally?" Alan asked. "You personally, what's your area of responsibility?"

"I am not at liberty to get any too specific with you," said Curtis. "But I am here to inform you," Curtis Clayton paused here for a moment before continuing. "I am here to inform you that this guy Voltaige is bad news—and he has got to go."

"What?" Alan Clayton exclaimed. "Are you crazy? Listen, I don't think you understand just who it is we are talking about here. This man—Monsieur Marcel Voltaige—has got pull—big time. He's got influence far and wide—all the way up to ambassadorial circles. He's an international figure. Really, a man of stature. I strongly suggest that you think twice about what you are saying here."

"And I don't think *you* understand," said Curtis. "Do you think I'm a fool? I don't discuss these matters casually. I've been thoroughly informed about this guy. I probably know a lot more about him than you do. He is cooperating with the enemy. He is actively supporting the enemy. His plantation is a hot bed of communist activity. We are sitting on a powder keg here. Voltaige is betting everything on the communists winning this little war. And he wants to carry on with business as usual. This guy has always lived like a king, and he plans to keep things that way no matter what—no matter who is in charge. Voltaige is on our list, I tell you. He is on our *list*. He has to go. Yes, go with 'extreme prejudice,' as they say. It might be a good idea for you and I—right now—to start thinking about his daughters. We might try to protect them, if we can. Perhaps get them out of here. I think that would be the best course of action."

Alan Clayton was pale and rather sick looking as he spoke. He had grown rather close to the Frenchman. He truly liked him. Again, Clayton spoke in a careful, measured tone.

"Personally," he said, "I don't like this business at all. And I don't want to have anything to do with it. I still believe that you should double check to make sure this—this what you are about to get into—is proper. That it's approved at the highest levels of government, and the proper course of action. I would certainly question this as being the proper course of action. We should do nothing precipitously out here. This could have wide ramifications. Yes, very wide indeed. I don't know who is behind all this, but it is bad business, I tell you. And someone should do some rethinking, some reconsidering."

"The matter has been thoroughly thought through—considered and reconsidered. And I understand my responsibilities," Curtis Clayton curtly replied. "On that you can rely."

"Well, I think you should watch yourself. That's my recommendation. And I'm serious," said Alan Clayton.

Curtis Clayton smiled slowly and then spoke.

"Nietzsche said that we should live dangerously. 'Erect your cities beside Vesuvius,' he said. 'The only truly free and complete man is the warrior,' he said."

Alan Clayton shook his head, looked down and away, and said no more.

It was about that time that Wesley Hobbes, the Bien Hoa hobo-gunslinger, disappeared. He and his crew spent the day at Les Trungs. And then when it was time to depart, around 6 p.m., his copilot could not find him anywhere, and finally, was forced to fly back to the airbase without him. Hobbes was reported MIA (missing in action). The next day an ARVN battalion carefully searched the wooded area surrounding Les Trungs. But Mr. Hobbes was never found.

Prior to Hobbes' disappearance, Lee Ann had complained to Becky that the aggressive American pilot was trying to force himself on her. Lee Ann was Collins' girlfriend. They planned to be married. And she thought that everyone was aware of that and respected the arrangement—but not Hobo Hobbes. He was an unusually irreverent and disrespectful person.

After Lee Ann complained, her fellow beekeeper, Becky, started to get a determined and rather sinister gleam in her eyes.

"Come," said Becky while reaching out to take Lee Ann's hand. "We shall mend this situation. This is not acceptable. He is only a little man. Come."

Becky, with Lee Ann, went directly to Hobbes. The pilot had been drinking beer—much more beer than he should have consumed before starting to fly again.

"Come," Becky said to Hobbes, reaching out to him. "You, come now with us. We have something for you. Yes, we have something very special for you. Something *very* special."

Becky, with Hobbes and Lee Ann in tow, led them through the kitchen and then down into the wine cellar.

"Oh, this looks like a nice place to spend some time," Hobbes said. "Yeah, I can handle this, I'm sure. This looks interesting. Yeah, what have we got here?"

Becky hesitated a moment, and then put her finger to her lips as if to warn the others to be quiet. Then the thin young woman dressed in black moved forward. She went to the farthermost corner of the wine cellar, looked at Hobbes with a special expression as if to say, "Now just wait until you see this. This is truly special."

Becky moved several boxes of empty wine bottles, then lifted a large canvass flap, and opened a small door in the back wall of the room. It was just large enough for the average person to enter if they were carefully bent over. Almost magically, Becky had revealed to Hobbes the entrance to a long, dimly lit tunnel. Before Hobbes could really react to this revelation, two young Vietnamese men quietly stepped out of hidden recesses in the wine cellar and grabbed him from behind. They struck Hobbes repeatedly with a pistol and a small black silk bag (which appeared to be filled with sand) several times on the back of his head. They then dragged him into the dark hole that marked the entrance to the hidden tunnel.

Hobbes was gagged, blindfolded, bound, and dragged down the tunnel. It seemed like he was dragged for quite some time and distance. Wesley Hobbes was a cruel and bitter man, and he was about to meet a cruel and bitter fate.

Finally, they came to a small storage room. Most of the supplies and medications in that room were from France. There were also medicines stored there that had been donated by the Quakers in Pennsylvania. And then they entered a larger room. They were in a Viet Cong medical clinic and this was the operating room. When the adjoining rooms were considered, this clinic could accommodate about thirty patients. The operating room was neat, tidy, and clean under the circumstances. The walls were shored up with large bamboo supports and a parachute canopy was suspended just under the ceiling to protect the operating room from any falling clay.

They were now in the presence of Dr. Vo Hong Dien. He was a self-taught surgeon, and one of the most remarkable men in all of Vietnam. This man was not only a talented physician; when necessary, he was also the tactical combat commander of the Viet Cong forces in this region.

The two young guerrillas quickly brought Hobbes before the Vietnamese surgeon. Hobbes was on his knees. They briefly explained the situation to Dr. Dien.

"It is said that this American is an unusually cruel man. He has boasted of torturing our men, and he has offended and abused our women. What shall we do with him?"

It was quickly decided that Mr. Hobbes should be not be allowed to live. He would be executed. So, there by candlelight, still bound, gagged, blindfolded, and on his knees on the floor, Mr. Hobbes' throat was slashed. One of the young guerrillas wielded the knife. After Hobbes was dead, his body was surgically dismembered and buried piece-by-piece in the walls of the tunnel.

Dr. Dien's little hospital was equipped with an oxygen tank and a fairly effective ventilation system. Electrical power was a constant problem. They were able to construct crude generators from bicycle and motorbike parts. X-ray machines could only be found in the safe areas just across the Cambodian border. The VC surgeons wore gowns, but had no rubber gloves. Their instruments were sterilized in pressure cookers. Like their American counterparts, the VC surgeons worked to the point of exhaustion to save lives.

In the aftermath of Operation Cedar Falls, Dr. Dien performed more than eighty operations during a period of three days and nights. Dr. Dien routinely used honey from the plantation as an antiseptic. The beekeepers were very supportive. Dr. Dien was also one of the primary reasons that people were relatively healthy at the Les Trungs Rubber Plantation. He became probably the best known and most highly respected Vietnamese leader in the III Corps area.

Blood transfusions presented the tunnel surgeon with special problems. Blood could not be kept without refrigerators, which were indeed rare. Dr. Dien invented his own system. Often times he attempted to return to the patient his own blood. For example, if a soldier had a belly wound and was bleeding, but his intestines were not punctured, his blood was collected, filtered, put in a bottle, and returned to his arteries. All of the Viet Cong medical staff had their blood groups checked. They analyzed the blood type of the patients brought to them. Staff member often contributed their blood directly when the types matched. On a number of occasions, Dr. Dien had contributed his own blood directly to one of his patients.

Lee Ann expressed her appreciation to Becky for her help with the aggressive American. She spoke of how she would forever be indebted to Becky and would happily be her friend always. Lee Ann also spoke to Becky of her powerful feelings for Robby Collins, the young door gunner. She said that she hoped to be his wife, and perhaps even travel to America with him some day.

Then two days later Lee Ann disappeared.

Chapter 24

What Is a Man, Anyhow?

The Top Tigers were just preparing to leave Loc Ninh. They were finishing up a long day of combat assaults, and everyone was happy to be finished and going home—back to the airbase—back to showers, beer, pretzels, and popcorn. And then they heard there had been a midair collision.

The collision involved two helicopters from one of their sister units within the battalion. They had just completed their last combat assault of the day and were heading for home. The unit had a new company commander—a Major Atkins. The new CO had been heard to say that he was going to "tighten things up" in that outfit. It was also said that he boasted that his company would soon be known for flying the tightest formation in all of South Vietnam.

As Major Atkins' company was flying back from Loc Ninh toward Bien Hoa that day, through low hanging scud-clouds, he kept urging his pilots to tighten up the formation. He seemed unusually impatient and demanding that day. The new CO was on the controls. He was flying the lead ship—and then it happened. Apparently someone tried to get too close to the demanding new CO. The two aircraft crashed together in a huge explosion, a great fireball of flying parts and pieces. And—in a flash—two complete crews were gone forever.

Captain Clark never met Major Atkins. But Major Atkins had complimented Clark on his performance the week before that collision. One day Clark had been filling in for Captain Phillips, the assistant operations officer, as pilot aboard the smoke ship. Just as Clark had finished laying down the smoke screens, Major Atkins—on short final for the landing zone at that time—came on the radio and expressed his appreciation for the cover.

"Good show, Smokey," he had said. "You do good work."

It was just a few words. But it was a public comment, an open compliment in that almost the entire battalion—to include Colonel Perry, the battalion commander—was tuned in to that radio frequency and could hear it. And it was not often that anyone did that sort of thing. And Clark would long remember it.

Sometimes in life, little things really do seem rather important somehow, he later thought. Perhaps he would always remember it, because the man who said those words was dead before Clark could meet him, speak with him, and express his gratitude face-to-face.

The following week a pilot from another of their sister companies was landing near the Top Tiger operations office at Bien Hoa Airbase when, somehow, he crashed into the sandbagged revetment which was designed to provide some protection for the choppers during a mortar attack. One of the rotor blades hit the revetment and broke off, throwing the system out of balance. Then the other heavier rotor blade swung around low with great force, sliced through the cockpit and decapitated the pilot in the left seat. The other crewmembers somehow managed to get out of the aircraft safely. The huge rotor blade cut the cockpit open like a great sword attacking a tin can—a very large brownish-green army C-ration tin can.

Captain Clark had been in the company orderly room discussing some paper work with Major Scully when they heard the aircraft crash. There was a terrible ripping sound that seemed to never end. Large parts of the helicopter were flung great distances from the crash site. In a low voice, Major Scully calmly said: "Uh, oh, you know what that is."

This scene was so awful that Clark started trying to shut it out of his mind as soon as he saw it. It was the kind of terrible bloodletting that goes beyond conversation, discussion, and description. Just as one has a sacred obligation to relate some things about the dead, one also has a sacred obligation not to relate certain things. They are best omitted. As Clark's heart leaped out with compassion for this fatally injured man, he saw there were others about who would photograph this gruesome scene. Clark would always remember it as one of the most repulsive things he ever witnessed. There was a small circle of men standing around the body of the decapitated pilot taking photographs. The body was still sitting upright, strapped in, and seated in the left seat of the helicopter. The only consolation Clark could find in this unutterably horrible scene was the fact that none of those standing there taking photographs were from his company. Those ghouls were not Top Tigers.

Everyone agreed later on that it was a miracle that more people were not killed or injured. Both small and large pieces of helicopter flew hundreds of yards in every direction of the crash site.

They soon heard that the pilot killed, Mr. Porter, had been very tired that afternoon. Someone else said he seemed to be in a hurry. They never knew exactly what caused him to crash into the revetment. He was an experienced pilot.

There was hardly anyone in the barracks game room-bar that night. The lights in the barracks seemed unusually dim and it was quiet. By a dim light Clark read in the news that the great American boxer, Muhammad Ali, had refused to be drafted into the U.S. Army. "I ain't got no quarrel wit' 'dem Congs," he said. The monsoon rains beat down on the barracks rooftop relentlessly.

The following week Clark and Bauer were flying ash and trash out of Tay Ninh City when they found a chance for a break. They clearly had more than an hour of daylight left when they were released to return to their home base.

"Okay, guys," Captain Clark said, "How about we make a quick stop by Les Trungs, the rubber plantation—the Frenchies' place?"

Collins was the first to speak.

"Hey, hey, man," he said, "sounds great to me. Groovy, man. Let's do it! Steer it on in there, cool captain. You are cleared to land."

"That's where it's at, man," said Sergeant Dotson, "You knows 'da place. It's all dahre' at Les *Chicks*—I mean Les Trungs. Come on, now, girls, get 'dem steamy towels ready. 'Cause here we come! Woo-wee!"

Clark looked over at his cool and concise copilot. Bill Bauer shrugged his shoulders.

"Might as well, I suppose," said Bauer with a friendly smile. Bauer had heard quite a bit about Les Trungs, but he had not previously had the pleasure of visiting the Frenchman's place.

"Well, okay," said Clark. "I believe the man said we are cleared to land. So, let's do it!"

As Clark turned to line up on the plantation runway for final approach he could hear the Righteous Brothers singing "You're My Soul and Inspiration," on the AFN radio station.

As usual, Monsieur Voltaige and his daughters were standing on the hill near the patio waiting to greet their Top Tiger friends. From a distance they waved. But their wave did not convey the usual vigor and enthusiasm. As soon as Clark got near enough to make out their facial expressions, he could see that something was not as it should have been. Something was wrong.

They all greeted one another warmly, as they normally did. Clark introduced Mr. Bauer. The young warrant officer from Tennessee appeared almost shy. He later told Clark that he had a deep and abiding appreciation for the female gender, but he was married and was determined to remain true to his wife (of five years).

"I will never leave you or forsake you," she had said to him at the airport as he was leaving for Vietnam.

After an awkward pause, Monsieur Voltaige put his hand on Captain Clark's shoulder and started to explain what had happened. Specialist Collins was still busy with Sergeant Dotson, helping to tie down the rotor blades and secure the helicopter down on the strip. The old Frenchman said that perhaps they should speak now before Collins joined them.

About two weeks earlier, Lee Ann had simply disappeared. They investigated and searched for her, but all to no avail. Now, just the day before, they had finally learned what had happened to her.

"She was murdered," said Monsieur Voltaige. His daughters covered their faces with their hands and walked quietly away toward the chateau.

Monsieur Voltaige went on to explain in detail exactly what had happened to Lee Ann. Someone had decapitated her and hung her head on a pole in front of the main entrance to the U.S. 25th Infantry Division Headquarters near Cu Chi. Two legs were crossed underneath her head skull-and-cross-bones style. Lee Ann's shiny long black hair was hanging down and touching the ground, touching the dusty grass at the bottom of the pole. The legs were the legs of a man—an American GI. They had belonged to an American infantryman who lost them to a land mine in the Ho Bo Woods, a VC-controlled area just north of Cu Chi. Shortly after the mine exploded the soldier was "dusted off," medevaced (medically evacuated) by helicopter. The soldier lived, but without legs. None of the Americans had taken the time to pick up the man's legs as the Dust Off chopper zoomed in and out again. But after the GIs departed the area, a Viet Cong guerrilla popped up out of a nearby spider hole and retrieved the legs. Just under Lee Ann's head was a crude sign printed on a piece of cardboard that had been torn away from a discarded C-ration box. The sign said, "She got too close to the enemy."

The officers, Clark and Bauer, were stunned. They were speechless. They could only look down and shake their heads while hot rage started to build up inside them. Clark knew that he would have to tell Collins. Just telling the young soldier that his sweetheart was gone was awful enough. Clark did not plan to reveal the details. He would do that maybe later—or maybe never.

Collins quickly noticed that all eyes were on him as he walked up the hill to join the group. Captain Clark immediately took him aside and told him.

"Lee Ann has been killed by the VC."

The words hit Collins like a gigantic hammer. He fell straight down—face down—in the red dust and bawled like a baby. A terrible long loud groan came from deep within him. His face was completely wet with sweat and tears, and he was soon covered with dark red mud. The mud on his face seemed to take on the appearance of half-coagulated blood. He was oblivious to the mud—and to everything and everyone else. He could feel only pain—hot, searing, piercing, merciless, unrelenting pain.

"Oh, God, no! Oh, God, no!" he kept saying. "Oh, God, no! Oh, God, no! It's not true. Oh, God no! Don't tell me this! No, God, no!"

Sergeant Dotson helped Captain Clark and Mr. Bauer lift Collins off the ground. Clark looked back at Monsieur Voltaige.

"I'm afraid that we have to leave now," he said. "We have to go. I hope we can see you again soon."

The Frenchman nodded gravely. He started to speak, but his voice failed him. He waved his hand faintly. As the Americans walked away it started to rain.

Ten days later the Top Tigers were lined up on the landing strip at the Cu Chi base camp. It was early. Everyone was topped off with fuel and the troops were all lined up and prepared to load up for a "damage assessment" mission in the Ho Bo Woods.

The Ho Bo Woods were only ten miles from the 25th Infantry Division Base Camp, and those woods were about to be hit by a B-52 strike. The

American troops had located countless tunnels in the Ho Bo Woods and it appeared impossible to explore and destroy them all. So the big bombers had been called in to do the job and do it properly. Eventually, carpet-bombing by B-52s would gradually succeed where the CS gas (riot control-tear gas) and demolition charges of the tunnel rats had failed to deny use of the tunnels to the Viet Cong.

The B-52 strategic bomber, the Super Stratofortress, was rapidly becoming one of the most potent and awful weapons of the Vietnam War. The VC later testified, when the war was finally over, that the B-52 was the most feared and dreaded weapon of the war. The B-52s of the Strategic Air Command, flying out of Thailand, operated under the code name "Arc Light." They were restricted to bombing suspected Communist bases in relatively uninhabited sectors, because their potency approached that of a tactical nuclear weapon. These huge, high-flying eight-engine aircraft were each capable of carrying in excess of twenty tons of bombs. They usually operated at an altitude of about 30,000 feet, and their deadly payload could take out almost everything within a target "box" approximately five-eighths of a mile wide by about two miles long. As the bombs rained down the landscape erupted with a fiery string of explosions, leaving a great swath of total devastation. They left huge craters up to thirty feet deep, and they left the landscape permanently scarred. Before the war ended much of the open area to the west of Saigon started to take on the look of a moonscape.

A flight of B-52s was scheduled to drop their 500-pound bombs on the Ho Bo Woods at seven a.m. When they did, Clark felt the earth tremble under his feet as he stood near his helicopter at Cu Chi base. A B-52 strike could be seen, heard, and felt for twenty miles. It was a thunderous symphony of destruction that could often be felt in Saigon. The bomb run lasted about ten minutes. The earth trembled the whole time. And then it stopped.

"Load up!" Clark heard someone shout. "Let's go! Load up! Load up! Move it!" It was the infantry company's first sergeant calling, "Let's go! Come on, move it! Get on them choppers. Let's go!"

Within minutes all the troops were aboard the armada of helicopters. They would be flying out in "sticks" or formations of twelve aircraft at a time. Everyone was ready to go.

Captain Clark and his crew were flying about midway back in a formation of twelve choppers. As soon as they reached an altitude of 500 feet they could all clearly see the smoke and haze over the target zone. Their mission was to fly right into that maze of bomb craters and debris, deliver the troops any way possible, and get out.

The two-mile strip right down the center of the Ho Bo Woods was a complete mess. It was a wild jumble of smoking craters and trees broken like thousands of giant match sticks. The craters mostly appeared to be about twenty to thirty feet deep. Most helicopters were unable to rest their skids on the ground. They hovered low over the edges of the craters and allowed the soldiers to carefully climb out and down. And then the pilots pulled in the power and were off again.

During the briefing that morning someone had made the comment that one good thing about a B-52 damage assessment mission was that the VC—even if they were not killed in the bombing attack—would be altogether too shell-shocked to put up a fight when the choppers went in. The Top Tigers were about to discover that was not always the case. Later Clark thought that rather than stunning Charlie, the bombers had stirred up a hornet's nest.

The Top Tigers' flight rapidly pulled back up to 500 feet, and they were starting a slow left turn away from the target area when they started to take fire. One of the first to shout, "Taking fire!" was Specialist Collins.

Somehow, between Captain Clark and Major Marker, in operations, they had managed to give Collins a few days off after he received the news that Lee Ann was dead. He was deeply hurt. For a time he was disconsolate. But now—on the surface at least—he seemed to be getting back to being the pleasant happy–go-lucky young soldier that he had been. Sergeant Dotson had been extraordinarily good at helping him get through his ordeal. Dotson treated Collins like a younger brother. James Dotson had just the right touch. He treated Collins with kindness and consideration, but not pity. Now Collins was back on the job and he could be counted on to perform his duties as expected—in a first-rate manner, as always.

"Taking fire!" Collins said again.

"Pop smoke!" said Mr. Bauer.

"Popping smoke!" Sergeant Dotson said.

"Popping smoke! Smoke's out!" said Collins. And those were his last words.

On the company radio frequency they could hear several other pilots report: "Taking fire!"

"Come on!" someone said. "Get some smoke on 'em!"

"Roger that! Popping smoke!"

Despite all those high-flying B-52s, Charlie was out to fight. The terrible concussions from the giant bombs had caused most of the guerrillas to suffer with bleeding noses and ears, but there was still a great deal of fight in them that day.

"Come on, Mustangs," Top Tiger Six said. "Get in here and put some fire on that smoke. Come on! Get on 'em. We need some suppressing fire *now*! Come on! Get on 'em!"

"Smoke's out," someone said. "Focus on the red smoke!" It sounded like Major Marker, the operations officer.

All of them could hear bullets snapping past their helicopter. Several bullets tore through the aircraft.

"Collins is hit! Collins is hit!" Sergeant Dotson suddenly shouted.

Clark looked back over his shoulder from the left seat. He was looking back and across the open aircraft. He saw Collins hold up his bloody and broken right hand—the hand with which he had just thrown the smoke canister. And then he fell back against the bulkhead of the chopper. The bullet had broken the two middle fingers on his right hand. He was gasping, kicking, and writhing. Was it his hand only that had been hit—or was it more? Was it something worse?

"Hang on, guys," Captain Clark said. "We're going to the hospital at Cu Chi."

Neither Clark nor Bauer could raise the hospital on their given frequency to alert them about the impending arrival of their casualty. They were unable to make contact with Major Marker. Their radios had been shot out. They could only talk on the intercom. They later found ten bullet holes in the aircraft. Four bullets went through the nose box. The nose box, which was just about two feet from the pilots' feet, was where the radios were located. One bullet went through the transmission area just behind Collins position. One bullet went through the top of the front door just above Clark's head. And four more bullets went into the tail-boom. Every helicopter in their flight had been hit that morning except for one. And that was the lead aircraft, Top Tiger Six. His luck was holding steady. The last ship in the flight, "tail-end Charlie," as they called him, got the worst of it—which was often the case. That crew counted twelve bullet holes in their chopper, but most of the hits were in the tail boom, and did not hit anyone or anything vital.

Miraculously, aside from Collins, there had been only one other casualty in the entire flight formation. Captain Gamble had been shot in the neck. But miraculously, he survived it. It turned out to be nothing more than a frightful flesh wound. It left an awful scar, but later Gamble was not handicapped in any way. He lived to continue his career as a pilot.

"We'll just have to go on in—with or without radio contact," said Bill Bauer.

"Roger that," Clark said. "Let's go. Let's do it. Let's go on in. Let's go."

They flew on in silence. Collins was still now. His eyes were closed. Sergeant Dotson held him to keep him from falling off the canvass seat. He was still connected to his "monkey strap"—the strap designed to protect door gunners from falling out of the aircraft while moving around with the guns.

They landed on the hospital helipad at Cu Chi Base Camp. Because they had no radio contact with anyone, they felt lucky in that they had not experienced any air traffic control problems. After a minute or so two stretcher-bearers came running out. They held the stretcher up to the open cargo door on the right side of the chopper, Collins' side. Sergeant Dotson tried to assist them with getting Collins limp body onto the litter. Just as it seemed that they were prepared to move away from the aircraft with Collins, somehow they dropped him. They simply tipped the stretcher to one side and spilled him off onto the ground. And he landed hard on the PSP.

"Oh, God!" Clark exclaimed. "Oh, God! If he's not dead already, they'll surely kill him."

The litter bearers gave the impression that they had never done this sort of thing before. They were like two guys off the street—one was black and the other white. Why was this hospital sending out unsupervised idiots to retrieve wounded soldiers? Who could be in charge of this sorry operation?

Clark was furious. He thought about getting out of the cockpit and striking out at the inept litter bearers. He was in a rage, but he felt utterly helpless. Bauer noticed Clark making sputtering, fuming, seething sounds. Bauer reached out and put a hand on Clark's arm and said:

"Wait. Hang on. Stay cool."

They both watched as Sergeant Dotson ran around the aircraft, pushed the stupefied litter bearers aside, gently lifted Collins in his arms, and carried him into the hospital. The hapless litter bearers gazed after Sergeant Dotson and walked slowly behind him as if they were lost and frightened. These two dolts appeared totally dazed and bewildered. These men were not fit to take out the garbage, and here they had somehow been assigned the duty of attending to wounded soldiers. How could this happen? The thought went through Captain Clark's mind: Were they on drugs? Could it be that these idiots are on drugs?

Bauer pulled the helicopter up to a hover and moved it off the main hospital helipad over to the side to await Sergeant Dotson. A few minutes later Dotson walked out of the hospital, looked about, saw the waiting aircraft, and walked toward it—head down and dejected. His whole demeanor told the story. As he neared the aircraft they saw him wiping tears away from his shining black face. He put his face close to Bauer's ear and shouted: "He's gone. He's dead. He didn't make it." Dotson put his hand over his own heart and said, "He was shot in the heart."

The bullet had gone through the fingers on Collins' right hand, breaking two of his fingers, and then it went into his heart.

"He didn't make it," Bauer shouted to Clark over the roar of the aircraft engine. "He's gone." Bauer paused. "Collins is gone," he said.

So, Collins was gone—gone at 21. He was 21 years old when he died. He was just old enough to legally drink beer in his home state.

"You'll make a really cool captain," he had said to Clark. "And you'll probably shoot right up there to bird colonel like in no time flat. Hang loose, Mother Goose, yeah, man! Cool captain, let's do it! Hey, Captain Midnight, let's pull pitch and *fly, fly, fly* on outta here!"

He lost his sweetheart to Charlie, and now Collins was a "KIA"—killed in action—shot through the heart.

What is a man, anyhow? Walt Whitman had asked that question in his "Song of Myself"—and so had many others. What was a man? *What a piece of work is a man!* With those four men before the nose of their helicopter, they had it all—the long and short of it. Here we have those two incompetents—the two unfit, inept, incapable, and dysfunctional litter bearers. Here we have the sightless, those altogether without eyes, leading the blind. And here we have the good, strong, and reliable Dotson, and the brave, blameless, kind, and worthy Collins. And there we have it all—the full range of possibilities, the complete spectrum of possibilities in that obsessive question: What is a man?

A man is a beast, a burdensome beast of burden that makes bile and bitterness, odious gasses and waste, anger and acrimony, ill will, malice, disharmony, and hate. But he was also an angel who carries fire and light. Elijah was a man just like us. And when it would not rain, he prayed earnestly and the heavens gave rain—and the earth brought forth her fruit, her abundant harvest. Man created soaring music, uplifting, awe-inspiring music, and sounds that would almost defy the laws of gravity. Beethoven when he created his *Symphony Number 9*, he was but a man—and a deaf man at that. The Handel who composed *Messiah* was but a man, right? Tchaikovsky when he created his *1812 Overture*, he was but a man. When Michelangelo painted the Sistine Chapel he was but a man. When El Greco painted *Toledo Before the Storm*, yes, he was just a man. Men composed great poetry, exalting works of architecture, striking and extraordinary public works. Look at the Roman aqueducts. Yes, look at them—they are still there. And they are still functional after two thousand years. Clark would always remember how quickly the American engineers had transformed that mosquito-infested swamp into a huge heliport there at Bien Hoa Airbase. And they did it at the blink of an eye. Men like Franklin, the New World Prometheus, pulled power from the sky. Men constructed Kitty Hawk-wings and defied the laws of gravity. Men mapped out trails to the moon and stars. Like mad falcons, men flew through hurricanes in order to warn their fellow citizens of the approaching danger. And men laid down their lives for their friends. *Greater love hath no man than this, that a man would lay down his life for his friends.* Yes, those were but men who sat calmly there and played "Nearer My God to Thee" as the *Titanic* went under the icy waves. Yes, men did rape, murder, mutilate, torture, loot, slander, pillage, and plunder. They brought with them their petty squabbles, and their criminal insanity, their neurosis, psychosis, and halitosis. Yes, men, they blindly sought freedom—the freedom to be free, the freedom of free color TV—500 channels of vacuous wasteland. But the secret channel—it was never there—the channel that led to Nirvana, *les champs*, to the Elysian Fields. No, that channel was never there. It was blocked out—scrambled. And yes, men did wondrous things. Man—they said he had a good heart, such a good heart, but it was defective in so many ways. It sought free TV in a lonely motel somewhere along the way. Man remained the missing link between the savage beast and all that which he could or should be. *Oh, Lord, what is man that thou art mindful of him?*

Man was a terrible mass of contradictions. Could that ever change? How could man be the measure of all things? As sons of Adam, are all men defective—fatally flawed? Would the day ever come when the key will be discovered, the key to wholesomeness, balance, unity, and good will? Where lies the oversoul? Where lies buried the keys to kindness, mercy, and love? Where lies buried the Rosetta Stone of the human soul? Will the day ever come when someone will utter the golden words, or discover the golden tablets, discover the magic formula that will quiet the human heart? Hush, man, and be liberated, the voice would say. Sit still. Hush, the Angel of Light would say. Take up your wings now and fly, fly away.

Mr. Bauer had just shut off the helicopter's engine. Somehow the whole machine seemed to sound tired—every pin, wheel, and rivet—as it started to unwind and cool down. The rotor and turbine blades were still slowly turning as they prepared to refuel. For a long moment Bauer gazed straight ahead through the Plexiglas into empty space. It seemed strangely quiet as Bauer started to quote from the Book of Isaiah.

Those who wait upon the Lord
Shall be renewed.
They will mount up
With wings as eagles.
They shall run,
And not be weary,
And they will walk
And not grow faint.

Perhaps two bumbling idiots did come for Collins, but he rejected them. His soul made a line in the sand. And he rode away *on the wings of eagles*. Collins was gone. They would not see the happy, laughing face of this young man again. He loved life—and everything in it that was "cool." He was busy now flying through cool thin air. He would not share with them again the jolly-olly orange drink and the C-rations.

"Okay, who's got the beans and wienies?" he had asked so often. "Who's got the Tabasco? Come on, now. Who's the wienie who's got the beans and wienies?"

This was a young man whose love for life shone in his eyes everyday. Robby Collins rarely ever said no to anyone. But Robby was gone. No, no, not gone, *not* gone. He had a good heart. It had been broken and pierced. But it would remain always a good heart. In his mind's eye Clark could see Collins emerging from that wall of thick white smoke. He was carrying the badly burned body of the scout pilot.

"They shall mount up with wings as eagles," Bauer had said. His friends would miss him, and they all quietly wept for him as they flew back toward their home base that evening.

Clark glanced back over his shoulder a number of times, observing Collins' empty place in the aircraft. The unmanned machine gun that would never again feel the hands of that gentle young man pointed downward and silently bounced and bobbed with the vibrations and movements of the helicopter. It would never again feel the affectionate touch of those attentive young hands.

A week later Major Scully told Captain Clark that a Soldier's Medal for Heroism and a Purple Heart had come down from Headquarters for Specialist Collins. The Purple Heart Medal was for his fatal wounds. The medals were mailed to his parents in Ohio.

For many years, from time to time, Clark would see Collins in his mind's eye. He could see him sitting smiling and "mission ready" behind his M-60 machine gun, attaching an empty C-ration can to the side of the gun to help the bullets feed properly into the firing chamber. He would see him looking like a madman chasing Dinky the monkey down between the rows of barracks. He would see him splashing and playing with Lee Ann in the sparkling waters of the swimming pool at Les Trungs. At other times he would see him, looking like the Angel of Deliverance, as he stepped out of that wall of smoke with the badly burned scout pilot cradled in his arms.

What is a man, anyhow?

Chapter 25

Underground

Lieutenant Cox entered the tunnel. He held a .45 pistol in his right hand and a flashlight in his left hand. Inside the tunnel it was dark and damp. Lieutenant Cox followed Sergeant Deloach. The NCO, Deloach, was a seasoned "tunnel rat," and he led the way.

They crawled a great distance that day, and toward the end they were both approaching total exhaustion. How much farther? the lieutenant silently asked himself. He hungered for fresh air—oxygen. And then they came to the first sealed trapdoor in the roof of the tunnel.

Sergeant Deloach was still. Sweat began to fill Lieutenant Cox's burning eyes. He was totally soaked with sweat. Sergeant Deloach sat under the trapdoor. A thin trail of dust filtered down from a crack along the edge of the door. The trapdoor was about ten inches above his head. He put his flashlight between his legs, shining upward. Then he put his hand under the door and exerted a modest amount of pressure. He carefully cocked his pistol. Lieutenant Cox held his pistol at the ready.

Sergeant Deloach took a deep breath, and then he violently pushed upward on the door. It yielded. With great speed and agility, the sergeant lifted his head and shoulders through the trapdoor and fired three shots into the black void before him. He heard a slight movement in the darkness. He shined his light around and could see a young Vietnamese man dressed only in black shorts lying not more than three feet away. The strong smell of cordite filled his lungs. He could see an ever-widening pool of blood on the ground near the body of the guerrilla soldier.

Sergeant Deloach had won another round with Charlie. The man was dead. "Got me another gook," he said when he resurfaced later that day.

Sergeant Deloach had the reputation of being a deadly "tunnel rat." Some of the GIs referred to him as "Terminal Tim." Most of them referred to him simply as "The Roach."

"The guy lives in the ground," they said. "You know, in the dirt."

He was the leader of the best team of American tunnel rats in Vietnam—and he took great pride in that fact. Sergeant Deloach's team could boast of a body count of over 100 enemy dead. And Deloach was also quite proud of the fact that he had never lost a man underground. He was now halfway through his second year—his second "tour"—in Vietnam.

"I love gettin' down and dirty with Charlie," he said. "They think they got it made down in them holes. Well, think again, gook. I'll show'em who's got it made and who ain't got it made," he said.

On one occasion Sergeant Deloach went under, quickly killed two Viet Cong, and then all the Americans were amazed to see 115 more VC file out of the tunnel and go—hands up—into captivity. Sergeant Deloach and the men assisting him were awarded Bronze Star Medals for their success in that operation.

Many—probably most—of the officers admired Sergeant Deloach. But some others thought that he had started to take an unhealthy pleasure in his job, his work of searching and cleaning out VC tunnels in the III Corps Tactical Zone.

Lieutenant Cox had just recently volunteered for the job of "Rat Six," officer in charge of the tunnel rat platoon. It was especially dangerous work, and it was difficult to find volunteers willing to become "tunnel rats." Cox had a desk job in the 3rd Engineer Battalion Headquarters at Lai Khe. Then one day the battalion commander casually asked him if he would like to become a tunnel rat—or rather the officer in charge of the tunnel rats. Then, without too much thought, he replied, "Well, sure. Why not?"

The battalion commander, "Castle Keep Six," gave Lieutenant Cox a long quiet stare. And then he went on, in a father-to-son tone, to explain that this could involve extremely hazardous duty. Perhaps the lieutenant should really think about it some more, he said, before finally deciding on this matter. However, the battalion commander, with the short salt-and-pepper-colored hair, went on to say that it was not really his policy for officers to go down in the holes. That would be left entirely up to the lieutenant. Also, Lieutenant Cox was told that the burden of responsibility on him should be somewhat lightened by the fact that they had a very strong NCO leading the tunnel rat platoon—Sergeant Deloach.

"Still, this also has its downsides, so to speak," the tall commander said.

"What do you mean, sir?" the lieutenant asked.

"Sergeant Deloach, or 'Terminal Tim,' as the men call him, runs that platoon with an iron hand. Like a lot of NCOs, he resents officers in general, but he specifically—and viciously—resents anyone who seems to be encroaching on what he calls his turf. They say this guy seems to be a natural killer. Some say that if he were not in the army, he would probably be a prison somewhere. Once, when he got the impression that a new enlisted man was challenging his authority, he challenged the man to a duel with bayonets. Fortunately, the new man took a pass on the knife fight, and Sergeant Deloach continued to rein supreme, so to speak. Yes, Sergeant Deloach is a pretty mean customer."

"I'll take the job, sir," said Lieutenant Cox, "and I'll give it my best shot."

The colonel spoke after a slight pause. He seemed—for the briefest of moments—somewhat hesitant. But then he spoke.

"I'm sure you'll do well," the tall commander said with a reassuring smile. He gave the lieutenant a friendly pat on the shoulder and shook his hand.

Lieutenant Cox felt better about himself immediately after taking the new position as "Rat Six." He was no longer just a staff officer—a "strap-hanger"—someone who was just tagging along for the ride. From here on he could take pride in his service. He would earn his combat pay.

Cox spent about a week getting to know Sergeant Deloach and the platoon. Counting Sergeant Deloach, there were ten of them. And these men were special. They were all volunteers and highly motivated professionals with a code of honor all of their own. Essentially, that simple code said something like this:

"We're here to beat Charlie at his own game and we never, *ever* leave a buddy behind." That was it—simple, direct, and to the point. That was from what Sergeant Deloach called the "KISS Principle"—"Keep it simple, stupid," as Deloach, "the Roach," would often say.

The tunnel rats were gung ho in a quiet, sullen sort of way. They clearly felt superior to the regular "grunts." They received an extra $50 per month as hazardous-duty pay. These men were combat experienced, and were mostly small. About five feet four and 150 pounds was considered ideal for a tunnel rat. Lieutenant Cox was solidly built and over six feet tall.

"You've got the wrong physique for a rat," Sergeant Deloach later said to him. It came out like a reprimand.

Sergeant Deloach required his men to keep in top physical condition. He taught his men contempt for the ordinary infantry soldiers who were in his opinion "over-fed, over-equipped, and under-eager to confront Charlie."

"Stay lean," he said repeatedly, "Stay lean and mean. Think lean and mean, and you'll be better off in this business—or any other business, for that matter, unless maybe you are interested in sumo wrestling. Those other guys, the ordinary grunts, they go out and try to avoid Charlie. We go out to *get* Charlie. And that we do. And we do it in spades. And we do it close up and one-on-one."

"What good will 500 tanks and helicopters do you," asked Deloach, "when you are down in a hole with Charlie? When you are fighting an enemy down in a hole in the ground the only things that matter are a man's cunning, his instincts, his patience, his guts, his brute strength, and luck. This what we're doing ain't no high-tech war."

Sergeant Deloach possessed what the colonel had referred to as "unrivaled expertise" in tunnel fighting. And Deloach strictly disciplined his men. Their vision and their sense of smell and hearing were very important to success in the subterranean theater of war. "Terminal Tim" forbade his men from smoking and drinking alcoholic beverages. VC prisoners had volunteered the information that GIs had a distinctive smell. They mentioned that they could very often smell the American cigarettes before the GIs were visible. Sergeant Deloach forbade his men from wearing after shave lotion or anything that might tip off the enemy to their presence.

"Don't be really stupid and eat garlic," he said. "If you want to survive and clean Charlie's plow," Deloach said, "then you've gotta know how to sit still and look, listen, and wait sometimes for thirty minutes or more before you make a move."

"I am at the point, I believe," Sergeant Deloach told Lieutenant Cox, "that I can actually hear Charlie's eyes blink in the dark down there."

One evening just at sundown, Lieutenant Cox sat near the airfield drinking beer with Sergeant Deloach.

"I think you are going to be okay," Deloach declared to Cox. "Yes, sir, I believe that you are going to be a first rate Rat Six—top notch."

"Well, I'm happy to hear that," replied Cox. "I feel like I've learned a lot from you and the guys. I'm grateful for that, and I plan to do my best."

"Oh, sure, I'm sure you will," said Deloach. "Actually, there's just one important thing to keep in mind. And that is, stay out of my way, don't push your luck and you'll be just fine."

"What do you mean?" the lieutenant asked, looking askance at the sergeant.

"Just exactly what I said," Deloach replied with a cold stare. "I think you know what I mean. I mean stay out of my way and you'll be just fine. And if you don't, well who knows? I might be dragging you out of one of those tunnels feet first. There's no rank underground, you know. And strange things can happen down there."

Lieutenant Cox felt a coolness surround him just as though he had suddenly stepped out of the sunlight and into a deep cavern.

Just as they were parting ways that night, Sergeant Deloach made one more pronouncement.

"But, actually, Six, I want to tell you how it is—how it really is. And it's this way, Six." he said. "You are just no killer. No, you are not a killer. That's your problem. You are basically a nice guy. That's your roots, your background. That's where you're comin' from." Sergeant Deloach said "nice guy" in a sort of incredulous tone.

"One day you will hesitate when you shouldn't—and that will get you messed up," said Deloach. "And you are not built right for this business—no, not at all. You are too big. Charlie hasn't killed one of us in quite some time. But if you are not careful, you'll mess up, you'll screw up—and then that'll be it. That'll be all she wrote."

Lieutenant Cox was determined to command the tunnel rats. He had an uncle who had served in the Korean War, and Cox could remember hearing that man say that the most cardinal rule of a good officer was to never ask your men to do anything that you would not do. That was a golden rule of sorts that would always stick with Cox.

The next day when the team was called in to check out a newly discovered tunnel, Lieutenant Cox volunteered to go in first. Sergeant Deloach appeared slightly surprised. But he shrugged his shoulders and said, "Sure, why not?"

Lieutenant Cox entered the tunnel, and Sergeant Deloach followed about six feet behind him. But after almost an hour they became convinced that it was a "cool" tunnel, an empty tunnel, and they resurfaced. Cox led the way into three other tunnels that week. They were all cool. But it did seem as though the tunnel rats were finding an increasing number of VC weapons being stored away. The tunnel rats started to talk among themselves, and they speculated that Charlie was up to something. Their bet was that Charlie was getting prepared for something big.

One day, before Lieutenant Cox could react, one of the enlisted men, a young man named Timmons, entered the hole just prior to Cox's arrival on the scene. Timmons was taller than the other rats. As soon as his feet had touched the bottom, a guerrilla stabbed the American repeatedly in the groin with his bayonet. The men quickly pulled Timmons out of the hole. Without hesitation, Sergeant Deloach—pistol and flashlight in hand—was in the hole and out of sight. Within minutes the men heard three shots fired in rapid succession, and then about ten minutes later, Deloach surfaced dragging a dead VC behind him. Timmons' bleeding was massive and they could not save him.

Two days later Lieutenant Cox and Sergeant Deloach were called to a tunnel entrance just east of An Loc, in rubber tree country. Lieutenant Cox quickly entered the tunnel. They crawled for quite some distance and found nothing. After an hour they resurfaced and took a break.

"There's something peculiar about this tunnel," Deloach said.

"What do you mean?" Cox asked taking a drink of red Kool Aid.

"Well, to be honest, I'm not sure," said Deloach, "But this cave seems so clean, so neat, so well cut, well made. For some reason, it just seems special—like it was developed for VIPs or something—for some special purpose, maybe. I think we ought'a take another look at it—check it out a little more carefully. You know what I mean?"

They re-entered the tunnel. This time Sergeant Deloach managed to get in before the lieutenant. Before re-entering the tunnel Deloach explained to the men on the surface that they would probably be gone for some time—maybe two hours plus. However, this appeared to be a special tunnel, and they believed that it should be thoroughly investigated.

"So be patient, guys," Deloach said. "Stay cool."

"Don't worry," the young sergeant named Wrenn said. "We'll be right here till we hear from you guys. Good luck and good huntin.'"

They continued on through the tunnel until, finally, they came to a fork. They decided to take the right branch. Then after awhile they discovered they were in a false tunnel, a decoy, a dead-end tunnel. They retraced their path and started off down the other branch. This time they had brought a compass along. They determined that the tunnel seemed to generally lead off in a southwesterly direction. After some time they came to what appeared to be a little break room. There appeared to be some water and some *nuoc nam* fish source stored in the corner or this room. Fearing that they might be booby-trapped, the Americans did not touch the large wicker-covered glass bottles.

After a brief rest and a drink from their canteens, they continued on down the main branch of the tunnel in a southwesterly direction. Deloach slowed and then stopped. He motioned for Cox to look ahead. About ten feet ahead of them there appeared to be a curve in the tunnel. One always needed to be on the alert before rounding a curve in an unexplored tunnel. The Americans got down on their bellies and crawled slowly toward the curve. Finally, Deloach was there. He paused for a couple of minutes and then slowly eased around the curve with his upper torso, pistol and light at the ready. Cox had his pistol at the ready.

Sergeant Deloach flicked on his light. There was something there ahead. There was a figure ahead. It was prone—lying parallel to the tunnel wall. Deloach instinctively fired a shot at the figure.

The noise was deafening and the acrid smell of burned cordite filled the air around the curve in the tunnel. But there was another smell in the tunnel now. What was it? It smelled awful. It smelled rotten. There was no reaction from the dark prone figure. Now Deloach could see what appeared to be the bright green luminous shining eyes of a small animal. It was a rodent. It was a very large rat, reared back on his haunches, showing his teeth and appearing to be ready to attack. Slowly, ever so slowly, the

Americans edged their way forward. The dark figure was quite still. Deloach instinctively felt that the person lying there just ahead of him was dead. There was a certain careless finality about the posture and position of the body.

Deloach finally arrived at the point where he could clearly view the dark body.

"Oh, my God!" he exclaimed.

"What is it?" Cox asked.

"This guy is dead alright. Not only is he dead," Deloach replied, "he looks as if he's been dead for twenty years."

Suddenly, the smell seemed almost overwhelming. It was the smell of rotting flesh.

"My God! The smell!" Deloach gasped.

"Hold your ears now," Deloach continued, "I think I'm going to have to shoot this rat. It seems to be tied on a line. He's tethered. He can't run away, and he looks vicious."

Deloach fired another round. Now the big rat was dead. They had discovered an old human cadaver and three dead rats. Also, nearby they found a syringe and small phial containing a yellow fluid.

After an exhausting return trip to the surface, Cox and Deloach enlisted some aid and went back down into the tunnel to pull out the awful looking corpse. After the tunnel rats had successfully cleaned out the tunnel and started to discuss their bizarre find, the Intelligence Specialists became involved. And then the Medical Specialists became involved. What they discovered was that one of the rats was a carrier of bubonic plague. And the corpse apparently had been a leper. There was a small leper colony not far east of Phu Loi. How did he get there—deep inside a tunnel in the An Loc area?

The next day the American tunnel rats heard from the Intelligence Specialists that what they had encountered was apparently some sort of terrible obstacle, or blockade, designed to frighten interlopers (or Americans) away.

"This looks to us like Charlie's idea of chemical and biological warfare," said the captain from G-2 (Intelligence).

"I mean, man, like, who wants to tangle with the plague and leprosy?" asked Sergeant Wrenn.

"Charlie is truly amazing, you know?" said the G-2 captain. "They eat rats, you know? And if they are not really careful now, they might be contaminating their own food supply."

"And it could very well be that you guys really should take another look at that tunnel," the captain from G-2 continued. "If they take the trouble to devise this sort of barricade in there, well, then maybe they've got something special they're trying to hide from us in there somewhere."

After a thoughtful pause, Sergeant Deloach spoke. "You see," he said. "It's like I've been saying all along. There's something special about this tunnel."

Everyone seemed to agree. Early the next day Cox and Deloach re-entered the tunnel. On this excursion Sergeant Wrenn went along with them. Traveling light was always important to the tunnel rats. Again they took along a compass, and because the tunnel was so long, they took along a little extra water. They each carried a pistol, a flashlight, a survival knife, and Sergeant Deloach carried one hand-grenade and a short piece of rope.

Cox and Deloach were familiar with a major portion of the tunnel now, so they were able to move a little faster this time. Sergeant Deloach was leading the way, he was the point man, and they seemed to be making pretty good time, and it was not too long before they passed the place where the corpse and the rats had been just beyond that eerie curve. Then after a short while the tunnel seemed to narrow down, and it came to an end. There at the end was an overhead trapdoor.

There was always a moment of tension before attempting to negotiate a trapdoor, especially an overhead trapdoor. This was the time and situation in which the tunnel rats were most vulnerable. This was a dreadful moment, and occasionally it was the final moment for the point man. If they failed to react quickly they could be stabbed or shot. When the trapdoor was in the floor leading downward, that did not seem so delicate to the seasoned tunnel rat. But in this situation, gravity worked against them. Charlie might simply smile, say his equivalent of "Gotcha!" and drop a hand-grenade down the hatch, and take off in high gear. And grenades did terrible things to men in the narrow confides of a tunnel. After a grenade explosion there would not be much left over to put in the body bag.

Sergeant Deloach sat down, put his flashlight shining upward between his legs. The three of them exchanged looks and nods that said, "Okay, get ready." Each man cocked his pistol. Deloach pushed up on the door. It yielded. His grimy face glistened in the dim light. Then he quickly burst through the little square door. It was a tight fit.

Nothing happened. There was no one there. So far, so good. The tunnel remained peculiarly cool, quiet, and empty.

They climbed up one level and started off again—still in a generally southwesterly direction.

– – –

At Les Trungs rubber plantation, Mai Bec, the young Vietnamese woman they called "Becky," was busy tending the bees. Suddenly a small boy ran to her and said in Vietnamese, "Come quick! Come quick! Doctor, doctor—Dr. Dien—he say you must come now!"

Mai Bec quickly ran to the wine cellar, deep inside Monsieur Voltaige's chateau. She quickly moved the boxes of empty wine bottles. The messenger boy, Pham, who was only 10, and who now accompanied her, had already moved most of the boxes. Mai Bec opened the hidden door and entered the tunnel. The boy remained behind to conceal the hidden door. A few minutes later Mai Bec was standing before Dr. Dien in the center of the underground clinic.

"Quick! Quick!" the tunnel surgeon said, "The Americans are coming! They are getting much too close to us here. Much too close. Go now and stop them. I will send two of my people with you. But the Americans must be stopped! Stop the Americans! Stop them!"

A young man armed with an AK-47 Kalashnikov automatic rifle was prepared to accompany the beekeeper. Mai Bec walked to one corner of the room and opened a large basket. From the basket she quickly produced a net-bag in which she put a .45 pistol and one hand-grenade. Mai Bec handed the bag to the young woman who had been assigned to accompany her. She also handed the young woman a flashlight. Before leaving the clinic area, Mai Bec looked carefully in another corner of the room, and then finally emerged carrying what appeared to be a small spear. It was a sharpened bamboo stick. One end of the stick had been sharpened to a fine point and then the point had been hardened by fire.

Mai Bec, with a flashlight in one hand and her homemade spear in the other—still dressed in her flowing pink and white *ao dao* outfit—was quickly off down the tunnel in a southeasterly direction with her two companions. She knew where she was going, and she had to get there quickly.

About twenty minutes after climbing through the first overhead trap-door, the Americans came to another. Again, they followed their standard preparation procedures. The tension was there just as before. The pistols were cocked. The eyes burned with copious sweat. Lieutenant Cox thought, "This is what I would call a really grotesque game of jack-in-the-box."

Then Sergeant Deloach burst through again—to find nothing nor any-one—only cool, dank darkness. The three Americans climbed through to the next level and continued. They had been underground two hours now. Now there was something different about the way they moved and glanced at one another. They all instinctively felt that soon they would make a discovery—if nothing else, then perhaps a remote exit from the underground superhighway.

Again, after about twenty minutes they came upon another overhead trapdoor. Sergeant Deloach was about to start preparing for his ritual overhead trapdoor break through, when Lieutenant Cox softly put his hand on Deloach's arm and said: "Okay, you've had your two trapdoors. It's my turn."

Those were the rules. So great was the stress and tension, that the rules called for a change in the point man after two trapdoors. Sergeant Deloach looked groggily at Lieutenant Cox. Their sweating faces were not six inches apart. Deloach was exhausted. He shrugged and allowed the lieutenant to edge past him and get situated underneath the trapdoor.

Lieutenant Cox carefully put his flashlight—shining upwards—between his legs. He looked back at the two sergeants. They appeared to be ready. They all hungered for fresh air—for oxygen. The lack of oxygen seemed to slow everything down—their movements, their thinking process, everything. Cox cocked his pistol. The two sergeants—in almost exact unison—cocked their pistols.

"There's something special about this tunnel," Sergeant Deloach had said.

"One day you'll hesitate when you shouldn't," Sergeant Deloach had said to him that night while they were drinking beer out by the airfield. "You'll screw up," he had said.

Lieutenant Cox looked straight up at the trapdoor that was not more than a foot away from his face. The door was small. Cox would have to contract himself to the maximum degree to pop up through that hole. These holes were cut for Vietnamese bodies not American bodies. The sweat burned in his eyes. He placed his hand on the door and gave it a gentle push. It yielded. A trickle of dust fell through into his face.

"I can even hear a gook blink his eyes in the dark down there. Trust me. I know what I'm talking about," the sergeant had said.

Lieutenant Cox gripped his pistol. "You'll screw up," the sergeant had said. The adrenaline surged through the lieutenant's body. "*You'll screw up*!" And then with a crushing explosion of energy, Lieutenant Cox sprang upward, hitting the door with all his might.

The hole was narrow, but he popped through. He felt a sharp pain in his left shoulder. His head was through the hole but he was having trouble getting his arms through the small opening. Someone was there—nearby. He could instantly sense the presence of someone else nearby. A bright light shone in his eyes and blinded him.

Mai Bec, with her sharpened spear held firmly in both hands, lunged forward and with all her strength she plunged the bamboo spear through the American's neck from front to rear. The young girl standing slightly to the side and rear of Mai Bec kept the light focused on the American's face. The spear entered the front of the lieutenant's throat and exited through the back of his neck. The spear was plunged half way through the man's neck. His warm blood flowed and quickly accumulated in a large pool on the tunnel floor beneath the girls' feet.

Sergeant Deloach and Sergeant Wrenn did not know what had happened. But they knew that something terrible had happened. There was no sound except for the sound of a brief scuffle and a strange choking sound. But now they could see the blood flowing down the big lieutenant's body. Lieutenant Cox had been unable to get his left arm through the opening. His flashlight had dropped to the tunnel floor and now they could see a pool of blood forming underneath his body. He writhed and kicked for a few moments more, and then he was still. The two sergeants could not get the lieutenant's body through the hole either way. The spear rested on both sides of the shaft. The lieutenant's large body was wedged in the trapdoor. He was impaled.

"Never *ever* leave your buddy behind," they said. But they had to leave their "main man" behind. They had to leave Rat Six behind.

The beekeeper, Mai Bec, sometimes called "Becky," had stopped the Americans. And her weapon was simply a sharpened stick.

"This ain't no high tech war," Sergeant Deloach said again later.

Mai Bec had sealed the tunnel—-and she sealed it with the body of an American lieutenant. This was the same tall young lieutenant who—just six weeks before—had told his tall graying commander:

"I'll take the job, sir. And I'll give it my best shot."

Chapter 26

The Termite Hills

The rainy season was over. Now it was hot and dry—extremely hot and dry.

"You know," Mr. Bauer calmly said to Lieutenant Clark as the sweat dripped off the end of his nose, "I really believe this place is hotter than Hades. Yep, sometimes, actually, I think that is precisely where we are, in the pit, in Hades."

Bauer lifted the helicopter up to a four-foot hover and dust and ashes from the "prepped" landing zone flew about them wildly like a demonic tempest just released from some nefarious netherworld.

The Top Tigers had been doing one combat assault after another for over a week now. Mostly they were supporting the 1st Infantry Division and 173rd Airborne Brigade and working in War Zone D—mostly in an area to the southeast of Loc Ninh. On this day in late November, they had been flying since dawn. It was 3:00 p.m. now and everyone seemed worn out.

They were in the process of extracting a company of 173rd Airborne soldiers from an unusually large landing zone in the middle of nowhere—this was LZ "Hammerhead." The tired, grimy, sweaty soldiers were all loaded up now and the helicopters—12 of them—were lined up abreast across the wide LZ at a low hover, and ready to lift off. If they had been in the old horse cavalry, one could describe their formation as "stirrup-to-stirrup on a broad front." The choppers kicked up a wild storm of dust and ashes. Yes, their mounts pranced and pawed the earth in eager anticipation of the charge, in eager anticipation of flight.

"Okay, guys," Top Tiger Six came on the line. "Are you guys ready to go? Is everyone ready for lift off?"

Immediately there were several "Roger that" replies on the radio. No one reported any problems or any reason not to lift off.

"Let's get outta here and go to the house," Sergeant Dotson said on the intercom from his station just behind Captain Clark.

"I'll drink to that," Captain Clark said. And he could have been speaking for everyone.

"Yeah, man, come on, let's do it, *do* it!" Specialist Gutierrez said. A young man from Texas, Ramon Gutierrez, was their new door gunner. He was seated in Collins' place. Gutierrez was small and he was always smiling. He was consistently good humored and mission ready. They were happy to have him aboard. But they would never forget Collins. Later Sergeant Dotson would confide to Captain Clark that he was concerned with Gutierrez being overly distracted by and fascinated with "pot"—hashish.

"Okay, guys," Top Tiger Six said, "let's do it. Let's go, Top Tigers. Pull pitch. Let's get outta here."

Captain Clark was on the controls. He pulled in additional power, simultaneously balancing the pressure on the pedals and slightly dipping the nose of the aircraft. Twelve choppers, all with the golden tiger head emblazoned on their noses, roared and moved forward, rapidly gathering power and increasing speed as they moved across the landing zone. The air temperature was high and the aircraft were heavily loaded as they raced eastward across the landing zone toward a high tree line.

They were fast approaching the tree line when Clark glanced down to check the power gage. Not much power left to pull, he thought. Heavy load, hot, dry air—this lift off would take a lot of power, he thought. Those trees ahead look awfully tall. The aircraft roared towards the tall tree line, which was now only a short distance ahead. The Top Tigers were in their fast-forward mode.

Then things started to happen—and happen fast.

"*I've got it*!" Bauer suddenly shouted.

It happened so quickly that Captain Clark could almost not take it all in. He was speechless. Clark's eyes were locked on the high tree line dead ahead and in his tunnel vision the images of imminent danger only just partially registered. There was a blur of helicopter main rotor blades whirling by before his eyes. It seemed to be over and done in a blink of the eye.

"I've got it!" Bauer said as he seized the controls. "I've got control of the aircraft!"

Mr. Bauer pulled the stick back, simultaneously pulling the nose of the aircraft upward at a sharp angle. He pulled in additional power. And then there was no more power to pull, and so he started to gently "milk" the collective pitch, lightly, cautiously pumping the lever up and down, slowly and carefully, working to find more power, more additional lift.

"*Power, power! More power*!" The words were written in adrenaline in the hearts and minds and on the lips of both pilots.

Their helicopter popped quickly up towards the top of the tree line. Simultaneously, Clark got a glimpse of another chopper turning in toward them sharply from the right. They popped over it. Miraculously, the ship veering in from the right did not collide with anyone.

Now they were on top of the tree line. They could almost reach out and touch the treetops. The rest of the flight was moving off now ahead of them. This left them in rough, turbulent, "dirty" air. They needed time and space to milk in more power, to gain more forward air speed, and to gain more lift. They needed altitude. They were altogether too close to those high treetops. Ahead of them the jungle canopy was wavy, like an ocean of green. Bauer looked for low places in the swells, the canopy-top, the roof of the jungle. He would aim the aircraft for the low spots, dip down into them, gently letting the collective power lever down, gain a little air speed, gain more RPM, and then again gently pull in full power, and try to gain more forward air speed.

Suddenly, there dead ahead, they saw an open space. It was a small open field filled with strange upright cones of dirt. They were giant termite hills—hundreds of them. Most of them appeared to be about four to five feet tall. It was a small forest of giant termite hills. The GIs usually referred to them as "anthills." Bauer dipped the chopper down toward the open space and the aircraft quickly gained the much-needed air speed, power, and lift.

Everyone took a deep breath. Now, for a moment at least, they could relax. Captain Clark glanced back at the grunts. They appeared to be quite relieved. There was a great deal of head shaking going on as well as low-key swearing. Later one of the grunt lieutenants would tell Clark that they considered their chopper rides, the insertions and extractions, as the most dangerous part of their missions.

"That doesn't say much for your confidence in us," Clark replied.

"Oh, well, that's just the nature of things, I suppose," said the sinewy little lieutenant.

They were easily gaining altitude now and the power setting was stabilized in the normal cruising range. Everyone seemed to feel better now. This was expected to be the final mission—or "lift"—for the day.

"What was all *that* about?" Clark asked Bauer. "What happened?"

"That was Captain Cutler," Bauer replied. "Evidently he decided at the last second that he didn't have enough power to make it, and he cut right in front of us."

"Amazing," Clark commented. He was thinking something like this: "Well, if the guy had to commit suicide, couldn't he have the decency to leave us out of it."

It did not really occur to Clark until later that Bauer had saved his life. Bauer had saved all of their lives. Clark talked with Bauer about it later.

"By the way," he said, "thanks for saving my life back there. Thanks for saving *all* of our lives. I must admit that I was totally focused on that high wall of trees dead ahead of us. I did not see Cutler turning into us from the right. I didn't see a thing until I saw his aircraft go wheeling underneath ours. Thanks for being alert. Without you we would not be here today."

"Well, that's what a copilot is for," Bauer replied.

Clark thought for a moment and then spoke.

"Yes, true," he said. "But how many copilots would have reacted so quickly and so well. You pumped the clutch in just the right way, and made that machine do just exactly what it had to do. No, friend. Regardless of what you say, *my* copilot is someone special."

Bauer simply smiled his humble smile. Here was a man of rare virtue.

What they did not know was that Captain Cutler was desperately low on fuel. His fuel warning light had been on for almost fifteen minutes now.

Before joining the company for this extraction, Cutler and his crew had been on an administrative mission flying some colonel on an air reconnaissance. Major Marker had contacted Cutler on the radio and told him to hurry and join the company at LZ Hammerhead. In his rush to join the company for the extraction at Hammerhead, Captain Cutler had neglected to refuel when he had the chance. That omission turned out to be a serious mistake. His crew chief, Sergeant Manning had almost said something at that time. Manning thought that they should take the time to take on some fuel. But he thought twice about it, held his tongue, and did not say anything.

"Captain Cutler is an experienced pilot," Manning thought. "I suppose he knows what he's doing. Sure he does."

Captain Cutler was now hovering in the center of the LZ getting ready to make another run at the tall tree line. Even though he was low on fuel, the aircraft seemed, to him, to be overloaded. That day he just happened to be flying about half of the mortar platoon, and they carried a heavy load—base plates, tubes, and pack-boards with fin-tailed mortar rounds. And, as if this were not enough, Cutler was flying an aircraft that he considered under powered and a "hog"—a gas-guzzler.

Now Captain Cutler's aircraft was the only one on LZ Hammerhead. He pulled in the power and made a long run toward the tree line. Because his was the lone aircraft on the LZ at that time, Cutler and his crew enjoyed the advantage of clean air and no turbulence. So it was much easier to gain lift, power, and altitude this time and get up and over the tall trees on the eastern side of the LZ. Cutler was over the tree line now and starting to gain altitude, and then something happened.

The engine suddenly started to sound strange and the controls suddenly felt soft and spongy—the machine was not responding as it should. He looked ahead and saw the opening, the field covered with giant termite hills. The engine was fueled starved. They were going in. As the engine stopped, Captain Cutler abruptly pushed down on the collective pitch and prepared to autorotate down on to the field of termite hills.

Even though Captain Cutler executed a good autorotation—a power off emergency landing—the helicopter was bound to crash because of all of those tall solid termite hills. These things had been baking in the rain and sun for years. If the enemy had been there devising anti-helicopter landing traps, they could hardly have developed anything more effective than these strange towers of dirt.

The chopper came down in the top end, eastern end, of the field. It was a crash landing, but at first it did not appear to be too violent. The rotor blades beat themselves to pieces as the aircraft tipped over to the left. Everyone got out of the helicopter except Captain Cutler. A couple of the grunts were seriously injured but they survived.

The men tried desperately to get Captain Cutler out of the aircraft, but were unable to do so. He was unconscious and pinned in. Led by the crew chief, Sergeant Manning, the men systematically tried a number of different approaches to the problem. But it seemed hopeless.

Bitterly, some of them were starting to see that it *was* hopeless. And then the chopper started to burn. The men tore desperately at the metal walls pressing in on Captain Cutler. They tried everything physically possible to pull his body this way or that. But nothing worked. The wrecked aircraft held the man firmly in its clutches. It was not going to release him. This machine was not going to release the man who had denied her fuel when she so desperately needed it. Now the fire, the heat, was intolerable. The aircraft might explode at any moment.

The men, all covered with sweat and dirt and blood slowly backed away, half-crazy in their wild desperation to save the ill-fated captain. Sergeant Manning was a strong man and adrenaline surged through his body. But he had been unable to free his captain,—this moment would haunt him for the rest of his life. The men had to pull him away from the burning machine. He struggled against them in a kind of helpless, hopeless, defeated, and pitiful way. The hair was singed off his face.

There was only a minor explosion because the fuel bladder was empty. But the aircraft burned completely. And so did Captain Cutler.

Major Ratcliffe and his Mustangs came in to pick up the survivors. The wreckage burned on late into the night.

Chapter 27

The Tiger Pit

The next day Clark made a low pass over Les Trungs. He could get only a quick glimpse of the patio area near the pool, but Clark thought that he could make out Curtis Clayton sitting there at a table with Major Ratcliffe, Monsieur Voltaige, and his daughters.

Clark glanced up ahead at the airfield and he could see two gunships parked at the top of the red dirt strip. Yes, the 68th Buddha, traveling in the form of a light-fire team, was present.

Clark had a free day and he had succeeded at arranging to spend it at Les Trungs. And rather than simply dropping Clark off there at the Frenchman's plantation, the rest of the crew had decided to spend their day off there also.

"I mean, like, man, what else can you ask for?" Sergeant Dotson had said. "It's all 'dare. D'at Frenchy's got it all, man. I mean he's got it all."

"Hey, man," Gutierrez said, "you know where it's at, man. Groovy, man. Yeah, yeah, you know the way, man!"

They all came out to meet Clark and his crew—Bauer, Dotson, and Gutierrez—as they walked up from the red dirt airfield toward the chateau. And now Clark could clearly see that indeed he was correct: Curtis Clayton was presently visiting Les Trungs. Also, Sergeant Moses Merlins was there, and he was in the midst of preparing some of his extraordinary barbecue.

Standing nearby were two Vietnamese servant women holding and dispensing those wonderful warm face towels. The Americans always found this ritual to be extremely refreshing. Returning to Les Trungs—and to Genevieve—was always exhilarating to Clark. It was better than returning home, he thought. It was like suddenly flying beyond Shangri La and being safely delivered onto the Elysian Fields. But he could not avoid the feeling that Curtis Clayton was becoming a large fly in the enchanted ointment that was Les Trungs.

They were soon in the sparkling waters of the swimming pool. And they spent most of the day there, in or near the pool.

For lunch they enjoyed some of Sergeant Merlins' delicious barbecue. During the luncheon on the patio near the pool, Curtis Clayton started to chat with Clark.

"I understand you are considering becoming a teacher," he said, "just like your father and mother. Nothing like supporting the old family traditions, I always say. What are you going to teach?"

"History," I believe, said Clark.

"Oh, History," said Clayton. "Now, there's a topic. You know what Henry Ford said about history, don't you? He said it's more or less bunk. Yeah, worthless."

"John Kennedy said that history was important. He said, 'If we don't know where we have been, then we can't know where we are going,'" Clark replied.

"Actually, you know, I've been told that many of our schools nowadays don't even teach History anymore. They say it seems to be too contentious, too divisive—what with Thomas Jefferson and all of his mistresses and slaves and so forth. They supposedly teach something they call 'Social Studies.' And in Social Studies I've been told that they teach everything from how to use condoms and the U.S. Constitution, all in the same period of instruction. Now that must be challenging—that kind of teaching."

"Well, who knows?" said Clark. "Perhaps I will have to teach Social Studies. But I'll do it my way."

After a wonderful lunch, Clark managed to be alone with Genevieve in her room for a couple of hours. Again, he asked her about Curtis Clayton.

"Why is he here?"

"I don't know," Genevieve answered. "Honestly, I do not know why he is here."

Clark enjoyed watching her nostrils flare when she became exasperated or emotional.

"Please understand and believe me," she continued, "when I tell you that I have made it clear to him that I have no interest in him whatsoever—none. And I have tried to make it clearly understood that I *am* interested in *you*—and only you. You are all that matters to me now.

"But he," she tentatively continued after a moment, "he has tried to tell me that I am very young and perhaps I do not know what is best for me. And now he seems to be trying to tell me that it is important that I leave here soon and return to Paris. He is really quite insistent on this—on my leaving Les Trungs. I have told him *no.* I have told him that I plan to remain here—for now.

"When I leave here," she said in a carefully measured tone, her nostrils flaring again, "I want to have you with me. I *will* have you with me."

They kissed again. The deep, insatiable hunger they shared remained unchanged. The magic well was deep. It was bottomless—as unbounded as the universe. And the music that emanated from it was supernatural. It was sweet, wondrous, and serene. Again, he leaned over her to taste the intoxicating nectar that was her love. Their souls were entwined with all of the creative forces of the universe, and they were now immortal.

"I hope…" Genevieve continued. "It is my hope, yes—my only wish is that we can be together for the rest of our lives. I love you desperately. But also, I must say that I wish that Monsieur Clayton would leave soon. *Oui*, I wish that he would leave us alone. I am starting to feel very uneasy about him. And my father also feels this way, I believe. You know my father is almost always a totally calm and serene person. But now I sense that he feels rather ill at ease or uncomfortable around this man. And, yes, my father has described this man as peculiar.

"*Oui*, he should go away!" she said in a sudden fit of pique.

But then she seemed to grow calm once again. And after a long pause she spoke.

"But we should not concern ourselves," she said. "Monique, my dear sister, has said that we should not be concerned about this man. She says that he will soon depart. She knows. He will soon leave us. *Oui*, *oui*, he will soon go away. And my sister is a very well informed person. She always knows what is going on—always."

Genevieve said this regarding Clayton's departure with a certain air or tone of finality. It was like the last word—no more discussion on this topic was required.

"We should not concern ourselves," she said. "Hold me in your arms. Come to me."

— — —

"Teaching history does not really sound like much of a career, now does it—honestly?" Curtis Clayton said with a sarcastic smile and a wink when he saw Clark on the patio a little later.

Clayton seemed to be enjoying Major Ratcliffe's company. Clark heard them laugh as he walked away from them. Clayton walked with the Major Ratcliffe down to his helicopter after the evening meal just prior to the Mustangs taking off and heading back towards Bien Hoa and the airbase.

Sergeant Merlins and most of the enlisted men were flying back with Major Ratcliffe and his light fire team.

After the evening buffet, Clark had a chance to speak alone with Monsieur Voltaige for a short while. And the subject of Curtis Clayton soon surfaced.

"*Oui, oui, mon ami*," the little Frenchman said to Clark, "I have this odd feeling that somehow there is a certain amount of animosity between this man, Curtis Clayton, and myself. And no, no, I am not at all certain of what is causing this difficulty, this odd feeling of discomfort. It is most unusual—most unusual. It is not so pleasant. No, I must say, it is not so pleasant.

"Strangely enough," Monsieur Voltaige continued, "I have been led to believe that this man was offended by my remarks regarding American politicians. Come now! Did I offend you? No, of course not. I am certain of it. And you are an American. Humor is something we should all have, *n'est-ce pas*? Without humor I think life would be very long and dry—like a desert—not much fun. What, I ask you, is the matter with this man? He looks like a normal man on the outside, does he not? This man, Monsieur Clayton—this Curtis Clayton—he should stop and think for a minute—just one moment. *Oui*, he should think. What was it that our friend Voltaire said? *Oui*, the great Voltaire said, 'Ridicule is the best test of truth.' Of course. How true! This great man, Voltaire, the founder of the Age of Reason, reminded us of so many eternal truths—things we instinctively knew but needed only to be reminded of. And what was it that he said about government? He said, 'In general, the art of government consists in taking as much money as possible from one class of citizens to give to the other.' Oh, yes, I believe that I see clearly the spirit of our age. And the spirit of our age seems to be much more about taking than giving. The all-wise Voltaire said, 'Who has not the spirit of his age, of his age he will have all the unhappiness.' *Oui*, and this is what I believe this man, this man Monsieur Clayton, has—only unhappiness. He is discontent with his life. He is totally focused on taking and not giving. He should learn to love life and trust fate. We should cultivate our garden—mind the art of good living.

"Monsieur Clayton should remember, I believe," Monsieur Voltaige continued, "the proverb, 'A merry heart doeth good like a balm, a medicine. But a broken spirit drieth the bones.' Is that not correct, Monsieur Bauer?"

"Yes, that's true," Bauer replied. "And, 'He that is of a merry heart hath a continual feast.'"

"*Tres bien*, Monsieur Bauer! "Very good!" said the little prince with sparkling eyes and a broad smile.

"No, *mon ami*," said Monsieur Voltaige. "I am no ideologue. But I must say that when it comes to political philosophies I like very much what your landsman, Joseph Priestley said. You recall Priestley, I am sure. He was one of the co-discoverers of oxygen—and he was a friend of your Benjamin Franklin, the master of electricity—yes, the electrical philosopher. Priestley taught this one sacred truth—that the greatest happiness of the greatest number is the foundation of morals and legislation. *Oui, oui, mon ami*, this I firmly believe."

After a long pause Monsieur Voltaige spoke again.

"Voltaire—yes, again I must mention that great man, our friend, Monsieur Voltaire. He disagreed with the great religious philosopher Pascal and said that the purpose of life is not to reach heaven through penitence, but to assure happiness to all men by progress in the sciences and the arts, a fulfillment for which our nature is destined."

The little Frenchman suddenly seemed quite melancholy. He gazed at the patio tiles under his feet for a moment and then spoke in a dispirited tone.

"Yes, that for which our nature is destined," he said thoughtfully and then, almost reluctantly, he began to speak again.

"No, no, *mon ami*, I am no ideologue," he continued, "But honestly, sometimes I believe that there should be a special place in hell for those men who rekindled this fire—this bloody war. And all this for politics—for political purposes.

"Oh, but what does it matter what we think—what we believe? Matters seem to come and go as they will. The Buddha…Buddha said that all our suffering comes from craving—our craving for that which we cannot have, and in all likelihood, that which we do not need. Perhaps we should not crave so much and then we would be happier.

"And perhaps I talk too much," Monsieur Voltaige continued. "Talk, talk, talk! I supposed that sometimes I am guilty of being terribly unsophisticated—and sometimes a bit sentimental. This business makes me think of the words of the Emperor Charles V, Charles the Wise. He said 'I speak Spanish to God, Italian to women, French to men, and German to my horse.' So, you see? I suppose I should speak German with Monsieur Curtis Clayton."

Clark had recently noticed that Sergeant Dotson no longer seemed to be entertained by the beekeeper, Becky. Dotson now seemed to be playing the field, enjoying the company of several of the girls who were usually present at poolside. Clark later overheard Dotson speaking with Gutierrez about Mai Bec, the woman called Becky.

"Hey, man, what's going on with Becky?" Gutierrez asked.

"Dat woman crazy, man. She crazy."

"Crazy? Hey, man, what do you mean?"

"She *crazy*. She like snakes, man. Yeah! *Snakes*! She plays 'round wit' snakes. She showed me her pet snake. She said, 'Here now, you touch.' And I said, 'No way, baby. I'll see you 'round the block. But now I'm cuttin' out. Bye, baby. Goodbye, to you.' And, hey now, I ain't got *no* time for no snakes. You understand me? You know what I'm sayin'? No way, man. I ain't got no time for no snakes. She crazy! She not normal is what I'm sayin'. No way, man—no way."

Captain Clark and Mr. Bauer decided they had to leave and return to Bien Hoa Airbase at nine that evening. Monsieur Voltaige saw them off like a father, assuring them as they went that they were always welcome at Les Trungs.

"Stop by anytime—anytime. It could be for ten minutes or ten days, but you are always welcome here. We love your company. The Top Tigers are our American-born, corn-fed *cavaliers*. The Top Tigers are really, as you say, *tops*. God bless them, and may they fly safely through the skies of our little empire—our empire of *delices—yes,* of delights."

Mr. Bauer later confided to Captain Clark that he was really quite fascinated with Monsieur Voltaige.

"But there's something about him though that does not seem right to me. I can't put my finger on it. I don't know, but it's like...well, it's like he's from another planet or something," Bauer said the next evening at the barracks-room bar.

"Say, that's funny that you say he's from another planet," said Clark. "The Little Prince was from another planet. And his creator was a Frenchman—a man named Antoine de Saint Exupery."

"Yeah. Say, isn't he the guy that flew so high that he said he saw the face of God?" Bauer asked.

"He's the one. He was shot down and lost in World War Two," said Clark.

"He must have flown awfully high...to see God's face, I mean," Bauer said.

"Yes, absolutely. It must have been awfully high," said Clark. "I wonder just how high our little Huey will fly. What do you think?"

"Why, I think it would go all the way—all the way to the stars so long as we have enough JP-4."

"Well, here's to ample supplies of JP-4," Clark said with a wry smile. "Here's to high, high, *high* fuel bladders in the sky."

As Clark said goodbye to Genevieve she had tears in her eyes. He tried to cheer her and reassure her, but she suddenly seemed depressed.

"Come on," he said, "I'll be back soon. It will only be a week or so. What is it? Why are you suddenly so sad?"

"I don't know," she said, looking down and avoiding his eyes. "I am starting to get this strange feeling. This...this...how do you say? This premonition...yes, this premonition of bad things. I have this feeling of something hanging over us—something like a storm, something that might harm us, something that might interfere with our being together."

"Don't be down. Don't be such a pessimist," Clark said. "Our glass is not half empty. It's half full. And it will be completely full when I get out of the army and we are together—together every day. You know and I know that our love is something special. It is special and beautiful—and it is powerful. It has a life of its own, and it will bind us together—forever in a blanket, no, in a sweet cocoon of love and bliss. Don't worry, sweetheart. Put those peculiar premonitions out of your lovely little head. I will see you again soon. I promise you that. Remember: great beauty makes its own rules, and our love is magic."

"My father is now saying that perhaps I should return to Paris for awhile," she said.

"What?" asked Clark, a bit incredulous. "Now come on. I know your father. And you know, he is very much like a father to me. He's my friend. He's a wonderful man. And he knows we are in love. He is not blind. And I feel certain that he would not separate us against your will. He is concerned about your feelings. Yes, of course he is. Tell him that you wish to remain here, and I am sure that he will grant your wishes. He's a good man—certainly one of the best I have ever known."

"Yes," replied Genevieve, "of course. He is a good man. I love my father dearly. And he loves you. He agrees that you are special."

Clark held her hands in his. He looked down at her hands as he spoke.

"Lady fingers," he said. "Perfect lady fingers."

He kissed her hands, kissed her lips, and then walked away toward the airstrip.

— — —

While Winston Clark was saying goodbye to Genevieve, Mai Bec, the beekeeper called Becky was speaking with Curtis Clayton. They were standing in the shadows just off the patio near the changing rooms.

"Please," the young Vietnamese woman said to Clayton. "Please, you must come to me. I have information for you. Yes, you can believe me. I have important information for you—very important. *Very* important."

"What are you talking about?" Clayton asked. "What information? Just what is this information you are talking about? Come on. Get precise."

Mai Bec put her finger to her lips and glanced about furtively as if to say, "I can't talk now."

"Please, you must trust me," she said. "We cannot speak freely here. I must not be seen speaking with you. You should meet me behind the generator house at eleven o'clock. Please. It is very important. You must meet me behind powerhouse at eleven. I will tell you everything then. Very important information. Yes, for sure. So, I must go now. I must, I must!"

Mai Bec quickly moved away and faded into the shadows.

Curtis Clayton sipped his white wine and thought about his situation.

What about this girl, this Becky? he thought. What could she have to offer? Who knows? It might be something useful. It could possibly be something about what's going on here at this place, here at Les Trungs. It might be something about the local VC infrastructure. One can just never know. It might be nothing. Maybe she is simply peddling sex. Actually, she is a rather attractive girl. But, on the other hand, it might be a trap. How much does she know about me? These people…well, it's hard to say. Sometimes these people seem to be amazingly well informed. They have their bamboo network and it sometimes works wonders. Well, either way, I'll be there. And I'll have my little snub nosed .38 there under my shirt. Yes, I'll be there. Wouldn't miss it for the world. And I'll be ready, he thought. Yes, I'll be ready—prepared for all contingencies.

Curtis Clayton thought about Monsieur Voltaige, and he thought about his brother, Alan. They had continued to disagree about the

Frenchman and his role in the community—and the war. Curtis said that he had enough information to hang the Frenchman from the highest tree on his plantation.

"Don't you get it?" he asked Alan. "This guy's a—he's a—Well, you could say that he's a VC agent. He's a rotten Commie. That's what he is. He's supporting the other side. And he can't have it both ways. We cannot look the other way. We cannot afford to do that. I don't care who he is. We've got to take him out. There is just no getting around it."

"I won't have any part of it," Alan had said. "I am telling you this man has influence. He's somebody, I'm telling you. I mean he's like an international person. Everyone knows him and he knows everyone. He is highly respected—everywhere. If you do anything crazy…well, I think you will have the whole world coming down on you. Everyone needs rubber, you know. Listen, I say back off and take another look at this whole situation. Don't ask for trouble. You should double-check everything—all of your information. Everything. You need to know what you are getting into. I certainly will not have any part of it—no part. No, thank you. Not me."

"No one's asking you to have a part in it," Curtis Clayton replied. And with those words he left his brother never to see him again.

Mai Bec stood in the moonlight behind the powerhouse. She was not alone. The new beekeeper, the girl who replaced Lee Ann, was there also. Her name was Can Tay. (The Americans called her "Candy.") Can Tay stood nearby out of sight in the breadfruit trees. And all was ready. Everything had been carefully prepared.

More than one type of bee was nurtured and harbored at Les Trungs. There were the bees that produced the honey that everyone enjoyed, and then there was another type of bee in South Vietnam that did not produce honey. In Vietnam there exist an especially fierce type of bee. They are more than twice as big as ordinary bees, and their sting is terribly painful. Some people called them "killer bees." Mai Bec and her friends studied these bees very carefully. These bees always have four sentries on duty and if these are disturbed or offended, they call out the whole hive to attack whatever or whoever disturbs them. On numerous occasions these hives would be set up near a road or a trail. And when an enemy patrol came along and hit the trip wire—or string or earth colored twine—the bees would immediately attack with great ferocity. The troops—either ARVN or American—usually stampeded like a herd of buffalo and ran right into the carefully prepared *punji* traps that lay awaiting them. The Viet Cong considered these fierce bees to be quite special—a very special "low-tech" weapons system, one might say.

All was prepared. Earlier that evening Mai Bec and her friends had dug a hole, a "tiger pit," in the trail which led away from the powerhouse towards the forest of rubber trees. The hole was certainly large enough for a full-grown tiger. It measured roughly seven by seven feet. It was about five feet deep. And it was filled with *punji* spikes—hardened bamboo spears stuck in the ground at the bottom of the hole with the pointed ends up. Mai Bec and her friends gently covered this hole over with a minimal frame of small bamboo sticks, straw mats were laid over that bamboo frame, and then a little dirt, sand, straw, and palm leaves were strewn over the straw mats.

So, the carefully constructed tiger pit was ready and waiting. And the beehives were properly placed, the sentries posted, the trip wire was laid out—and, yes, all was in a high state of readiness. Can Tay would attend to the bees, and Mai Bec would attend to the American.

Mai Bec was watching carefully. She was alert and prepared to move quickly. Now! Yes, now she saw the big American, Mr. Clayton—Mr. Curtis Clayton—the American agent of death. He was walking slowly toward the powerhouse. Mai Bec quickly moved away from the rear of the generator house. She moved a short distance down the path and stopped, stood as still as a statue, and waited there in the radiant blue moonlight.

Curtis Clayton nervously touched the revolver under his shirt as he walked to the area just behind the powerhouse. The little black revolver was there and loaded and this was always reassuring to him. Where was she? Where was the girl?

"Pssst! Pssst!" Mai Bec made soft sounds to attract the American.

Clayton looked in Mai Bec's direction, and he saw her standing there alone on the path in the moonlight.

"Oh, *there* you are," Clayton said in a low tone.

"Come!" she said. "It is urgent! You must come with me. Be quiet and hurry! We don't have much time. Come now! We must not be seen. Please, hurry!"

"Well," he said. "Okay. Hang on."

Mai Bec backed away a few steps. Clayton hurried down the path to join her. He had walked only about fifteen feet down the path when he hit the trip wire. The hive was disturbed. The sentries led the attack on the intruder. Within seconds, the fierce bees were all about Clayton's head and on him—in his hair, his eyes, his nose, his ears, and down his collar. Mai Bec disappeared into the shadows. Clayton charged another ten feet down the path, and then—with a low growl filled with anger and anguish—he crashed through the straw matting into the tiger pit and onto the sharpened spikes below.

— — —

The owl screeched that night. The snow owl from the old Clayton mansion back in Watauga screeched at Winston Clark as he lay sleeping and dreaming on his bunk that night at Bien Hoa Airbase. "Taking fire," someone said in the distance. "Taking fire. We've got a man hit! Got a man hit!" And the owl screeched and flew off into the retina of the great Cao Dai eye.

In his profound unease Clark awoke. From some distant place in the darkened barracks he could hear the low-volume late-night radio sounds of the Beatles singing their hit song "Help!" Their supplication seemed forlorn and monotonous.

— — —

Mai Bec heard only the buzzing of the bees, a brief sound of anguish—and then it was silent.

A short distance away Can Tay held her hand high in the pale moonlight and made a soft cooing sound. She spoke softly to the bees, and herded them back down the way to their hives. Mai Bec stood at the edge of the pit. The big American fairly filled the pit. She reached into a small black bag she carried. Slowly she pulled out a snake, a bamboo viper. The snake was about three and a half feet long. Holding the viper just behind the head, she held it up toward the full moon. Some of the Vietnamese called Mai Bec *Ran Co*, "Serpent Woman."

"And now a special treat for you, little one," she said in Vietnamese. She then threw the viper onto the body of Curtis Clayton. "Enjoy yourself, little viper, little friend. Go now and get to know the big American—the agent of doom who lost his way."

The GIs in the area called these vipers "one-step, two-step snakes." They said that after being bitten, one could take only one step or two before dropping dead. The little vipers were sometimes quite worrisome to the tunnel rats. Occasionally the Viet Cong would take a piece of bamboo, only a foot or so long, then take a small viper, tie the snake by his neck, insert him into the bamboo tube, and then put the tube in the ceiling of a small narrow tunnel. When the GI, the tunnel rat, would brush up against the tube, it would fall, and the snake was on the hot, tired, soldier. The tunnel would not allow for a great deal of maneuver space, and if the GI shot the snake, then the guerrillas were forewarned of the Americans' presence. It was another fine example of an outstanding low-tech combination booby trap and warning system.

As Mai Bec was speaking softly to the moon and the serpent, someone nearby stepped out of the shadows from behind her. Quietly and gently the man moved toward her as she stood there in the moonlight beside the pit with her back toward him. It was Captain Torres, the "long eagle" adviser who had occasionally been seen traveling about with Curtis Clayton.

From behind Torres quickly and firmly put his hand over Mai Bec's mouth and pulled her to him as he stabbed her in the small of the back with his razor-sharp survival knife. He felt her stiffen and then struggle for a moment. She tried in vain to bite his fingers, and then made a low noise like a trapped animal and went limp.

Captain Torres pushed Mai Bec gently forward and she fell into the pit and onto the spikes there beside the impaled body of Curtis Clayton. Torres made a quiet motion to someone in the trees. He was a completely casual person. It was almost the same as if he were sitting in a bar and wanted to catch the attention of a waiter. Two Vietnamese soldiers appeared and walked quickly to him. The three of them gazed down into the pit.

Then Torres spoke to the soldiers in Vietnamese. The men quickly produced two spades from the tree line, and they started to fill in the pit. Captain Torres again quietly disappeared into the shadows. In a short time the hole was filled, and later people would speak of Curtis Clayton and Mai Bec vanishing—simply disappearing from the face of the earth. Some would speak of them as MIA. Some of the Americans would wonder aloud if the two of them might have run away together.

Not far away, Can Tay was speaking to the bees in the moonlight. She cooed and breathed gently, lovingly on them, and told them they were good bees, and that she was very pleased with them. She loved her work with the bees. She had always heard that it was good luck to tell the bees about the important things in one's life. Bees were said to be mediators with God.

"Go tell it to the bees," she had often heard Mai Bec say.

Also Can Tay remembered hearing the Frenchwoman called Monique say that the Prophet Mohammed had declared that both the bee and the ant would certainly be allowed into Paradise—the ants for their strength and industry, and the bees for their sweetness and industry.

"You are patriots," she said to them as the bees slowly crawled over her slender fingers. Both her fingers and the bees appeared pale blue in the moonlight.

"Yes, you know your duty, and you do it well. You do not hesitate. You have no fear of the big Americans. You have no fear of anyone. Yes, yes, you are precious little patriots, and you will be well cared for. I promise. Yes, yes, I promise you that. Go now, go home and sleep well. Sleep well for you are sweet patriots. Yes, sweet, sweet patriots."

Chapter 28

Tet Was a Sacred Holiday

Jan 31, 1968

The violent predawn explosion knocked Clark off his bunk onto the straw matting and concrete floor of the barracks. He felt the earth shake—and it shook again, and again.

When he thought about it later, he was not really sure if the power of the explosion—which was about half mile away—had knocked him off his bunk, or if that was merely the violent reaction of his body being so drastically startled and shocked out of deep sleep. The movement was something like a great spasm. He went instantly from the bunk to the floor—a supersonic no-frills flight of which he could remember nothing.

The same thing had happened to his copilot and roommate Mr. Bauer. Even in the dark, he sensed that Bauer was lying there not two feet away from him.

"Goo-ooo-ood *morning*, Vietnam!" they heard Captain Thedeibeau from his place on the floor down the hallway, greeting the day, but in a rather half-hearted, apathetic way.

They could all hear bottles crashing to the floor and breaking all along the line in the barracks and especially down at the end of the hallway in the game room-bar. Glass was breaking and things were crashing to the concrete floor all the way up and down the barracks. Clark looked at his watch. It was six minutes past three in the morning. It was January 31, 1968. And it was suddenly and terribly evident that the Tet truce was over.

The ammunition dump at Bien Hoa Airbase had exploded. And it continued to explode—thousands of bombs, rockets, grenades, and bullets for hours to come. For the Top Tigers this was the beginning of the historic Tet Offensive. For the next 48 hours or so there would be constant explosions, and the air would be filled with mortar rounds and tracer bullets. Shortly after the ammo dump went up at Bien Hoa, the ammo dump at the huge U.S. base camp at Long Binh went up as well.

Tet was Vietnam's sacred holiday period, the lunar new year festival on January 31. Traditionally, during the long Vietnam War, there would be an unofficial truce or "stand-down" for at least a week—but not this year. That was not to be in 1968. Firecrackers were allowed that year. With 493,000 U.S. troops in the country at that time, the Saigon regime felt secure enough to authorize the traditional firecrackers at Tet, a custom that had been forbidden for a number of years to prevent the Viet Cong from using the firecracker noise as a cover for gunfire. And now the bullets and mortars were flying everywhere. The top general in Saigon later complained about the enemy "deceitfully taking advantage" of the Tet truce to "create maximum consternation."

Normally it might be considered almost sacrilegious to order a general offensive at this time. It would be deeply resented by the ordinary Vietnamese. However, just as with General George Washington's attack against the Hessians at Trenton in New Jersey on the day after Christmas in 1776, the improbability of an attack would be its best concealment. ("They make a great deal of Christmas in Germany," wrote one of General Washington's aides, "and no doubt the Hessians will drink much beer, and they will be sleepy in the morning.") The Battle of Trenton was

Washington's first really successful battle. At Trenton in 1776, was George Washington guilty of "deceitfully taking advantage" of the Hessians in order to "create maximum consternation?" Tet '68 would be another case of history repeating itself. In 1789, Vietnamese patriots had used the same trick on the occupying Chinese in Hanoi.

The offensive was planned in complete secrecy. In January of 1968, the war in South Vietnam was to be taken from the countryside—the rice paddies, rainforests, and the jungles—to the towns and cities, where, it was hoped, the people would rise up against the government and the Americans. Hopefully they would quickly rally to the side of the National Liberation Front. And the war, the North Vietnamese leaders decided, would end in a blazing historic victory for the Communists. Short of that breathtaking supposition, perhaps in a U.S. election year, this explosive offensive would convince the American public that the war was futile and un-winnable.

The enemy wanted to "create maximum consternation," the man said. And that they did. They succeeded in creating consternation beyond anyone's wildest dreams—or nightmares. This was the helicopter war, some said. And it was certainly the television war—on that almost everyone would agree. For years Americans were turning on their televisions to watch American soldiers fight their way across rice paddies and through thick jungles. And they saw their own fathers, sons, and brothers bleeding and dying on television. But they had never seen it so concentrated as it was with Tet '68. The whole world was watching—and the effect of that primitive Tet blitzkrieg was awesome and electrifying.

Prior to the thunder and crash of Tet, there were hints that something was about to happen, but no one seemed to really notice until it was all over and most of the American top brass in Saigon was looking stunned and foolish. The tunnel rats were finding more weapons stored away in the tunnels west of Saigon—mostly in Cu Chi Province. They were finding more of everything—food, supplies, and ammunition. But they did not see any more Viet Cong. The tunnels, caves, jungles, and rain forest continued to hold their secrets.

The trail watchers, the Oscar Team LRRPs, were seeing more people entering the country from the direction of the Ho Chi Minh Trail. And these people were NVA, from the North Vietnamese Army. They were better dressed and better equipped than the local VC. But not much was made of this intelligence. Some interpreted this as business as usual or actually as good news. To some in G-2 this merely meant that Charlie in the III Corps Tactical Zone had been pretty much wiped out and now he was being forced to call on his cousins in the North to reinforce him before the bottom fell out of the war effort entirely. Subsequent investigations would determine that there had been serious intelligence failures just prior to Tet '68.

The Americans and the ARVN were reeling. They simply did not know what had hit them. Only recently, on a stateside visit, the top American general had repeatedly announced that the Americans had turned the corner, that they could see the light at the end of the tunnel. All this was supposed to mean that the Americans were clearly winning the war. Did someone maybe get it all wrong? What was going on? Charlie was supposed to be on his last leg. Did someone forget to tell Charlie that he was finished—all washed up? The elusive Charlie seemed to have come back to life with a vengeance. The enemy seemed have multiplied by a thousand and now he seemed to be everywhere at once.

Just shortly before the ammunition dump had blown at Bien Hoa, a platoon of specially trained Viet Cong had blown a hole through the compound wall and charged into the U.S. Embassy in Saigon, their automatic rifles firing as they ran. Five American guards were killed in less than five minutes. The U.S. Embassy was a newly constructed six-story concrete structure on one of the city's main boulevards. The edifice was ensconced behind thick stucco walls and thought to be quite defensible. The Vietnamese guards supposedly fled at the first hint of violence. It took almost seven hours of intense fighting to clear the embassy of Viet Cong commandos. An American soldier raced up to the side of the building and tossed up a pistol to a colonel who was standing at a second floor window. And, as they met on a stairway, the colonel shot and killed the last of the enemy commandos.

One well informed American journalist and historian, Stanley Karnow, wrote that this operation was staged and planned "near a rubber plantation" about forty miles northwest of Saigon. The enemy commandos concealed arms, ammunition, and explosive in truckloads of rice and tomatoes, which were easily driven into Saigon and stored in an automobile repair shop whose proprietor was a VC sympathizer. One VC strong point was a Buddhist pagoda. Weeks before, with the collusion of the monks, the guerrillas had dug a bunker under the pagoda and stashed weapons and ammunition there. It would take over a week for the Americans to regain control of Saigon. And farther up north, it would take the hard-fighting U.S. Marines almost a month to re-take the old imperial capital of Hue.

Almost everyone involved in the Tet Offensive seemed to be suicidal—and extraordinarily brutal. In many of the villages and cities that they occupied during the Tet campaign the Communists slaughtered hundreds of minor government functionaries, as well as many other innocuous figures, such as foreign doctors, schoolteachers, and missionaries. The Communists succeeded in occupying Hue for twenty-five days, and there they committed countless atrocities.

In Hue, an American civilian who worked for the U.S. Information Service was captured while visiting the home of a Vietnamese friend. He was shot and left in a nearby field. A German physician teaching at a local medical school was seized with his wife and two other German doctors, and their bodies were later found in a shallow pit. And despite their instructions to spare the French (President Charles de Gaulle had recently announced to the press that he thought the Americans should get out of Vietnam), the communists arrested two Benedictine missionaries, shot one of them and buried the other alive. The Communists also killed

Father Buu Dong, a popular Vietnamese Catholic priest who had entertained Viet Cong agents in his rectory, where he kept a portrait of Ho Chi Minh, telling parishioners that he prayed for Ho because "he too is our friend." Many Vietnamese with only the flimsiest ties to the Saigon regime suffered a similar fate.

During the months following the Communist occupation of Hue, the remains of approximately 3,000 people were exhumed in nearby riverbeds and jungle clearings. Paradoxically, the American public hardly noticed the stories about these atrocities, because they were preoccupied at that time with news about an American atrocity—the My Lai massacre—the awful incident in which American soldiers, at the direction of their officers, killed approximately 100 Vietnamese peasants—women and children among them.

Some in the North Vietnamese Communists hierarchy believed that a full-scale offensive at that time would be foolish. But most of the top communists in Vietnam seemed to conclude that Ho Chi Minh was getting old. He had not been in good health for some time. And most of the key communist leaders agreed that they should do something to speed up the war and try to win it before the death of Ho Chi Minh.

Ho Chi Minh died at the age of seventy-nine on September 2, 1969. And his death seemed to inspire renewed zeal among the Vietnamese Communists.

The famous Tet Offensive was an extraordinary military operation. And historians will perhaps disagree for many years on whether or not it was wisely planned and conducted. Nevertheless, it clearly had historical significance, because it turned out to be the turning point of the war. The top American officers in Saigon seemed stunned and almost speechless. This blockbuster of an offensive just did not seem possible. Journalist Neil Sheehan described the Tet Offensive as the "masterstroke" that would have the will-breaking effect on the Americans that Dien Bien Phu had on the French back in 1954. It was indeed a masterstroke. It was fanatical, brutal, and thoroughly blood-soaked—but, yes, it was undoubtedly a masterstroke.

One highly placed American general later said that the Tet Offensive was a "tactical defeat for the Viet Cong, but it was a psychological victory" for the enemy. The world seemed to shout back at him as if to say, "Well, which is more important in war—especially a guerrilla war? The psychological victory, of course. General, do you recall Yorktown in 1781? Well, the British Empire was not exactly defeated there, but they were quite embarrassed and seriously discouraged."

The Communist Vietnamese seemed to better understand the power and effectiveness of the media in shaping the will of the American people to support this faraway war. The U.S. top brass in Saigon never seemed to understand the value of truthfulness and honesty in dealing with the press.

Only weeks before while on a visit to Washington, the top general from Saigon had said, "the enemy's hopes are bankrupt." Now, just after the U.S. president, the U.S. Congress, and the American people had been reassured that the famous "light at the end of the tunnel" was visible, the entire country of South Vietnam seemed to explode in a carefully concealed and coordinated attack of massive proportions. Then suddenly the world was viewing dead American soldiers being picked up by the truckload off the streets of Saigon and the ancient capital of Hue. Everyone seemed quickly convinced that something had gone terribly awry. Someone had been misinformed, misled.

The big American president from Texas was thoroughly sick and tired of hearing about the tunnel or the "light at the end of the tunnel." Toward the end of his tenure, after hearing that tired metaphor for the ten thousandth time, the president, in a most dejected mood, looked down and muttered to a close aide: "We don't even have a tunnel. We don't even know where the tunnel is."

This was the very portrait of a proud man brought low and speaking in bitter despair.

Fifteen Viet Cong battalions, approximately 6,000 Communist troops, had moved into Saigon and its suburbs in a period of just a few days. One of these battalions was a sapper battalion of 250 who had been living in the city, working at such lowly jobs as taxi and pedicab drivers. These men knew the city intimately. Simultaneously, the Communists invaded thirteen of the sixteen provincial capitals of the populous Mekong Delta. At the end of January, U.S. and South Vietnamese government installations were attacked at over one hundred cities, towns, and bases. Ten provincial capitals fell under temporary Viet Cong control. And two long sieges—one at remote Khe Sanh in the far north, and one at the citadel in old imperial capital of Hue in the central part of South Vietnam—would prolong the agony of Tet '68. At this point the VC seemed to have abandoned their flexible tactics and often defended untenable positions to the last man. None of the twenty Viet Cong commandos assigned to seize the U.S. Embassy survived the attack.

Ben Tre, a Mekong Delta provincial capital, and a city of about 35,000, was hit hard by the Viet Cong during Tet '68. During the fighting there, in an effort to defend a small American compound of advisers and the province chief, the city was almost obliterated. At least 500 civilians were killed. The U.S. had spent millions since 1961 trying to make Ben Tre a Delta showplace of security and prosperity. This was where the journalist Peter Arnett wrote the absurd and ludicrous line, a quote from a local U.S. officer that, "We had to destroy the town to save it."

One of the lasting and most violently haunting images to come out of the Tet fighting in Saigon was the photograph snapped by Associated Press photographer Eddie Adams, of the Saigon police chief putting his short barreled revolver against a young prisoner's head and firing. The man grimaced and then fell backwards, blood gushing from his head as it hit the pavement. The young guerrilla wore black shorts and a checkered sports shirt. His hands were bound behind him.

One day just prior to Tet '68, Clark had asked Linville what he imagined the outcome of the war would be.

"Oh, I think we'll win—eventually," Linville said almost without hesitation. "I think what's going to happen is that this place, this whole country will end up being paved over, wall to wall, with GIs and all their stuff, their equipment—tanks, planes, helicopters, and guns."

"The solution, I believe," Major Ratcliffe interjected, "is more bombs, more shells, more napalm, more B-52s, until the other side cracks and gives up—flakes off."

Men like Major Ratcliffe, it seems, would never believe it, but it was becoming increasingly apparent to most that there was not enough napalm in the world to make the Vietnamese people give up their struggle. War had become a way of life for them.

Increasingly Clark was hearing other officers saying words like the words he had recently heard from Captain Thedeibeau.

"This is crazy," Thedeibeau said, "Didn't any of those guys at the top in Saigon ever play a game of craps? Well, my old daddy used to say to me, 'Son, remember, don't ever throw good money after bad—know when to fade. You bet, know when to fade. And know when to pass.'"

Bill Bauer said he thought that big general in Saigon should read, or reread, the Book of Job—especially that part about the mountain and the water wearing away the stone. Bauer quoted the passage. It went like this:

But as a mountain erodes and crumbles
And as a rock is moved from its place,
As water wears away stones
And torrents wash away the soil,
So you destroy man's hope.
And he will be brought low,
As his life ebbs away.

During the weeks prior to the Tet Offensive, Clark was increasingly overcome by a feeling of melancholy when he though of Genevieve, Voltaire Six, and Les Trungs. Something seemed to be going awry. Clark could not be certain what it was, but something was amiss. Somewhere there was a serpent hiding in the folds of Paradise. He continued to have a strange feeling of foreboding about the Frenchman and his plantation, his "empire of delights." Clark's heart told him that all was well in Paradise. But his stomach told him that the apple might be wormy. Genevieve told Clark that her father appeared depressed over the disappearance of Curtis Clayton. The American investigators continued to return repeatedly to Les Trungs, and they endlessly questioned her father and almost everyone else there. She said that Monsieur Voltaige seemed more and more to believe that this Clayton man had put a curse on their happy estate. The little Frenchman told his daughters that increasingly his American friends in Saigon seemed to be inclined to avoid him.

"*Mother Courage and Her Children,*" Genevieve said one day.

She mentioned to Clark that her father had recently commented that he was starting to think of himself in terms of Bertolt Brecht's *Mother Courage and Her Children*, a well intended but ill-fated figure exposed to the capricious forces of war.

After a recent debriefing in the operations building, Top Tiger Six announced that Les Trungs, the Frenchman's plantation, would be off limits to all company personnel in the future. He did not go into details as to how or why this decision had been made. But he appeared to be very firm and grim on this topic.

A little later, Clark overheard Major Marker discussing the matter with several other officers—and Major Ratcliffe was among them. Major Marker said he was not really sure what the problem was, but drug abuse was increasingly a problem in the unit and it had been said that the men were getting the drugs at Les Trungs. It was about that time that a highly placed American official revealed that a recent study indicated that as many as 30 percent of the U.S. troops in Vietnam had experimented with either opium or heroin. Also, Mr. Hobbes was still listed as MIA, and more recently the civilian Foreign Service officer, Curtis Clayton, had disappeared, and both of these cases seemed somehow to be related to the Frenchman's place, Les Trungs.

The pitch black night sky was filled with fireworks as Captain Clark trotted toward his helicopter. He looked up and saw hundreds, thousands of .50 caliber tracers crisscrossing the night sky. And the fire in the sky carried a message that night. The message was written across the nighttime sky in flames. Now he could make it out. It was written in the universal tongue of grief and desperation. On the trail of flaming .50 caliber bullets it said:

"You know these words. Yes, they are written on your heart. *You are a stranger in a strange land.* And you have become an unwholesome guest—a corrupt sojourner. Now you must go. It is time. Time has found us—and found us wanting. Yes, both of us fell short of the measure. We have both shed our honor. Something important got lost in the most remote part of the rainforest, in the deepest, murkiest part of the Delta, and in the back streets of Saigon. The price of reckless adventurism is abject humiliation. And the adventure is over. It is time to stand at the bar of judgment and be violently banished. Yes, banished, humiliated, and shamed. Serious damage has been done. Let us pray that it is not irreparable. Go now and perhaps one day we can be friends again and laugh together. But do not remain here now—no, not now. If you remain, together we will dictate some terribly shameful pages of history. If you remain we will fall just this side of genocide. If you remain we will lie down and die together in a fast embrace of pestilence, corruption, shame, and death. So, heed this message and go. Be a friend to yourself and to everyone, and go, and go now—and go gracefully."

Tet represented a new year—and a panoramic new perspective for everyone.

Chapter 29

No Survivors

Viet Cong assault groups had penetrated the bunkers around the eastern end of Bien Hoa Airbase. Commandos were dashing for the hangars; the helicopter gunships, the Mustangs, were swooping in after them. The running figures disappeared under an intense hail of machine gun, rocket fire, and dust.

Captain Clark and Mr. Bauer were soon in the air with a flight of eleven other helicopters heading westward for the U.S. 25th Infantry Division's main base camp near Cu Chi. The air was still filled with tons of hot flying lead and parachute flares. The Top Tigers pulled in additional power and climbed on up to 6,000 feet for more safety. They flew using only their running lights.

It was a terribly dangerous night to be out flying, but the flight was a fairly short one, and they were soon letting down for a landing on the PSP landing strip at Cu Chi base.

Major Marker conducted a quick briefing at Cu Chi to tell everyone that for the next ten or twelve hours or so they would be ferrying troops into Saigon. There they would be landing at the racetrack—and also later at the soccer field. These troops were tasked to clear the VC out of Saigon, Cholon, and Tan Son Nhut Airport. By the time the Top Tigers, flying eastward now, started to let down at the racetrack, it was growing light.

They spent the entire next day ferrying troops into the Saigon area to retake the city and its airport, Tan Son Nhut. They flew one load after another of U.S. troops out of Cu Chi, and then they flew load after load of ARVNs out the PSP airstrip at Trang Bang, which was just to the west of Cu Chi.

Toward nightfall, because of a slight delay in refueling, Clark and Bauer found themselves flying in the "tail end Charlie" position—bringing up the rear of the formation as they took off from the soccer field. While refueling at Cu Chi they heard that they had lost a Mustang crew—shot down just off the main highway not too far from Bien Hoa. Some VC with machine guns had holed up in a strong position in a filling station about midway along the main highway between Bien Hoa and Saigon. Major Ratcliffe had been attacking that position with a light fire team when his wingmen—Mr. Sykes and Mr. McClain—had been hit and gone down. They reported "taking fire" and then went in across from the filling station with a big explosion. The entire crew was gone. There were no survivors.

Just as Clark was taking off from the soccer field he got a call on the radio from Major Marker.

"Clark," said Marker. "Are you tail end Charlie today?"

"That's right. That's us. What's up?"

"Major Rats has got something going on the other side of town," Marker said, "and he has asked for a slick to help him out. Can you take the mission?"

"Sure," said Clark. "We'll take it. Where is he?"

"There's a firebase over there about twenty-five miles east of Saigon on the road to Vung Tau," Marker said. "It's a little place called Phu My.

They've been under heavy attack now for about four hours. Get in touch with Rats as soon as you can and find out what he needs. See what you can do for him."

"We'll do it," Clark said. "We're breaking off and heading east for Phu My."

Clark pulled in additional power and flew the aircraft up to about 5,000 feet, and after about ten minutes they had Major Rats, the Mustang Buddha, on the radio. The sun was rapidly setting in the West. Major Ratcliffe said he was on station over Phu My with a light fire-team. They were trying to break up an attack on the ARVN compound there, he said, and now things did seemed to be quieting down somewhat. However, the American advisor in the compound, call sign "Bushwhacker," said that he had a number of wounded that needed to be "dusted off," medevaced. As Clark and Bauer approached the outpost they could clearly see a number of bodies dressed in black pajamas lying about in the concertina wire around the post perimeter.

"I think it's safe to go in now," Major Ratcliffe said to Clark. "You guys go on in and pick up as many wounded as you can. We don't have much ammo or fuel left. After you pull outta there, we'll go in and pick up all we can, and hopefully that will do the trick."

It was dark by then and the landing area inside the compound was extremely small and surrounded by high wires and antennas. Clark made a slow approach to the compound. The tension in the chopper was palpable. As they crossed over the wire they expected to take some fire—and they did. Just as they crossed over the wire they heard some bullets snapping by the aircraft. But they were lucky. Later they found eight bullet holes in the aircraft, but no one was hit and the damage was minor—an easy job for the men in the Sheet Metal Section of the Maintenance Platoon. Most of the hits were in the tailboom. Fortunately a flare lit up the nighttime sky just as they were coming in over the compound walls. Dotson and Gutierrez were on their door guns and putting down some good protective fire while they were at their most vulnerable point.

Shortly thereafter, Dotson and Gutierrez were quickly outside the chopper supervising the loading of the wounded. They took onboard five wounded ARVNs, two women, and three small children. They all just seemed to pile up in the middle of the chopper and hold on for dear life as the aircraft lifted off. It was a little tricky getting over the wires again. But at least they did not hear any bullets snapping around them this time. They were soon climbing out and rapidly gaining airspeed and altitude.

Major Ratcliffe and his wingman also went in and each picked up a load of wounded. Flying eastward Clark could soon see the lights of Vung Tau, the coastal city where he had once enjoyed residing at the Pacific Hotel. They were very low on fuel, and Clark could not help but think about what a mess it would be if they crashed with all of the wounded Vietnamese and their families piled up loosely in the middle of the aircraft—mostly not strapped in, but just hanging on.

As they approached the Vung Tau airfield from over the bay the fuel warning light came on. Clark became a little uneasy. Maybe we should get ready to ditch? he thought. Maybe we should get unbuckled and get out from under these chicken plates? Then again, maybe we should get tuned in to that airfield up there and get focused and ready to land.

They made a safe landing and hovered to a position near the tower where an ambulance stood by ready to take the wounded off to the hospital. Both Clark and Bauer agree that being low on fuel had made the aircraft much lighter and therefore made takeoffs and landings much easier at the Phu My compound. But they were also thoroughly convinced that it was the closest they had ever come to running out of fuel, and did not wish to repeat that performance again in the near future.

Dotson noted that it took a great deal of fuel—236 gallons—to refill the bladder.

"Jus' fumes," he said. "We came in here on jus' fumes, man."

"Yep, Ultimate Six was with us again," Bauer said with a tired smile as they took off and flew over Dead Man's Beach, where Clark and Mel Meeks had enjoyed a swim together a long time ago.

That night upon returning to Bien Hoa Airbase they were able to get some sleep. Early the next day they were sent back out to Cu Chi base for more troop movements, and then in the late afternoon they found themselves at the airfield in Tay Ninh. The advisers there had taken some hard pounding and had suffered a number of casualties. Clark and Bauer took two wounded Americans and four wounded ARVNs to the hospital at Long Binh. As they turned onto their final approach to land at the hospital pad at Long Binh, they could hear Petula Clark singing "Don't Sleep in the Subway, Darling" on AFN radio. Winston Clark could not avoid thinking at that moment how sweet it would be to say hello to Petula Clark and to sleep in the London subway for awhile right at that time. They quickly refueled and then returned to Tay Ninh. It had been a long day—an infinitely long day.

Roughly an hour and a half later, while Captain Clark was standing near the helicopter as it was being refueled on the airfield near Tay Ninh City, he looked up and saw the "Lone Eagle," Captain Torres, approaching him. They made some small talk. And then Torres thanked Clark for the support with the wounded, and he talked about how he very much appreciated the Top Tigers, and especially the gunship support from the Mustangs.

"We had a lot of action over at Suoi Cao last night," Torres said. "And we lost some good people. But then your friend, Major Rats, and his guys showed up just in time. They fired up Charlie in the wire. Yeah, they brought smoke. This morning our guys counted over fifty dead Charlies around the perimeter over there. And, yeah, they're giving the gunships credit for most of those. Yes, it's true. You guys do good work. We owe you some beer—a whole hell of a lot of beer, I would say."

Clark thanked Torres for his generous remarks. And then he asked about Major Ratcliffe. Where was he—had he returned to Cu Chi?

"Oh, you mean you didn't talk with him?" Torres asked.

"No. Why? What's up?"

"Oh, well," Captain Torres said rather pensively, "it's like this. While Rats was here he met up with Major Wilson. You remember Major Wilson. He used to be Rats' platoon leader. Well, now he's the CO of the Sidewinders. He's Sidewinder Six now. Their former CO was shot—took a round in the head the other night. Well, anyway, Wilson also knew that civilian guy, Curt Clayton. You know, the guy that disappeared over there at the Frenchy's place—that civilian guy. Major Wilson spent a year flying with Air America, working for the agency, the company, you know. And during that time he got to know Clayton, who also worked for the agency."

Dotson and Gutierrez were just about finished with refueling the helicopter. Bauer walked over and joined Clark and Torres in their conversation.

"Well, one thing came to another," Torres continued, "and then I decided to let them know what happened to Clayton. I was there," said Long Eagle. "I heard what was about to happen that night. But I arrived a little too late to prevent it. So, I'll tell you about it too, but it's confidential. Actually, I mean it's more like top secret. Don't ever say anything about it or I will certainly deny it. You got me? Well, I told them that Clayton was killed over there at the Frenchy's place. And that pilot, that warrant officer, Hobbes—remember him? Well, he was also killed and buried someplace around there."

"Well, Rats and Wilson seemed to get pretty steamed up about this when I told them about Clayton and Hobbes. I also told them about us losing Lieutenant Littleton last night," Torres went on, "and then they said—on the spot—that they thought they just might pay the Frenchman a little visit."

"Wait now," said Clark. "It was not the Frenchman, Monsieur Voltaige, that killed Clayton and Hobbes, was it?"

"It was the beekeepers—they did it. They killed them both," said Lone Eagle, his voice coming down an octave. "And who is the keeper of the beekeepers, might I ask?"

After a long pause Torres continued.

"We've captured a number of prisoners during the last couple of days and one of them told us quite a bit about Voltaige, the Frenchman. He said that some of the main attacks on Saigon were planned over there at Les Trungs, the Frenchy's place. And this prisoner said that the attack on Suoi Cao was also planned over there. And we lost some good people at Suoi Cao. That's enough for me. I think someone needs to make the Frenchy pay the piper. Some say that the Frenchy is so well connected that he will never have to bite the bullet. But I'm not so sure about that. Your man, Rats, well, he…well, he's pretty spontaneous—a bold operator, you know. And he's headed over that way right now."

"You make it sound like Buddha is out for blood," Bauer said.

"Well, with your Buddha—with Rats—you never know now, do ya'?" Torres asked with a sardonic smile.

"Now, let's see if I got this right. Are you saying that Voltaige is a Communist?" Bauer asked.

"Listen," said Lone Eagle, showing a hint of impatience. "You can call him what you like—Communist, Mouseketeer, or Tooth Fairy. Whatever. But can't you see? The bearded lady is really a man. That guy's pulling a lot of strings. And some of those strings have got nasty little surprises tied to the end of them. We lost Lieutenant Littleton over there at Suoi Cao last night, and they tell me now that he was badly mutilated. And this Frenchy and his plantation are at the very center of enemy activities in this area—the area between the end of the Ho Chi Minh Trail and Saigon. Sure, he's chummy with everyone we know, but he is working for the other side. It's that simple. And it's high time he got shut down—put out of business. Wrapped up. Terminated."

There was a clear spark of malevolence in Torres' eyes when he pronounced that last word—"*terminated.*"

"Come on, Bill," Clark said to his copilot with a sudden sense of urgency. "Let's go. Let's take a quick swing by Les Trungs and see what's going on over there."

"Okay, sure. Let's go," said Bauer without hesitation.

They quickly started the machine, ran it up to operating RPM, did a sharp pedal turn, pulled pitch, and took off. To the west, toward the Ho Chi Minh Trail and Cambodia, the sun had just dropped behind the endless sea of jungle canopy. It was getting dark fast. Clark pulled in some additional power and in less than fifteen minutes they were approaching Les Trungs. They could see some lights in and around the chateau. They could also make out the blinking of a rotating beacon attached to the roof of a helicopter in the vicinity of Les Trungs

— — —

Genevieve was in her room lying on her bed near an open window. She would soon be preparing for the evening meal with her father and her sister, Monique. But now she was writing in her diary. This was something she had done a great deal of lately. She wrote of her loneliness. She wrote of the strange beauty of Vietnam and the uncertainty of life. She wrote of the Vietnamese people and their intensity in their everyday struggle to survive. And she wrote of Winston Clark. She talked of his sweetness, his kindness, and his thoughtfulness. This man, this American, seemed different. He seemed well informed and interested in everything. Yes, such a range of interests! And most of all he was interested in her. He wanted to know all about her—what she had been like as a small child, and what her world was like. As a young girl, who was it that had impressed her most and why? What sort of school did she attend? How did she envision her adulthood? Who was her first love? Everything about her interested him. He wanted all the details—the little things. It all mattered.

Ah, oui, the scope of his interest knew no bounds, but at the same time, he seemed so uncomplicated. Her father had said that Clark had the heart and the simplicity of a great man—a noble soul. They—Genevieve and Winston—could dance and talk all night long. They had done so on several occasions. She never tired of him. This man could do anything—and do it with the greatest of ease and grace. He could ride a horse, play tennis, shoot skeets, dance, write poems—and fly a helicopter. Yes, he could fly like an eagle. And he learned different languages quickly. He was rapidly learning French. And it was he who always acted as an interpreter between his friends and the Vietnamese. The Vietnamese seemed to take an immediate liking to him. He was so friendly and open. He gave the children candy and—filled with laughter and joy—they taught him their language. Being with him was like being on a journey through an unknown land, a fantasyland. She did not know where the journey would lead, but she would not think of that now. Regardless of the unknown, she would gladly travel with this man, this Winston. Traveling with this man was blissful. And she would gladly agree to accompany him anywhere. She would happily face the unknown with him. He was an endless source of wonder to her. He was like the sun with the blinding beauty of his spirit, his soul. No, he was like the moon. One side was dark and mysterious, and the other side open, shining, glowing with golden warmth—and sweetness. Yes, sweetness. This man was sweetness itself. He was the essence of sweetness. Everyone loved him. No one could not love him unless that person was entirely evil. Yes, this man was sweetness itself.

The last time that her father had stayed up late and drunk wine with them, he had said:

"D'Artagnan, I must tell you—you are like a son to me. And I entrust to you my most precious daughter, Genevieve. Take good care of her."

Monsieur Voltaige seemed sad and somber that night.

"I will, *mon ami*," Clark had replied. "I will take good care of her. And I will love her always."

Genevieve suddenly put her pen down in the crease of her diary. She gazed at the open window, and yes, there in the distance, she could hear a helicopter—probably several helicopters. By the sound she could tell it was of the type that the Americans flew. Her father's helicopter was parked near the airstrip. The helicopter sounded as if it were approaching Les Trungs—their airstrip. Yes, it was! Could it be him? Could it be Winston? Could it be her love?

As light as a bird, Genevieve flew quickly down the stairs. She met her father and her sister at the door, and together they quickly walked out onto the patio to watch the approaching helicopters.

Major Ratcliffe approached the south end of the airstrip at Les Trungs. The airstrip was lighted, not well, but well enough that he could clearly make out the triangular outline of the strip on final approach. Ratcliffe made his approach to the center of the dirt strip.

"This place is a viper's nest," Ratcliffe said to his copilot, Mr. Gibson.

Major Wilson was flying in Major Ratcliffe's wingman position. And now, as Major Wilson and his crew were on short final approach to the south end of the airstrip, Ratcliffe heard someone come on line and report, "Taking fire!"

Major Wilson's crew chief and door gunner reacted quickly and laid down good suppressing fire on the area below and to the sides of the helicopter. But something was going on with Major Wilson's copilot, Mr. Oakley. Major Wilson now noticed that he had blood on his gloves, his clear visor was sprinkled with spots of blood. And soon he would see there was blood on the radio console and on the ceiling of the machine. Mr. Oakley had been shot in the upper right thigh and was bleeding badly. Blood was splattered all over the cockpit.

"We gotta man hit!" Wilson reported on the radio to Ratcliffe as he glanced nervously over at Oakley, who was writhing in pain.

"Is it bad?" Ratcliffe asked.

"Yeah, it looks pretty bad. We're gonna have to break off," Wilson reported. "It's Oakley. He's been hit in the leg. He's bleeding quite a bit. We've gotta get to a hospital right away. We're breaking off."

"Yeah, sure. Okay, then go ahead. Break off. I think I would take him to Cu Chi, if I were you," said Ratcliffe.

"Roger that," said Wilson. "We're breaking off—heading for Cu Chi."

"We will soon be following you," Ratcliffe said after a pause. "First I think I want to check on something here. I gotta check something out here, but we'll be coming on in behind you soon."

Major Wilson pulled in additional power and flew away in the direction of the Cu Chi base camp.

Major Ratcliffe, still at a high hover, now started to slowly move his chopper up the dirt airstrip toward the chateau. He stared hard toward the patio, and yes, there he thought he could make out several figures moving about. He hovered slowly forward.

Just at that moment Clark and his crew were on short final approach over the south end of the airstrip. Clark and Bauer could see Major Wilson's aircraft moving off in an easterly direction rapidly gaining altitude. Clark and Bauer were tuned in to the same radio frequency as were Ratcliffe and Wilson, so they had heard the report of "taking fire" and of the casualty—Mr. Oakley. Clark had also overheard Ratcliffe's comments on "checking out" something there at Les Trungs.

Major Ratcliffe was now at the north end—the top end—of the airstrip. He could see a small group of people standing on the patio near the swimming pool. He pulled his chopper up to a slightly higher hover. He flipped on the landing light and focused it—spot light fashion—on the group standing on the patio. And now he could clearly make out who was there. It was Monsieur Voltaige with his daughters, Genevieve and Monique, at his side, and standing slightly behind Monique to the right was the Frenchman's pilot, Paul Picair.

Major Ratcliffe pulled in additional power and hovered higher and closer to the patio and the people standing there transfixed in his spotlight.

Clark had completed his approach to the center of the airstrip, and now he was rapidly hovering toward Ratcliffe and his aircraft at the top of the strip.

"Hey, Mustang Six, what are you doing? What's up? What's going on? What are you up to?"

There was no answer from the gunship. Major Ratcliffe seemed to be hovering ever closer to the people on the patio. His tailboom wagged slightly as he lined up with them—face to face. The tailboom of the helicopter seemed to wag in a menacing sort of way. To Clark it seemed to bring to mind a cobra preparing to strike.

"Hey, come on! What's happening? What's going on?" Clark asked on the radio to Ratcliffe. In Clark's tone it was clearly evident that he was concerned that something was not right—not as it should be.

"Okay," Ratcliffe responded to Clark. "You guys back off. That's right. I said just back off. Back off."

Clark, now only a short distance behind Ratcliffe's hovering chopper, put his aircraft down in the red dust.

"Bill," Clark said, "take the controls. Okay?"

"Sure," Bauer responded. "I've go the controls."

Clark quickly unbuckled his seatbelt, unplugged the radio line from his helmet, slipped off his chicken plate, and climbed out of the machine.

"Hey, where ya' goin'?" Bauer asked just before Clark disconnected his helmet radio line.

"I'm really not sure. But hang on. I'll be back soon. Just hang on for a couple of minutes, okay?" said Clark.

Bauer nodded. "Okay," he said.

Major Ratcliffe again focused on the group there not more than twenty yards in front of his aircraft. He shined his spotlight in their faces. Their clothing blew violently about their bodies from the helicopter's powerful downdraft. The girls tried to protect their faces from the wind and dust. Major Ratcliffe was carrying almost a full load of rockets. He had expended only four earlier that day. Now he had a load of ten rockets—a pod of five on each side of the aircraft. Ratcliffe put pressure on the chopper pedals. The aircraft's tailboom wagged slightly as he lined up on the group directly ahead on the patio.

At that moment, as from no where, a ghostly parachute flare popped directly over the Frenchman and his group. Monsieur Voltaige stood there as though he were a performer at center stage. He seemed to be looking Ratcliffe directly in the eyes. With one hand Monsieur Voltaige attempted to protect his face and with the other he gave the Americans a friendly wave. Genevieve stood on his left side. Monique stood on his right side, and Paul Picair stood slightly to the rear of Monique. Picair was wearing a pistol in a shoulder holster.

Major Ratcliffe flipped off the safeties. He flipped another switch activating the weapons system—the rockets.

"This place is a nest of vipers," Ratcliffe said.

"Buddha!" Clark shouted desperately as he ran toward Ratcliffe's helicopter.

"Buddha, no, no, *no*! Buddha! No!"

Major Ratcliffe pulled the switch and fired a full salvo of ten 2.75-inch rockets at the small group of people standing there before him on the patio. And they all vanished in a fiery explosion.

"BUDDHA! NOOOOOOO!"

"Oh, Buddha, no! Nooooo!" Clark screamed as everything before him exploded and transformed itself into a wall of flame and searing heat. It was too late. It was done. It was all over. He faced a wall of roaring flame—a violent and withering wall of death and destruction. Genevieve, the angel of life, was gone—completely gone. Vanished. Voltaire Six was gone. He was irrevocably gone. Gone. Completely and forever. The delicate little prince, the man who personified the art of good living, was gone forever. The little man who possessed such a powerful, surging, indestructible life force was now gone. And suddenly, it was as though he had never existed.

Clark stared toward the chateau, toward the patio where Genevieve had just been standing with her father, her sister, and Picair. He faced a wall of flame. The very air was on fire. They were gone. Gone. And there on the patio where they had been Clark saw only grief, disaster, red raw pain, revulsion, and death. Now the chateau was burning. He could feel the heat. And his heart and soul were afire with Les Trungs.

"Oh, no! Oh, God, no!" Clark said as he fell to the earth there at the end of the red dirt runway. He fell almost as though he had been shot, hit by a flurry of deadly, silent, invisible, and intangible bullets. They were bullets that did not cause the blood to spill and flow, but they incapacitated just the same.

Major Ratcliffe did a slow one-hundred-and-eighty-degree pedal turn to his left. He coolly glanced at his copilot, Hoot Gibson. Ratcliffe hardly noticed Clark lying face down in the dirt.

"They cooked off," said Ratcliffe. "You know how that goes, guys, if anyone should ever ask you. Those rockets—these things just cook off sometimes, right? The electrical system is tricky at times. We all know that, right?"

Everyone quickly agreed with Major Ratcliffe, their aircraft commander. Those rockets—sometimes they would just cook off. Electrical impulses, or something—it happens. Major Ratcliffe pulled in additional power and started to move around Bauer's aircraft and down the runway for a takeoff to the south.

"Hey, what's going on down there?"

Suddenly Mr. Bauer heard Mr. Lang's voice on the radio. Lang's voice, as always, seemed husky and reassuring.

"What's going on?"

"I'm not really sure," Bauer replied. "It looks to me like someone just fired a full salvo of rockets directly into the Frenchman's place."

Simultaneously, as Mr. Lang was approaching the airstrip at Les Trungs, Major Ratcliffe was in the process of taking off. As his aircraft approached the south end of the airstrip with ever-increasing velocity, Ratcliffe suddenly came on line.

"Taking fire!" he said. Again, "We're taking fire!"

His voice conveyed urgency, but not panic—never panic.

Then there was an enormous explosion. Mustang Six had gone in—crashed and was burning in the trees just past the south end of the airstrip.

As the fire at the chateau spread and grew in intensity, both Dotson and Gutierrez jumped out of their positions in the Huey and trotted forward to where Captain Clark was lying face down sobbing in the dirt. With one standing on each side, they gently helped the captain up from the ground.

He wept like a baby—a helpless, hopeless child. He choked on his sobs. His grief was massive—a black, bottomless pit of disabling pain and despair. Where he had once known a bottomless well of love, now he knew a bottomless pit of grief. His face was completely smeared with sweat, tears, and dark, blood-red mud. He was blind with tears and mud. He had been lying there weeping at almost exactly the same spot where Collins had wept three months earlier, after being told that Lee Ann had been murdered. And like Collins, he kept saying, "Oh, God, no! Oh, God, no! This can't be. This cannot be happening. No, God! Please, please no, God! Please, no! Don't let it be."

"Come on, now," Sergeant Dotson said. It was like he was speaking to a small child. "Come on, now. We gotta go. We gotta get outta here. This ain't no place to be. No, not now. Not no mo'. No, it's time—it's time to go."

They helped Clark get back into the left seat of the helicopter, and they strapped him into the seat. Mr. Bauer pulled the aircraft up to a hover and slowly hovered southward down the runway. Slowly, carefully, he moved closer to the burning wreckage of Major Ratcliffe's gunship.

Not far away from Major Ratcliffe's burning wreckage stood Can Tay, the beekeeper known to the soldiers as Candy, and a young Vietnamese man. In her net-bag Can Tay carried a .45 pistol wrapped in a black scarf and the young man carried an AK-47 automatic rifle in his hands at the ready. Can Tay and the young man stood concealed in the brush just off the eastern edge of the airstrip and carefully watched the Americans.

Now they could see that Mr. Lang had landed nearby. Mr. Lang was flying with a young new warrant officer named Hammonds. And in spite of the intense heat, they had landed near the burning wreckage, and Mr. Lang had pretty much patrolled on foot all around the wreckage. And now he trotted over to the place where Mr. Bauer had just put his chopper down, on the edge of the south end of the strip.

Mr. Lang approached Captain Clark's side of the helicopter. Clark held his face in his hands. He could not look anyone in the face.

"No survivors," Lang shouted to them through the open window on the left side—Clark's side—of the cockpit. "There were no survivors," Lang said.

The 68th Buddha was dead.

Lang asked about the fate of the Frenchman, Monsieur Voltaige.

"No survivors," Bauer said simply. "Let's get outta here."

The chateau was engulfed in a great storm of roaring fire as they took off and flew away in an easterly direction. And for a long time Clark continued to hear those words.

"No survivors."

Chapter 30

The Wings of Salvation

Only one month after the massive Tet Offensive, a high North Vietnamese official ordered further attacks, and yet more throughout 1968, to try to "sustain the momentum of the war."

Even after the Viet Cong ranks had been so badly decimated, they succeeded in February of 1969 in penetrating the "highly secure" perimeter at the U.S. 25th Infantry Base Headquarters near Cu Chi and wreaking havoc on the Americans encamped there. After slowly and carefully working their way through the minefields and barbed wire, thirty-nine Viet Cong, three squads of thirteen—some of them women—entered the base. Their primary aim was to destroy what one of them later described as their enemies' "most feared and hated weapon—the helicopters." And they knew exactly where to find them. Using satchel charges, the guerrillas blew up fourteen of the big troop-carrying CH-47 Chinook helicopters on the ground, *all* those at Cu Chi base at that time. The realization that the VC were inside the wire created panic among many of the Americans.

The defenders fired ghostly parachute flares into the air to illuminate the base and help spot the attackers. Firing broke out on all sides. Thirty-eight Americans were killed, but the attackers lost only thirteen of their original thirty-nine. The others safely melted away before dawn.

In April of 1969 the American troop strength level peaked at 543,000.

Even after taking fearsome casualties, the Viet Cong would keep coming back for more. Twenty years earlier, Ho Chi Minh himself had warned the French: "You can kill ten of my men for every one I kill of yours, but even at those odds, you will lose and I will win."

This had something to do with what the top brass called "kill ratio"—something else the Americans could never get quite right.

Early in March of 1968, the U.S. Command reported that some 2,000 Americans had died since the start of the Tet Offensive a month earlier. Approximately 4,000 South Vietnamese soldiers had died during that period. And over 50,000 enemy troops died in the Tet Offensive. It was during the Tet Offensive that American casualties surpassed those of the Korean War—34,000.

The financial cost of the war had reached $33 billion a year. This had provoked an inflation that was beginning to seriously disturb the U.S. economy. Some of the top men involved in managing the war suddenly came to see the impact and the extent of the psychological victory the Vietnamese Communists had won with Tet '68. Some were now saying that the Tet Offensive had broken the will of the American people and the administration. It was said that the president was ready to crack.

Early in 1967, the famous and charismatic Southern preacher, Civil Rights Movement leader, and Nobel Peace Prize winner, Dr. Martin Luther King, denounced the Vietnam War as "one of history's most cruel and senseless wars." And now he was calling on young people to boycott the war altogether by becoming conscientious objectors to military service.

After Tet '68, America's most highly respected journalist, Walter Cronkite ("an American icon," they called him), decided that the United

States should give up their efforts in Vietnam. His coverage of the war had always been balanced. Early on he had been a firm supporter of U.S. efforts in Vietnam. But he visited Vietnam during the Tet fighting, and he came back a changed man. He rejected the official forecasts of victory, predicting instead that it seemed more certain than ever that the "bloody experience of Vietnam is to end in a stalemate." He stated that at some point there is no shame in a nation saying simply that "we have done the best we could, and now it is time to move on."

In late March 1968, the president listened to his handpicked assembly of "wise men" recommend that "we take immediate steps to disengage" in Vietnam. Five days later, the president went on live television and renounced any possibility of another term in office.

In November of 1968, the United States elected a new president. He was distinctly different from the big man from Texas. The big man from Texas was expansive and he loved to be with people. The new president was from Yorba Linda, California. And he did not seem at all expansive. The new president seemed to be a lonely man torn by much inner conflict. One distinguished journalist said early on that this man would not do well in politics because he was obviously uneasy around people. And it was said that the man from Yorba Linda lacked the inner conviction and self-confidence that are the hallmarks of natural leaders and governors of men. The new president seemed to be a clever man, but an unwise man. This man, this new president, said he had a "secret plan" for winding down the war and ending it "with honor." Later, he confessed to a distinguished journalist and historian that he really had no such plan.

However, some historians later were to write that the president's so-called secret plan was to threaten the North Vietnamese with nuclear weapons. But supposedly, that did not work out. The Vietnamese were willing to call his bluff. They played the game, and took their chances, counting on the Americans not being prepared to commit moral suicide.

However, the new president did start to reduce American troop strength. But simultaneously he widened the war into Laos and Cambodia. And the war went on for another seven years.

At long last, a cease-fire agreement was signed between representatives of the United States and North Vietnam in Paris in 1973.

On April 21, 1975, 40,000 North Vietnamese troops overran Xuan Loc, thirty-five miles northeast of Saigon on the road to Bien Hoa. The battle had raged for two weeks—the only engagement during the South Vietnamese government's last phase, in which its forces fought well, as their aircraft inflicted heavy casualties on the Communists. Surging forward after the breakthrough, the North Vietnamese divisions quickly turned the corner at Bien Hoa and headed south for Saigon.

Then the U.S. mission had finally set in motion its emergency withdrawal plans. North Vietnamese rockets had started to land on the riverfront area of Saigon. The repeated playing of a recording of Bing Crosby singing "White Christmas" on AFN was the final signal for everyone to grab their bags and move out—"White Christmas" in April. Some 50,000 Americans and Vietnamese had departed during the previous weeks.

On April 29, with the Communists rocketing the Saigon Airport, the ultimate alternative, "Option IV"—the largest helicopter evacuation in history—was initiated. Over a span of eighteen hours, shuttling back and forth between the city and the aircraft carriers riding offshore, a fleet of 70 U.S. Marine choppers, assisted by some U.S. Air aircraft, lifted more than 1,000 Americans and nearly 6,000 Vietnamese out of the beleaguered city—2,000 of them from the U.S. Embassy compound.

It had come at last: the day of reckoning, the day of retribution, the day of refuge, and the day of deliverance—on the wings of salvation.

Finally, all that was left to be seared into the American collective memory of the war were those chaotic evacuation photographs. There were the wild and frenzied photographs of the men aboard the offshore ships pushing helicopters overboard to make more room for people. And there were those especially painful and humiliating photographs of

Americans and Vietnamese fighting to board helicopters in the courtyard and on the rooftop of the American Embassy in desperate last minute efforts to flee the country on that last day in April 1975.

"Suddenly, it was over," a top CIA agent had later mused to a friend over drinks in a Washington bar. The man he was speaking with was a veteran of the Vietnam War. His name was Torres. This was the Torres who had once befriended the 68th Buddha, the Torres who had been referred to as Lone Eagle and who and lived and worked in the shadow of Nui Ba Den.

"I was stunned," the CIA man said. "It was one of the saddest days of my life. I felt an awful mixture of guilt, pain, and sorrow. I grieved over South Vietnam. By early morning of the 30th, the last helicopters had left the embassy's rooftop. It was over. I felt like weeping. I thought about all the sacrifice, the sixty thousand Americans dead, over three million Vietnamese dead, and the countless billions of dollars in cost. The Arab-Israeli war of 1973, the oil shortage, and the presidential resignation—all these things, these ingredients spelled the end for South Vietnam. And after the fall, after all that loss of life, resources, and blood, I was never asked to testify. I was not even debriefed."

"The Vietnam War," he continued, "was like a curse—like a poisoned apple. No one wanted to remember it. No one wanted to discuss it. It was over and everyone wanted to forget."

Chapter 31

The Watauga Express

Just before Clark departed Vietnam, he lost his second door gunner. The seemingly always happy, joyful, and "mission ready" Gutierrez committed suicide.

Gutierrez came into the barracks late one night and stopped by a group of friends who were enjoying a late game of poker.. He laughed and joked as usual, but then he told them that he was going to kill himself. Everyone laughed and scoffed at him. He laughed with them. He forced one man to take some money, and he told that man to be sure to pay his laundry woman what he owed her.

Gutierrez then went down to his cubicle, lay down on his bunk, and shot himself in the throat with a carbine. The bullet went through his neck and ricocheted through the next cubicle giving the man sleeping there an awful fright. A closer look would show that the weapon used by Gutierrez was the old homemade carbine that had once belonged to Mr. Hobbes. The little rifle had eight notches cut into the wooden stock.

"Dat dope did it. He kept on playin' 'round wit' 'dat dope. And, Lord know 'dat did it—'dat dope. Yeah, man. You can believe 'dat."

Sergeant Dotson maintained that drug abuse was at the heart of Gutierrez's problem. But no one ever knew why he killed himself.

The last thing Gutierrez had said to Dotson was, "Oh, man, I don't get no, no satisfaction." But he said it, as always, with a smile.

About a week prior to the young door gunner's death, Captain Clark had been conversing with him. Clark mentioned the fact that he thought perhaps one day he would write a book about his experience in Vietnam. Gutierrez was enthusiastic about the idea.

"I had an uncle," said Gutierrez. "He told me there is an old Spanish saying that says a man is not really a man until he has done three things. Number one, he must grow a mustache. Number two, he should father a son, and number three, he should write a book. So, yes, I think that is a very good idea. You should do it. Cool, man. You should write a book. That's good—that's good, man. Good."

Captain Clark was flattered to hear that Sergeant Dotson also endorsed the idea.

"Dat's good," he said. "Yeah, man, you go on and do it. You write 'cho book. I know you can do 'dat. You's got da' soul of a poet. A poet. I knows 'dat. And I knows you. You knows da' words. You know what I'm saying now? I'm talking 'bout soul power, too. Yeah, *soul* power, man. Go to it, man. Yes, sir, you go on and do it. You's da' man. Don't let us down. Write 'dat book, man. Write it. Yeah, man, write it. Put it down on da' paper, man. You can roger 'dat. I'll be seein' you on the newsstand—the bookrack. Yeah, the rack, man. I know I will. Do it, man, do it."

The Emperor Le Loi had said: "Every man should accomplish some great enterprise."

Some weeks after that terrible night at Les Trungs, that night at *Les Delices*, when the delights were consumed and lost forever, Winston Clark packed his bags to leave Vietnam. After the destruction of the stone hearth and altar, after the golden bowl was broken and the pitcher was shattered at the well, Clark boarded a "Freedom Bird" at Saigon's Tan Son Nhut Airport. He was about to fly off eastward back to a different world and a different life. Michael Linville, "Lucky Lindy," and Bill Bauer accompanied him to the airport to say goodbye.

"Well, Winnie," said Linville, "we'll miss you. You are a real gentleman and a scholar."

"Thanks, Michael," Clark said. "Actually, that's just what I always wanted to be."

"You take care," said Linville. "I will be out here boarding one of these big birds myself next week. Oh, man, we're practically on our way. Hard to believe—the time has finally arrived."

And then Linville blessed him with his favorite Irish blessing.

May you have warm words on a cold evening,
A full moon on a dark night,
And a downhill road
All the way to your door.

Then he added:

And my your prop wash always
Be pure and clean
And your down draft
Soft and serene.
Happy landings,
You lucky man,
And kiss all the girls for me
Back there in freedom's land.
Oh, yes, back there in freedom's land,
Kiss all the girls for me back there
In sweet Lady Liberty's lovely, lovely land.

"Keep the faith," Bill Bauer said as he shook Clark's hand firmly. "God's speed—and I hope we meet again."

The soldiers all gave a great cheer as the airplane's wheels lifted off the runway. "Houston, we have liftoff," someone said. They were disengaged. For them the war was over. They were on their way back to "the world." They had, as one said, a "new lease on life."

D'Artagnan was on his way back to Gascony on the Watauga Express.

Chapter 32

Across an Ocean of Time

Years later, as an older man, as a professor at a prestigious old southern university back in the United States, Winston Clark would sometimes think back on his time in the Far East—the Orient. He would think back on his time in Vietnam.

Yes, the NVA had taken Saigon, the Pearl of the Orient, and changed its name to Ho Chi Minh City. Time passes and cannot be restored. The pearl became a peanut.

Clark had become a teacher of history and a writer of books of poetry. For quite some time he had chosen not to be like Lot's wife. He did not look back. But finally he did look back, and he wrote that book about his experience in Vietnam and his book had met with considerable success. The book was dedicated to the Top Tigers.

Clark's last book of poetry had included a short poem concerning the saga of Mr. Tucker's toe. One of the poems was entitled "Taking Fire," a poem about the death of a door gunner. And the thin book also included another brief poem that some said brought to mind Randall Jarrell's World War II Eighth Air Force poem, "Death of the Ball Turret Gunner."

This poem was based on an incident recounted to Clark by Mr. Lang one night while drinking beer in the game room. A relatively new and young pilot had been out on a mission in a two-seater observation chopper (a Bell H-13 "bubble") when his passenger, an artillery major, had been shot and killed. The young pilot looked shaken and blanched as Mr. Lang approached him on the flight line. The medics had just taken away the major's body. The young pilot looked at Mr. Lang and then looked back inside the aircraft. Both doors were wide open and the cockpit was filled with blood. It was especially thick on the floor on the observer's—the major's—side and down in the chin-bubble.

"Okay, so, what do I do now?" the young pilot asked with a slight tremble in his voice.

Mr. Lang paused only briefly before replying.

"You wash that cockpit out and get back out there on your mission. That's what you do. Get out there and finish your mission. Any questions?"

The young warrant officer, looking somewhat bewildered and afflicted, did just as he was directed. With the help of the crew chief, he was soon busy washing the thick blood out of the delicate little aircraft and checking his blood-spattered maps to make sure they were still legible.

Mr. Lang went on to tell Clark that had he been in the young pilot's place, he would never have asked what to do.

"Somehow, one way or another," Lang said, "I think I would have taken the rest of the day off."

Lang remained forever afterwards somewhat amazed and astonished that the young man did indeed heed his order. Wan and grim, he washed away the blood and—with the smell of blood and death still fresh in his nostrils—he checked his engine RPM, pulled pitch, lifted off, and went on with his mission. He was off toward the Big Red One's base at Lai Khe.

Sometimes in the fall, when the sun was warm and the leaves were old gold, painted with patches of green and scarlet, Clark would sit on a bench in a quiet corner of the campus and think back about his life—and *life* in general. It seemed that there—when the warmth of the autumn sun and the color of the leaves were just right—time would condense itself, and then pour itself, filled with stardust and moon-flakes, into his ear at 90 knots. The secret kaleidoscope would start to turn and do its magic. The colors and shapes fell into place. Effortlessly, in a somewhat chimerical and visionary way, he peered down a long enigmatic tunnel and beheld a clear pattern—the delightful scheme of things.

Sometimes he would remember his final high school football game. His team, the Wildcats, had defeated their rivals, the Bears, 28 to 6, and he had scored two touchdowns. As Clark walked off the field his father met him, smiling broadly. He proudly put his arm over his son's shoulders, and they walked off the field together. It was one of the sweetest, most cherished moments of his life. The memory was priceless. And now it seemed to Clark that being a good parent was really and truly a piece of cake—incredibly simple.

"Elementary, my dear Watson," he thought. If you loved someone, you must simply demonstrate it. There are not many clairvoyants around. Love should be communicated, illustrated, demonstrated. One need not be secretive about love. It should be clearly communicated and demonstrated. Love should be a visible part of our lives. Otherwise it might be lost in the baffling logarithms of time and space.

Sometimes Clark would suddenly find himself flying back across an ocean of time. From his little corner of the campus—and the universe—he would look about the campus around him and think:

There are no land mines out there.

This is an ambush-free zone, he thought. And, hopefully, there are no free-fire zones out there. There is no plague, no leprosy out there. Fortuna and fortuitous fate, he thought, do we have the eyes to see what we have here? Still now the spirit of Odin, the one-eyed Nordic god of warriors, was hovering about the Great Eye on the Cao Dai Temple. Odin had traded one of his eyes for wisdom and insight.

"Sacrifice," he said, "Yes, nothing good can come to you without it—without sacrifice."

Clark thought of the Top Tigers, an assault company with halos, perfect halos hovering over their aircraft as they glided through the early morning mist above a boundless jungle canopy. He remembered a roommate who had said to him, "Be sure you tell'em I died for nothing."

He thought about the death of a door gunner. Actually, he thought of the death of two door gunners.

And he thought of Bill Bauer, his steadfast copilot and the man who had saved his life that day at LZ Hammerhead, the day that Captain Cutler died among the termite hills. Bill had been killed on his second tour in Nam. That was in the spring of 1970. He was shot down on a night mission. His last words were, "We're taking fire."

Bill's wife, Gwen, had telephoned Clark just as he was preparing to go to bed one night. The news hit him like a body blow. And he wept like a baby. The tears and grief washed over him instantly. It was overwhelming—almost breathtaking. There was no holding it back. The pain and tears washed over him in fiery waves of molten anguish.

"No," he said, "not Bill. Oh, no, please, God, not Bill. Please, God, not Bill! No, no, no! Please, God, not Bill! No, not Bill!"

He was sitting on the floor leaning against the side of the bed, and—with all his heart and soul, with his entire being—he was talking directly to God, helplessly pleading with God.

"Oh, no, God, no, no, please, God, no! Not Bill! *NO*! *Ahhhhhh. God, NO*! NO, NO! Please, no, God! Not Bill!"

Molten flames of anguish burned him through to his core.

Bill Bauer had been such a thoroughly good man. As Linville had said, there was "not a bad bone in his body."

"Keep the faith," he had said. "Keep the faith."

One roommate had said don't forget to tell them I died for nothing. And the other roommate had said keep the faith.

Sometimes the snow owl would still come to Clark in the middle of the night and scream at him and flutter its wings in his face. And he would hear the echoing call:

"Buddha, no!"

"NO, BUDDHA! NOOOOOO! NOOOOOO! NO!"

He thought about a vision of the Angel of Deliverance, the angel with the Purple Heart, emerging from a wall of smoke and flame. He thought of a scout who could not find a place to hide because he was burning and being followed by a trail of smoke—his own smoke—smoke from his own burning body. He was a burning bush. And Clark thought about the Angel of Light and Life—the angel with perfect ladyfingers—the angel who had rubbed his back and listened intently to the magic song of the monsoon.

"Is there a key or a formula?" Clark thought. Is there a master plan? He thought of the strange twists and turns in the labyrinth of life. He thought of the extraordinary feats of which men and women were capable—all the things men could and could not do. Men could be so powerful, so awesome, and yet, at the same time, they were so very fragile, so delicate, so perishable. The frail heart was beating there just under the skin—just behind that thin shield of ribs. Beating. Beating. Squirming for air—for life.

As the colorful dry leaves would blow around Clark's feet and out before him, across the well-manicured fields and walkways of the broad campus, sometimes he would think of Alexander, and Caesar, and Machiavelli, and Shakespeare, and Voltaire—and *Les Delices*. Oftentimes he would vividly remember to remember Major Compton, Top Tiger Six, Major Marker, First Sergeant Rodriguez, Major Ratcliffe, the 68th Buddha, the legendary John Lang, Bill Bauer, Michael Linville, Dotson, Collins, Hobbes, the Hobo Kid, Melvin Meeks, the Claytons. And he would think of Lee Ann, and the pretty smiling girl at Rock City, Len Lee, and the Montagnard Chingachgook in his clean white shirt. And there was Voltaire Six, and Genevieve.

"I was a stranger in a strange land and you took me in," Clark thought.

The leaves? Were the leaves speaking of a master plan? Were they whispering something to him? Was it a cryptic formula or some sacred text—the sacred key from the sacred tree—the tree of knowledge? Did he have the ears to hear, the eyes to see? Could he find the rhythm of the sacred symphony? As he moved through the invisible labyrinth the leaves moved before him—rustling and whispering. When conditions were just right the leaves would speak to him. And it was reassuring. When conditions were just right he could still see the great halos of ice, perfect halos over the rooftop of the wet early morning jungle. What does it signify if on one hand you have a man who says, "Let's go do it. Let's go fight. Let's bring smoke. It ain't much of a war, but it's the only one we've got"? And on the other hand you have a man who says, "I ain't got no quarrel wit' no Viet Cong?" This formula would, in all likelihood, give you a man in the middle that would say, "Be sure you tell 'em I died for nothing."

The Top Tigers could not thrive on Dead Man's Beach. Fortuna remained off shore. They could never understand why things simply would not add up, nothing seemed to mesh, and no operation was ever complete, or conclusive, or final.

"We keep doing the same thing over and over again," the Mustang pilot had complained. "We're goin' 'round in circles."

And the vicious circle was awfully vicious at times. Nothing was final but the zip of the body bag. The body count never seemed to tally. No body count would ever seem to really count. Charlie defied systems analysis quantification. No armada of helicopters was great enough. And no downdraft was ever powerful enough to drive away the demons, the killer bees, the rats, the vipers, the mist, and the plague. The jungle air was sulfuric for them, the Top Tigers. Even the hashish-eaters could find no solace. The hunters always became the hunted. Their Moses was unable to get them out of the wilderness.

Drained and depleted, their sad eyes gazed up at him and they asked, "Hey, sir. What are we gonna do with these webbed-feet?"

Some had said that the war was lost not in the Mekong Delta, but in the Mississippi Delta. But someone or something was being redeemed. Something was being rescued, reclaimed, dusted off, liberated, rediscovered, and sustained. Shortly before the end of his life, speaking not far from the delta, the Mississippi Delta, that famous charismatic black Southern preacher had said: "I have come to believe that unmerited suffering is redemptive."

The tropical symphony could find no harmony for them, the rainforest soldiers. No Valkyries would ever retrieve them and carry them off to Valhalla. No Homer would ever sing of their barren expedition. There would be no Song of Roland for the lost Top Tigers. No Herodotus would ever write about their heroic deeds, their guileless sacrifice. They sat down to weep by the rivers of Babylon and called it the Mekong. Some called it *The Lost Crusade.* Surf City became indifferent. Good vibrations went still—became inert. And "Go-ooo-od morning, Vietnam," lost its resonance.

But doggedly, something inside Clark still sought to unscramble the 500th channel of his free TV. Where is the hidden turtle that supports the cosmic elephant—and the world? Somewhere in the deepest part of the murky delta there was a huge faceless oracle that told him—that shouted out to him—that all that sacrifice was not for naught. This powerful oracle was more ancient, more esoteric, and more insistent than the ancient icons of Angkor Wat. And that powerful voice, a voice as ancient as the mud-man of Genesis, remained with Clark, always insisting that the sacrifice was not for naught.

"You are not just tigers," the Aussie had said. "You guys are *Top* Tigers." Professionals. Coolheaded, good-natured Wildcats. Benign Hellcats. Cats that deliver. Hellcats with halos. They dwelled in chicken-coops. They were courageous tigers who dwelled in chicken coops.

Clark recalled the best of the Top Tigers. And he could still see the perfect halos, the smoke rings, and he felt the pull of the leaves and the labyrinth and the master plan. He was unable to translate the sacred text and yet the powerful current of some undisturbed underground stream caused his heart to move and to believe there was a formula, a matrix, a key. Somehow it all made sense, he concluded.

No, it could not be articulated. But it made sense. The oracle at Delphi did not offer the Greeks an explanation. It spoke in simple declarative sentences. This too, the Golden Age, is not forever. This too is fleeting. Even Job, the blameless and upright man from the land of Uz, was not offered an explanation. But he persevered and was blessed. *Keep trying,* the shabby old sign had said. The subterranean stream rushed and propelled the rhythm of it all into his bloodstream and it filled his heart. And whatever it was, it surpassed knowledge and wisdom.

"No, Mel," Clark said aloud to the fields, the leaves, and trees before him. "I will not tell them that you died for nothing. No, I will not do it."

Mortal man can offer only so much. They perished in the seamless roof of the jungle, where no human eye could see them. The leaves hardly fluttered, Clark thought. But Ultimate Six knows your face, your name, and your number. No one is listed as MIA with Ultimate Six.

Collins stepped out of the wall of smoke and said, "You'll be a really cool captain, really cool, Captain Midnight. But stay that way—stay cool."

He still dreamed of Genevieve, his Minerva, Dulcinea, and Athene. He had dreamed of her just last night. He could see her standing there on the Champs Élysées with the Arc de Triomphe in the background—the girl from the Elysian Fields, the Angel of Light who brought with her the triumph over spiritual corruption. But now she stood with her back to him. He reached out. He put his hand gently on her shoulder. She put her soft warm hand on his. Precious ladyfingers, he thought. She turned her head and smiled, standing quite still, she displayed her angel's profile. Helen of Troy.

"Just walk beside me and be my friend."

Her love was to him what water was to a dying man in a desert. It was the elixir of life. Magic fireflies came to him from the heavy vapors of time and space and sang in his ears. Cut the lines. Launch the canoes.

Keep me, keep me as the apple of thine eye,
Hide me under the shadow of thy wings.
Harbor me.
Love me.
Love me.

"Take care of my little girl," said Voltaire Six, "Cultivate your garden. And remember, as the red man would say, we are blood brothers." And the clay pitcher was shattered at the well.

Fate had smiled on Winston Clark, and now he was happily married and had fathered children. His love for his family was complete and unconditional. Clark listened to the whispering of the pines overhead—the sweet voice of nature. He had suffered a minor heart attack the year before. And, for a while there, he did think that he might finally see that infamous light at the end of the tunnel. He could vividly recall the small army of his students who stood—with his family—just beyond the emergency room door—beyond the veil. Still he could clearly recall his vision of the Angel of Deliverance and the Angel of Light. They also stood watch over his recovery.

Clark felt the warm sunshine on the back of his shoulders. He thought of his kind and thoughtful students and his wonderful family, and he mused aloud, "This must be at least almost as good as being a poet and living in Italy."

Watching as the golden brown leaves fled frantically in the wind before him as he walked away, Clark inhaled the clean fresh autumn air and marveled at the rich fullness of life.

"D'Artagnan," someone said from far away.

Voltaire Six, the happy philosopher, smiled across an ocean of time.

"*Au revoir*," said the little prince, standing alone in a circle of light.

"*Au revoir,*" he said with a broad smile as he walked off into the nighttime streets of Saigon.

"*Au revoir.*"

About the Author

John R. Cooke served as a helicopter pilot during the Vietnam War. In addition to serving there as a pilot (with the Top Tigers) in 1967, he served two additional years in Vietnam in staff positions. After leaving the army in 1978, he taught History with the University of Maryland (European Division), and then later at Brunswick Community College in Shallotte, North Carolina. He now resides with his wife, Astrid, in Wilmington, North Carolina. *Voltaire Six* is his first published novel.

Glossary

AFN	Armed Forces Network-the U.S. military radio station in Saigon.
AK-47	Russian-designed Kalashnikov 7.62 mm automatic rifle.
APC	Armored Personnel Carrier.
APO	Army Post Office.
ARVN	South Vietnamese Army (Army of the Republic of Vietnam). Pronounced "Arvin."
B-52	Strategic high-altitude bomber converted for conventional bombing raids in Vietnam.
Charlie	Short for "Victor Charlie," meaning VC, Viet Cong, the Communist guerrilla fighters in South Vietnam.
Chinook	CH-47 cargo helicopter.

Chopper	Helicopter.
CIA	Central Intelligence Agency, often referred to as "the agency" or "the company."
Clear visor	Helicopter pilots have two visors built into their helmets. One is tinted and is used in bright sunlight. The other is clear and is used at night or on foggy days to protect the pilot's eyes from shattered Plexiglas, etc.
CO	Commanding Officer.
Cobra	AH-1G attack helicopter.
Collective pitch	The control lever which is pulled upward to add more power, and pitch (or angle) to the rotor blades to enable the helicopter to take off or climb. ("Let's pull pitch," means "Let's go." "Let's get out of here," in helicopter pilot's jargon.)
C-rations	Combat rations (quick cold canned food).
CS	Riot-control gas, or "tear gas."
Cyclic control stick	The control stick which determines the attitude of the helicopter with regard to going up or down, or left or right.
DEROS	Date eligible for return from overseas-the end of a serviceman's tour of duty in Vietnam.
Dust off	Medical evacuation by helicopter.
Free-Fire (Strike) Zone	Area where everybody is deemed hostile and a legitimate target by U.S. forces.

G-2	General staff, intelligence section.
Getting tickets punched	Fulfilling career objectives.
Grunt	Slang for U.S. infantryman.
Gunship	An armed (attack) helicopter.
Huey	HU-1 (Bell) Army "Iroquois" "Huey" helicopter, the workhorse of the Vietnam War. (HU-1 stands for "Helicopter, Utility, Model One.")
IFR	Instrument Flying Rules-flying by instruments during inclement weather, as opposed to VFR, Visual Flying Rules used during clear weather.
III Corps Tactical Zone	ARNV military region-the land between the Mekong Delta and the central highlands of South Vietnam.
JP-4	Jet petroleum, aviation fuel.
KIA	U.S. military abbreviation of "killed in action."
LOCH	Light Observation (Scout). Helicopter.
LRRP	Long Range Reconnaissance Patrol.
LZ	Landing Zone.
M-16	Standard U.S. infantry rifle (5.56mm).
M-60	U.S. machine gun (7.62mm).
MACV	Military Assistance Command, Vietnam.

MEDCAP	Medical civil action program-free treatment for villagers by U.S. and ARVN medical support teams.
Medevac	Medical evacuation by helicopter (Dust Off).
McGuire rig	Sometimes called a "Jungle Penetrator," this is a heavy metal rig equipped with three legs that are folded up when lowered on a hoist. The legs are folded out and straddled by the person being rescued (lifted out of the jungle).
MIA	U.S. military abbreviation for "missing in action."
NCO	Noncommissioned officer—a sergeant.
NVA	North Vietnamese Army (Communist).
OH-6	Observation Helicopter, a small "scout ship."
ORWAC	Officers Rotary Wing Aviation Class. My aviation school class number, for example, was ORWAC 66-2.
OSS	Office of Strategic Services.
P-38	Small standard manual can opener that come with c-rations.
PFC	Private First Class.
Phoenix	Code name for an intelligence-based campaign (organized and managed by the CIA-Central Intelligence Agency) designed to eliminate the Viet Cong infrastructure.

Point	The leading man on a patrol or tunnel exploration mission.
PSP	Perforated Steel Planking—material used to line and reinforce temporary airstrips and helipads.
Punji stake	Sharpened bamboo sticks used in primitive booby traps.
R&R	Rest and recreation. An R&R break was usually one week;, each serviceman was usually allowed to enjoy one-sometimes two-R&Rs during his/her one year tour of duty in Vietnam.
Roger	Military radio code talk for (message) "Received."
RPM	Revolutions per minute.
Six	Military radio code designation for a commander.
Slick	Troop carrying helicopter, usually a Huey.
Specialist (SP4)	Roughly the equivalent of a corporal, but a technician, and not considered an NCO.
Sgt.	Sergeant.
Tet	Vietnamese (and Chinese) lunar new year festival, celebrated as a national holiday.
UHF	Ultra high radio frequencies.
VHF	Very high radio frequencies.

War Zone C (and D)	Densely forested (jungle) areas within the III Corps area that were generally considered Free Fire Zones, hostile areas.
WIA	U.S. military abbreviation for "wounded in action."
XO	Executive Officer.

0-595-23275-2